RYDER'S SURRENDER

HELL YEAH!

By
SABLE HUNTER

Other books in this series:

Cowboy Heat
Hot on Her Trail
Her Magic Touch
A Brown Eyed Handsome Man
Badass
Burning Love - Cajun Style
Forget Me Never - Cajun Style
I'll See You In My Dreams
Finding Dandi - Cajun Style
Skye Blue
I'll Remember You
True Love's Fire
Thunderbird - Equalizers
Welcome to My World
How to Rope A McCoy
One Man's Treasure-Equalizers
You Are Always on My Mind
If I Can Dream
Head Over Spurs
The Key to Micah's Heart
Love Me, I Dare You!
Because I Said So (Crossover Texas Heroes Book 6)

Sable Hunter

CONTENTS

CHAPTER ONE
PROLOGUE

The Path Begins in Childhood

Ryder - Love Enough for Two

"Please, Papa, I want them both," Ryder pleaded with her father, looking up at him with big, blue eyes shimmering with tears. She clutched two squirming puppies tight to her chest. "I can't just leave one by himself, he would be so lonely."

Christian McCoy dry-scrubbed his face. "Your sister and brothers each chose one apiece. Why do you have to have two?" He let out a long sigh, meeting his beautiful wife's amused gaze, as she watched on indulgently. "Two horses, two puppies, two dolls. What will be next?"

"Let her have them, dear." Carolyn sat on a bale of hay, sewing a button on Tennessee's shirt. "This boy is so rough on his clothes. He seems to rip off a button every day."

"All right, go." He held up his hand and pointed toward the house. "Don't let me see you with both of those dogs up in the bed, Ryder. Make them sleep on the floor."

"Yes, Papa." Ryder jumped up and scampered off, her long, brown braid flying in the wind behind her.

"What's up with our oldest daughter? She's never satisfied with one of anything. Two cookies, two chicken legs, two candy bars. Ryder seems to think she has to grab onto everything with both hands or she won't have enough."

"All of our children are special, Christian. Ryder has a big heart; she has love enough for two."

Christian went to his beloved wife and pulled her into his arms. "She must have inherited that trait from you. You make each member of our family feel like they're the most special person in the world."

Carolyn laid down the shirt she'd been darning. "Do you need to feel special, husband?" She glanced around. "We are alone…in a barn…with hay."

A gleam came into his eyes. "Hell yeah." Taking his wife by the hand, they climbed into the hay loft.

Life was good.

Samson and Gideon – A Way of Life

"Let's race." Gideon challenged as he took off toward the beach at a run, holding his surfboard under his arm.

Samson was only a microsecond behind his brother. "The waves are high tonight. I bet I can stay up longer than you."

"Does everything have to be a competition?" Their mother smiled indulgently while she watched her boys head out into the sparkling ocean. "Work together. Share. You are brothers."

"My, Leilani, you are so wise." Solomon Duke picked up his wife's hand and kissed it.

"Thank you, husband." Leilani gazed into a pair of golden eyes so like her son's. Samson was the mirror image of his father.

"Our wife is not only wise, she is beautiful." Kona gazed at Leilani with devotion. "Both of our sons are lucky to have such a wonderful mother."

Descended from Polynesian royalty, Leilani was raised in a household with two males to protect and love her mother, as was her mother before her, and her mother before her. Now, in more modern times, they did not flaunt their chosen lifestyle, but it worked for them. Her sons also would find one woman to love. It was the way they were raised; it would be their choice and their destiny. "I have seen the woman who'll love my sons. She will be a strong woman, a woman who'll be willing to sacrifice everything for them. I shall begin to prepare them, so they'll recognize great love when they see it."

Watching her boys as they surfed the waves, she was reminded how fortunate she was to live in paradise - a paradise not defined by the fact that she lived in one of the most beautiful places on earth, rather the perfection of her existence was due to being surrounded by the people she loved.

CHAPTER TWO

"I'm so tired of being told what to do, Pepper." Ryder pulled on her boots. "I'm twenty-one years old. An adult!"

Pepper watched her sister get dressed. "It's a little late to go riding. Heath won't like it."

Ryder visibly fumed, her cheeks flushing, her eyes flashing. "Heath can take his arrogant Neanderthal opinions and stick them where the sun don't shine." She grated each word out between clenched teeth, still tugging on her Lady Justin's.

Ducking her head, Pepper tried to hide a laugh. "You're trying to put your boots on the wrong foot."

"Dammit!" Ryder snatched the offending footwear off and started over. "He's got me so mad, I can't think straight!"

"Just give it a little time, he'll find something else to worry about." Ryder's sister tried to console her. "You knew he wasn't going to go along with you moving to Austin." Flouncing on the bed, she put her arm around Ryder's shoulders. "I didn't want you to move out either."

Lying back on the bed, Ryder stared up at the white ceiling fan making its mesmerizing revolutions. "Moving out wasn't really the issue. Going to Europe with my friends isn't really the crux of the matter either." She turned her head to look at her beautiful, golden-haired sister. "Our family is so overprotective; I don't feel like I can breathe sometimes."

Pepper placed an arm around Ryder's waist and laid her head on her sister's shoulder. "I know the feeling. They just love us, you know. With Dad's condition and our losing Mom, our brothers rallied around us like pioneers circling the wagons."

Ryder calmed a little, scooting closer to Pepper. "I know; I shouldn't resent it so much." With a mischievous grin, she whispered, "What are they going to do when we fall in love? Can you imagine?"

Pepper covered her eyes. "Oh, I can. We might have to elope."

Ryder sighed and sat up straight, her eyes moving around the tastefully decorated room. Most women would consider this a haven. The family provided her with everything she could want or need. She'd torn a photo out of a magazine and Heath had instructed the builders and decorators to bring Ryder's vision to life, a cool, blue, French country sanctuary with Audubon prints that reminded her of Louisiana. Her home was beautiful; her life was perfect. So, why did she feel as if she was suffocating?

"I still think I'll take a ride. Could I borrow Star?"

"Sure, Star would love a good run." Pepper gave Ryder a quick hug. "I know you miss Honey and Chelsea. You can ride my mare anytime you'd like. We'll go to the sale and pick you out a new horse soon. In fact, we'll pick you out two."

"Thank you, Pepper. Honey and Chelsea both lived a good, long life, I just wanted to keep them forever. I can't believe I lost them so close together." Just thinking of her loyal mares made her sad. "Anyway, I need to calm my nerves. Do you want to go with me?"

"I can't." Pepper sat up, pushing a strand of long hair over her shoulder. "I have a paper due tomorrow. This is my last semester, you know."

Yes, Ryder did know. "And then what?" The question was directed as much to her own ears as it was to Pepper. "What does the future hold for us?"

"I don't know, Sister." Pepper pulled Ryder to her

feet. "But I'm sure looking forward to finding out."

A few minutes later, Ryder was mounted on Star and headed down toward the lake. Riding next to the water always calmed her. Highlands, their ranch, bordered Lake Buchanan on one side and Heath's Canyon of the Eagles resort on the other. As she rode, she patted the mare's neck, feeling a little guilty. Ryder knew she had a good life and shouldn't resent being loved and cared for by her family.

She also knew something was missing.

Knowing Star knew the landscape as well as she did, Ryder closed her eyes and just listened. The lapping of the waves soothed her. Cattle lowing in the distance sounded like home. An eagle's cry overhead thrilled her. A satisfied smile settled across Ryder McCoy's pretty face as she exhaled a breath that seemed to release a ton of tension from her body. What could possibly be missing in her life?

Adventure. Purpose.

A man.

Holding the reins of her mount lightly, she let the palomino mare choose her path down to the sandy beach. The breeze off the lake was picking up, blowing the wispy clouds quickly across the evening sky. A spectacular Texas sunset spread before her, a panorama of red, orange and pink. The dying sun shone like a fading citrine jewel sinking into a cobalt blue sea. "Okay, I'm here. Where are the cabana boys?"

Her only answer was a call of an eagle as he sailed through the air. Honestly, Ryder wouldn't have been surprised to hear the deep voice of her older brother rising from behind her. *Don't take any chances, Ryder. Remember everything I've told you.*

Not that she didn't love her family, she did. Even now, surrounded by the lush beauty of all outdoors, Ryder felt the pull of the ties that bound her to them as clearly as if actual silken bonds stretched across the way. "Not here, Heath," she answered the disembodied ghost haunting her thoughts. "I'm trying to clear my head."

No matter her protest, countless memories, a lifetime of devotion, and unquestioning loyalty tethered Ryder to the big white columns that graced the front of their Louisiana-style plantation home as firmly as any anchor ever could. The house they lived in now was merely a replica of the one they'd grown up in, the original being lost in Hurricane Katrina along with their beloved mother. To Ryder, those familial cords had always proved comforting – but now she longed to break free – to fly – to spread her wings and truly live.

Ryder was weary of being and doing only what her family expected. Always the good girl. Always the peacemaker. In her heart of hearts, she wanted to experience everything, for her days to be as full and vibrant as life could offer. And now was as good a time as any to begin.

With a laugh of pure bliss, she nudged Star into a run, heading toward the far edge of their property. Always at home on horseback, Ryder gave into the amazing sense of freedom, throwing her arms out and embracing the wind. Her absolute immersion in the experience was dashed when the mare stopped, whinnied, and reared up on her hind legs.

There was really no time to panic.

Ryder tightened her knees against the mare's body and held onto the saddle horn. "What's wrong?" she cried, beginning to slowly pull back on the reins.

"Whoa, girl!" the exclamation rushed from Ryder's lips as she was thrown from Star's back. She didn't have time to think before her body hit the ground with a thud, knocking the breath from her lungs. A few seconds passed before she could ascertain that nothing was broken – except her pride maybe. "Star? What happened?"

Ryder sat up and tried to get her bearings – and that was when she heard it. The unmistakable castanet sound of a rattlesnake preparing to strike. "Oh, God, no," she breathed, trying to figure out where the threat was and how much of a distance lay between her and the serpent.

Star danced away, keeping her eye on a point behind Ryder's back.

Honest to God, she was afraid to move, expecting to feel sharp fangs sink into her flesh at any moment.

Closing her eyes, she began to pray for a miracle…and a split second later she was no longer in harm's way, swept off the ground and into the air, clasped against the broad, hard chest of a large, very handsome man. He held her safely with one arm while aiming a rifle with the other.

Crack! Boom!

A gunshot rang out, silencing the ominous rattling. Ryder nearly jumped out of her skin, burying her face against his jacket.

"Hey, beautiful, it's all right. I've got you. Are you okay? Any broken bones? Did he bite you?"

His strong, gentle hand was moving across her body, rubbing her shoulders and arms.

"No, I'm okay," she whispered as he picked up her left hand and brought it to his lips.

"No ring. Good. Look at me."

"I hate snakes. I hate snakes," she chanted.

"Look at me, sweetheart. You're safe."

Surrendering to the command in his voice, she obeyed. Breathing became secondary to staring into a pair of the warmest amber eyes she'd ever seen. "Thank you for saving me."

He smiled and Ryder's heart rate shot through the

roof.

"My pleasure. I've always heard you don't know what you're looking for until you find it."

"What were you looking for?" All her brothers' warnings about making herself vulnerable to a strange man flew out of her mind. He still held her close and she could feel his heart beating against hers.

"You."

"No." She blushed. "I mean what were you looking for when you found me."

"Oh, okay." He chuckled. "One of my bulls tore through the fence. I live at Falconhead."

Falconhead? She knew the place. A veritable castle on the cliffs overlooking Lake Buchanan. "I didn't know anyone lived there." Maybe she'd hit her head when she'd fallen. This man looked to be from another time. He wore a brown leather jacket with fringe and had shoulder length blond hair. "You're trespassing," she blurted out as a blush tinged her cheeks.

Her champion threw back his head and laughed. "Lucky for both of us."

She was beginning to agree with him. Capturing his left hand, she clasped it in her own. "My name's Ryder. Ryder McCoy."

"And I am Samson Duke." As he spoke, he carried her to her mount. "You have a good horse; she didn't run away." Ryder thought he was about to lift her into the saddle, but he surprised her when he sat her down. In the next moment, he mounted Star, then lifted her up to sit in front of him, sidesaddle.

"What are you doing?"

"Taking you home."

"Oh, thank you." Ryder let herself relax, enjoying the feel of his strong arms around her. When he started off, it took her just a bit to realize they were headed the wrong direction. "I thought you were taking me home."

"I am. With me." When she tensed in his arms, he gave her his full assurance. "Don't be afraid. I wouldn't hurt you for the world. I just found you, don't ask me to let you go so fast. There's someone at Falconhead I want you to meet. Okay?"

Reasons to say no tumbled through her mind, like boulders rolling down a hill. She didn't know him. He could be dangerous. Heath wouldn't like it.

Ryder rejected them all.

"All right, I'll go home with you, for a little while. I've never been to Falconhead. Pepper and I used to walk up to the gate and pretend it was a castle. I always wondered if my Prince Charming lived there."

"Well, they do," he answered simply.

They? Ryder frowned. His comment didn't make sense. Oh well, maybe she misunderstood. "How long have you lived there?"

"Not long."

When he looked down at her, the evening shadows made his face look mysterious. Ryder had the oddest feeling, like she'd met him somewhere before. A sense of recognition.

"Who's Pepper?" he asked before she could formulate a question of her own.

"My sister. My only sister, but I do have four older brothers," she said with a bit of a huff to her voice.

"Yes, four brothers. You would have four brothers." Her Greek god chuckled. "Actually I've heard of the McCoy brothers. Heath is a formidable businessman. We have some things in common, I think."

Ryder didn't want to talk business or about her brothers. "Who do you want me to meet?"

He smiled mysteriously, capturing his bottom lip in his teeth. "My brother, Gideon. He's going to think you're amazing."

"I'm sure I'll like him too."

"Look." He pulled her closer to him so she sat more upright. "Do you see the eagles? They've made a nest high in the trees right next to our home. Their taking one last flight before calling it a night. And look at the bulls, they've come to greet us."

She gazed into the dusk, not seeing the eagle clearly but hearing the flapping of his wings. At the fence, she could see the hulking form of large animals. They did seem to be waiting for something. She could hear their heavy breathing and the way their feet shuffled on the ground. "What do they want?"

He patted his pocket. "I carry treats. Ah, look who else is waiting for us on this side. Nestor, did you decide to come home?" Laughing, he dug in his pocket and took out a nugget. Ryder watched in fascination as he held out his hand until he got close enough for the big, black, prodigal bull to take it from his fingers. "Now, let's go in." He leaned over to unfasten the gate. They let the bull go through first, then he nudged Star forward to follow him through.

"Aren't you going to give them all something? They did come to welcome you home."

"They're all beggars. Here, help me." He gave Ryder a couple of nuggets and they doled them out to the eager bulls, who accepted them like children enjoying candy. She was surprised Star stood so still while being surrounded. The mare was used to cattle, but not this close. Maybe it was Samson himself. He was big, powerful and undeniably in charge. Like Ryder, Star probably knew nothing would happen that he didn't will it to be so.

When one bull licked Ryder's palm, she laughed. The noise went right straight to Samson's cock. "Okay, enough. Let's head to the house. Gideon was about to grill steaks and I'm sure he'll be able to add one for you."

"Oh, I don't want to intrude. You've done enough for me. I'll call one of my brothers to come give me a ride home and someone will come collect Star tomorrow."

Ryder shivered when he wrapped a hand around her neck, collaring her gently. "Not yet. Stay. Just a little longer. I can't bear to part with you so soon."

His words sent chills all over her body. What was happening to her? Ryder had dated before, but no man had ever affected her the way this one did. "Tell me something about you," she said quickly, needing to know more before her emotions carried her right over the cliff and into the unknown.

"Well, my brother and I are from Hawaii originally."

"You are? How exciting! I've never been," she whispered with envy. "You don't really look Hawaiian." Or at least she didn't think so. "I'll look at you better in the light."

Samson laughed. "You can look at me all you want to." He rode up to the barn, then dismounted. "If you'll let me return the favor. I want to look at you too."

"Why?" Ryder hoped she knew the answer. "Do you think I'm pretty?"

"I think you're gorgeous. Now, come here." He held out his arms and she slipped into them like she belonged there.

She held onto his shoulders until he set her on her feet. "What about Star?"

"We'll take care of your horse."

"She belongs to my sister. My horse passed away. She was very old, we brought her from Louisiana. My mother gave her to me before she died."

"Awww, baby, I'm sorry." He kissed her on the forehead. "No worries. Skeet! Will you bed down Miss

McCoy's horse for the night, please?"

Automatically, a man with salt and pepper hair and a close-cropped beard came out of the barn to take the reins. "Yes, sir. I'll take care of it."

"And get a few men to check out the fence and ride the perimeter. I got our missing bull back in, but I'm sure another one or two will venture over onto our neighbor's property if we don't get it fixed soon."

The ranch hand took off to check things out based on his boss's orders.

"Could I borrow a phone? I didn't bring my cell and I probably need to call my brothers, they'll be worried, Samson."

Samson gave her a stern look. "You don't go anywhere without a cell phone anymore. Do you hear me?"

His concern did two things – it thrilled her that he would care, and it reminded her of Heath. "I don't need another brother telling me what to do."

Her emphatic response to his worry made him laugh. "You can be assured, my feelings toward you are not brotherly, in the least." Without asking permission, he found her hand and tucked it in the crook of his arm. "Of course, let's go inside and I'll give you a cell to phone home."

Ryder shivered, so aware of the man beside her that she felt weak. "I wish the sun were shining, I'd love to see the grounds." She peered across the yard, seeing islands of light illuminated by gas lamps highlighting beds planted with a profusion of flowers: purple and blue plumbago, orange peacock flowers, and mounds of purple sage.

"The landscaper did a good job." He pointed at a fountain. "They even put koi in the water. There's a stream that leads from that spot and goes all around the house. I asked for a water feature and they built me a damn moat."

Laughing, Ryder skipped a step or two. She felt so happy. "A moat. How romantic, makes me feel like a princess."

"Princess." He playfully scoffed. "In this house, you wouldn't be a princess, you'd be a Queen. But until then…Princess it shall be."

Ryder stared at him. The man literally took her breath away. When they mounted the front steps, Samson didn't have to knock, ring a bell or even reach for the knob. As soon as they drew near, the door opened and an older gentleman in a black suit greeted them. "Mr. Samson, Mr. Gideon is waiting." He nodded at Ryder. "Madam. Welcome."

"Thurgood, this is Miss Ryder McCoy, she'll be joining Gideon and me for dinner. Could you bring her a phone so she can contact her family? And bring us a drink." Samson touched Ryder in the small of the back. "What is your pleasure, sweetheart?"

You. She wanted to say 'you' so badly she ached. How had this happened? This man had her wrapped around his little finger so fast she felt like her head was swimming. "A glass of white wine. Not very dry."

"Bring a bottle of the 2010 German Riesling."

Thurgood raised one eyebrow. "The Ego Muller-Scharzhof Scharzhofberger Riesling Trockenbeer-enauslese?"

Samson nodded his head. "Yes, Thurgood. That Riesling. Only the best for Miss Ryder." He hid a smirk. His butler was protective of the five-thousand-dollar bottle of wine.

Once the butler had left them alone, she looked up at Samson. "I have no idea what he said."

Samson threw back his head and laughed. "The wine

does have a long name, but I assure you it is wonderful. A fine vintage produced on the banks of the Moselle River in Germany's Rheingau vineyard."

She nodded, impressed, but unable to add anything to what he said except for a confession. "I'm afraid I don't know much about wine."

"I can teach you whatever you want to know."

The intense look he gave her made Ryder quiver, she didn't think he was referring to just wine. "You can?"

"I can and I shall." He breathed the words right into her ear and she gasped. "This way." He steered her from the marble vestibule, past a grand staircase, and through a formal dining room. Ryder knew everything she was passing deserved closer inspection, but she couldn't bring herself to take her eyes off Samson Duke.

"Your wine, sir." Thurgood was waiting for them in the kitchen. "And a phone."

Ryder accepted the cell from the butler. "Thank you."

"You make your phone call and I'm going to join Gideon at the grill to tell him we have company." He went to a massive French style refrigerator, opened it and took out a package wrapped in white butcher paper. "I'll be right outside if you need me," he said, pointing to a fully equipped outdoor kitchen where she could see another man standing by a brick bar.

"Okay." Ryder swallowed nervously. She couldn't help but wish she and Samson were going to be alone.

But this wasn't a date...this was just a neighborly dinner.

Pressing the numbers, she placed a call to Philip. She always called him when she thought she might be in trouble. He was, by far, the calmest of her brothers.

"Where are you?"

So much for calm. "I'm fine. I went for a ride and ran

into a neighbor."

"A neighbor? Who? Where are you, Ryder?"

She heard a louder growling noise.

"Give me that damn phone!"

Heath.

"You tell me where you are right this damn minute, Missy, or I'm grounding you for a month of Sundays."

"Heath, I'm fine. I'm with friends."

"What friends?"

Her older brother was beginning to get on her nerves. "I'm twenty-one years old, Heath. Technically, I don't have to tell you who my friends are."

If Ryder had been nearer a north facing window, she would've probably heard the explosion. The growls and grumbles coming from the phone were loud enough. Seeing Samson and his brother heading toward the door, forced her to make a quick decision. "I can't discuss this with you right now, Heath. Just take my word for it, I'm fine. I'm just next door. I'll call Pepper to come pick me up when I get ready to come home."

Click.

Samson opened the door, carrying a platter of grilled vegetables. Behind him, came a very handsome man. The resemblance between them was subtle. Where Samson was golden, Gideon was dark. Both were looking at her with unmistakable heat in their eyes. Ryder felt a bit confused.

"Ryder, this is my brother, Gideon. Gideon, this vision is Ryder McCoy. I found her and I'm planning on keeping her."

Gideon held her gaze, then stepped forward to take her hand. "Remember what mother taught us about sharing, brother."

She didn't quite understand his sense of humor, but she did love Gideon's voice. It was deep and husky, making her nerves dance. "Hello, Gideon. Thank you for having me."

The grin he gave her took Ryder's breath away. "Oh, when I have you, Ailana wahine nani, you will thank me."

Ryder blushed. Was he coming on to her? Cutting her eyes toward Samson, she expected to see jealousy on his face. But she didn't. He appeared to be pleased that his brother was flirting with her. Did Samson invite her here for his brother?

"I'm not sure if I should stay." She backed up a few steps.

"Oh, no. No." Samson took her by the arm. "Please, stay. Don't let Gideon scare you off. He's harmless."

"Yes, my apologies, Ryder. I was teasing you."

Samson and Gideon exchanged a look that Ryder couldn't read.

"Come, let's eat. Thurgood has brought us a wonderful bottle of wine." She let the brothers lead her to the kitchen bar. In this fancy of a home, eating at the more casual spot seemed perfect.

Samson filled a plate to place before her and Gideon pulled out her stool. "Are you okay after your spill, Ryder?" Gideon asked.

"Yes, I'm good. If your brother hadn't come along when he did, I would probably have been snake bit." Ryder shuddered at the thought.

"Sometimes, we're in the right place at the right time for a reason." Samson handed her a glass of wine.

"Tell us a little bit about yourself, sweet girl." Gideon held her gaze, his eyes warm and friendly.

Ryder searched for something interesting to say about herself. "Well, I'm your next-door neighbor. I live at Highlands Ranch with my sister and four brothers. My father is still alive; he lives in Austin. I graduated from U.T. a few months ago. My degree is in business. I've been helping Philip with the business side of the ranch and I might end up working for Heath at his energy company before it's all over."

Samson nodded. "I am sure you would be an asset to any company."

"I hope so." She waved her hand a bit self-consciously. "I'm pretty much a homebody. I do a little volunteer work at the local hospitals, but I'm really happiest puttering around the kitchen and working in the flower beds." Ryder frowned. "I look forward to having a family, I want children and my only real hobby or interest is writing poetry." She blushed. "Isn't that silly? I don't sound very exciting, do I?"

"Nonsense." Samson took a drink and placed his glass down on the bar. "Sounds like some amazing talents – a businesswoman, a philanthropist, an artist, and a caring woman. You sound perfect to me. Doesn't she, Gideon?"

"I was thinking the same thing." Gideon leaned forward, seeming to hang on to every word that was being said.

Ryder felt self-conscious being the full focus of the two men. "Samson tells me you are from Hawaii?" She directed the question to Gideon. Where Samson didn't appear to be from the island, his brother definitely looked the part.

"Yes, our family owns the Lani Ranch. Much like Highlands, we raise cattle and horses." He smiled. "We also raise pineapple and have palm trees. The northern boundary of our property borders a volcano and the southern stretches all the way to a sandy beach."

"I'm fascinated." Ryder was serious, caring far more about learning about her hosts than eating their delicious food. "Tell me more about your home and your family."

Gideon seemed pleased to share with their guest. He

threw a napkin in his lap and began to cut his meat into bite size pieces. "Well, our mother is descended from Polynesian royalty. She is very beautiful, like you. Her name is Leilani. My father's name is Kona. I am full blood Hawaiian, while my brother here is half. His father is a man named Solomon Duke."

"Yet, you have the Duke name also?" she asked. "You were adopted?"

Gideon shook his head. "Our family dynamic is a bit complicated. Suffice it to say that we are one happy family. Protected. Loved."

Ryder tried to imagine living in such a place. "I love where we live and Falconhead is gorgeous, but why would you leave paradise for this?"

"Work." Samson answered simply. "Our home on the islands will always be important to us, but we needed to be nearer Houston and other cities that cater to our business needs. Our work is in the space industry and there was a lot of talent and resources here that we couldn't find on the island. We have a home in Houston, but we wanted a taste of the country life too, so here we are." He winked at her. "And now...I'm more convinced than ever we made the right decision."

Ryder laughed nervously, getting the point that he was talking about meeting her. "Sounds...very interesting." She wanted to know more, but she stopped to enjoy a few bites of her meal. "The steak is very tender. Delicious."

"Are you dating anyone, Ryder?" Samson asked, placing his hand over the one that held the stem of her wine glass.

Ryder didn't move a muscle, she loved the way their hands looked joined. "No, not seriously. I dated a little in college. A casual thing."

"Good...maybe we --."

Whatever Samson had been about to say was cut off by a horrendous noise coming from the front of the house.

"Sirs...sirs...I need to announce you, sirs." Thurgood's raised voice and frustrated tone caused them all to look toward the front of the house.

"Where is she?"

"Ryder!"

"Where's our sister?"

Ryder groaned. There was no mistaking those voices.

"Sounds like a storm's coming," Gideon said dryly.

"Hurricane McCoy, I'm afraid." She covered her eyes, maybe if she couldn't see them they would disappear. "How embarrassing!" When would they ever realize that she was a grown woman?

The sound of cowboy boots making heavy steps would've shaken the kitchen had Falconhead not been a veritable fortress.

"There you are!"

Ryder parted her fingers and peeped through. Heath stood there like a huffing bull. He was flanked on either side by Philip and Jaxson.

"Just three of you? How in the world did you manage to get away without Tennessee?"

As angry as their crashing her private dinner with the Dukes made her, she couldn't help but see the humor in the situation. Her three brothers reminded her one of those old-timey westerns that featured three brothers like the Cartwrights of the Ponderosa or the Barkleys of Big Valley. In fact, Heath reminded her a little bit of Hoss.

"Headed to Big Bend. He got called out on a rescue mission." Heath narrowed his eyes, glaring at Samson and Gideon. "Who are you?"

The Dukes were already standing, just waiting for an opportunity to get a word in edgewise. "Samson Duke." He offered his hand to Heath, and Gideon followed suit.

"Gideon Duke."

There was handshaking all around and Ryder felt compelled to finish the introductions. "Samson, Gideon, these hotheads are my brothers; Heath, Jaxson and Philip McCoy. Brothers, be nice to my new friends."

After being halfway civil, Heath crossed his arms over his chest. "Now, what are you doing here with two strangers?"

Philip stepped up and whispered to Heath. "I think I recognize these guys."

Heath tilted his head. "You do?"

Samson and Gideon locked gazes and tried to hide their amusement. *Keep your cool, Gideon. She's worth it. You might be right.*

Their twin connection was deep. Even though they had different fathers, they'd shared a womb and now they shared their thoughts.

"This is Samson and Gideon *Duke*." He emphasized the last word. "Those Dukes. The OuterLimits Dukes."

"Do tell..." For Heath, it was hard to mellow, but he tried. After all, he'd submitted a proposal to partner with these space pioneers to provide them with the cryo, solids and kerosene used to propel their rockets into outer space. "Sorry, I didn't recognize you. Wasn't expecting to find you…in my backyard with my sister." His voice had gone from congenial to gruff in a heartbeat, despite Philip giving him a hard elbow jab to the ribs.

"I wouldn't exactly call Falconhead our backyard, brother," Jaxson whispered. "This house is a fuckin' citadel and the Dukes are gazillionaires."

"Not gazillionaires." *Billionaires.*

Be humble, Gideon. Keep the prize in sight.

"Ah, yes, Ryder." Gideon said her name, acknowledging both Heath's comment and Samson's thought. "Luckily, Samson came upon her when he did.

Her horse threw her right into the path of a diamondback rattlesnake."

Philip moved quickly. "Are you all right?" He pulled Ryder into his arms.

"I'm good." She hugged her brother. "If Samson hadn't come along and shot the snake, it would have bit me though. He showed up just in time."

"Thank you." Philip addressed the Dukes. "We are grateful you rescued Ryder and brought her back safely."

"Why didn't you just bring her home?" Heath grumbled.

"I wanted her to meet my brother, I also had a bull that pushed through a fence onto your property and we managed to get him back where he belonged."

"Hmmm," Heath didn't look like he was convinced. "Well...I do thank you for helping Ryder. She shouldn't have been out riding so late or alone." He nailed his little sister with a pointed glare. "But, I'm glad you were there when she needed you. Now, it's time to get her home. Ryder, you're coming with me. Jaxson, you ride Star home."

"I was having a good time." Ryder protested, forcing herself not to whine.

"Sure, I can do that," Jaxson agreed.

"We could bring Ryder home when she is ready to leave." Samson suggested, although he was aware this was a skirmish they weren't going to win. No matter, their time with the beautiful Ryder McCoy was just beginning.

"No." Heath was adamant. "I'll feel better if she goes home with us."

"I'm so sorry. Thank you for everything." She took Samson's hand, then moved to Gideon. "And thank you, Gideon, for making me welcome."

Disregarding the McCoy brothers' watchful eyes, Samson and Gideon both kissed Ryder's hand, ignoring the growling noises that were coming from her elder brother. "We'll be seeing one another again soon, I'm sure of it." To ease the situation, Samson did something he'd been planning on doing anyway. "Heath, why don't you give me a call on Monday and we'll go over some numbers on the fuel. I've been doing my research on your energy company and I appreciate what you're doing in the conservation area."

Heath's business would never be more important than his family, but he did manage half a smile. "I'll do that, Mr. Duke. I look forward to doing business with you."

"Thurgood!" In about five seconds, the butler appeared at the kitchen door. "Will you see the McCoy family to the door?"

"Yes, sir." He bowed and did his duty.

Ryder felt like a recalcitrant child who was being sent to her room. She was about to follow her brothers when Samson captured her hand and pulled her close.

"I'll be in touch, beautiful. We Dukes don't give up easily."

His voice made her shiver. She locked her gaze with Samson, then glanced at Gideon. He gave her a wink as if confirming what his brother said to her.

Alarm bells began to go off in Ryder's head. Maybe it was a good idea she was going home right now, she certainly needed time to think. Ryder was confused…and very, very glad she'd met her new neighbors.

* * *

Samson and Gideon stood at the window, watching the McCoys head down the drive. "I don't have to ask you what you're thinking," Gideon muttered at Samson's side. "I can feel it."

"Yea, she bowled me over. Tonight wasn't the right

time, but I think we should make our move." Samson leaned his forearm on the window sill, gazing out into the night. "She's sweet, soft, smart, and sexy as hell."

"Just the thought of something happening to her and we never got the chance to meet her...to touch her." Gideon turned abruptly, heading to the tray and pouring himself another glass of the expensive wine.

"Unthinkable," Samson agreed. "Our only problem will be convincing her to accept us both."

Gideon laughed. "If you think that will be our only problem, you didn't meet the same group of cowboys that I did tonight. Those McCoy men would die for their sister. And I have the feeling they're pretty traditional."

"I guess we'll just have to convince them, as well as Ryder." Samson drained his glass and set it on the tray.

Gideon stared at his brother. "So...you're not viewing this as just another sexual partner, another conquest." The Duke siblings weren't promiscuous, they tended to focus on one woman at a time. All vetted. All discrete. But none serious.

Samson crossed his arms and shook his head. "I don't know, Gideon. This feels different. How do you think we should proceed?"

Gideon tried to ignore his cock, which had been hard anytime she was near. "Slowly and with as much finesse as possible."

"Ryder is not like the other women. The idea of both of us will surprise her. Should we be honest from the start or should just one of us pursue her first and...?"

Gideon interrupted Samson. "Gradually get her used to the idea of a threesome?" The brothers could always finish one another's sentences. From the time they were born, their connection was inexplicable to other people.

"Yes, I suppose." Samson mused.

Gideon heard his brother's unspoken concern.

"We've done that in the past and I don't think it's a good idea with Ryder. I prefer we were honest from the beginning. This may be too important – she may be too important. If Ryder can't accept us for who we are, there's no use investing more than we can afford to lose in a dead-end relationship."

"I'm not sure she picked up on it, but we didn't exactly hide it from her tonight." Samson recalled all that had been said. He also remembered how she felt in his arms, how beautiful her face was, and how her curvy little body was beyond delectable. They would give her more pleasure than she'd ever dreamed.

"True." Gideon laughed. "I wish I could read her thoughts as easily as I can read yours."

"Damn, I'm going to bed." Samson clapped his brother on the back and headed up the stairs to his suite.

"I'm right behind you," Gideon called out, knowing he'd be doing the exact same thing his brother would be doing.

Fantasizing about Ryder McCoy.

Upstairs, Samson shed his clothes, tossing them in the hamper. Even though they had household help, he was by nature a neat person. He and his brother enjoyed sharing their women, but each had their own private space. Since moving to central Texas, they hadn't participated in their favorite form of eroticism, but the size of their beds certainly allowed for the possibility. Samson and Gideon were big men and their choice of furniture reflected the amount of room it would take to play with their woman of choice. Custom made beds, oversize chairs, and an en-suite hot tub were just a few of the built-in luxuries they'd had installed in their new home. Needing to relax, Samson grabbed a towel and headed for the Jacuzzi tub. As he passed the bed, he imagined Ryder stretched out between them, her beautiful body bare to their hands and lips.

"Ah, yea." He rubbed his cock. "Making you feel good would be such a pleasure." Stepping over the side, he lowered himself into the bubbling waters and sighed. The warm water churning against his skin felt incredible. Leaning back against the side, Samson closed his eyes and took his cock in hand, remembering how her breasts had rested on his forearm as she'd nestled against him while on the horse. As he stroked himself, he thought of Ryder's sweet scent. He couldn't wait to see her breasts, suck her nipples, find out how sweet her little clit would be on his tongue. "Fuck, baby." She'd said yes to his phone call, he prayed she'd say yes to seeing them again. Up and down, he pumped his dick. The silkiness of the hot water against his skin a poor substitute for the creamy heat of Ryder's pussy.

For years, they'd searched for the one woman they could call their own, one who would love them both, be receptive to their needs and desires – want them as much as they would cherish her. "Oh, yea, let me love you, baby." As he worshiped Ryder in his mind, his whole body bowed, shafts of fire licked at his balls. His hips bucked in the water, sending little waves beating against the sides. "Ryder!" he shouted as his cum boiled up, jetting out of his body in white ribbons of ecstasy.

Meanwhile… In the opposite wing, Gideon was having a similar fantasy. He stood in the shower, his back against the smooth marble wall, fisting his cock. Tonight, they might have met the woman of their dreams. He treasured the memory of how his lips had felt on her skin. Drops of water glistened on his heaving chest as he let go, sending plumes of cum shooting across the tile. "I'll take you to heaven, baby. Just give me a chance."

After finishing his shower, Gideon dried himself off with a Roma bath towel from Neiman Marcus, which his housekeeper had informed him cost a hundred and sixty dollars when she'd found it wadded up in the tub. He pulled on a pair of Hermes woven boxers with two fourteen karat gold buttons on the waistband which had been on sale at five hundred dollars a pair. The sheets on his bed were one thousand thread count made by Charlotte Thomas, the price for these bed linens per his decorator's invoice, were a cool twenty-four hundred dollars. No creature comfort had been spared in their home and their five-car garage held a Bentley, an Aston Martin, a Lamborghini, a Porsche, and a King Ranch pick-up. The Duke brothers wanted for nothing money could buy.

Yet – something was missing.

The value of material things fades fast if there's no one to share them with – no one to make smile.

That night, as they closed their eyes in sleep, both would have given most anything they owned to have Ryder McCoy lying next to them.

CHAPTER THREE

"I can't believe they did me that way!" Ryder fussed as she put the finishing touches on a salad for supper.

Pepper giggled at her sister's obvious nervousness. "You can't say you were surprised. They acted totally in character."

"They embarrassed me in front of the Dukes." Putting a hand on her hip, Ryder frowned at Pepper who was climbing up on a stool and stretching upward as far as she could. "What are you doing?"

"I want Mama's platter for the pork loin."

Hearing her strained voice and seeing that she was on the verge of falling on her ass, Ryder stepped up, jumped a few inches, and grabbed the serving dish. "Here, short stuff. Just ask next time."

Pepper huffed. "I like to be independent." Taking her mother's dish, she took a second to hug it close before placing it on the counter and lifting a succulent piece of meat onto its smooth white surface. "So, tell me Ryder Leigh, which of the luscious Dukes do you have your eye on?"

Peering into the refrigerator, Ryder searched for the Catalina salad dressing that Tennessee preferred. She was trying to ignore her sister's question. Mainly, because she didn't have a ready answer.

"Ryder, I Googled them, they're both hot as hell. Samson is so dreamy with that lion mane of honey-blond hair and that dark scruff on Gideon makes him look like such a bad boy. Which one did you click with?"

When Ryder delayed her answer once again, Pepper pulled her out of the fridge and slammed the door. "Ryder McCoy! She-devil! You can't have both!"

"Oh, don't be silly, Pepper. I don't want both." She looked sheepish. "I'm just not sure which one I do want." She twisted her body while standing on one foot, like a little girl. "They both seemed to like me. How shall I choose?"

"You sound just like you did when you were young. I can't believe you!" Pepper swatted Ryder on her arm. "Isn't Scott Eagleton still calling you?"

"Yes, but I'm just not interested in him." She squirmed a little and frowned. "I know the family approves of him – he's rich, powerful, and shares Heath's values and love of green energy. I don't know what it is, there's just something about him that makes me uncomfortable."

"You have all the luck, Ryder. I'm the one who sits dateless on Saturday nights."

"Oh don't tell me that, I saw the way Judah James looked at you at that party at Jimmy's Dushku's. Are you going to his concert in Dallas in a few weeks?"

"I want to." Pepper went all dreamy-eyed.

"Well, do it! Did you know most all of our friends are engaged, married, or at least going steady with some guy?"

"Yea, I just got an invitation to Dana Oliver's wedding. I can't believe she's getting married, not after what happened with her fiancé." Pepper began to set the table, then stopped and turned to face her sister. "You've done a good job trying to change the subject, but I am not going to forget your dynamic duo and the fact that you seem destined to be the female-filling in a sexy cowboy-sandwich."

"Oh, hush." Ryder began to pour the tea. "You don't know what you're talking about."

"Oh, I do too. I know how you've always inhaled those ménage romances! M/F/M! Every woman's dream!

Having a threesome is on your sex bucket list! You've always wanted this. This is one of your dream fantasies"

Ryder stared at her sister. "You've been reading my diary again."

"Yea, you might as well just 'cc' me on every entry."

The sound of a door opening and shutting drew the girl's attention.

"Something smells good." Philip smiled at his sisters.

"Pork loin with all the trimmings." Pepper grabbed a bottle of water to hand to her brother. "You look sunburned and exhausted. Is something wrong?"

"Oh, we've got a mess out there. We had one crazy cow kick down a fence post that was loose and now fourteen calves are loose and headed in fourteen different directions. You ought to see it, it's like one of those crazy video games out here. Once we round them up, we still have to repair the fence and tag them. If you two could fix us some sandwiches, we'd appreciate it. I bet it'll be midnight before we're finished."

"Sure, of course." Ryder instantly began to gather bread, condiments, and sandwich baggies.

Pepper pitched in. "I'll run them out to you as soon as I get everything together, Philip."

"Thanks." Glancing at his watch, he frowned. "I was supposed to take a run out to that mine I discovered on the land we own near Enchanted Rock. I swear someone's been messing with my gear out there. Oh well, it won't be today. Family first."

"Do you think you've struck gold this time?" Pepper asked.

"Silver, maybe." Philip shrugged. "As a professor, I'm more interested in the history, of course." He started to leave, then glanced back at Ryder. "Are you all right after last night?"

"What do you mean?" Ryder asked. "From my fall? Yea, I'm good. This wasn't the first time I've taken a tumble off a horse." She shivered. "I don't like snakes, thankfully it didn't get a chance to bite me."

"No." Philip held onto the doorknob, delaying his departure to study his sister's face. "I'm more concerned about your encounter with Thor and Aqua-Man."

Pepper snorted over Philip's description. "Christ Hemsworth and Jason Momoa. He's right, that's exactly who they look like, with their long hair and bedroom eyes."

"Whoa!" Philip reacted with horrified surprise, holding his hands up. "Don't put words in my mouth. I did not see any bedroom eyes!"

Even though Ryder had no desire to discuss the Dukes with Philip, she couldn't help but laugh at his reaction. "Philip, we've all wondered why you've never gotten serious about a girl."

Philip scowled. "I might be more serious than you think. I've met someone and her name is Shell."

Before Ryder or Pepper could ask him a question, he was gone.

"Shell?" Pepper repeated. "Like Michelle or clam shell?"

Ryder shook her head. "I can't believe he just dropped that bomb...*shell* and walked off."

Giggling, Pepper helped her sister get the sandwiches ready to take to their brothers and the ranch hands. Just as they were finishing, the house phone rang. "You get that and I'll bag these up and take them to the barn," Pepper offered.

"Thanks." Ryder wiped her hands on a towel and grabbed the phone from where it sat on the bar. "Highlands Ranch."

"Ryder?"

The husky voice was familiar and it only took her a moment to place it. Her nipples and clit recognized Samson Duke before her brain got the message. "Yes." Her whispered response was so low; she was sure he wouldn't hear. She grasped her throat and tried to find her voice. "Yes, it's me."

"Hey, baby. How are you today?"

Ryder grabbed for the bar stool before her knees gave way. "Samson? I'm good. How are you?"

"Better now that I've heard your voice. What are you doing?"

"Pepper and I just finished making sandwiches for the men, they're tagging calves." She covered her eyes, knowing she was telling him things he probably didn't care anything about.

"Do they need any help?"

His offer of aid surprised and pleased her. "No, I think they've got it in hand. Thank you, though."

"Okay, well, the reason I called was to see if you'd be free for dinner tonight. Last night we were interrupted and we didn't get to spend as much time with you as I wanted. How does a moonlight ride and a picnic sound? Can I tempt you?"

"Yes." The answer erupted from her lips before her brain could present an argument. Her brothers might have something to say about it, but right now they weren't here and she wanted this...she wanted it badly. "I'd love to see you."

"Good." Samson's voice sounded immensely satisfied. "Could I pick you up at six?"

Ryder glanced at the clock. "Sure. I'll be ready." Her heart was thumping hard in her chest at the idea of spending time with this exciting man. Like Pepper, Ryder had grabbed her laptop when she'd come home last night to see what she could find online about the Duke brothers.

What she'd discovered had both intrigued her and made her nervous. They were the real deal – self-made men with roots that bound them to the cowboy world as well as a tropical paradise. Their holdings were massive, but that wasn't what impressed Ryder. Samson and Gideon seemed to be good men. They were very active in charities and sponsored groups like Make-A-Wish Foundation and cancer research. The one thing she didn't enjoy seeing was the pictures of them at society functions with a beautiful woman on their arm. Nevertheless, she was the woman Samson was interested in at the moment…and she intended to enjoy herself. "Should I bring anything?"

"Just your beautiful self. Until then?"

"Until then." She held the phone to her ear even after he'd disconnected the call.

Glancing at the clock, she saw that she only had a couple of hours to prepare. Not bothering to wait on her sister or speak to her brothers, she went to get ready. She'd leave Pepper a note and with some luck, she'd be back before her brothers even knew she was gone.

* * *

Ryder was dressed early. She'd checked her makeup three times and changed tops twice. Now she was standing at the front window and staring down the road, watching for Samson. Her eyes were so focused on the window, that she noticed she could see herself in the glass. Turning sideways, she checked out her own reflection. These jeans made her look fat! Drats! Ryder was just about to whirl around and run upstairs to change when she heard the powerful roar of an engine. Her eyes flew up to see what was making the noise and she gasped at the sight of a low-slung, ice-blue Lamborghini. "Oh, my stars and garters, that machine is pure sex on wheels."

Ryder stared at the foreign sports car until it came to a stop, but the man who stepped out of the luxurious Italian vehicle was far more magnetic than his car. She froze, mesmerized, until their eyes met and then she bounced back, ashamed he'd caught her mooning over him like a lovesick teenager.

She'd barely regained her composure when the tap came on the door. A small part of Ryder's subconscious told her to escape, to run up the stairs and forget she'd ever met the gorgeous Greek god who was, even now, standing outside her home.

Knock! Knock!

Any reservation she'd entertained fled as her feet started toward the door, seemingly of their own volition. Her mind might not be fully onboard with this date, but her body wasn't listening. When she arrived at the wide front entrance, she stopped, took one deep breath and opened it. "Samson. Welcome."

He didn't say one word, just stepped into her space and placed a big hand on the side of her face, bending to claim her lips with his own. Ryder acted on pure erotic instinct. Their mouths collided, their tongues clashed, and Samson proceeded to kiss her with a thoroughness that took her breath away. She didn't care if she passed out from lack of oxygen – everyone had to die sometime.

Waves of bliss rolled over Ryder as she succumbed to his passion. She was so immersed in the pleasure, that it took her a few seconds to realize he'd pulled back, leaving her on tiptoe, with lips parted slightly and eyes closed. Only his chuckle brought her back to reality.

"Open your eyes, lovely."

Ryder obeyed, her breath coming in little pants. "Hi." She gave him a sweet smile. "I'm glad to see you."

Pulling her close, Samson hugged her tight. "I'm glad to see you too. Are you ready to go?"

"Yes, I am. I'm excited."

A small growl came from Samson's chest. "Me too." He took her by the hand and led her to his car, holding Ryder's hand while she eased in. "Buckle up, beautiful."

She did and spent a few seconds admiring the interior of the amazing car. When Samson settled next to her, however, he claimed her full attention. "Did you have a good day?" she asked.

As he started the engine and put the car in gear, Samson cut his eyes toward Ryder, giving her an indulgent, sexy smile. "I did. Gideon and I flew to Houston to meet with some engineers. We're in negotiations with NASA to take some cargo and crew up to the International Space Station."

"That's incredible. It's hard for me to wrap my mind around what you're saying. Space travel used to be relegated to governments and now I find out my neighbors regularly launch rockets and plan missions to faraway places in the galaxy."

"Well, not too far, not yet. Although we do hope to get to Mars in the near future." He pulled out of Highland's drive and started toward the main road.

Ryder shook her head. "I could ask so many questions, but the one bothering me most is…when you have exciting things like happening in your life, why are you wasting time with me?"

"Are you serious?"

Ryder was surprised that he looked somewhat offended. "Well…it crossed my mind."

"Let me put your mind to rest." He gave her a sharp glance. "There is no one in this world I'd rather be spending time with than you."

Ryder gasped, finding she had no comeback for that at all.

Samson checked in his rearview mirror and when he

saw there was no traffic on the narrow two lane road, he pulled over onto the narrow right-of-way. Putting the powerful car in park, he unlatched his seat belt and turned in the seat to face Ryder. "From the moment I saw you, I felt an irresistible pull. I'm a man of action, I don't waste time. When I see something I want, I turn the world upside down to get it."

Ryder was mesmerized, looking into his handsome face, his intense eyes. "And you want me?"

"I want you." He bent to kiss her. "I want you very much."

His words both thrilled and scared Ryder. Her experience wasn't vast and her dealings with men like Samson and Gideon Duke was nonexistent. Her brothers were cut from the same cloth, but they'd made it their life's mission to shield her from the world, to ensure that no man took advantage of her. Only a certain type of man was good enough for their sister. Well…for the first time, Ryder wasn't sure she wanted their protection. She craved to know what it would be like to belong to a man like Samson Duke, what it would feel like for him to hold her in his arms – to touch her, to…

Her imagination made Ryder blush.

She felt her nipples bead at the images coming to her mind. "I don't know what to say."

"You said yes when I asked you to spend the evening with me, that's all you need to say."

With that, he resumed the trip. The drive from Highlands Ranch to Falconhead didn't take but a few minutes and when they drove through the gate, Ryder's eyes were wide, trying to take it all in. Samson and Gideon's home was magnificent. Her last visit had been at night and she hadn't been able to appreciate the landscaping or the care that had gone into the renovations and design. There was so much glass, native stone, and architectural detail that made her feel like the house had sprung up, fully built from the land around it – it all just seemed to fit.

Samson pulled into the circular driveway and he'd no more than stopped, before a uniformed gentleman came to help them from of the car. He opened the driver's side door, but Samson came around to open her door. "What did you do today, sweetheart?"

Ryder took the arm he offered, and they began a leisurely stroll to the barn. Beneath her fingers, she was super aware of the hard muscle of his bicep. Walking next to him, she felt ultra-feminine, and having his attention focused on her made butterflies swarm in her stomach. "I spent the morning studying."

He covered her hand on his arm with his own hand. "You've graduated, right? What were you studying?"

"Yes, I completed my BBA degree at UT with a major in accounting and a minor in finance. I took a year off before graduate school." She glanced up at him and smiled. "My plans were to go to Europe with my college roommate, but my brothers squashed that idea."

"You want to travel?"

Ryder held his gaze. His eyes were so kind, and he seemed truly interested in every word she had to say. "Yes, I think I'd enjoy seeing the world. I haven't really done much of that; my brothers weren't of two women traveling overseas with no man to protect them."

"Well, I'm going to be selfish and be happy you're still here. If you'd gone to Europe, our paths might not have crossed."

A pang of loss knifed through Ryder's chest. "I'm glad that didn't happen." She let out a sigh. "Anyway, I'm planning on going back to school for my MBA, but right now I'm studying for the CPA exam."

Samson looked at her with admiration. "Smart as

well as gorgeous, I like that."

Ryder blushed. "I tried my hand at selling real estate for a while, but that didn't seem to fulfill me."

Coming to the barn, he held open the door. "Seeing you fulfilled is a fantasy of mine."

His easy teasing made her whole body tingle. "Samson…" she chided him playfully with one word.

"Ryder…" He mirrored her tone exactly.

Even though Skeet was there to help them with horses and gear, Ryder felt like she was the center of Samson's attention. "I know you're a good horsewoman, you've been practically raised on one. Am I right?" he asked, while placing a steadying hand on her back as she mounted a beautiful black mare.

"Yes, my fall yesterday was a fluke, I assure you." Ryder wanted him to think of her as graceful.

"Anyone would've taken a spill, very few horses will walk past a snake." Once she was astride the horse, he accepted the reins of a large white stallion. "We'll be back in a few hours. Is everything set up and ready?"

"Yes, sir," the hand answered. "Mister Gideon made sure of it."

At the mention of Samson's brother, Ryder felt her heart jump in her chest, then a wave of guilt hit her. She was with Samson, not Gideon.

"Good, thank you, Skeet." Samson took hold of the horn and swung into the saddle. "Ready?" he asked her.

"Yes, lead on." She gave him a nod and a smile.

In a few moments, they ventured from the spacious barn and rode out into the waning daylight. Skeet moved ahead of them and opened a gate, closing it once they'd ridden through. The sun was still high enough in the sky to illuminate their path – and what a glorious sight it was. This part of the Texas Hill Country was Ryder's home, but Falconhead seemed to display a collage of the area's greatest beauty. All around her were unexpected gems; a shallow river that wound through a grove of bald cypress trees before emptying into the shimmering lake cupped by limestone canyons. Stirring vistas, expansive pastures that she knew would be covered by dense spreads of bluebonnets and Indian paintbrushes in the spring. When they rode close enough to the fern-lined cliffs, springs bubbled into a moss decorated grotto. "This is a wonderland, Samson."

"I can't take any credit for it, all of this was here before we came."

"I know, but now that you possess the land, you can protect it from developers. Our two ranches encompass some of the most beautiful country in the world, we're very lucky."

"You're right." He gave her a sensual look. "I feel very blessed right now." They rode deeper into Falconhead land where the trees were thicker – ancient live oaks and massive pecans whose branches hung low enough to be used as benches or places where small children could climb up and lay down for a nap, warmed by the dappled sunshine. "Look."

Ryder let her gaze follow his pointing hand and what she saw made her gasp with wonder. Ahead lay a small clearing lit by thousands of tiny white lights that had been strung in the trees. A table and chairs sat in the middle adorned with flowers, a white tablecloth and candles. "How beautiful," Ryder breathed. The closer they came, the more she could see, the table was set with china and dishes covered with silver domes. All of it looked like a fantasy scene that had jumped right off the pages of a magazine...especially the dark, handsome man who stood there waiting for them.

"Gideon."

"Yes, Gideon is waiting for us."

Everything Ryder thought she knew and understood about what was going on between her and Samson flew out the window. Wasn't this a date? What was his brother doing here?

"I...don't understand," Ryder muttered as Gideon stepped forward to meet them, coming to Ryder with a smile on his face. His dark hair tousled in the 'I don't give a shit' fashion that he wore so well.

"Hello, Ryder. It's so good to see you. I'm glad you could join us."

Ryder looked at Gideon, then back at Samson. "Hello." Her mind and heart were in turmoil. She shivered with excitement, but that excitement was accompanied by a sinking feeling in the pit of her stomach. Truth slipped from her lips before she could call it back. "I wasn't expecting to see you here."

Instead of seeming disturbed, Gideon gave her a heated look, reaching up to lift her from the mare's back. "You didn't tell her I'd be joining you, Samson?"

Ryder allowed his hands on her body. Truth be told, she enjoyed his touch. Confused, she looked from one brother to the other. "What's going on?" She couldn't fathom their motives. Was this some kind of joke? Were they having fun at her expense? Despite the holdings and wealth her family had accumulated, she wasn't sophisticated – she was just Ryder. "Are you two making fun of me?"

Samson dismounted and came to stand near to Ryder. She was surrounded by two men who overwhelmed her senses. Each in their own way – one light, one dark – each possessed enough raw male beauty to take her breath away.

Samson's smile faded and his expression became completely sincere. "We would never make fun of you. You, Ryder McCoy, have captured our complete attention in a way no other woman has in a long, long time."

"He's right," Gideon whispered. "You've taken over our dreams, overwhelmed our senses. I've been able to think of nothing else."

"I don't understand." Ryder shivered as she felt Samson run his hand beneath her hair, caressing her neck. He wasn't the only one touching her, however. His brother ran a finger down her arm from elbow to wrist, causing frissons of excitement to rise along its path. "I thought Samson and I were here on a date. And now…" She closed her eyes and swallowed nervously. "Am I supposed to choose?"

Samson chuckled. "No, Princess. This isn't some kind of weird competition between us."

"No, Ryder, no competition." Gideon took the same finger he used to caress her arm and lifted her chin so he could look into her eyes. "We share."

Ryder heard his voice, but she couldn't process the meaning of his words. "Share?"

"Surrender to us, Ryder," Samson whispered, his lips branding the sensitive skin of her neck. "We'll give you more pleasure than you ever knew possible."

"Just a chance, Ryder," Gideon murmured as he kissed her palm. "You'll be the center of our attention, the focus of our passion. There's nothing we wouldn't do for you."

In a haze of confused excitement, Ryder trembled at their touch. "Both of you want me?"

"More than you'll ever know." Gideon pressed her small hand between both of his, engulfing it in secure warmth.

Fantasies warred with expectations. Ryder's heart raced as a wild, raging desire rose within her, trying to override all she believed, all she'd ever held to be true. "I can't."

"Oh, yes, you can." Samson moved in front of her, taking her face in his hands, capturing her mouth with his. Giving her one long kiss after another, only pausing so they could take a breath.

"Don't kiss me, please." Her voice didn't sound convincing, as she blindly sought Samson's mouth again with her own.

"We have to," Gideon teased in her ear, "look at all the mistletoe."

"What mistletoe? It isn't Christmas," she whimpered, her body on fire, her nipples as hard as river washed pebbles.

"Look up, beautiful, it's all around us." Samson pressed his lips to the upper swell of her breast.

In an erotic daze, Ryder lifted her head and saw the hundreds of green clumps hanging from the branches of the oaks, like lush decoration. Her action exposed the creamy expanse of her neck and Gideon took advantage, blanketing her from behind. As she gave herself over to Samson Duke's hunger, his brother's lips blazed a hot trail across the tender flesh of her shoulder. "You won't be sorry. We'll worship your body, fulfill your every fantasy."

As surely as she could feel their excitement, their hard, aroused bodies pressing against her front and back, Ryder could feel her resolve slipping. She wasn't afraid of these two men, they'd never hurt her, they'd proven that. She was afraid of herself, afraid of what she wanted – of what she couldn't have, of what she shouldn't want...

"No! This is wrong." Pulling away, she broke apart from them. They didn't try to stop her, they only stood watching, an unspeakable sadness on their faces. "I have to go. I shouldn't be here. I'm not the type of woman you need."

"You're all we need," Samson beseeched her, holding out his hand. "Let us show you how good it can be."

"Give us a chance, Ryder." Gideon stared at her with a hooded, intense gaze.

"Why would you do this?" She gestured at them pointing between the two men. "Why would you want just one woman together; it doesn't make sense. You're both amazing! You could have any woman you wanted! Is this sort of game to you?" She began to back away. "Oh, I've fantasized about this. A lot of women do, but it's just a fantasy." Wiping tears from her cheeks, she looked at Samson accusingly. "I thought you were serious, you're just playing with me."

"No, Ryder, you've got it wrong." Samson was aghast at her accusation.

"Did Pepper put you up to this? She did, didn't she? After what I told her, after what she read, she thought this would be funny. Didn't she?" Ryder began to cry harder. "But it's not."

"No. No." Gideon moved toward her. "We've never spoken with your sister. This isn't a game; this is who we are."

At his admission, Ryder stuck her chin in the air. She wasn't so sure she believed him, all of this was just too…unbelievable. Too wild. "This is Texas! They shoot people for stuff like this down here."

"Our private lives are private." Samson began…

"I know. I know." Ryder glared at them. "You're different. You are super wealthy and whatever you do in this ivory tower," she gestured at Falconhead, "is your business. Well…I'm not like that, I have a family and friends. How would I explain you?"

Samson and Gideon looked at her with sadness on their faces. "Ryder, please. Let us explain." Gideon moved toward her, his voice imploring.

"I wish I could…I wanted…" With a choked sob, Ryder turned and ran from the grove of oak trees, catching the horse's bridle. Through a haze of tears, she mounted and rode back to the Highlands as if the devil himself were on her heels.

"Well, we blew that like a 4th of July fireworks display," Gideon muttered softly.

"Yea, I don't know what went wrong," Samson said, his voice full of regret. "I was so sure…"

Gideon placed a consoling hand on his brother's shoulder. "This isn't your fault. Not everyone is wired the way we are. Ryder is just one of those people who wouldn't be able to accept what we do as a lifestyle, she might enjoy thinking about it, but living it in a day to day situation isn't something she could handle."

Meanwhile…Ryder saw nothing she passed – not the Falconhead gate she rode beneath, not Jaxson leading a breed bull by a bridle, not Tennessee driving a huge tractor from the hayfield, Ryder was intent only on reaching her house and the sanctuary of her room.

Entering Highland's barn, she gave an apologetic glance at one of the ranch hands. "Would you make sure this horse is tended and returned to Falconhead, Hanse. I don't feel well."

"Of course, Miss Ryder."

Without looking back, Ryder ran across the yard, barely glancing at the rose garden she and her sister lovingly tended in their mother's memory. She only hoped Pepper wasn't home. At the moment, what she needed most was to be alone with her thoughts.

Flinging open the door to her suite, she flung herself on the bed and let the tide of despair wash over her. What they wanted from her wasn't something she'd hadn't heard or fantasized about. She loved to read ménage romances, they gave her a special thrill – but this was real life, not a fantasy. Her sexual experience was small, becoming involved with two men like Samson and Gideon Duke was like throwing a goldfish into a barracuda tank – and she was the goldfish.

Sitting up, Ryder pushed her long hair over her shoulder and rubbed her arms, trying to dispel the chill she felt. Even now, she could feel their lips, their touch. Shivers of awareness raced over her body. There was no way she could lie to herself, she hadn't run because she didn't want them, she ran because she wanted them too much. "Stop it," she chided herself. "You did the right thing." If she succumbed to the great temptation they offered, to take her places she'd only dreamed – Ryder knew exactly what would happen. She knew how she was, she never did anything by halves. Ryder had a tendency to jump into everything with both feet.

If she allowed herself to become involved with the Duke brothers, she would fall in love with one of them or even worse - both of them.

* * *

Ryder's eyes flew open. Her bed was bouncing. "Too early, Pepper," she moaned. "Come back in an hour."

"No. We've got a lot to do. The chili cook-off is today. Remember?"

"Like I could forget. I get heartburn just thinking about it. Heath is making his boudain chili again, isn't he?" She pulled the pillow from atop her face and stared at her sister who was looming over her, her perfectly coiffed hair making Ryder feel like a ragamuffin.

"He is. In fact, he just carried a big pot of it to the outdoor kitchen so he could watch it while he finished supervising the setup of the booths and tables."

"All right, I'll get up and we'll get started making the

sides. Coleslaw, baked beans and brownies. Is that the plan?" Ryder started to sit up, but Pepper pounced on her, holding her down. "Hey!"

Pepper gave her a mischievous smirk. "Not so fast. How was your date with Mr. Duke? Did you stay up all night writing poems about him?"

The mention of last night's fiasco hit Ryder hard. "No, I didn't. And I don't want to talk about it." She tried to dislodge her sister so she could rise.

She failed.

"Have you met me, Ryder?" Pepper quipped. "You know that's not how our relationship works. We have no secrets."

"We should. We're grown women, not children." Even as she said the words, she knew she didn't mean them. The relationship Ryder had with her sister had gotten them both through the toughest times a girl can have – the loss of their mother. At Pepper's stubborn glare, she relented. "All right. All right. The date was a disaster. I ran away. I told them I didn't want to see them anymore."

"What?" Pepper sat back. "Them? What are you talking about? You look guilty as hell."

Ryder just laid there, watching her sister's face as she worked it out in her mind.

"Oh, my God!" Pepper covered her mouth. "Did they…"

"Yea, they both came on to me. Apparently, the Duke brothers share their women."

Jumping up, Pepper began to charge around the room, fanning her own feverish face with an outstretched hand. "Wow. They told you that?" She didn't give Ryder a chance to answer, instead she turned and flounced on the bed. "Tell me everything. Everything!"

"You really don't want to know. I threw a McCoy

sized hissy fit. I even blamed you."

"Me?"

"Yea. I thought you had put them up to it all, like you were punking me or something." Ryder dragged herself up to sit on the side of the bed.

"I wouldn't do that," Pepper denied. "Was it all bad? Tell me." She came to Ryder and ran a comforting hand over her hair.

"No, it wasn't all bad. That's the problem. Samson was perfect, I thought we were hitting it off great. When we got to Falconhead, Gideon was waiting on us. They'd created this fairyland for a picnic, lights in the trees and an elegant table set up in the middle of it all."

"Sounds dreamy."

"Oh, it was. The only problem was that there were two Prince Charming's instead of one. They weren't even subtle about it. Both were super attentive, both of them completely open and honest about what they wanted."

Pepper stared at Ryder wide-eyed. "And what they both want is…you."

"Yea, me." Ryder rose and trudged to the bathroom. "I felt like I was in the middle of some kind of movie."

"Yea, some kind of fantasy, erotic, romantic movie. And you told them 'no'? Are you crazy?"

"We don't live in a movie, Pepper. We live in a family dominated by chauvinistic males, in a society that judges everyone at the drop of a hat."

Pepper waved her hand dismissively. "You can't live for others, Ryder. Are you sure you want to deny yourself this experience?"

Standing at her closet, Ryder realized her focus was shot. She couldn't decide which blouse to wear, much less which man she wanted. "Part of me does want this, Pepper. But these are powerful men. Movers and shakers. They're used to getting what they want. They can have any woman in the world. Why would they want me? Why would either of them want me?" She sighed, ignoring her sister's murmurs of protest. "At the most, all I'd be is a momentary distraction. I'm not wired like that; I don't think I can treat sex that lightly. I'd get emotionally involved…with both of them." Ryder laughed wryly. "And let's just say they fell for me too."

"Why wouldn't they? You're a wonderful, beautiful woman."

Grabbing a pair of jeans off a hangar to go with a red sweater, she giggled as she faced her sister. "If everything worked out and we became serious, can you imagine what our brothers would say? Can you imagine Heath's face?"

Pepper held her sides while she laughed. "I don't wish you anything but happiness, but it just might be worth it to see our big brother's reaction." She tried to make herself big, holding her arms out, hands into fists, and making a face. "Two men!" Pepper bellowed. "Are you crazy, girl?"

"All of them would have something to say," Ryder murmured as she dressed. "After all, we're a conservative family. This is the South. We live in Texas, land of pickup trucks and tea party values." She stooped to select a pair of shoes from the bottom of her closet. "Honestly, I don't even know how it would work. Can you imagine the family reunions? The Christmas card portraits? The rest of the family and…Ryder with her two men."

"I'm sure you would be a very stunning couple, triple…" Pepper laughed. "We'd have to come up with some new words."

As she followed her sister down the stairs to begin their day, Ryder didn't mention how good those words had sounded to her ears.

Ryder and her two men.

* * *

"I wish Heath would meet someone. Since that vile snake, Amy, left him at the altar he's been so angry. I think he lost confidence in himself." Pepper mused as she pulled a huge batch of brownies from the oven.

"I know. I want him to be happy, Pepper." She covered the big pan of baked beans with aluminum foil. "Plus, if he had his own romantic life to think about, he'd be less likely to focus on ours. Did you check the guest list and the entrants? Are there are any likely prospects coming that might give us a chance to play Cupid?" Ryder was proud of herself, she was managing to function normally and not dwell on the Duke brothers – much. She couldn't deny that thoughts of them kept flitting through her brain. Their whispered words, seductive touches, and tender kisses would be hard to forget.

"I haven't looked at it in a while, let me check. Heath's secretary has been good enough to help us keep up with this stuff. Remind me to send her flowers when this is over." Pepper walked to the laptop and pulled up the file. "Julie Stevens is coming. She always had a thing for Heath."

"I think she's seeing someone, Pepper. Anyone else?"

"Hmmm, Christine Pace, maybe?" She continued to look. "And your not-so-secret admirer is on the list. Scott Eagleton."

"I don't care, I'll just avoid him."

"Oh, my God! Oh, my God!" Pepper exclaimed, then exclaimed again. "Oh, my God!"

"What's wrong?" Ryder threw down a dishtowel and came over to where her sister was standing.

Pepper slammed the lid shut. "They're coming, Ryder. They're coming!"

"Who's coming, Pepper? The British?"

With eyes bugged and mouth agape, Pepper grabbed her sister by the arms. "The Dukes just entered the chili contest, Ryder! They even gave their address and telephone number to confirm."

"Oh, Lord." Ryder let go, gripping her stomach. "Why would they do this?"

"Well, isn't it obvious?" Pepper beamed, clearly happy about the situation. "They're not giving up on you."

Ryder opened the laptop to look for herself. Sure enough, Samson and Gideon Duke were registered as a team. "The dish they're entering is called, *Hot Stuff – Hawaiian Style.*" She almost choked. Apt name for them or their dish. "I can't believe this."

"Things are about to get interesting..." Pepper teased.

...A few hours later, Ryder had to admit Pepper was right. Things were getting interesting. As usual, a big crowd was gathering. Heath's best friend, Jimmy Dushku, arrived with his entourage. Like normal, he'd brought several celebrity friends with him, a varied crew consisting of actors, a professional golfer, even a member of the band Coldplay. Christine Pace did have Heath cornered at his chili pot and Tennessee had returned, looking like the cat that had swallowed the canary. Plus, she'd managed to evade Scott Eagleton – just barely escaping his clutches behind the Pavilion when she'd gone to the restroom.

But the most interesting thing was the two men who were approaching her from across the lawn, leading a beautiful, prancing Arabian between them. As they came, the crowd parted and Ryder understood why. Three more magnificent creatures she could never imagine. Why were they here? She doubted the billionaires had recently developed a need to express themselves by preparing culinary delights.

"Samson, Gideon, I didn't know you two were coming." Ryder stepped forward, wanting to put some distance between herself and her brother, Jaxson, who was all ears behind her.

"Ryder, you look beautiful." Samson bowed gallantly. "There were several matters we didn't get to discuss with you last evening, our plans to come to the cook-off was one of them."

"We would like to talk to you, Ryder." Gideon reached for her hand. "Please."

Seeing them again was more than embarrassing. "I said too much last night. I'm not sure what we have to say to one another now." Seeing their adamant attitude, she relented. "Well, not here. Everyone is watching us."

"Let's go down the hill toward the paddock." Samson suggested. "Our girl might need a drink of water."

Even though she was confused and upset, Ryder couldn't deny the obvious. "She's beautiful." Her hand seemed magnetically drawn to stroke the majestic animal, her fingertips grazing the mare's face and neck. "Did one of you ride her here bareback?"

"No, Skeet delivered her for you." At Ryder's confused expression, Samson explained. "Vashti is yours now. She is royalty, her bloodlines are impeccable. We wanted to give you a gift as amazing as you are."

Ryder stopped in her tracks. "A gift? Why would you do that?" She faced the two men and the gorgeous horse. "Last night was a disaster!"

Gideon took Ryder by the hand, leading her down the hill. "Let's get out of earshot. What we have to say to you, is not for everyone's ears."

Ryder went with them, more aware of the two men than ever. "I told you how I felt last night." Her tone had cooled, she was trying to hold onto her anger, but it was hard in the light of their kindness.

"Yes, you did," Samson acknowledged as they came to an area adjacent to the barn, one shaded by several big oaks. "Now, we need to tell you how we feel."

They stood on either side of Ryder as she met Vashti. "I've never seen a more beautiful horse. She must be worth a fortune. Why would you give her to me?"

"Samson told me that you'd lost your horse. We wanted to present you with a lifelong friend, we thought you'd enjoy her."

"Oh, I will. I would." She hesitated. "I don't think I can accept such an expensive gift...especially after what I said to you."

"Ryder." Samson touched her back. "We wanted to apologize to you. We are so sorry to have scared you. Looking back, I handled all of this so wrong."

Ryder didn't know what to say, she tugged on the bottom of her linen top. "I don't know what you mean."

"We meant you no disrespect, Ryder," Gideon interjected. "We wouldn't hurt you for the world."

"That's correct." Samson handed her Vashti's reins. "We hope you accept our gift and our apology in the manner that we mean them. Goodbye, Princess." He gave her one last wistful glance. "And if you ever change your mind, you know where to find us." With a tender kiss to her forehead, Samson gave her a slight bow. And with that courtly gesture, Ryder was shocked to watch them begin to retrace their steps, leaving her alone with her beautiful gift.

* * *

After Ryder introduced Vashti to one of their men, so the mare's needs would be seen to, she returned to the festivities - completely unsettled. When she'd seen the

Duke brothers striding toward her, her first thought was that they were going to refuse to take her 'no' as an answer. Heck, they'd even brought the horse to carry her off into the sunset.

But the horse wouldn't hold three.

"Stop it," she chided herself. What was she complaining about? They'd accepted her wish to not see them again. The Dukes had given her exactly what she'd asked for! They hadn't even argued about it or tried to change her mind.

So, why wasn't she happy about it? Damn them!

The truth was much more complicated.

As Ryder climbed the hill toward the crowd gathering around the chili cook-off booths, she only had eyes for Samson and Gideon Duke. While people milled around, sampling the chili, she was amused to hear how many people were loving the tropical themed chili. "What's in this?" one lady asked. "I think I taste ground pork and pineapple."

Her companion took another bite. "Whatever is in it, this stuff is amazing."

"Not nearly as amazing as the men who cooked it. Did you get an eyeful of that man candy?"

Ryder couldn't help but smile. Heath's reign as the indisputable winner of the Highland Chili Cook-off seemed to be over.

Needing a little time, she decided to take a walk to clear her head. All around her were happy people, loving couples, and contented family groups. Laughter rang out. This annual celebration was more than just a chili cook-off; it was the McCoy's way of thanking their employees and welcoming their neighbors by providing a day filled with good food and many ways to have fun. There was a live band playing on a stage down by the lake. Games were set up for the children and other activities were available for the adults to entertain themselves, everything from target practice for the men to free spa treatments for the women.

But as she made her way through the throng, Ryder felt isolated. Separate and apart.

She was immersed in a sea of happy people – and she had never felt more alone.

As she topped the hill, gazing down toward the area where the guests' vehicles were parked, Ryder noticed a man milling between the rows, looking to the left and then to the right. For a moment, she smiled, having been in his predicament before. If she had a nickel for every time she'd lost her car in a big parking lot, she's be a wealthy woman in her own right. She felt sorry for the guy, almost deciding to call out to him and ask him to describe the type of truck or car he was looking for. From her vantage point, she had a good view of them all.

But then, he stopped and knelt down. She stood on her tiptoes, curious as to what he was doing. Ryder was a bit surprised that he seemed to be doing something to Samson's Lamborghini. "Hmmm, maybe he's just a car buff, checking out the tires." She watched him until he stood up, glanced around, and took off in a semi-run. He didn't seem to see her, so Ryder watched until he made his way out to a dark sedan, hopped in, and drove off.

"Hey, Ryder!" Pepper called some distance away. "Time to announce the winners!"

"Okay!" With one last questioning glance at the departing sedan, she went to join her sister.

"Guess what?" Pepper held the basket of small trophies and ribbons.

"What?" She couldn't help but notice the twelve-deep throng of people standing around the Duke's booth. Most of them women. A spark of jealousy rose in her breast and she forcefully tamped the errant emotion down.

"Your guys won. Heath came in second and Scott Eagleton came in third."

"Oh, no." She dreaded how unhappy Heath would be and she also dreaded having to present Eagleton with a ribbon. "They aren't my guys, Pepper."

"Yea, I believe you. Men who don't like me, they bring me prize racehorses all the time."

Ryder didn't stop to ask how her sister had found out about Vashti. The woman had eyes in the back of her head. "Come on. Let's get this over with."

As the crowd looked on, she and Pepper presented the prizes to the winners of the cook-off and the other races and contests that had been held during the day. As predicted, Heath was one disgruntled cowboy. To give him credit, he didn't show it, offering the winners a congratulatory handshake. Scott Eagleton tried to draw her in for an embrace, but she slapped the white ribbon on his chest and moved on. When it came time for Ryder to present the first-place award, her voice shook when she whispered her congratulations. The chaste kisses Samson and Gideon pressed to her cheeks burned like the sweetest fire.

"Thank you, pretty lady. Being welcomed at your home was a pleasure."

When they walked away from her, leaving her alone, Ryder felt bereft. Even though the crowd pressed around her, people trying to speak to her – Ryder's hungry eyes followed them as they walked down the hill.

Murmurs about them met her ears.

"I can't believe they were here."

"Do you know who they are?"

"Yes, those are the billionaire brothers who send rockets into space. I wouldn't mind them putting me into orbit."

"Did you hear they're in some kind of feud with the Russians and the Chinese?"

"I heard on the news that they've received some kind of death threats."

The comments were going in one ear and out the other until Ryder zeroed in on the last two. An unbidden image of the unknown man kneeling by Samson's car came back to her. What if? What if someone were to try to… "Oh, my God!"

"Samson! Gideon!" She screamed and began to run. There was a chance she was wrong, but if she were right… "Samson! Gideon! Don't get in the car!"

Ryder ran as fast as she could – pushing people aside, tears streaming down her cheeks. Why hadn't she realized? Why hadn't she put two and two together before? If something were to happen to them, "I would die," she whispered in agony.

At the bottom of the hill, Samson opened his car door while Gideon went to the other side. "Did you hear that?"

"Hear what?" Gideon asked, opening his door.

"I thought I heard Ryder's voice." They both looked up to see her running to them, her eyes wide, crying out.

"Don't get in the car! Please! Stop!" She held out her hands to them.

Without shutting their doors, they came right to her. "Ryder? What's wrong?"

She was crying so hard, that they pulled her into their arms, both holding her close. "I was afraid for you."

"What do you mean, sweetheart?" Samson kissed her tears away.

She held onto them with both arms, nestled between them. "I didn't think anything of it at the time, but I saw a man at your car earlier. He was kneeling down looking under it. Something a woman just said reminded me, and suddenly I couldn't breathe. I had to stop you."

Gideon pulled away. "Take her and get back, brother."

Samson followed his sibling's direction, enveloping her in his arms and moving farther up the hill, shielding her from whatever might happen. "Be careful, Gideon," he called out loud, then asked in his mind when Gideon got closer to the car, "*what do you see?*"

Gideon knelt at the back of the Lamborghini, peering far enough under it to see a small electrical box with a flashing light. "*Good God, it's a bomb.*" Aloud, he yelled. "Call 9-1-1! Clear the premises!"

No sooner were his words set loose in the air, that Ryder was swept along in a maelstrom of chaotic activity. Highlands security converged on the spot, her brothers came running, men began the systematic and careful process of moving everyone to a point of safety. When Samson left her, she felt abandoned, so scared for him and Gideon she could scarcely breathe. From a safe vantage spot, she strained to see, hungry for any glimpse of the two men who'd come to mean so much to her so fast…

Ryder covered her mouth, gasping at the realization of her feelings. "Oh, God, what have I done?"

… Samson spoke tersely on the phone. "We've got a situation, Gabe. Bring the whole crew. We've got a bomb."

"They're just going to say 'I told you so'," Gideon observed dryly as his brother hung up from talking to their head of security. "Our keeping the guys at arm's length is over as long as this launch is being threatened."

The brothers stood back, watching as the authorities began to gather.

"God Almighty," Heath McCoy whispered, "My chili cook-off has gone to fuck." He stared over the tree line as two helicopters came into view. "Here comes the bomb-squad."

"We're sorry, Heath." Gideon offered.

"Hell, it's not your fault, Duke. I've been on the receiving end of a couple of crazies in my life." He grinned at the brothers. "Almost married one of them."

As quickly as possible, the attending crowd was escorted off the ranch. Celebrities like Eagleton and others were flown out on helicopters. Over the next hour, experts gathered and a deadly bomb equipped with a mercury switch was carefully removed that would've detonated after the car had been driven no more than a few feet.

"She saved our lives, Gideon," Samson whispered as they watched Gabriel Khan and his security team converse with the state police.

"I know." Gideon stared at the ground, his mind full of horrendous possibilities. "With no care for her own life, she ran right into our arms to save us."

Samson locked his gaze to his brothers. "She's the one, she's the one Mother always told us about. The one who'd be willing to sacrifice everything to be ours."

Gideon let out a heavy sigh. "I know Mother always told us about her vision, Samson. I believed it when I was a kid, but how can we trust something like that? Ryder saved us, yes, we owe her our life, but that's not going to change her or how she feels about us." As much as Gideon would like to grab onto this hope with both hands, his innate tendency to face the facts, no matter how bitter, came to the forefront. "Don't make more of this than there is."

"Boss, we've brought another car. Are you ready?" Gabe stood a few feet away, a mountain of a man who was ever ready to take a bullet for Samson and Gideon Duke if it was necessary.

They were about to walk away when Samson heard it…

"Wait! Wait! Please!"

Gideon and Samson wheeled around, just in time to see Ryder flying down the hill again. This time she raced toward them, throwing herself in Samson's arms. "Are you okay?"

"We're fine, precious. Thanks to you." He glanced at Gideon, his eyes conveying a distinct message. *Everything's changed.* Then, Samson cupped her face in his hands and kissed her in front of God, the McCoys...and Gideon.

We came prepared to let her go, Samson. Gideon hung back, waiting to see if she would come to him too. His heart was hammering harder than it did when his face was inches from the explosive device.

"Oh, Gideon," Ryder moved from Samson's arms into his. "I'm so sorry that I didn't think to tell you quicker."

Gideon cradled her close, breathing in the clean, sweet scent of her hair. "You came just in time, baby." She moved closer to him, pressing herself so hard against him that he could feel every soft, sweet curve.

"What if I hadn't stopped you, what if I...?"

"You saved our lives, Princess." He kissed her face, mindful of those who were watching as she embraced first one Duke, and then the other.

Samson's mind linked to his brother's. *And now, Gideon, what now?*

Ryder shook in Gideon's arms and he hugged her tight, absorbing her fear, reassuring her with whispers of thankfulness. Meeting his brother's gaze, he conveyed a distinct message. *I don't know, I know what you want, what I'm afraid to want. But I don't know if it's right.* He closed his eyes and let his body memorize hers.

"Ryder, come quick!" Pepper came running up.

Ryder stepped back from Gideon, quickly dashing

the tears from her cheeks. "What's wrong?" She could tell whatever worried Pepper was serious, her sister didn't give Samson or Gideon more than a passing glance.

Pepper leaned near her, keeping her voice down. "A detective is here to talk to Philip. They've just discovered a body at the mine where Philip was working."

"Someone was killed in the mine?" Ryder was confused.

"Yes. Someone was murdered on Highland's property and they've come to question Philip."

"They can't suspect Philip." Ryder's heartrate picked up. "Philip wouldn't hurt a fly."

"Come. We need to be there for him," Pepper urged, her face clouded with worry.

"Of course." She turned to the Duke brothers. "Excuse me, I need to go."

"We understand," Samson said, reaching out to touch her arm. "We'll call you."

"If there's anything we can do, just ask," Gideon promised.

With one last fleeting glance, Ryder took off with her sister.

"What are we going to do?" Gideon asked his brother as he raised his hand to summon Gabriel.

"About the bomb? We find the son-of-a-bitch who did it and whoever is behind it and we crush them," Samson said as they began to walk toward the limousine that had pulled up a few feet in front of them.

"You know I'm not talking about the bomb." Gideon nodded at the chauffeur who held the wide door open for them.

"Yes. I know. Home, Gervis." Samson settled in, closing the window between the front and back seat. "You're talking about Ryder."

"Yes, Ryder. I can feel hope rising in your heart."

As the limousine left Highlands land and made its way to Falconhead, Samson spoke to his brother. I can't give up. I just can't." Swiveling to face Gideon, Samson asked, pointblank, "How about you? Are you as drawn to her as I am? Do you want to see this through? See where it will take us?"

"I am as blown away by her as you are, yes. I'm just afraid we're all going to get our hearts broken. Do you think what happened today is going to change her mind about dating us?"

"I don't think her head is ready to accept what her heart wants. It's up to us to change her mind."

"And how are we going to do that? Ryder lives at home. If we go after her with no holds barred, her brothers will immediately be involved. I'm not sure how this can happen without doing the one thing she fears the most – alienating her family."

"I guess we'll have to be subtle. Show her we can be her friends, someone she can depend upon, before we try to take on a role as her lovers."

Gideon held his brother's gaze as long as he could, then turned toward the heavily tinted window, running his finger across glass, and staring at his own reflection. He could feel his brother's determination, Samson intended to pursue Miss Ryder McCoy full force. "I guess we have our work cut out. None of this is going to be easy, Samson."

"Nothing worth having ever is, brother."

CHAPTER FOUR

A trouble filled year later…

"Sometimes life throws you a curve ball, sometimes it throws you a dozen and you just have to throw your arms up and hope you don't get knocked out by one of them." Ryder stood by her sister Pepper who was crying her eyes out. "I know you think the world just ended, but it didn't. Life goes on. You just need to forget him and move on."

"How can you say that? Judah James, the man I love, is getting married to someone else!" Pepper buried her face in the pillow, her voice muffled. "Just because you've given up on being happy doesn't mean that I have to."

Ryder felt a knifelike pain lance through her heart. "I haven't given up on being happy, I just made a decision that was best for everyone. The family had to come first. Look at all that's happened to us. Philip was arrested for murder. Tennessee married, divorced, and remarried. Jaxson lost his leg in a horrible accident. We discovered a whole new branch of the family, then promptly lost one when he was kidnapped by a Mexican drug cartel. Does that sound like I've had time to pursue a romance that can go absolutely nowhere?"

Pepper sat up, her face red, and her usual glorious hair a total mess. "Yes, but look where we are now, Ryder. Heath has found love, he's married to Cato. Together, Cato and Zane solved Dalton Smith's murder and Philip was exonerated. Tennessee is back with Molly, true love won out for them and now they're about to have a baby. Jaxson is better, nothing can keep him down. And the whole family worked together to rescue Aron, he's home and the McCoy's are stronger than ever. Love conquers all. I don't intend to stand by while Judah makes the biggest mistake of his life, I'm going to him. He's marrying Ivana Paul for all the wrong reasons, he can't love her, he just can't. He loves me!"

"All right." Ryder handed her some tissues. "I'll go with you. Get up, wash your face, and let's go."

Pepper knew Ryder was baiting her. "You know I can't." She began to cry anew. "I don't know where he is. He canceled the concert in Dallas."

"Call him. He'll take your call, he always does."

"All right." She pushed her hair over her shoulder. "I will, but you need to get in touch with Samson and Gideon too. I know they've tried to reach out to you."

Ryder almost wanted to put her hands over her ears. Pepper didn't know the half of it. From the day of the cook-off, when she'd alerted them to the car bomb, not a day had gone by that Samson and Gideon had not reached out to her in some way.

Her sister continued to make her case for Ryder's would-be suitors. "They sent you those beautiful roses, which you kept in your room. You throw Eagleton's bouquets away at the door. And all the tabloids say Samson and Gideon have stopped dating completely, the speculation is endless. The gossip rags talk as much about the Duke's lack of a love life as they do the controversy over their space travel. Samson has even ridden up in our yard, like a knight on a white charger. It seems as if they're just waiting for a word from you and they'll step in to fight anyone who dares to stand in the way of you being with them."

Ryder turned her back on Pepper. "I have to consider other people. You don't." Even as she stated the sad fact, memories began to filter through her mind. A year had gone by, twelve months, a little over three-hundred sixty-five days, and during that time Samson and Gideon had never ceased to surprise her. The first indication that they hadn't given up came only two days after the cook-off. Ryder had taken Vashti out for their first ride together and, like déjà vu, Samson had joined her, galloping up to ride alongside her...

"Hello, sweetheart, how are you two beautiful ladies this morning?"

Ryder couldn't deny the thrill she felt at seeing him. "Samson, what a surprise. How are you and Gideon? Are you safe?" She couldn't keep the concern out of her voice if she'd tried. Her own family probably would've reacted more strongly to the terroristic episode on their land had it not been for two things: Sheriff Carroll had assured them that the incident was directed strictly to the Dukes, and second – finding out Philip was a serious suspect for the murder of Dalton Smith. No arrest had been made in the case, but just knowing their brother was being investigated made the whole family nervous. Each member dealt with their concerns as best they could – Ryder's way had always been on the back of a horse.

"We are safe. Our security team is on top of this, no need for you to worry."

As Samson's mount fell into step with hers, Ryder didn't waste the opportunity to drink in his presence. "I can't help it." She shook her head as if trying to dispel a bad dream. "When I think of what could've happened, it's horrifying."

"I won't bore you with details, but we're taking precautions." He reached into his jacket pocket. "And one of those precautions is making sure that you're protected."

"Me?" Ryder was shocked. "What do you mean?"

Samson's amber eyes held hers. "You'll learn very

quickly, Princess, that the Dukes protect their friends. Don't worry, the steps we're taking won't infringe on your freedom, your family won't even be aware. Since Highlands borders our property and the only road going in and out of the area goes by Falconhead, it will be fairly easy to make sure you're secure."

Ryder was flabbergasted. "You're assigning a bodyguard to me?"

"In a way," he smiled. He pointed to Falconhead's high tower. "From that high vantage point, we'll monitor any traffic around your home." At her raised eyebrow, he held up a hand. "Don't think of this as spying on you, they'll be looking for specific things. This is protective surveillance only."

"So, our meeting wasn't a coincidence. Someone informed you I left the house."

Samson had the good grace to look sheepish. "Yes, I was called the moment you headed to the barn."

"Is that all?" She didn't know whether to be angry or flattered.

He gave her a smile and Ryder couldn't help but notice he had the sexiest dimples. "No. When you leave your home alone or with someone else, a car will discretely follow you."

"Now, wait a minute, Samson..."

She pointed one elegant finger at him and Samson's hand shot out to capture it. "No, you wait. What kind of men would we be if we didn't make every effort to keep you safe? We're alive because of you. The security guards who'll follow you will keep their distance, you won't even know they're there unless something happens and then you'll be glad to have them close."

"But why would you think I was in any explicit danger? What do I have to do with any of this? The man didn't see me. How would he even know I was involved?"

"Ryder, we can't be sure who is involved. There could've been someone else at the cook-off watching to see what happened. They might think you could identify one of them."

What he said made sense, she just didn't like it. "Don't I have a choice in the matter?" How was she supposed to move on, supposed to let go what she was feeling for the Dukes if they wouldn't let her forget? "You can't do this; you don't have the right."

"You gave me the right when you put your life on the line for me. When you ran straight into our arms, the deal was sealed. And the only choice you have is whether we guard you in the way I'm laying out or if you move in with us - lock stock and barrel - so we can protect you ourselves."

She pressed her lips together. "I can't believe this."

"Believe it." He handed her what, at first glance, looked like a cell phone. "Keep this with you."

"I have a phone," she muttered, but took it from his hand, raising it to her eyes to examine the item closely.

"You don't have a phone like this, it's a satellite phone. It will work anywhere at any time. My number is programed under #1. Gideon is #2. Gabe Kahn, our head of security is #3. 9-1-1 is #4 and your brothers and sister are programmed also. We will contact you often, but we expect you to contact us if you need anything…anything. Do you understand?"

Ryder shivered. She didn't understand. "Why are you doing this? We don't have a future together."

Samson hung his head briefly, then raised his eyes to hers. "Neither one of us can be sure what the future holds. Gideon will tell you that I never give up." He moved his mount close to Vashti, leaned over and stole a kiss. "I choose to believe we do have a future. Someday." Samson gave her a smile. "I think it's written in the stars."

Pepper's irate voice penetrated her daydream. "What do you mean, you have other people to consider and I don't? My family is your family."

"This is primarily between you and Judah," she explained. "The family wouldn't really think twice about you two getting together." Ryder walked to the window and looked out, trying to shake off the wave of memories that were bombarding her brain. From the day Samson informed her of the steps they were taking to protect her – everything changed. While they'd been right, the watchful eye his team kept on her was unobtrusive, the twins themselves made no effort to hide their concern. They never pushed her to have a relationship, but they did remind her at every opportunity that they were going nowhere. They were waiting.

For her.

One day when she'd driven by Falconhead, Gideon had been waiting at the side of the road with a lei. When she'd slowed to a stop, he'd come to the car window and placed it around her neck. "Aloha, nani."

"Nani?" she'd asked, repeating him, mainly because she was too tongue-tied to think of any other words.

"Nani means beautiful, and you are." He'd kissed her, told her to be careful and sent her on her way.

Another time, Samson had met her on a walk, presenting her with a golden charm bracelet, and the brothers had taken to hiding charms for her in the fork of a tree where they'd met her more than once on horseback.

And as much as she was drawn to them, Ryder explained - more than once, "I can't date you, you know that, I explained how I feel."

"Who's dating?" Gideon had said. "We're just trying to be good neighbors, Princess." As he'd kissed her hand, her arm, her shoulder. "Aren't we being good neighbors?"

During the discussion with her sister, she played with the chain around her wrist – fingering the small charms that meant so much: a crescent moon, a star, a rocket, a heart, a horse, a crown, and the number 3.

Pepper stood and straightened her clothes. "Don't be so sure," she muttered. "Heath said he didn't trust *that singer* to put me first in his life." Pepper hugged herself, feeling a chill coming on. She didn't know if she was coming down with something or if this was just nerves. "Something more is going on with Judah, either he thinks he's protecting me from God knows what or he doesn't care anything about me at all." She walked to her dresser and stared at her tear-stained face in the mirror. "I just don't know which it is."

"You won't know until you try to find out."

"How about you? Are you going to just abandon your hopes and dreams?"

"Our circumstances are different, Pepper." Ryder just wished she could convince her heart of what her mind had been forced to accept. Every time she built up a wall – they'd show up and tear it down. Over the past months, she'd lost count of how many times they'd made a point to see her – on a walk, a ride, or casually running into her on shopping trips, church, even once the library. Never pushing and usually bearing gifts. Sometimes these presents were costly by her standards, other times they were simple, like a journal Gideon gave her to record her poetry. Once she'd returned the favor by buying them gloves after they'd joined her for a ride on a blustery day and came barehanded. The small gesture seemed to mean more to Samson and Gideon than if anyone else had given them a million dollars.

"Exactly. Judah is pushing me away and the Dukes would do anything to win you."

"If Heath and the others found out the truth about

Samson and Gideon, it would be World War Three around here." This belief, that her family couldn't accept the Dukes, was really her only argument against being with them. Ryder had become so used to – or maybe addicted was the better word – to their impromptu appearances that when they didn't show, she worried. The few times she'd used the satellite phone was to check on them when she felt they'd gone longer than usual in contacting her. Once she'd learned Gideon was sick, so she made him soup and took it to him. He'd seemed so touched and honored, she sat with him while he ate. Another time when she'd contacted them, the brothers were traveling in the Middle East and Samson had immediately contacted her via Skype so she could see for herself that they were okay. Her efforts to reach out to them were always rewarded. The next time they saw her, they would shower her with praise and affection – and lots of kisses. All of this seemed so surreal to Ryder. Were they just good neighbors? Friends? Did she want more?

They'd been careful, in accordance with her wishes, to keep their visits and meet-ups secret. Her family, including Pepper, had no idea what was going on. Sometimes Ryder felt like she was living in two worlds – one real and one a fantasy.

Whirling around, Pepper faced Ryder. "I know you pushed them away, but they've never stopped trying. The three of you are at a romantic stalemate. They've reached out to you, and you want them, I know you do. I can see it in your eyes. What are you waiting for?"

What was she waiting for? A miracle! Ryder hated to lie to her sister, but she saw no other way around it. Her family wouldn't understand. She didn't even understand. In her frustrations, Ryder picked up a pillow from Pepper's bed and hurled it across the room. "How would this work, Pepper? Two men. No matter what I might want, you know how the family would feel about this. Hell, it might kill Daddy. He's had a series of strokes already. Do you think I want that on my conscience? Sometimes you must do what's right, not what you necessarily want."

"Even if it breaks your heart, Ryder?"

"Yes. Even if it breaks my heart."

"What would it take to change your mind?"

Ryder wished Pepper would just let the whole idea go. "A miracle. A divine intervention. Maybe if they just kidnapped me and I had no choice." She couldn't help but smile at her own ridiculous suggestions. "That might be fun."

"Well, since I'm praying for a miracle of my own, I'll just add a few extra novenas for you." Pepper assured her with a smile, a rather sneaky smile.

…At Falconhead, the Dukes were having a family discussion of their own. Nothing throws two grown men off their game like having their mother come visit.

"I want to meet this woman." Leilani sat primly at the kitchen table. "Invite her to tea."

Samson looked thunderstruck. "I will not invite Ryder to tea so you can grill her, Mother." He'd made the mistake one night of pouring his heart out on the phone, telling his mother about their secret rendezvous with Ryder, and what a toll the emotional distance they were forced to maintain from the woman they were fast falling in love with, was costing them.

"This is a problem neither our money nor our mommy can fix." Gideon chuckled sadly, leaning his chair back on the tiled floor.

"Sit up straight, son. You underestimate me. I don't intend to push; I just intend to subtly find out how she feels."

Thurgood arrived with a silver tray, heavily laden

with refreshments. He sat it down, then proceeded to serve them, pouring coffee for the men and tea for the lady. "May I order a car for you, madam?"

Samson cut his eyes toward their old butler. "Don't encourage her, Thurgood. We don't need mother to fight our battles for us." The last time they'd spoken to Ryder, just the night before, he could tell she was also feeling frustrated by their odd predicament. While they were trying to abide by Ryder's wishes, his patience was wearing thin and he knew Gideon's was also.

"Yes, sir." He leaned over to whisper to Leilani. "They require assistance in this romantic stand-off."

Leilani laughed. "Very well. My flight to Paris doesn't leave until tomorrow. We have plenty of time."

"Mother, no." Samson was insistent. Pressuring Ryder wasn't the way to go. They ought to know, they'd been stalking her like predators for a year without much success. Oh, they'd handled her with kid gloves, but they'd left no doubt in her mind that they wanted more. And…if there was any doubt, when she saw the new name of the rockets they were about to launch, that doubt would be blown sky high. Pun intended. Ryder-I and Ryder-II were set to be put into orbit within the month.

"Fine." She held up her hands. "I will behave. I just want a chance to meet your neighbors. A woman gets hungry for female companionship. This place is like home, too much testosterone."

You might as well let it go, Samson. She's going to do what she wants to.

Nothing's changed. Right?

"How are our fathers?" Samson asked as he checked his phone. Text messages kept popping up like ant hills.

"They are good. The ranch keeps them busy. You must visit soon and see the changes they are making. We are thinking of opening the main house to visitors."

Leilani sipped her tea, munching on a lemon cookie.

"Why in the world would you do something like that?" Samson asked, clearly upset at the notion.

Leilani spread her hands. "For history. Our family is descended from the island's royalty, we have much to share, much we can teach the children."

Gideon placed his hand over his mother's. "Let's discuss this before we decide anything. Until we're convinced all threats are contained against us, we don't want to have to worry about you and the dads. Also, our way of life is not understood. I'm not sure shining the spotlight on it is the best thing to do."

"Mother, we'll have dinner together tonight." Samson stood, picking up his hat. "Right now, we've got to make a conference call."

Following suit, Gideon rose, then leaned over to kiss his mother. "You behave, Makuahine."

She gave him a complacent smile. "What fun would that be?"

"That's what I'm afraid of." Samson growled good naturedly as they headed for the hall. "We're in trouble, aren't we?"

"I suspect we are," Gideon mused, opening the office door and stepping through. "Mother's on a mission, changing her mind would be impossible at this point."

"I wish she wouldn't. I feel as if we've made some progress with Ryder and I don't want Mother to jeopardize that progress."

"I'm not so sure we have made any significant progress." Gideon sat down at a large mahogany table, opening the lid of a computer. "We've got her more used to being around us, but I still don't think she's ready to let us into her life in any meaningful way."

"I'm not giving up," Samson stated flatly, crossing his arms and staring at the screen while Gideon placed the call. "I can't read her mind like I can yours, but her face lights up every time she sees us. And if we don't call at our usual time, she gets antsy."

"Shoot, you don't give her a chance to get antsy." Gideon barked a low laugh. "Look, we might not have a choice but to give up. She's still turning us down if we even hint at anything more than a causal meeting."

"Ever the pessimist, aren't you?"

"That's my role, not everyone can be a cockeyed optimist like you." He pointed at the computer as the face of a man appeared. "I fear it's going to be far easier to get this astronaut and the payload to the International Space Station than it will be to get to first base with the sweet girl next door."

* * *

Ryder stood on the balcony outside her bedroom, staring at the rooftops of Falconhead Manor. What were Samson and Gideon doing this morning? Did they miss her? They'd taken to calling her right about bedtime every night. Just hearing their voices gave her strength to get up in the morning. She hugged herself tightly, trying to ignore the ache in her chest. No matter what Pepper said, this was an impossible situation.

Her attention was drawn to a car coming down the hill, a red convertible. Ryder watched as the car turned off the main road and came down the drive toward Highlands Ranch. Knowing she was here alone, she turned to make her way downstairs to greet the visitor.

When she opened the door, Ryder was met by a beautiful woman with dark hair, impeccably dressed in a golden sarong-like garment.

"Hello, may I help you?"

The woman nodded graciously. "I'm sure you can. You are Ryder McCoy, are you not?"

"Yes, I am." Ryder studied her face. There was something familiar about the woman. "Do I know you?"

"No, but it's time you did. My name is Leilani. I am Samson and Gideon Duke's mother."

Ryder's mouth opened, she almost forgot her manners. When she'd opened her eyes this morning, meeting Leilani Duke was the last thing she thought would happen. "Won't you come in?" She stepped back, making room for her regal visitor to enter. "To what do I owe the pleasure?"

Leilani took the time to survey her surroundings. "You have a lovely home." She gave Ryder a warm smile. "And you are a lovely girl. My sons have good taste."

Ryder went weak in the knees. "Let's sit down in the drawing room. Could I serve you a drink?"

"Yes, please. Water would be nice."

Ryder accompanied Leilani to the sofa, then hurried to the kitchen to get her a glass of water. The McCoys had never hired a fulltime maid or housekeeper, so she wondered how this mother of billionaires would view her doing the serving. Scurrying to grab a piece of crystal, fill it from the tap, all without dropping the glass or tripping over the rug was quite a feat. What was she doing here? Ryder couldn't even begin to fathom.

"Here you go." She presented the glass to this woman who epitomized what she'd always presumed royalty to look like. Straight back, graceful air, perfect features. Ryder felt gauche and unprepared in contrast. "If I'd known you were coming, I'd have dressed…" She ran her somewhat damp palms down the sides of her faded blue jeans.

"You look beautiful. You're exactly what I expected."

Leilani's compliment didn't do much to settle Ryder's nerves.

"So, you're visiting your sons?" Obviously. How lame.

"Yes, I am." The matriarch nodded. "I'm on my way to Paris. I try to stop in and check on my children as often as I can. Leaving my ranch and my two husbands isn't something I enjoy doing, but since they have chosen to live half a world away from me, I do the best I can."

"I can't imagine being that far away from my folks." Ryder spoke calmly, even as her mind was spinning. Two Husbands?

"You love your family, don't you?" Leilani smiled indulgently. "Loyalty is a very valuable quality. Tell me about yourself, Ryder, my dear."

Ryder wished she'd brought water for herself. Her mouth was as dry as cotton wool. "Well, I have one younger sister and four older brothers."

"Very protective, I'm sure."

"Yes, they are." She didn't want this woman to get the wrong impression. "Believe me, they can be a pain, but when our world fell apart, my brothers stepped up and built a life for us." At Leilani's quizzical expression, Ryder went on to explain. "Our childhood home was a plantation in South Louisiana, one that my mother inherited. We had an idyllic childhood. I can remember my parents being head over heels in love."

Leilani touched her hand. "What happened to destroy your world?"

"Hurricane Katrina stole our home and our mother. My father fell apart, he suffered a massive stroke, he's only just now beginning to recover. Heath, my older brother, took the reins. Philip, Tennessee, and Jaxson were equally supportive and protective." She shrugged. "I would be lost without them."

"And in your own way, you're very protective of them. Am I right?"

Ryder studied her own unpainted fingernails. "I don't like to disappoint them."

Leilani gazed around her. "As beautiful as your home is, could we walk outside? I need to stretch my legs."

"Certainly." Ryder rose and led the way. "I must tell you that your two sons have been very kind to me."

Leilani laughed. "I'm surprised you brought them up. I guess they are the huge elephant in the room. You had to know this wasn't just a neighborly visit, no matter what I told Gideon and Samson this morning."

"They know you're here?" Ryder was growing more confused by the minute.

"They know, but they don't approve. Samson and Gideon did not want me to interfere." She raised her hands imploringly. "But when you see that your children are hurting, what else is a mother to do?"

Ryder frowned, leading her guest near to the rose bed they'd planted in their mother's memory. "I can't believe they are hurting, Mrs. Duke. Your sons are men of the world and I'm..." What was she? A distraction? A challenge? Ryder immediately felt guilty. If they'd done nothing else, they'd proven they were good men. "I'm their friend."

"I do not pretend to speak for my sons, Ryder, but I do know them well. The impact you have made on their lives has been momentous. They told me of you after your first meeting, when Samson killed the serpent about to strike you."

"Yes, he saved my life." She felt once more the unexpected connections she'd felt to Samson first, and then to Gideon.

"And in turn, you saved theirs. They told me you risked your life to stop them from crawling into that death trap of a car."

"Of course I did, anyone would have."

Leilani waved her hands. "You know how self-absorbed and selfish people can be. Most people don't notice what goes around them, much less intervene when it means putting their own life on the line." She paused to smell a rose. "Ah…fragrant. My sons have also told me that they haven't stopped seeing you as you will allow, despite what your family thinks."

Ryder matched her stride to Leilani, who was quite a bit shorter than she was. "Okay, I'll admit our acquaintance has been rather spectacular and unorthodox. But your sons live in a different world than I do." In more ways than one. "I'm nowhere near being in their league. I don't travel in their circles. We have nothing in common."

"Hmmm, I don't know." Leilani looked around. "You share a love of the land. Your properties share a common boundary." She looked Ryder straight in the eye. "And I think you share other things as well."

Ryder gulped. "Your sons are very charming, very handsome, and true gentleman. You raised them well." She closed her eyes, then tripped over a rock and Leilani had to reach out and grasp Ryder's arm to keep her from falling. "Forgive me, I'm clumsy."

"Come, let's sit." Leilani picked up the mantle of her maternal instinct and guided Ryder to a covered arbor. "May I be frank? I think we're skirting the issue."

Ryder bowed her head. "Mrs. Duke, I don't know if I feel comfortable speaking about these matters with you."

She paused, then began speaking softly. "My sons were raised in a household where love abounded. Yes, I have two husbands. Two wonderful husbands." She laid her hand over Ryder's, which trembled on the cool wood. "This is our way. I am descended from a line of Polynesian Queens who have always been blessed to possess the protection of more than one man. This does not discount their devotion or our loyalty. Love is not a commodity that decreases the more it is given. Just as a woman can love a dozen children completely and equally, so can a woman love two men equally, sometimes differently, but always completely."

Ryder was shocked. "I thought their proclivity for sharing was rooted more in a sexual preference, not a…"

Leilani laughed. "I'm their mother. Despite my beliefs, I don't want to go there. What I'm telling you is that they meant you no insult."

"I didn't take it as an insult, Mrs. Duke. If I were to be honest, I was frightened by my own desire."

Leilani rose gracefully to her feet. "I will not keep you. My visit has been fruitful."

"How so?" Ryder rose to her feet also, amazed at how beautiful this woman was, with her smooth tanned skin, her clear dark eyes and the gracefulness of her lithe, still youthful body.

Leilani placed a warm hand on Ryder's arm. "I needed to see for myself what type of woman you are. You may be the one who claims the hearts of my sons." She folded her hands in front of her. "I needed to also make sure if you were the type who could accept and understand our lifestyle."

Lifestyle. Ryder's head spun. "I still think you're overestimating your sons' fascination with me. What they feel is probably merely friendship and gratitude." Shutting her eyes, she recalled the words they'd whispered to her only last night.

Ryder, we will wait for you.

Give us a chance, Ryder.

And singly.

I dream of no other. Samson told her.

And Gideon's plea. *Allow me to make you happy,*

Ryder.

As they began their stroll back to her car, Leilani dismissed Ryder's assumption. "Samson and Gideon may be grateful you prevented their climbing in the booby-trapped car, but they know their own mind. This tradition is deeply rooted in our past. The men from whom they are descended offered their lives and their love to protect their woman."

"I think I can understand, but that doesn't mean my family would ever be able to accept it. And even…if I were to want be a part of something like this…how could I turn my back on my family?"

Leilani nodded. "We will have to trust the gods to work this out." When they reached her car, Leilani took Ryder's hands. "As I take my leave, remember this, Ryder McCoy. To be loved by one good man is to be blessed, to be loved by two – is paradise." To Ryder's shock, Leilani went on tiptoe and kissed Ryder's cheek. "Don't close your mind and heart to something that might very well be your destiny. The next time we meet, I trust you'll be wearing white."

As Samson and Gideon's mother drove away, Ryder stood still, with the uncanny feeling she'd just been hit by a very small, very elegant, tropical steamroller.

* * *

"Pepper, what's wrong?" Cato, Heath's wife, asked from the bottom of the stairs.

Holding her phone in her hand, Pepper raised her head to look at her sister-in-law. There was no hiding the fact that she was crying. Knowing Cato read lips and wouldn't be able to understand her if she didn't speak clearly, she swallowed back a sob and took a deep breath. "I just talked to Judah's manager. He's going to be filming tonight at Austin City Limits. This might be my only chance to talk to him before he marries that woman."

"Oh, honey." Cato went to her, sitting down on the step beside Pepper. "Do you want me to go with you?"

"Where are you two going?" Molly spoke up from behind them.

Cato, not seeing Molly, continued to comfort Pepper. "I bet Molly and Ryder would go with us. You shouldn't have to do this alone."

Molly squeezed by and came to squat down in front of the sad pair. "Wherever this field trip is taking us, count me in."

Pepper looked at her very pregnant sister-in-law. "Do you feel like driving down to Austin in your condition?"

The beautiful Hispanic girl patted her swollen middle. "Are you kidding? I'm craving some Mexican food from Chuy's. If you'll promise me a taco, I'll follow you to the border and back."

"I can spring for tacos," Pepper promised with a wan smile, then bowed her head. "I know I'm being stupid. Judah has made it crystal clear how he feels about me. He says what we shared that night wasn't real. He says those lyrics he wrote don't refer to me, but I know they do." She grabbed Molly and Cato's hand. "Why is he doing this? Why is he marrying that woman? He can't love her, he just can't."

Cato hugged her and Molly gave her a pep talk. "Don't cry. You are such a wonderful person, Pepper. Any man who can't see that is blind."

A door opening behind them, caused Pepper and Molly to turn and see Ryder approaching them. Cato, seeing where their attention was directed, stood up and smiled. "Pack your bags, sister. We're going on an all-girl field trip."

Ryder, who hadn't talked to any of her family since she spoke to Leilani Duke, was more than curious.

"What's going on? And when did you all get back?"

Pepper and Cato scooted to one side, so Ryder could come down the stairs and sit by Molly. "If you wouldn't sleep all day, you'd know what's going on," Pepper teased tearfully.

Ryder twisted a lock of her hair around one finger. "I didn't sleep well last night." She couldn't get all the things Samson's and Gideon's mother had said out of her mind.

"Tennessee and I had a good time in Marathon. His wind turbine farm is coming right along. He thinks Thunder-Hawk will be producing electricity by the end of the year." Molly's pride in her husband's accomplishment was obvious.

Cato laughed. "Well, Heath and I went on a wild goose chase. He was supposed to meet this Russian guy named Boris Anatoly who has been promising Heath he would invest in some green energy project that my husband has been trying to get off the ground for months. We were supposed to have dinner with Anatoly in Dallas and he didn't show." Cato sighed dramatically. "To say Heath was pissed is putting it mildly."

"Is he still doing business with our neighbors?" Ryder asked casually, making sure no emotion showed on her face.

Cato's eyes narrowed. "You don't know?"

"What do you mean? Don't know what?" She wanted Cato to tell her, just in case something slipped. Samson and Gideon has shared the news with her a few evenings before in their ten o'clock phone call.

"Heath signed a contract with them. He's not only providing the rocket fuel, he's also working on some environmental programs with OuterLimits, something to do with oceanic debris."

"That's great, isn't it? I'm sure they'll be able to open

a lot of doors for Heath. They have contacts all over the world."

"So, will you go with us?" Pepper asked, refocusing their conversation.

"I still don't know where we're going." She surveyed her female relatives with curiosity.

"Austin," Pepper stated. "I'm going to see Judah and I'm going to need all the support I can get."

"What are you going to tell our brothers?" Ryder knew this was a sore topic, it was certainly one with her. Still, this was the way they were raised and neither of them would be changing anytime soon.

Pepper fidgeted. "Well, I thought we could stay with Racy Monahan. She has that big house in Westlake and we have a standing invitation. After we stood up for her that day in the quad, when that guy was bullying her, the girl thinks we hung the moon."

"So, what I hear you saying is that we're going to visit a friend," Cato interpreted.

"Exactly." Molly grinned. "The guys will barely notice we're gone anyway."

"Speak for yourself, Molly." Cato giggled. "My husband will definitely notice if I'm not in his bed."

Pepper covered her ears. "TMI, Cato."

Molly just shook her head. "Tennessee will notice I'm gone too, but they will be distracted when the organizers for that cattle drive come to visit." She poked Ryder. "Remember? There's a plan to celebrate the one hundred fifty-year anniversary of the Chisholm Trail by driving four hundred Longhorns eight hundred miles from San Antonio to Abilene, Kansas. Our Tebow McCoy cousins are coming too; the whole family is helping sponsor the event. After all, it was our ancestor, the first Joseph McCoy, who made the dream of transporting cattle from Texas to the Eastern United

States possible."

"Wow, I'm impressed," Ryder said, with all sincerity. "Not only do you know your stuff; this is a damn good plan. You're right, the guys will never even notice we're gone."

Pepper sighed. "Remember, this isn't going to be all fun and games. My heart is on the line, here. If I don't stop Judah from marrying this Hollywood bimbo, my hope to win the love of my life is over."

"Oh, sweetie, don't look at it that way. Things just have a way of working out like they're supposed to." Cato gathered her sisters-in-law into a huddled embrace.

As they hugged, Pepper plotted. She knew Cato and the others meant well, but she didn't plan on just hoping things worked themselves out. It was time to take the bull by the horns. There were two things she planned on doing. One – she was going into the 'divine intervention' business and call her handsome neighbors to tell them where they could find Ryder in Austin, if they chose to do so. And second – she planned on confronting Judah James and asking him to his face whether he cared anything for her or not.

CHAPTER FIVE

The drive from Lake Buchanan to Austin was fraught with emotion and laughter. At the first of their journey, as they passed Falconhead Manor, Ryder nearly broke her neck staring back toward the big house.

"Do you want to stop and check on them?" Molly asked as she browsed through the Sirius stations on Pepper's radio.

Ryder, who was sitting in the back with Cato, denied everything. "I wasn't thinking about them at all. I was watching one of the eagles sail over the trees. She has a nest nearby."

"What did Molly say?" Cato asked, hitting Ryder on the knee. "I couldn't see."

"She wanted to know if I wanted to stop and see the Dukes, she thinks I was gazing toward their house with longing," Ryder explained patiently.

Molly turned and looked at Cato between the seats. "Sorry, Cato."

"No problem, Molly. And she was thinking about the Dukes, I could tell."

Cato's remark made Ryder giggle and pull her sister-in-law's hair. "You're a toot. No wonder Heath is going gray."

"Oh, he looks distinguished. He's going to be my Silver Fox one of these days," Cato said dreamily.

"They're not home, anyway." Pepper piped up.

"Who?" Molly asked.

"The Dukes," Pepper said, then pressed her lips together. Oops.

"How do you know?" Ryder asked, a hint of suspicion in her voice.

"Oh, uh," Pepper hemmed and hawed. "I saw a report on one of those gossip shows this morning. They're in France."

Ryder sighed, but said no more. They hadn't told her they were going to France. She tapped her toe in agitation. Of course, she hadn't told them she was going to Austin, either. At least she didn't have her private goons following her anymore. After nine months of no threats, the Dukes had finally relented on the security detail that had been her constant, yet unseen, companion. Of course, with all the trouble they'd been through, the family had stuck pretty close to home, or at least close together. This was the first outing the girls had taken without one of their husbands or brothers along as chaperones.

Pepper just stayed focused on the road. If she said too much, she'd end up confessing how she'd talked to Samson Duke for a good half hour before they left home. The big man had thanked her and told her they would fly in immediately, that nothing was more important to them than another chance with Ryder. She smiled sadly to herself. She'd give anything in the world for Judah James to feel about her the way the Duke brothers felt about her sister.

"What's up with Jaxson these days?" Molly asked out of the blue.

"Why? What have you heard? Anyone want something to drink?" Ryder faced Cato, offering her a bottle of water from the bag at her feet.

"Thanks." Cato accepted it, as did Molly and Pepper. Ryder handed their waters to them, reaching between the two front seats.

Molly began to speak again. "All I know is that he came home last night and threw a plate against the kitchen wall. He broke the dish and knocked the chalkboard down."

"Wow, I hope nothing's wrong." Ryder worried aloud. "He's been doing so much better, completing rehab and volunteering to help out at the hospital."

Pepper pulled down her visor and opened the makeup mirror so she could see into the backseat. "What could get him that upset? Did you ask him?"

"I did," Molly admitted. "Ten was with me, but he wouldn't talk to either one of us."

"Dang." Ryder breathed out a sigh. "I wish we could all be happy at the same time for once."

"Yea, I agree." Cato took a swig of water. "Philip seems much better, at least. I think he went to visit a woman yesterday."

"What woman?" Ryder asked at the same time Pepper spoke up.

"Oh, really?" Pepper asked, glad to have something to think about other than her upcoming confrontation with Judah. "Do you know who?"

"No, I don't. All I know is that he had lipstick on his collar when he came in last night," Cato murmured, all smiles.

"Wow. I thought he'd gone to do a guest lecture at A&M," Pepper mused, keeping her eyes on the road. She was nearing the intersection where she needed to hit the interstate.

"Oh, he did," Molly injected. "Ten spoke with him before he left Bryan-College Station. He wanted Philip to go by the Blue Bell factory store and buy a case of that new flavor they have – get this – Camouflage."

"Seriously?" Ryder laughed. "What's in it? Deer meat and bullets?"

"No." Molly turned around. "Actually, it's good. I tasted it. The flavors are pistachio, milk chocolate, and cream cheese. And get this, it's green, brown, and white. The container is even camo colored."

"Good grief, every hunter's dream," Cato said, shaking her head. "We should have carried some on that hunting trip we went on with Libby and Aron."

"I heard about that trip from Libby. You two were nuts. She said she fell down on her butt and accidentally shot a duck and you caught a fish in your tube top," Pepper said laughing, feeling better.

"I enjoyed them so much, I can't believe your two families never knew the other even existed. The idea that Christian and his twin brother, Sebastian, was separated at birth after their parents divorced is just unreal. Their parents did not treat those children fairly. They lost out on a whole lifetime of knowing one another." Cato was still suffering over their recently discovered family history.

"Well, I think there may be more to the story than we know. Daddy said something really strange the other night," Pepper confessed quietly.

"What?" Ryder asked, but all the girls leaned toward her, not wanting to miss a single word.

"Well, I'm not exactly sure what the details are, but he said he and Sebastian had seen one another on at least three occasions. One was their mother's funeral and the other was when Dad almost died after Mother was killed. He said Sebastian also came to see him in the hospital, this was just before Sebastian and Sue drowned in that flashflood."

"All of this was before we supposedly met them all for the first time?" Ryder gasped. "Why didn't he tell us? Why would he lie about it?"

"I don't know." Pepper mused. "What he said shocked me so bad, I didn't know how to ask him to explain."

"How sad!" Molly rubbed her arms. "That gives me chill bumps. After losing my mother the way I did, it just breaks my heart to hear of others who let their time together slip through their fingers."

Ryder swallowed a lump in her throat. She knew Molly had lost her mother when she committed suicide, jumping off a steep cliff on the Rio Grande river to her death. "You're right. We'll talk to him about it when the time is right." Visions of Samson and Gideon kept coming to mind. What if she was making the biggest mistake of her life?

After that remark, the girls grew quiet, all lost in their own thoughts.

When they arrived in Austin, they first went to Racy's house where they were joyously welcomed by the excited woman. "I am so glad you all came! We can have a slumber party tonight!"

"Thanks, Racy, we owe you one." Ryder hugged their old friend. "Are you seeing anyone these days?"

With a wry laugh and a frown, Racy waved her hand. "Are you kidding? I'm having to beat them off with a stick!" When Ryder looked surprised, she hugged her. "No, honey. I'm still an old maid and will one day win the title of oldest virgin in Texas."

"Ah, I don't know, Racy. I may be competing for that prize myself," Ryder whispered once Racy was out of hearing range.

Once their hostess showed them all to their rooms, Pepper slipped off to check her messages. Sure enough, Samson had texted that they were back in the States and on their way to Austin. She messaged that they had arrived also and everything was on schedule. Now, if things would only go as smoothly with Judah.

* * *

"Where is she, do you see her?" Samson asked as they made their way through the crowd.

"No, not yet," he spoke loudly, trying to make himself heard over the music.

"Do you think she's going to be glad to see us?"

Gideon couldn't help but smirk and shake his head. Less than twenty-four hours ago, Samson Duke had made a French government official shake in his boots for having the audacity to question the motives of OuterLimits quest for interstellar space travel. Now, that same man sounded like a timid teenage boy. "She might not show it right away, but yes, I think she'll be glad to see us." At least he hoped he was right. Everything had seemed off since Ryder had put a quietus on their relationship. The emotional bond they'd shared after the near-disastrous car bomb experience seemed a lifetime removed from where they were now.

"Let's go backstage. I bet we'll find her back there. Her sister's not answering my text messages." Samson led Gideon around the perimeter of the building, never considering for one moment they wouldn't be allowed entrance.

He was right. The Dukes were some of Austin's most famous residents.

"Here are your passes, Sir. Just be wary of the 'On Air' lights to indicate when we begin filming."

Samson nodded and Gideon lifted a hand in salute. They eased down the dark hall, seeing if they could spot Ryder in any of the rooms.

They didn't have far to go before they ran into a scene they weren't expecting.

"Please, Judah, stop! I don't understand." Pepper pleaded with Judah James who stood against the dark wall, staring at her with anguish in his eyes.

"Pepper, I beg of you. Stop haunting me!" He turned to walk away from her and she followed, almost reaching him, her hand outstretched.

Samson and Gideon stayed in the shadows, not wanting to draw attention to themselves at such an inopportune moment.

"Judah, please listen to me. I love…"

Before she could say more, a door opened and a gorgeous woman stepped out clad in a sequined jumpsuit. Samson immediately recognized her. *Ivana Paul.*

I see her.

"Judah, you need to get rid of this overzealous fan. I'm ready to start my honeymoon, aren't you, baby?" She grabbed Judah by the collar and pulled him close for a kiss.

When Gideon started to step forward, Samson held him back. *Pepper wouldn't appreciate our interruption. Just wait.*

"Judah?" Pepper asked, her heart in her eyes. "Why?"

Judah tore himself from Ivana's arms and turned to face Pepper McCoy. "You need to go back where you came from, little girl. Be it my dreams or be it my nightmare, I don't know. There is no place for you here. No reason for you to stay. You and I will never be. All of this is just in your head! Can I be more clear? I DO NOT WANT YOU!"

Gideon watched Pepper sway. *To hell with this.* He rushed forward. By the time he reached Pepper, Judah and Ivana were gone. "Hey, come with us. Let's get you out of here."

Pepper sank against him, resting for just a minute, her whole body shaking with emotion. "He doesn't want me. God, he's already married." She clutched Gideon's jacket. "I need to leave. Molly and Cato are in the lounge with Ryder. Could you ask them to meet me at the car?"

"Of course." Samson walked away to follow her instructions. "Gideon will take you outside, we'll join you shortly." If he ever met Judah James in a dark alley, he was going to rearrange that pretty boy's face.

"And tell Ryder not to worry about me."

Samson heard Pepper's voice and understood. She still intended for her sister to spend the evening with them. *Take care of her, Gideon. And wish me luck.*

Hell, your batting for both of us, brother. I wish you Godspeed.

…In the lounge, Ryder was bored. She was surrounded by famous musicians and a myriad of groupies, band members, and their crew. Liquor and drugs were being passed out hand over fist. She, Cato, and Molly sat on the couch like three little monkeys. Ryder's eyes were covered, she had no desire to see two people fornicating on the pool table right in front of her. Molly's mouth was covered, because she felt queasy from the smell of pot and vomit. Cato's ears were covered, and since she couldn't hear anyway, it had to be because her hair was about to stand on end. With eyes wide open, it was apparent Mrs. Heath McCoy didn't want to miss a thing.

"My gosh, I don't think we get out enough. This is shocking the refried beans out of me. How about you?" Molly whispered to Ryder.

"Same here. Just as long as it doesn't shock the baby out of you," she murmured. "What time is it?"

Molly glanced at her watch. "A few minutes after ten."

An uneasy feeling wiggled around in her middle. Why hadn't Samson or Gideon called or texted? She tried to ignore it, but the more she thought about it, the more worried she became. "Excuse me," she spoke to her companions. "I'll be right back." Ryder rose and went toward the restroom, weaving her way through the crowd. The music was so loud she couldn't think. When she rounded the corner, she pulled out the satellite phone and tapped out a message to Samson.

You didn't call.

Just down the hall, Samson felt his phone vibrate. When he picked it up to look, he smiled.

You miss me?

His question instantly made Ryder feel better. Maybe it was the events of the day, but before she could question her motives, she answered.

Yes. Are you okay?

Look up and see for yourself.

Ryder's head jerked up and her eyes met his. Her heart immediately leapt in her chest and her feet began to automatically head straight for him through the crowd. "Samson? What are you doing here?"

He placed an arm around her shoulders and gave her a hug. "We came for you." Before she could voice a question, Samson added. "Gideon took Pepper outside. She's upset and asked for you to get Cato and Molly to meet her at the car."

"Oh, no." Ryder's heart immediately sank. "She talked to Judah?"

Samson nodded. "And his new wife."

"Damn, Judah James, damn him to hell," she murmured heatedly. "I hate the way he's jerked her around."

Samson didn't know the whole story, but he did know he would side with Ryder. If she would but allow him, he would always take her part.

"What's going on?" They were joined by two women. Figuring they were Ryder's sisters-in-law, he introduced himself. "Hello, I'm Samson Duke. I'm so pleased to meet you. I've come for Ryder. Pepper is outside waiting for you."

The women shared a quizzical look between them,

but they all hurried out of the lounge and exited through the back. "What happened with Judah?" Ryder asked as they walked along.

Samson hesitated to say. "Not knowing all the details, all I can tell you is that he didn't let her down gently."

"Bastard!" Ryder exploded. She stopped. "I ought to go back and…"

"No, come here, baby." Samson enveloped her, holding her close, while Cato and Molly continued on to where Pepper and Gideon were waiting. "I think your sister is better off without that individual. No man who values a woman treats her the way James just treated Pepper."

Ryder softened. "I know, but she thinks she's in love with him."

To Samson's absolute delight, Ryder rested against him, allowing him to cradle her close.

He could no more keep from placing a gentle kiss to the top of her head than he could prevent himself from seeking his next breath.

"How did you know how to find me? Find us?" she asked in a whisper next to his chest. "I still don't understand what you're doing here."

"Your sister called me yesterday to tell us where you'd be tonight. We flew back immediately; on the off chance we could talk you into letting us kidnap you for a few hours."

"So, this is divine intervention." Ryder raised her head and grumbled with a sad half-smile on her face. "No wonder she knew you were in France." Looking in the direction of the car, she whispered, "I need to go to her."

"Let's go." He led Ryder across the parking lot, wanting to say so many things, knowing this wasn't the time.

When they caught up with the others, Ryder took her weeping sister into her arms. "I'm so sorry, honey."

"Don't be." Pepper hugged her close. "I needed to do this. I needed to look him in the eye and hear him tell me that all of this was just my imagination. That he cared nothing for me."

"Do you want to go home?" Ryder asked. "I'll take you."

"No." Pepper pushed away. "I want you to go to dinner with Samson and Gideon. This trip was to kill two birds with one stone. My goose is cooked, but yours is still chirping." Her awkward analogy made both sisters laugh sadly. "Go talk to them. You've been as miserable as me. Why don't we see if one of us can find happiness?"

"You're a meddlesome little minx." Ryder pushed a lock of light blonde hair from her beautiful sister's face. "I'm wasting their time. I can never be what they need. You know that and I think they know that too."

"I know nothing of the kind and they're crazy about you. I wish you could've heard Samson when I spoke to him on the phone. Don't you know I would give anything in the world for Judah to love me like that? Don't waste this. Please." She pushed Ryder gently. "Go to them. Don't worry. Molly and Cato will take care of me. We'll spend some quality time with Racy."

Ryder looked over her shoulder and saw the brothers waiting for her.

"Are you sure you're going to be all right?" she asked Pepper, seeing Molly and Cato waiting just a few feet away.

"Skedaddle. I'll call you if I need you." Pepper kissed Ryder's cheek. "I won't wait up for you. I'm going to cry myself to sleep."

Ryder took Pepper by the shoulders. "Don't waste your tears on that guy, he's not worth it."

Pepper nodded. "I'm sure I'll feel that way soon." She kissed her sister on the cheek. "Don't do anything I wouldn't do."

Ryder laughed. "I guess I have a wide range of options, don't I?"

Pepper started to laugh, then bit back a sob. "Go!" She yelled at Ryder as her sister started to hug her again.

Ryder backed up two or three feet, then turned and walked toward the Dukes. As soon as they saw her coming, they each held out a hand and Ryder didn't hesitate to accept them both.

* * *

"Where are we going?" Ryder asked, sitting between Samson and Gideon in the back of their stretch limousine.

Samson picked up her hand in his and rubbed his thumb over the palm. "To the Driskill Hotel. We've reserved a private dining room."

Gideon bent his head to hers. "We would never expose you to gossip, not intentionally. Protecting you will always be our priority."

"What are we doing? It's awfully late to eat."

Samson squeezed the hand he held. "I can tell you're nervous. You have no reason to be. Have you eaten?"

Ryder shook her head. "No."

"Well, we're taking care of you, that's all," Samson muttered. "Isn't that right, Gideon?"

"Absolutely. When Pepper called, she seemed to think that you wanted to see us as much as we wanted to spend time with you. She thought this was our perfect chance. Was she wrong?" While he still had serious reservations, Gideon had been unable to stem his own rising hope that they could make this work between them.

"I don't know. I don't really feel like having a good

time, knowing that she's hurting." When she'd set out on this trip, her only thoughts had been for Pepper. Now, Pepper's heart was breaking and Ryder was about to be wined and dined by two men who, if things were different, could make all her dreams come true. Ryder didn't know whether to be happy or cry.

Ryder's words worried Samson. "I don't want you to be unhappy." He bent over and buzz kissed her cheek. "What if we just agree not to have a good time."

A giggle burst from Ryder's lips. "Silly."

Gideon hugged her. "I don't know about you, but just the possibility of spending a few hours with you is incredible. All we're asking you to do is join us for dinner. Perhaps if we all get to know one another better, we can work through this maze of emotions we're feeling."

Being so close, sandwiched between them in the seat, Ryder felt excitement, an edgy eroticism. But she also felt secure, like nothing could possibly harm her. Her feelings of being so sheltered were odd, considering the attempt on their life. "Did you ever get any more news on the car bomb? Did you ever find out who did it?" This was one topic that they always managed to dodge, but now that they were together, maybe she could get some answers.

Samson and Gideon exchanged a look.

How much should we say? I don't want her to be worried.

At this point, I think honesty is a must, Gideon.

Speaking in an even tone, full of confidence, Samson assured her. "We do know who did it, yes. There is a group of people, backed by a Russian faction, who would like to prevent us from sending our unmanned mission to Mars in a few months. We don't know the mastermind behind the plot, but we will soon. You, my beautiful girl, foiled their attempt and possibly saved mankind. When this world is threatened by drought, famine, or alien invasion – whatever - we'll have laid the groundwork for a whole new habitable world. And don't worry, we've taken aggressive action to make sure they don't get within striking distance again."

His positive attitude and sure words eased Ryder's mind to a degree. "Good. I can't stand the thought of anything happening to either of you and I sure didn't enjoy those bloodhounds you kept on my trail."

"Huh." Samson chuckled. "I'll have to tell Gabe that Ryder likened him to a droopy faced dog with long ears and a mournful voice." What he didn't tell her was that she was still being monitored and if she agreed to their arrangement, she always would be.

As the limousine arrived at the Driskill Hotel, Ryder wondered what the evening would bring. "This is a beautiful place, thank you for bringing me."

"You're more than welcome, it is our pleasure." Gideon climbed out as the chauffeur opened the door, then held out his hand to assist Ryder to her feet.

Flanked by the Duke brothers, Ryder entered the opulent lobby of the hotel. Despite the late hour, the place was hopping. Heads turned when they entered, fingers pointed, and a few cameras flashed. "I feel out of place," she whispered, her hands working at the hem of her top. "I'm not dressed for this."

"Your beauty and grace puts the rest of them to shame, sweet girl." Samson placed a possessive hand on the small of her back. He guided her through the morass of people while Gideon stepped ahead to tell someone they had arrived.

Ryder's eyes widened. She'd been to the Driskill before, but it's beauty always amazed her. The magnificent columns rising to the stained-glass ceiling drew her eye and she didn't know where to look next, there was so much to see.

"This way, Ryder." Gideon led her to a private elevator. "Our suite is ready."

"Suite?" she squeaked.

"This is our Austin home-away-from-home; we have many meetings in the private dining room of the penthouse suite." Gideon tried to reassure her, even though he and Samson both hoped the evening ended up with Ryder between them in the big king-size bed.

The ride up in the elevator was tense for Ryder. She hugged herself, rubbing her arms.

"Chilled, darling?" Samson immediately blanketed her back.

"We'll warm you up." Gideon promised, moving to her front, mirroring his brother's stance behind her.

Ryder shivered, not from the cold but from arousal. "I feel a little crowded."

Samson chuckled, giving her a little space. Gideon wasn't as giving. "Sorry, baby, we're just so happy to be here with you."

The elevator opened before she had to respond. "After you." Samson held the door and Ryder was surprised to find they were inside the suite, not an entrance hall.

"Oh, how magnificent," she breathed, taking in the fabulous room. This might be a suite, but the focal point was a huge artisan bed. Pillows seemed piled to the sky. She took one glance at it, then almost put a crick in her neck, jerking her head the other way. A blush rose in her cheeks. The bed was big enough to hold all three of them and then some. "Oh, look at the fireplace." She hurried into the sitting room, admiring the furniture. The colors in the room ranged from a regal alabaster to a rich gold. All the floors appeared to be hand-scraped hardwood and the ceilings were vaulted.

Samson and Gideon shared a smile. *Our beautiful girl is nervous.*

"The dining room is this way and everything should be waiting for us." Gideon led the way into an adjoining room with an intimate table set for three with a dramatic candelabra overhead.

The setting for three, the significance of it, was not lost on Ryder. This was really happening – she was dating two men, together.

"The bathroom is equally luxurious; perhaps we'll take advantage while we're here," Samson told Ryder. "There's an oversized whirlpool tub and a massive rain shower." When Ryder looked at him with wide doe eyes, he changed the subject. "There's also a balcony with views of 6th and Brazos Street. If we want, we can check that out while we have an after-dinner drink. Now, come sit down and see what we have for you."

Ryder approached the table and Gideon pulled out her chair. There was no way she could miss how handsome they looked. Both were clad in black jeans and black jackets, with Gideon in a dress black shirt and Samson in a dress white one. Neither wore ties, but they did have their signature Stetsons, Gideon's black and Samson's gray. "I think I might be too nervous to eat," Ryder confessed.

As the men joined her, one on either side, Samson tried to put her mind at ease. "You have no reason on earth to be nervous. You are with two men who would die to keep you safe. We only want to please you, not to cause you one moment of discomfort."

His words were meant to soothe, but Ryder trembled. "Thank you." While she watched, they uncovered dishes and served her filet mignon adorned by a shaved black truffle sauce, balsamic bacon brussel sprouts, and smoked blue corn grits. "This looks too pretty to eat."

Gideon laughed. "Nothing looks too pretty to eat, not even you." He picked up a bottle of wine and filled her glass.

Gideon's teasing comment lit a fire in Ryder. She felt parts of her warm, from her cheeks, to her breasts, to her sex. *Yes, she was in trouble.* Picking up her fork, she took a bite of the warm grits.

Don't tease her, Gideon. Patience and finesse is required.

I'll try. I'm sure you want her as much as I do. And I ache, brother.

"How many other women have you brought here?"

The brothers were so in their own head; Ryder's question took them totally by surprise. Samson recovered first. "Don't judge us for our past, sweetheart. Judge us by how we've conducted ourselves since meeting you."

Ryder sipped her wine, looking from one to the other of them.

"We've been with no one else, since meeting you, Ryder," Gideon explained, holding her gaze. "No one."

Feeling contrite and shocked, Ryder folded and refolded the napkin in her lap. "Sorry, since meeting your mother the other day…"

Gideon groaned. "So, sorry about that. You have to know it wasn't our idea. We have little to no control over Leilani Duke."

Samson was about to apologize too, but Ryder stopped him. "No, she was totally charming. She made me think. I found myself wondering a few things."

"We want to answer any questions you might have, but first…a toast." He raised his glass and the other two followed suit. "I want to tell you, Ryder McCoy, how perfectly exquisite you are."

"Yes," Gideon clinked his glass to hers, "and I want to tell you how hard my heart is beating in your presence."

Ryder blushed anew, wondering how this all came to be. "Thank you. I was hesitant to even hope to be with the two of you like this again, but I'm glad I am." She lowered her glass. "I must tell you I was surprised at what your mother told me. When we first met, and I became…" She cleared her throat, then continued. "When I became aware of your preferences, I assumed this was a form of kink for you, a fetish. Your mother implied it was much more."

Gideon nodded at Samson, who laid down his fork. "I don't know how much Mother told you, but, yes, this is more than indulging in a fantasy for us. Our sharing a woman is part of our family's tradition. This custom is our sacred way."

"Yes, it is hard to explain but we are linked, Samson and I," Gideon explained, "we're linked as all pairs of males born in our family have been, dating back generations."

Ryder was confused. "You're twins?" She looked from one to the other of them.

"Yes." Samson smiled. "One pair of twins, two fathers. Rare, but entirely possible. We've always shared more than just our hopes and dreams. We share our thoughts."

"What? Are you psychic?" Ryder asked, the frown on her face showing her confusion and surprise.

"We share the bond that many twins share," Gideon added. "Only we share more. I feel what he feels and vice versa. We also know what one another's thinking at times. It's a trait we inherited from our maternal grandmother. She was a trip."

Ryder audibly gasped at Gideon's revelation. "No wonder you share women. I can see why that gift would be a problem if you were with other people."

Samson shrugged. "True, but it will make being with you even that much more satisfying for us all."

Discussing intimate matters with these two was almost more than she could handle. "Wine. I need more wine." She held out her glass and Gideon refilled it with a smile.

"There's only one thing you need to truly understand. The woman who'll be in our life will be the center of our universe. We will honor her, protect her, and love her all of our days."

Ryder visibly shivered. "I think I need to go to the powder room."

Both men stood and Gideon jumped to pull out her chair.

"Excuse me." She smiled and fled the room, needing air and some water to cool her face.

"Of course, Princess, take your time."

Samson's voice followed her into the restroom. She made for the large marble vanity with its two copper bowl sinks. She turned on one of the crystal faucets and splashed cool water on her cheeks. "What am I going to do? All they have to do is look at me and I want to fall at their feet."

Outside…the brothers talked quietly.

"Let's check on her sister, that will help her feelings, I think." Samson took out his cell and called Pepper.

Meanwhile, Gideon rose and walked to the balcony, looking out over the lights of downtown Austin. If the truth be known, he was on pins and needles. There was no doubt Ryder was important to them both, she held their hearts in her small hands. This was a woman he could see himself being happy with for the rest of his life. But Gideon had never seen Samson like this before. His brother was already head over heels in love with this woman. Gideon could feel the surge of emotion raging through Samson at every glimpse he had of Ryder. And as much as he wanted to find happiness himself, for them both together - Gideon wanted happiness for his brother more.

After all, Gideon owed Samson his life.

Some nights, he still awoke in a cold sweat, reliving the night he almost drowned. When the powerful wave had pushed him under, when the surfboard had come crashing down on his head – when he'd been dragged down by the current, water filling his lungs – it had been Samson who'd dove in after him, Samson who'd swam to his rescue, and Samson who had pulled him to safety, working with him until Gideon had begun to breathe once more.

Yes, if only one of them were meant to be happy, Gideon wanted Samson to be the one. He would sacrifice his own self for his brother in a heartbeat.

While he and Samson had been busy on their plans to send a rocket to Mars, Gideon had spent whatever extra time he had researching Ryder's family. The McCoys and the Dukes shared some similar characteristics – a love of the land, an astute business acumen, and a fierce love of family. Despite their common ground, there were also some distinct differences in the two clans' outlook on life. In essence, they really were from two different worlds, more so than just liberal vs. conservative. Ryder was close to her family, they'd been through some hard times together, many in the past year, which only served to strengthen the bonds between them. Considering all of this, Gideon was mighty afraid that their sweet Ryder would never be able to wholeheartedly give herself to both of them – not publicly and not for the long term. She would end up feeling torn in two, between her heart and her family.

Hiding things from Samson wasn't easy, he had to

perform some mental acrobatics to build a wall that he could hide some of his feelings and intentions behind. Over the years, Gideon had found blocking his brother from some of his feelings was essential. Gideon had a dark side, not evil – not mean, but sometimes he saw shadows where his brother only saw sunlight. Maybe it had to do with his near-death experience, and maybe it was something he'd inherited from his father. Whatever the cause, he didn't want to color Samson's life with his harsher palette. Samson, while brilliant, was the most positive human being that Gideon had ever encountered. And Gideon wanted Samson to stay that way. The world needed as much goodness as it could get.

. So…he'd made a decision, a decision that he couldn't share with his brother. In order to preserve their future relationships – just in case their plan didn't work out – there would be some boundaries he would not cross tonight.

"I'm back." Ryder announced, surprised to find both brothers had moved from their spots.

"Good. We missed you." Samson greeted her with a kiss. "I just talked to Pepper. You'll be glad to know that she and your sisters-in-law have gone out on the town with someone named Racy. They seem to be doing well, despite their hostess's unusual name."

Ryder let out a small giggle. "I'm glad. Racy is nothing like her name. She's a doll, but the only way Racy is fast is when she's behind the wheel of a car. Believe it or not, she's on the Indy 500 circuit. Racy is Rachel Monahan."

The name immediately clicked with Samson. "Well, I'll be damned. She's good. I've seen her race."

Gideon watched Samson and Ryder. They looked good together. "Who's ready for dessert?" He picked up the house phone. "Cherries Jubilee sound appetizing?"

"Oh, yes." Ryder almost clapped in delight. "My favorite dessert!"

"Your sister gave us a head's up," Samson admitted with a smile. "So, while we're waiting for our sweet to arrive, how about some more wine."

They moved from the dining table to the sitting area, a large cream sectional sofa, big enough for them all to be comfortable. They talked casually until the dessert arrived, then they teased Ryder by taking turns feeding her the luscious dish.

"Anything else you want to discuss, beautiful?" Gideon asked, settling back on the couch to the left of Ryder.

Ryder scooted back, her skin tingling at their nearness. *In for a penny, in for a pound*, she thought. "Well, I've read some books, some ménage books."

"I remember you telling us you did. That's a good sign," Samson muttered with a satisfied smile. "Did you like what you read?"

"Yes, but I wouldn't expect what we might share to be like a romance novel."

Gideon took a risk, placing a caressing hand on her knee. The initial touch of her skin made his palm tingle. "No, it will be better."

"How?" she couldn't help but ask.

Samson leaned closer. "If we were to be allowed to love on you, we would do everything in our power to please you. Sometimes we would bring you to the heights together, and sometimes we'd crave our own time with you. But at no time would you feel anything less than cherished."

Ryder felt her reservations fading. There was only one more question bearing on her mind. One she had to ask. "You two are every woman's dream. You travel in circles that I could never attain." She looked down at herself. "I do own a mirror and I have a sister who looks like a Hollywood starlet." Gideon tried to interrupt her, but Ryder persisted with a held up hand. "My question is, why me?"

Again, Samson and Gideon seemed to speak to one another with their eyes.

Gideon took her hand. "While we have had other relationships, of course, we always knew they were temporary. Those associations were to be honored, to be respected, but not to be sustained. From the time we were small, our mother told us of a blue-eyed goddess who would come into our life and give it meaning."

"Do you know how many women have blue eyes?"

"Billions," Samson answered. "But there is only one you. Our mother also told us that this woman would risk her life for ours. While we were attracted to you from the first, we did not recognize you as our soulmate until you ran into our arms after saving us."

She couldn't wrap her head around his mother's vision. Although, after having met her, she wouldn't be surprised to find out she was an oracle to the ancient gods. What did stand out in her mind was their attitude of indebtedness. "So…this is gratitude, maybe?"

Gideon gave her a smile hot with promise. "Gratitude has nothing to do with how we feel about you."

"Let us show you, Ryder." Samson ran his hand underneath her hair. Ryder trembled, but didn't move from her place between them. "You don't know what seeing you all those times this past year has been like, loving to be with you, yet aching to touch you."

"Just say the word, baby." Gideon came closer, moving to face her. They were so close; she could feel their warm breath on her face and neck. "Let us give you a taste of paradise."

Ryder tried to think. Did she want this?

Oh, yes. She wanted Samson Duke. He was so powerful, yet so gentle. When he looked into her face, she felt like she was home. The very thought of his hands on her body made her weak with desire. She looked at his lips and felt her own part with need.

"You're so soft, so sweet." Gideon's whisper drew her attention.

And yes, Ryder wanted Gideon too. So much. She could almost drown in his dark eyes. Every time he touched her, a sizzle of heat danced across her skin.

"Surrender, Ryder, let us show you how much we want you, how much we need you." Samson clasped her nape and turned her face to his. The first touch of their lips made her whimper. But his weren't the only lips she felt...Gideon picked up her hand and kissed the palm. Ryder's whole body felt alive with electricity, her nipples swelled and grew hard, poking through the thin material of her bra and silky top.

"I want to surrender," she whispered. "I want to, so much." The idea of being with these two was daring – wild. Her nerves sizzled beneath her skin. Curiosity and want churned within her.

"Do it, baby," Samson whispered back. "Fall and we'll always catch you. Run to us and our arms will always be open for you. Trust us, we'll never let you down."

"I do trust you. I just don't know if I can trust myself."

Samson could see her confusion; she was surprised at her own reaction to them. This endeared her even more to him. "Kiss her, Gideon. See how sweet she is."

With one finger to her chin, Gideon turned her face toward his and he captured her mouth, consuming Ryder with his kiss. When she strained toward him, Gideon felt his cock grow long and thick, filling with desire for this woman.

Samson leaned in and twisted a lock of her hair around one finger, lifting it. Lowering his face, he kissed the warm, sweet flesh of her neck that he'd exposed. "Let's go to the bed, stretch out, get comfortable, and play a little. Just a little. Okay, Ryder?"

Ryder's breath was coming hard and fast. Being touched by both men was almost too much excitement for her to process. The slow burn of their fingers on her body caused a blistering spiral of desire to rise within her body. She didn't know what to do...who to touch...when... "I don't know how. I'm not experienced. How could I possibly please two men like you?"

"By breathing, angel. Just by breathing," Samson muttered as he tilted her head toward his to receive another kiss.

Ryder was overwhelmed. Between these two men she felt small, protected and utterly feminine. The tomboy was gone and Eve of Eden had taken her place. "Show me, please."

Her simple request enflamed them.

We'll have to go slow, she's skittish, Samson.

As slow as we need to, this is all about her.

Gideon swept her up into his arms and Samson led the way to the big bed that awaited them. Once his brother had pushed aside most of the pillows, Gideon laid her down and the brothers began to unwrap the gift that was Ryder McCoy.

Repeating what he'd told Gideon in his mind, Samson assured her. "This is all about your pleasure, love. Our pleasure is solely dependent on yours."

Ryder shivered as they undressed her. Two pairs of hands, twenty fingers, made short work of a few buttons and a zipper. As more skin was unveiled, she wanted to hide, to cover her nakedness. "Are you sure you want me?"

"My God, baby," Samson muttered. "Look at me," he held out his hand, "I want you so much, I'm shaking for you."

Gideon went to one knee on the mattress, his eyes raking over her graceful curves and golden skin. Her breasts were twin mounds of perfection, topped by succulent, puffy nipples that he couldn't wait to touch and taste.

Ryder moaned, unable to take her eyes off the men as they pulled off their shirts. They were so incredibly handsome. One light. One dark. In their clothing, they were sexy – half-naked they were lethal. Her eyes skated over the huge bulge in their jeans. She'd never seen a man nude, except in photos on some friend's Facebook site, but even in her inexperience, she knew they were exceptional. Big. Too big. "I don't think you're going to fit." A shiver of apprehension sent chill bumps over her body.

"You're made for us, Ryder. When the time comes, we'll not only fit, it's going to feel perfect for all of us." Unable to resist, Samson went to his knees at the side of the bed, claiming a kiss, his tongue sweeping in, taking her mouth in a kiss so passionate and possessive, it rocked Ryder to her toes.

Gideon lay down beside her, one hand stroking her body, his lips on her neck, her chest, feathering gentle kisses over her breast. When Samson would relinquish his position to allow his brother to sample her sweetness, Gideon would claim her lips, breaching, invading - conquering. She was almost overwhelmed by his intensity. And when they took turns – Samson teasing and Gideon demanding, she was never satisfied, constantly aching for more.

At last, Samson chose to begin scattering kisses all

over her body, beginning at Ryder's shoulder and working his way down. She tried to pay attention to everywhere he touched, but it was almost more than she could process.

Gideon's tongue still tangled with hers, exploring her mouth, demanding that Ryder respond with everything he craved. The man tasted like sin as he coaxed and teased her with licks and nips, cajoling her to join in his erotic play. And every time their gazes clashed, she was jarred by the hunger she saw in his eyes. Needing to touch him, she wove her fingers into his long dark hair, grasping it, holding him right where she wanted him.

While Gideon worshiped her mouth, Samson made himself happy at her breasts, running his hands over them, circling them, tweaking and pinching her nipples. "Look how beautiful and soft she is." *Touch her Gideon, they feel so good.*

Now, Samson had her attention. Her breasts had always been sensitive. When she touched herself, her breasts were one place she loved to tease. As he played with her, Ryder's nipples tightened, she couldn't be still, her hands roving over his arms and chest – relishing the soft as suede male skin. Ryder arched her back, thrusting her breasts up in an open invitation.

Gideon heeded the call, leaving her lips and letting his mouth blaze a trail to one breast while his brother suckled at the other. Writhing with pleasure, Ryder held on to them, a hand on each of their heads. She'd never dreamed of being so aroused, with two powerful sexy men feasting at her breasts. Ryder closed her eyes, melting – mewling, almost fainting with pleasure as their hands began to skate down her sides, on down her thighs, caressing and stroking.

Samson swirled his tongue around one hard-candy nipple, feasting on its sweetness, scraping it with his teeth. "Oh, Samson!" She was coming alive in his arms, her hunger unmistakable. Knowing what she needed, he let one hand slide over her stomach to touch her mound, then delve between her thighs. Her hips bucked in silent supplication.

God, brother, she's so creamy. Wet. Hot.

Kiss her, taste her, Samson. Together we can take her to the stars.

"Open wide, love."

She obeyed. With her legs splayed open, Ryder felt completely vulnerable, a living breathing invitation to whatever they wanted from her. Samson ran his fingers through her soft, wet folds, seeming to memorize their texture – their heat. And while he explored, Gideon watched his brother with a heated, dark gaze. Knowing they were sharing the experience, taking pleasure in what the other was doing was fascinating to her. With their undivided and ardent attention, Ryder felt more desirable and feminine than she ever had in her life. She burned, literally shaking with need. "Please," she keened.

"Please what, love? Ask for what you want." Samson's touch was as electric as his voice while he rubbed her swollen labia, just teasing the opening of her empty, aching channel. Ryder's mind was fevered, her lips unable to form words. As he stroked her pussy, she lifted her hips, wanting more and more. Finally, Samson used his big fingers to fill her, to stretch her. "I want…"

She's too innocent to know what she wants, brother. Just make her cum.

With pleasure. Samson flashed an answer to his brother as he went to his knees between Ryder's legs, parting her thighs even farther. Bowing at the altar of her femininity, he began to kiss and lick and suck, teasing her clit – using his mouth and tongue to drive her certifiably insane.

Gideon heard his brother groan, he felt Samson's excitement and satisfaction as he tasted Ryder for the first time. While his brother pleasured their woman, Gideon held Ryder in his arms, loving how she moved, how she undulated when Samson lifted her hips so he could spear his tongue deep within her. To soothe her, tempt her, let her know he was part of the process, Gideon kissed her repeatedly – her lips, her breasts, the corners of her eyes, whispering words of adoration. "You are so beautiful, baby girl. You are ours. Did you know that? You're mine!"

"Samson!" Ryder whimpered, then looked up into Gideon's eyes. "Gideon, help me." Magical sparks brushed her skin, her whole body was crying out for release.

Suck her clit, Samson. She's burning alive.

Desperately needing to be a part of sending Ryder over the edge, he bent to take her mouth in a kiss ripe with erotic possession, his fingers pinching and tweaking her nipples, his erection helplessly pumping at her side. Gideon swallowed the sweet sounds of her keening, as Samson gave her what she craved. God, she was beautiful when she surrendered – arching between them – letting herself go in complete abandon.

She cried out, the blush of sweet release flushing her body to a rosy hue. Samson thought her response was the most beautiful thing he'd ever seen. She'd gone up in flames at their touch. Undoubtedly, she was the woman they'd been waiting for all these years.

Trembling at her side, Gideon wanted to take her – possess her – shove his cock so deep inside of her that he'd touch her soul. But he couldn't...not yet...not until he was sure this wasn't going to go up in flames.

Samson wanted her just as much. *She's so tight, so perfect. If we played with her just a little more, she'd be begging for us to claim her.*

Ryder was on the verge, the very edge of reality. "Samson? Gideon?"

We need to give her time. There can be no regrets, Samson.

You're right. "We must stop," Samson whispered.

Ryder reached for them. "Why? Did I do something wrong?"

"God no, baby." Gideon tenderly kissed her cheek. "You were perfect. Being with you was heaven. We just want you to be sure before we go any farther."

She heard their words, but she also saw the evidence of their desire beneath their clothing. They were both hugely aroused. There was no way they could be comfortable, much less satisfied. Ryder wanted to touch them, to bring them the same pleasure they'd given her. "Are you sure?"

"We're sure that we want you to be happy." Samson pulled the covers back while Gideon went to the bathroom and returned with a damp cloth and a fluffy towel.

"Let me clean you up, darling." Gideon sat beside her, coaxing Ryder to open her legs once more. As he tenderly ministered to her, he gave her a sexy wink. "Next time, maybe I'll be the lucky one kissing you here."

Ryder blushed. "I can't wait."

Gideon shuddered, he had to fight himself to keep from accepting the invitation in her eyes. After he'd wiped her and patted her dry, he gave himself one more indulgence – he bent low and placed one soft kiss on the pearl of her pleasure. To his absolute delight, Ryder lifted her hips for more. It was hard to tear himself away, but he did.

"Thank you, beautiful. I've never enjoyed anything more."

Ryder was so swamped with pleasure; she was finding it hard to think. When she saw her almost lovers begin to put on their shirts, she began to feel self-conscious. Ryder didn't understand, they'd given her everything and asked nothing in return. Pulling the sheet up to cover her body, Ryder reached for her underwear. As their backs were turned, she wiggled underneath the sheet and began to shimmy into her purple panties and matching bra.

Look.

Samson turned to see what Gideon saw. He couldn't help but smile. "If I had my way, I'd keep you naked and in my bed, but if you're going to get dressed, I think we have something we'd like to add to your outfit."

Get the necklace, brother.

Ryder sat up, finding her skirt and top one of them had laid neatly on the bed next to her. She wasn't sure what they meant. She pulled on her clothes, then sat in the bed, her knees drawn up to her chin. "I'm not sure how to feel? Is this real? What did we just do?"

"Hell yeah, it's real." Samson came to her, putting one knee on the bed. "We just laid our world at your feet. How you feel about it is up to you."

Gideon rejoined them, a square velvet box in his hand. "This time we came to you, Ryder. We really didn't give you much choice."

"That's right. We want you to think about this carefully." Samson ran a finger down her velvety cheek, cupping the side of her face. "Next time, we need for you to come to us."

"And here is your assurance that we'll be waiting." Gideon opened the box to show her a necklace, a beautiful necklace with three diamonds, one Princess cut in the center, flanked by two round, one on either side, each stone at least two brilliant cut carats.

Samson took the golden necklace from the box, went behind her and placed it around her neck. "For you."

"Samson, Gideon…" She didn't know what to say. "Oh, my God. I can't accept this. It's just too much."

Gideon stilled her hands as she tried to reach back to remove it. "No, it's not too much. We're prepared to offer you everything we have, everything we are, this is just a token of the total love and affection we have for you."

Ryder placed a hand over the three stones, pressing them into her flesh. "You've overwhelmed me."

Samson placed his arm around her and pulled her back against him, kissing her neck and the side of her face. "We wanted this chance to be with you, to show you how good it could be. And this is just the beginning."

Gideon stood by, letting Samson have his moment, a moment he was dying to share. "We'll be waiting for you, Ryder. For your decision."

Ryder bent her head and rested her face against his forearm. "All right. I know it's late, but I think I need to go be with Pepper."

When Samson let her go to call Pepper's cell to see if they were home, Gideon offered her a hand up, pulling her right up to his body. "Don't make us wait long, baby." This time he didn't hold back, he layered his mouth over hers and drank deeply of her sweetness.

Ryder's arms rose of their own volition to cling to his shoulders.

"Ryder."

Samson's voice broke the moment; his tone didn't sound right. Breaking away from Gideon, she met his brother's eyes. "What is it? Something's wrong with Pepper?"

"No, she was just about to call you. They're on their way to Seton Hospital to meet your family."

"Who is it?" Ryder's heart was in her throat.

"It's your father. He collapsed."

CHAPTER SIX

"Come on, let's go." Gideon took her arm. "We'll take you to your father."

In a scared daze, Ryder let them lead her out of the suite, into the elevator and down to the hotel lobby. Samson had called his driver and the limousine was waiting at the door.

"Did she say what they think is wrong with him?" she asked when she finally found her voice.

"No." Samson took her hand. "She didn't. Has he had problems in the past?"

"He's had health problems," she spoke lowly and slowly, her eyes unfocused, staring straight ahead. "Strokes. The first one occurred right after my mother died, he was in rehab for a long time. We thought he was recovering," she gave them a vague half-smile, "he's even been dating his nurse."

"Don't worry, sugar," Gideon told her, solid and warm at her side. "Just as soon as we find out what's wrong with him, we'll fly in the best doctor we can find in the world to take care of him."

"Thank you." Ryder knew his offer was more than kind. "I just know he's had another stroke, and they said his body just couldn't take any more. He might not recover from the next one."

The Duke brothers held her hands as the driver sped from downtown Austin to the northwest side, exiting off 183 and pulling into the tree-lined parking lot. Following the signs pointing to the ER, Gervis pulled under the covered drive next to the glass entranceway and Samson sprung out, not waiting for help. Taking Ryder's hand, he led her in. Gideon moved ahead of them. "I'll find something out for you."

Ryder was shaking. Looking around, she didn't see any of her family. Could she have beat them here? "This way." Gideon motioned, a nurse waiting to escort them where they needed to be.

"How is he? Is he still alive?" She wanted to know and at the same time, she dreaded to find out.

"Mr. McCoy is in Intensive Care, an ambulance brought him in just under a half hour ago. You are the first of his family to arrive. The doctor will speak to you in just a few minutes."

"Pepper will be here soon, I'm sure." Samson tried to comfort Ryder as they strode down the hall toward a pair of large automatic doors.

"Heath and the others will be here too," Ryder said, not doubting that her brothers would drop everything to come. They'd done it before.

"Of course they will." Gideon kept a protective hand at the small of her back. "But until then, we're here and we'll move heaven and earth for you, just say the word."

Ryder wanted to cry. Fate seemed poised to place happiness in her reach with one hand and snatch it back with the other. "Thank you, I appreciate you both so much."

Moments later, the nurse stopped at a doorway, gesturing for them to enter. The waiting room was small with just a couple of couches and straight back chairs. "The doctor will be with you momentarily. "Thank you," she murmured. Ryder had no more than taken a seat before hurried footsteps could be heard coming down the hall.

"Ryder?"

Ryder rose as Pepper, Molly, Cato, and Racy burst on the scene. "Oh, I'm so glad you're here!" She hugged them all. "How did you find out?"

"Olivia called the house and Tennessee called me," Molly spoke up. "They'll be here soon."

Ryder nodded. "Olivia is Dad's nurse." She explained to Samson and Gideon.

Cato, ever Cato, walked up to the Dukes. "So, I don't think we've been formally introduced. I'm Cato McCoy, Heath's wife. I believe we're business partners."

Samson took Cato's hand. "We are so glad to meet you, Mrs. McCoy. I'm Samson and this is my brother, Gideon."

"How do you do." Gideon took her hand, also.

"I've heard a lot about you," Cato continued and Ryder wanted to crawl under something. Her brothers didn't know about her infatuation with these two men, but the females in her family hadn't missed a thing.

"I'm sorry, my manners are lacking." In order to quell her chatty sister-in-law, Ryder took the opportunity to introduce Molly and Racy to them also.

"The doctor's here," Pepper announced and they all stopped talking to meet the man who'd been caring for their father. "How is he?" She'd no more than voiced the question before the doorway was filled to overflowing by the male members of their family, all looking worried to death.

Ten and Heath gravitated to their wives, but not before Heath had zeroed in on the Dukes. Instead of asking a question, he pinned Ryder with a stare so sharp she felt like a bug about to be preserved in an entomologist's collection.

"Your father did not have another stroke or a heart attack."

The doctor's announcement took them all by surprise and they all began talking at once. He held up his hands for silence. "Your father is stable. We're doing some tests to ascertain the cause of this attack and to see if there is any damage to his heart. So, I suggest you all just try to relax." The doctor looked around the rowdy room as if he felt like that request might not be an easy one to fulfill. "You can begin to go in and see him, but just one at a time."

About that time, Olivia joined them and Heath went right to her to try and find out the details of their father's collapse.

"Are you okay?" Samson leaned in to whisper in Ryder's ear. "This is good news, is it not?"

"Yes, I'm breathing a little easier," Ryder said, nodding. "I want to see him, though." Waiting her turn proved to be hard. They let Heath go first, he insisted, and none of them would buck him.

Olivia came to sit by Ryder. "I was in the shower when I heard him fall. When I found him, he was gasping for breath." She began to cry. "He scared me to death. I was so afraid he was having another stroke."

Ryder embraced the older woman. "I know. I'm so sorry you had to go through that alone."

"I'm just thankful he's still alive," Olivia sobbed, taking Philip's hands as he came to sit on the other side of their father's companion.

"I brought you some coffee, Princess," Gideon whispered as he came to squat at her feet.

"Thank you." She accepted the cup gratefully, her attention splintered by all that was going on. "I'm so glad you're here."

"Where else would we be?" His eyes sought hers, seeking to convey all he was feeling. "We belong with you; you belong to us."

She gave him a sweet smile, conscious of many pairs of eyes watching what they were doing.

Heath came out and Tennessee took his place. Ryder was barely aware of the fact that Samson and Gideon stepped off to one side to talk business with Heath. After a while, she rose and paced for a bit, the movement making her feel better. She was aware that at least one of the Dukes kept her in their view, and she also saw that Racy had Philip cornered in one section of the hallway. This would have given her pause if she weren't so worried about her father.

"Ryder, baby, you wanna go in and see Daddy, now?" Jaxson called to her from a few feet down the hall.

"Yes!" she almost yelled the word, hurrying to meet her brother.

"He's asking for you." Jaxson took a moment to give her a hug. "He's not strong, but he's alive. We'll just have to hold onto that."

Almost afraid to breathe, Ryder pushed open the door and entered the semi-darkened room. The blips and beeps of machines sounded alien to her ears. "Daddy?"

When she rounded the door and saw him, Ryder almost collapsed. He looked so drawn, so pale. She could barely remember the big, robust man who used to carry her on his shoulders. When he'd lost his Carolyn in the horrible way she died, Christian McCoy had almost given up. "Oh, Daddy, I'm so sorry." She went to him, took his hand, and laid her head on the same bed to cry.

"Hey, none of that, sweetie."

His voice wasn't strong, but it was so dear, Ryder cried harder. "You scared me so bad. I can't lose you, Daddy, I just can't."

"You're not," Christian whispered. "I don't think this was anything but stress. A man with a big family like I have, there's always going to be something to worry about." He tried to laugh. "Heath is a rock, but he's so volatile and Tennessee almost lost out on being with his wife and baby." He reached up to wipe his eyes and Ryder jumped up to hand him a tissue. "I'd take Jaxson's pain away from him, if I could. He's still suffering. And Philip, just the thought of how close he came to going to prison, gives me nightmares to this day."

"Everything is okay now, Daddy. Our family is back on track." Ryder tried to comfort her father, kissing his hand.

"I'm old, I'm not blind and I am aware of things, little girl. Your sister is going through a rough time. She doesn't think I know, but I do. I can read our Pepper like a book."

Ryder tensed, wondering if he could sense her own turmoil.

"You're the only one I can depend on not to break my poor old heart, Ryder. You're my good girl. I never have to worry about you doing something crazy." He coughed and she handed him some water, not sure what to say in return. "I don't think I could survive another shock. Our family has had too many of them in the past year."

"You won't, Daddy. Everything will be smooth sailing from now on." Her father would never know that his words just shattered her dreams. How could she pursue a future with the Dukes? When, not if, he found out, the news and shock could be the thing that would hurt him the most.

"Will you get your little sister for me? I need to make sure she's okay. I know she was at that damn concert."

Ryder didn't ask how he knew, she was just glad he didn't have a clue what she'd been doing the same night. "Okay, Daddy."

On the way out, she momentarily rested her head against the cool wood of the doorframe. What was she going to do? How could she tell Samson and Gideon? As she walked the dozen or so yards from ICU to the waiting room, Ryder tried to come up with a plan. Was there any way they could all be happy? If there was, she couldn't see it clearly right now.

Watching her feet as she walked, deep in thought, Ryder almost walked directly into Samson's arms. "How is he? How are you?"

She wanted to rest against him, she wanted to ask them both to take her away – far away. Somewhere where they could escape reality and just live off of dreams. "He's awake, he's very fragile and I'm…sad," she whispered, surrendering to his embrace for just one precious moment.

"Samson!" The urgency in Gideon's voice caused both Ryder and Samson to turn.

"What's wrong?" she asked, hating the worried look on his face.

"There's a fire at the plant. We've got to go." He came to Ryder, taking her in a hug. "You take care and we'll check with you in the morning. Try to get some sleep, precious."

"What happened? What plant?" She didn't want to keep them, but she needed to know what they were facing.

While Gideon called for their car, Samson took a moment to explain. "The plant is in south Houston, where we build our rockets. We don't know what to make of it yet."

"Could it be terrorists?" Ryder asked, her eyes wide with concern.

"We don't know, but don't worry. We have a strict policy. We never negotiate with terrorists – no matter what. We won't be held captive by the dictates of others."

"I don't know about any of that," Ryder whispered. "I just don't want anything to happen to you."

"I'll call you and let you know something, if you'd like."

"Please do. I'll worry." She threw her arms around his neck. "Please take care of yourself and take care of Gideon." Kissing his cheek, she confessed. "I enjoyed myself so much with the two of you. I am the luckiest woman in the world."

Samson looked deep into her eyes. "You take care of you and your family." He touched the necklace with the symbolic three stones. "And don't forget that you belong to us too."

* * *

A few days later...

"We've got a get handle on this, Gideon. People just thought the space race ended in 1969, we've got a whole new competition now. Nasa, Putin and Roscosmos, China - I fear these folks will do whatever it takes to make sure we don't launch that rocket to Mars."

Gideon stood with Samson, looking out over the pool, watching their gardener as he scooped leaves out of the crystal clear blue water. "I don't have a good feeling about this. Just remember, Samson. We rely on our own wits and our security team. If we start meeting ransom demands, they'll have us over a barrel forever."

"You're right. I won't forget." Frankly, he didn't like to think about such things. "How much time do you think we lost with this fire?"

"None, if I have any say in the matter." He turned to reenter the house. "One of us needs to break away and go to the Ukraine. I'd bet my last dollar we could find out some information from those scientists who used to make the rockets for Leonid Oleg. If he's not behind this, I'll eat my Stetson. He and his cohorts, whoever they are, will do anything to keep us from making this deadline. It's not only a matter of pride with our competitors it's also a fortune's worth of contracts. Whoever lands a spaceship on Mars first will rule the space travel industry."

"Yes, one of us needs to go, it's just not a good time, is it?" Gideon knew exactly what Samson would say, he could feel his desperate anticipation as well as he could his own.

"No, not until we know where we stand with Ryder." Samson checked his phone for the thirtieth time today. "She was supposed to call an hour ago."

While they'd been gone, the brothers had been in constant contact with Ryder. Her father was out of the hospital and back in his apartment in Austin. They'd personally, sent him a fruit basket big enough to serve as the produce section of a small grocery store. She'd called them a few times, but she seemed afraid that she was being a bother. Both Samson and Gideon had assured her in no uncertain terms that any communication from her, at any time, would be more than welcome. And while they hadn't pushed her to give them the decision they were so anxious to hear, nothing was more paramount in their minds and hearts than learning whether Ryder had made up her mind whether she would begin an open and honest relationship with them.

"She'll call soon, but until she does, I think I'll ride out and check on that cow we were expecting to calve soon." Gideon pressed his hat tighter to his head. "Give me a call if she shows up or if you hear from her and I'll come right back."

"Will do." As Gideon headed to the barn, Samson went to the front room to wait by the window…just in case.

Down the road…

Ryder felt like her heart was being torn in two. "I can't choose. Don't make me choose." The tormented whisper echoed in the empty room, and even as she said the words, she knew the choice had already been made.

She wasn't considering a choice between Samson and Gideon. Her feelings for both men were so far beyond anything she'd ever felt or imagined feeling for a man, that denying them was impossible. No, she talking about choosing between what she wanted more than air...and her family. There was no question...a decision like she was tempted beyond measure to make would crumble the very foundation of the McCoy clan. Her brothers would never understand and the impact on her father could be deadly.

Sadly, Ryder walked to her car, realizing her happiness came with a price tag higher than she was willing to pay. She'd wrestled with this decision for days. Nothing in the world that she'd ever done, would be harder than what awaited her in the next few minutes. Opening the door of her white Lexus, she slid behind the wheel and just sat there for a few moments, wondering if she'd gathered enough strength to see her though the coming ordeal.

With a heavy heart, she started the engine and started off to Falconhead. The last week had been a nightmare. Their father had developed angina, which could easily lead to a heart attack if he didn't take care of himself. And one of those ways to ensure that he maintained his health was making sure the amount of stress he had to endure was at a minimum. How could she knowingly add to his worries? Before, she'd joked about her association with the Dukes killing her father and now she was faced with that possibility – if she chose to pursue the relationship. Ryder had worried the situation to death. Could she continue seeing them and just hide it? Ryder couldn't deny that she'd considered that possibility very seriously. But that wouldn't be fair to Samson and Gideon and she'd always been terrible at keeping secrets anyway.

Pepper, Cato, and Molly had agonized with her,

knowing she was almost at her wits end over the whole thing. To her sorrow, she hadn't seen anyway she could accept their advice – which was to throw caution to the wind and choose the path her heart desired. What they didn't understand – was that her heart was torn. How could she do something that might harm her father? How could she tear up their family by introducing something they couldn't begin to understand?

Since the drive was short, Ryder didn't have time to further debate her decision. When she turned into Falconhead's drive, the guard immediately granted her entrance. She didn't need to be told that she had a standing, open invitation. The brothers had been more than clear that she was to consider this home to be her home. With a heavy heart, Ryder pulled up to the door and greeted the man who came to help her from her car. She hadn't taken two steps before the door opened. Expecting to see Thurgood, Ryder raised her head to greet him, only to be swept into a pair of strong arms.

"You're here!"

"Sam…" The rest of the word was swallowed up in his kiss. She couldn't do anything but respond – he left her no choice with his consuming, passionate, possessive welcome. Ryder could feel his heart beating hard against his chest. When his mouth slid from hers, he continued kissing her face, her neck, holding her up off the ground, cradled against him. "Thank God, you're here. I've missed you like crazy. Can you spend the night?"

"Samson…"

One word.

One word, just his name.

One word and he understood she was about to break his heart. "Ryder?"

"Oh, Samson," she began to cry, "I can't. I just can't. Daddy's problem hinges upon leading a relatively stress free life. He said that I was his good girl, the one he didn't have to worry about, the one who didn't cause him any problems. How could I tell him? How could I break the news that I'm involved with two men? This just doesn't happen in our world, Samson. I don't know how to be what you want me to be without letting everybody in my life down."

Samson went to his knees. "You're walking away from us?"

Coming around the side of the house on his horse, Gideon heard their voices. Every word he heard tore a hole in his soul.

"If things were different, I could love you, Samson. I just can't love you both."

When Gideon heard that, he froze, flames of torment cascading over him at every word. With a harsh gasp, he turned his mount around and urged the stallion to run – he needed to get away, as hard and as fast as he could.

Ryder continued, wishing she could wipe the agony from Samson's face. "I could have loved just you," she repeated. "I could love, Gideon, too. So easily. Both of you speak to my heart in a way that I didn't know any man ever could. But I just can't allow myself to trust this. It goes against everything I believe in, everything my family believes in. Being with you both is a fantasy, but this fantasy can't exist in real life. Maybe we could hide our love affair or love triangle for a while, but eventually someone would find out. And then what?"

"Stop." Samson couldn't bear to hear more.

Ryder couldn't stop, not until she'd said everything she had to say. "Believe me, I've searched my heart and my soul, I want to be with you more than anything, but I don't know how to break all the rules!"

"I…I don't know what to say." Samson stood to his feet, spread his hands and looked off into the distance.

"There has to be something, someway…"

Ryder couldn't stand the pain she saw in his face. "I don't have the answer, Samson. I wish I did." She reached into her pocket and pulled out the necklace. "Please tell Gideon goodbye for me." With her eyes full of tears, she turned and fled to her car.

Filled with desolation, Samson watched as Ryder drove from sight.

…Riding alongside the shore of the lake, Gideon's pain was only matched by his brother's. He could feel Samson's hopeless, helpless despair. Ryder had turned them down – because of him. If Gideon were out of the way, his brother and Ryder could be happy.

* * *

Gideon stayed away until he was certain he'd built an impenetrable wall, a curtain to hide his deepest feelings. As much as he was hurting, he intended for the two people he loved most in the world to have a chance at forever. And he…he would put on a brave face and lick his wounds in private.

When he could face Samson and pretend he'd heard nothing of his and Ryder's conversation, Gideon returned home. The barrier he'd erected had cut off the 'knowing' he'd always relied on, the constant awareness of where his brother was, what he was doing, and how he was feeling. So, essentially, he was walking into the situation blind. This blindness prevented him from being prepared for what he found.

Crash! Crack! Crash!

Thurgood stood by helplessly with Samson, watching streams of red wine flow down the white kitchen wall like rivulets of blood. His brother had hurled the bottle like a ballistic missile, crashing with enough force to dent the stucco finish. Gideon felt his guts twist into a knot. For his usually placid brother to react like this, he had to be in immense agony. Gideon understood. He felt the same way.

But if Gideon was successful, Samson would never know it.

"What's wrong? Why are you playing target practice with a perfectly good bottle of Riesling?"

Samson turned, his face stricken. "Ryder said no. She turned us down."

Gideon knew what he said wasn't exactly true. Samson was rejected because Ryder couldn't accept the package deal that included him – Gideon. "Really? I'm so sorry." He went to his brother and put a hand on his shoulder. "I know you're disappointed."

Samson's expression when he looked at Gideon was full of questions and pain. "Disappointed? I'm not disappointed, I'm hurt. The woman I care most about in the world just walked out of my life!"

Gideon, putting on a performance worthy of an Oscar, walked away from his brother to look out the window. "I hate this has happened. I expected it. I do know you're hurting, but I think this was for the best."

"How can you say that?" Samson roared, his voice awash in desolation.

"What was her excuse?" He put just enough judgment in his voice to bring out Samson's protective instincts. Oh, yea, he was playing his sibling like a well-tuned guitar.

"This wasn't an excuse; she really feels trapped. What her heart desires and what she can live with are two different things."

Gideon looked down, shuttering his eyes as well as his mind. "I hate to say this, but I'm relieved. I've always enjoyed sharing with you, but I'm not ready to tie myself down to one woman. I went along with all of this because of you." He shrugged both shoulders up in the air. "Oh, Ryder is sweet. I'll give you that. I'd love to fuck her, but I'm not ready to just settle for one tight little pussy. Sharing a woman for a night is pleasurable, sharing one for a lifetime is nuts. I don't want a half a woman…."

Samson jerked Gideon around and hit him so hard, he knocked him into next week. "Shut your fuckin' mouth. You're talking about the woman I love!"

Gideon didn't fight back, instead he grabbed Samson's shoulders and looked him in the eye. "Go to her. Make yourself happy, this is your chance. We're not bound by traditions and rules. This is about you and Ryder, I'm out of the picture."

Samson stared at Gideon as if he were speaking a language he didn't understand. "Where the hell is this coming from? Why haven't you ever said anything?"

Gideon met his stare, cloaking the ache in his chest. "I don't know." He lied through his teeth. "I didn't want to rock the boat. I like sharing with you, double the pleasure and all that fuck – but, to tell you the truth, I've always had reservations. I'm like Ryder, in that respect, how would this work? We don't live on Lani, surrounded by people who are used to our erotic peculiarities."

"Don't be so off-hand with something we've respected our entire life, brother. Or at least I have. We are a product of that peculiarity. Our fathers are fine men, men who molded us into the people we are, laid the foundation so we felt the freedom to pursue our dreams," Samson said through gritted teeth, shaking his fist in his brother's face. "They love our mother unequivocally and, as far as I know, they've never regretted that decision a day in their life."

More lies. "As far as we know, yes."

Samson stared at Gideon as if he didn't know him. "What's gotten into you? Ryder is what we need to complete our life, and we lost her."

"She's what you need, Samson." Gideon managed to get the words out. "Nothing will change between us. I'm your brother, I'm your business partner. I will always have your back. I just don't want to share Ryder with you. You and she belong together. I want you to go to her and make this right. Tell her that I think she's amazing and that I understand."

He could tell Samson was listening, trying very hard to process this new information. He was also probing; Gideon could actually feel Samson's mind reaching out to him. Stoically, he shielded his thoughts, careful to emit the message that what he'd said was true. Samson needed to go to Ryder and Gideon needed to get the hell out of the way. The only pertinent fact he had to hide was how very much he wanted to stay.

"What will you do? This is your home. We're partners."

"We'll always be partners. I can find another home close by, or build one. You're never going to get rid of me." Gideon just needed time – time to heal, time to build an emotional front to match the one in his head, and Ryder and Samson needed time together to lay the foundation for a future together. "We've been needing to go to the Ukraine and check out Oleg and what he's might be up to. This is a good time to take care of that task and I'm just the man to do it."

Gideon gave his brother a smile. "Don't worry. Everything's going to be okay. Mother will fuss for a little while, but as soon as she sees how happy we all are, she'll come to terms with our new way of doing things."

Samson laughed and the sound was bittersweet to Gideon.

"Mother wants us to be happy, but she sure hates to be wrong." Letting out a deep breath, like a tremendous weight had been lifted from his shoulders, Samson clapped his brother on the shoulder. "I'll go to Ryder; I can't say for sure she'll listen to me."

"Oh, she'll listen. Didn't she say that she wished things were different, that she wished she was free to love you – just you?" Yea, he was pushing the envelope, but this was goddamn important. If he was going to sacrifice his chance at forever with Ryder, he at least wanted to know she and his brother had a chance.

And their only chance hinged on him riding off into the sunset…at least until the darkness had passed and the night was over.

One day, maybe not too long from now, they could all be together again. Samson and Ryder as a happy couple…and him as the happy-go-lucky third wheel, wearing a mask of indifference that they must never see him without.

* * *

"It's time! It's time!" Tennessee bellowed at the top of his voice and he ran out of his room, with one boot on and one boot off, his shirt unbuttoned and flapping in the breeze.

Doors began to open and heads popped out of rooms. "Time for what?" Jaxson bellowed, half asleep.

"The baby! The baby's coming!" Tennessee started running down the stairs.

Pepper and Ryder heard the commotion and grabbed their clothes, pulling on jeans and a T-shirt in record time. They met in the hall, along with Philip, Heath and Cato. As they all started down the stairs, seeing Ten at the door with a small suitcase, Ryder had to smile. "Are you forgetting something papa-to-be?" The joy she felt at the impending birth of her niece or nephew was a relief from the heartache that had consumed her since she walked away from Samson and Gideon only hours before.

For a moment Tennessee looked blank, then when the realization hit that he'd left his pregnant wife upstairs, he got a silly look on his face and headed back up the stairs, taking them two or three at a time. "I'm coming, Molly!"

"The man has lost his ever-loving mind." Jaxson chuckled as he and Philip started out the door to bring the SUVs around to the front.

"Just wait till Cato gets pregnant, Heath will be the world's worst." Pepper smiled.

"I will not, I resemble that remark," he good-naturedly grumbled as he watched the stairs as Ten came carrying Molly who was hanging onto his shoulders for dear life.

"How close are the contractions?" Ryder asked as they fell in line behind Ten and they all hurried out to climb into the vehicles. This was their first family baby and nobody intended on missing the excitement.

"Um…um…five or six minutes, maybe. My water broke." She was panting and smiling. "This hurts, but I'm so excited I'm about to burst!"

"Well, don't burst until we get to the hospital." Ten got to the car, then had trouble turning her sideways to get in. Philip jumped up to help him.

Finally, they were loaded up and on their way. As they neared Falconhead, Ryder thought of the untouched satellite phone lying on her dresser. She'd finally turned it off when Samson persisted in calling her over and over again. When the SUV came even with the drive to Falconhead, she couldn't look away, feeling like she'd left part of her heart and soul with the two men she'd walked away from. Each time Samson had called; she'd also wondered about Gideon. Ryder felt guilty because she hadn't talked to him in person. Right now, her biggest battle was trying to tamp down the resentment she felt…resentment toward her circumstances, society – and God help her - her family.

"Are you okay?" Pepper asked, her voice low. They'd huddled together over the last week, being there for one another the best they could.

"Yea, I'm looking forward to seeing that baby, aren't you?" Ryder didn't see any use rehashing her decision again, but she knew Pepper wouldn't give up, she'd push the envelope, it was just her way.

"Yes, I am. I still say you shouldn't give up on Samson and Gideon. Daddy would understand. The things that upset him were when we were in trouble. I think he'd be more worried that you were unhappy than he would be to know you were in love.

"With two men, Pepper. Two." She hugged herself tightly. "It doesn't matter now, I told them I can't do it."

"You're making a mistake, that's all I can say. Do you know what I got in the mail today? A restraining order. Can you believe it?"

"You're kidding me!" Ryder was truly horrified. "Why?"

"I guess his new wife didn't want me showing up backstage at one of his concerts again." Pepper tried to keep the hurt out of her voice, but she wasn't successful.

"I'm so sorry," Ryder sympathized with her sister. "We're having a hard time."

"What are you two talking about back there?" Molly asked from the front seat, huffing out the words as she made it through another contraction. "Make it good, I need a distraction."

"Boys. What else?" Tennessee asked. "They're talking about boys. They've been talking about boys for the last twenty years. I hope to God this baby is a boy. I don't think I could contend with a girl."

"Hush." Molly punched Ten. "We're going to be happy no matter what comes, boy or girl. Now hurry before I have him or her on the road!

The next few minutes, the McCoy's drove with hazard lights flashing. Someone had called the highway patrol and when the small convoy hit the main road toward Austin, an escort pulled ahead to carry the group safely on in to the hospital.

When they arrived, the family moved inside as a unit, holding doors, informing the nurse of their arrival. Someone came after Molly, sweeping her and Ten down the hall toward a birthing room. The rest of them had to stay in the waiting room. "Did anyone call Daddy?" Ryder asked. For some reason, she didn't want to be the one who did it, so afraid he'd detect something in her voice that would make him ask questions – questions she had no answers for.

"I did," Jaxson said, from his corner of the waiting room. "I told him we'd send a ton of pictures, but I think he's coming anyway. Olivia might be trying to stop him. I doubt she'll be successful."

She wasn't. In a few minutes, they were joined by a flustered Olivia pushing an excited Christian in his wheelchair. The big man might be an older, weaker version of his youthful self, but he was still a male McCoy who was used to getting his own way. "Is the baby here, yet?"

All his children converged on their father to welcome him. "No, Daddy. It might be a while, first babies sometimes have their own agendas," Pepper said, giving him a kiss, as Ryder hugged him from the side.

They tried to relax, tried to wait patiently, sharing coffee and news about whatever they were working on, but it was hard. Every few seconds, one of them would walk to the hall and gaze down toward the room where

Molly and Ten awaited the arrival of their first child.

"Can you imagine how spoiled this baby is going to be with all of us giving her everything her little heart desires?" Philip mused with a grin on his face.

"Don't call it spoiled," Ryder murmured. "Call it loved. We're all going to have a good time taking care of her."

"I think it's going to be a boy," Heath stated as he sat in the chair closest to the door, one leg crossed with his big black boot resting across his knee. "We need more boys. Do you realize it's tied right now?"

"What's tied?" Cato asked her husband as she sat by him, her hand resting on his thigh.

"The count of males and females. It's five to five, counting Olivia and Daddy. Four to four, if you leave out the old folks. That just won't do. We need more boys"

"Hey, whose old?" Christian piped up from next to the coffeepot. "I'll have you know that Olivia is young. I robbed the cradle!"

"Hush, Chris. You know I turned fifty last week."

"Fifty is the new forty, Olivia," Pepper asserted.

"Well, if fifty is the new forty, and we're all ten years younger, that makes you too young to date, young lady." Heath waggled a finger at Pepper. "Don't think I don't know you're going out with Oliver Pinkerton. That man is a good ten years older than I am. What's the deal? What happened to Music Boy?"

Ryder held her breath, afraid Pepper would just fold up like a morning glory facing the harsh rays of the noon day sun. But she didn't, Pepper stood up straight and glared at her brother. "Haven't you heard? Music Boy married someone else, Heath." She cut Cato a glance, to see Heath's wife shrug her shoulders.

"Sorry." She mouthed at Pepper. "I didn't tell him."

Heath swelled up like a puffer fish. "Married? Do

you want me to pay him a little visit? No man is going to lead my sister on, then marry somebody else!"

Pepper blushed. "Everything is settled. I don't need you to fight my battles for me. Oliver is taking me out to dinner. Don't worry. I'm just moving on, this is a casual date, nothing else."

Cato shook Heath's knee. "I didn't know we were dividing up, boys against girls. I thought you and I were on the same team."

Heath's eyebrows raised, realizing he'd worked himself into a corner. "I didn't mean it, that way baby." He kissed his wife's cheek. "Of course, we're on the same team. I just didn't want a gaggle…I mean, I'd like to see us have enough for touch football someday."

"Girls can play touch football." Cato defended her point. "And when Ryder brings in her two…"

"Cato!" Ryder jumped in front of her deaf sister-in-law. "Do you want to go to the cafeteria with me?"

Cato wasn't looking at Ryder, her gaze was focused on Ryder's shoulder.

"And one of them just walked through the door, Ryder." She pointed, a big smile on her face.

Ryder realized two things simultaneously – she needed to have a long talk with Cato and one of the Dukes had crashed their party. Whirling around, she came face to face with Samson. "What are you doing here?" Just the sight of him stole her breath, made her knees weak, and sent her hopes sky high. She couldn't help but glance behind him to see if Gideon were here. He wasn't - but that didn't do anything to discourage her foolish heart from pounding away.

"I know this is a special family time and I don't want to take you away from it, but I need to talk to you for a few moments. Please."

Knowing there were nine pairs of eyes watching

them closely, she maintained her composure. "Of course." Glancing around at her family, she included them all in her comment. "If you all will excuse us, I'll be right back."

Samson let out a breath he hadn't realized he'd been holding. "Thank you, Ryder." As he placed a guiding hand to her back, he tipped his hat at their wide-eyed audience. "Let's step outside where we can speak privately."

"I didn't know we had anything else to talk about, Samson."

He chose not to respond, not until he could get her alone. She looked adorable, her face completely devoid of makeup. Samson found that he preferred her this way – natural and so sexy he couldn't think straight.

When they were standing outside on the concrete walkway, bathed in the illumination of a security lamp, Samson took Ryder by the shoulders. "I couldn't stay away."

"Oh, my God," Ryder exclaimed, as the truth dawned on her. "Are you still having me followed?"

Security was a way of life in his world, he refused to feel guilty for protecting a woman he considered his. "I followed you myself tonight."

As he stepped closer to her, there was no mistaking the heat in his eyes. "What do you mean?"

"When you all came outside to go to the hospital, I had just arrived at your house. I didn't even have time to get out of the car before you all took off. So, I followed you." He kept his voice low, his gaze on her face, his hand lifted to touch her cheek.

"What were you doing coming to see me in the middle of the night?" Didn't he know how much this hurt her? "I can't change my mind, Samson."

"You wouldn't take my calls? What else was I

supposed to do?"

"Just show up at my door? Wake up my whole family? Was that the plan?"

Samson smirked, sometimes he amazed himself. "No, I was about to climb the tree outside your window and throw pebbles at the glass."

"No, you weren't." She had to fight a smile from blooming on her face. "You're a billionaire…you'd have someone do that for you."

"Oh, no." Samson took one step forward. "There are some things I want to do myself." He framed her face, threading his fingers into her hair. "I can't stay away from you, Ryder McCoy. I just can't." Nuzzling his lips at her temple, he rained kisses down her cheeks until he finally claimed her lips. Ryder was utterly motionless in his embrace, like she couldn't quite believe what was happening. "Breathe, baby." Samson kissed her mouth again, butterfly kisses, lapping tenderly across the sexy perfect bow of her lips that drove him insane.

Ryder obeyed on the wisp of a sigh, a parting her lips which gave him the access he'd been longing for. Samson didn't waste the opportunity, he delved into her mouth, a growl of satisfaction rumbling in his chest at the sweetness of her taste, the delicate movements of her tongue against his. Even though he hadn't made his case, her surrender gave him hope. She still wanted him. She still felt something for him.

Samson deepened the kiss. God, he needed her more than he needed air. He consumed her, exploring every inch of her mouth as she melted in his arms. Gathering her close, he relished the way she leaned into him, as if he were her rock, the barrier between her and anything that could threaten. Her hands slid between them, but instead of trying to push him away, she clutched at his shirt, insuring he stayed right where he was. Samson had never known anything sweeter than her trust.

"Am I enough, Ryder?" Samson whispered. "Could I be enough?"

Ryder didn't understand. "Enough?" She gazed him his amber eyes. "You're everything to me." This was one of the great mysteries to her, a mystery that she made no more attempt to understand than she did how the stars hung in the sky or how the waves found their way to the shore. Each of her men, God help her – they always would be – each of her men was everything. Enough. Yet…together…they were a miracle. "What are you saying? You know what I'm facing with my father's health. I explained to you, I don't think I can hide something so important to me from my family for very long."

"You don't have to, sweetheart. We can be together." He cradled her face, running his thumbs over the velvet beneath her eyes. Drowning in her eyes, he could stave off the pain of his brother cleaving himself away. "Gideon's gone."

Ryder felt her heart lurch in her chest. "What do you mean, gone? Is he all right? What happened?"

Gideon hugged her close, ready to absorb her shock. "When he returned, after you left, and I told him your decision, he confessed that he'd had reservations." As her body jerked from the emotional blow, he tightened his grip around her. "Not with you, never with you." Samson didn't know if what he said made things better or worse. "He isn't ready to commit himself to a relationship that includes me. He doesn't know if he ever will be." Tilting her head up, he kissed her lips again. "But I have no doubts, I know what I want, and what I want is you. Take my hand, baby, let's see what the future can hold for us. Please?"

Ryder felt like she was in the midst of a storm. Waves

of complete joy crashed against a seawall of complete despair. Could she throw away a chance at happiness just because she couldn't have it all? A glass half full or emptiness. Guilt swamped her. Who was she to call a chance with Samson Duke half a cup? He was worth everything. With him, her cup would overflow. Tucking the hurt of Gideon's rejection into a secret place, she understood his admission had opened the floodgates of opportunity for her and Samson. "Yes. I want to be with you."

Total relief buoyed Samson's soul. "You won't be sorry. I promise you, you'll never be sorry."

"Ryder! Come quick! The baby's here! Both of them!"

"Two!" A smile came to both their faces when they heard Pepper yelling out the door. Ryder threw her arms around Samson's neck and hugged him. "I know I won't be sorry. I can't wait to see what tomorrow brings."

"Good. Now, let's go see what the stork brought tonight."

Taking her by the hand, Samson led her back into the hospital to greet the newest additions to her family.

Inside, they hurried down the hall to assemble with the rest of the McCoy clan in front of a large glass window, peering at Tennessee, who stood with a baby in each arm, beaming. Two heads of dark hair peeped out of pink blankets. "Twins!" Ryder exclaimed.

"Yes, apparently, Molly knew there were two babies all along. The doctor helped her keep Ten in the dark as a surprise. That's why she always slipped off to the ultrasound visits alone." Philip explained as the watched the happy scene.

"And they are both girls!" Ryder was so amazed; she just couldn't keep from shaking her head in disbelief.

"Yay! Two more for our team!" Cato pumped her fist

in the air.

"What's their names?" Pepper asked Tennessee through the glass.

The proud father spoke to the nurse, then came around the side and out to join his family. He went straight to his father, filling the old man's lap with two tiny girls. "McCoys, meet Ava and Ella."

Over the next few minutes, everyone in the room admired Molly and Ten's babies. The girls took turns looking in on Molly, and Ryder managed to get one photo of the happy parents with their twin daughters.

Gradually, things calmed down and they started to realize an extra was sharing the moment with them. Heath made his way to Samson. "Duke." He held out his hand. "I'm surprised to see you here."

Samson shook Heath's hand. "I came to see Ryder."

Heath folded his arms over his chest. "What you had to say was so important, it couldn't wait for good daylight?"

Samson stood nose to nose with Heath – as big, as tall, as powerful. "No, it couldn't wait. I'm going to be keeping company with your sister."

Ryder blushed at the old-fashioned way Samson stated his claim to her.

"Oh, really, and here I was thinking that you'd come to keep company with me." Heath's voice was friendly, but there was an underlying edge, a hint of a warning to his tone.

Samson didn't blink. "As business partners, I always welcome an opportunity to pass a little time with you." He leaned in nearer to Heath. "But I don't really have a desire to date you."

"Good thing, this hunk's taken," Cato inserted, linking her arm to Heath's. "Come on, darling, leave Ryder's beau alone. You've got your hands full with me.

I think I might be pregnant too."

Cato's announcement turned Heath's head, completely monopolizing his attention. "Pregnant?"

"Yea, let's go home and make sure." She led her husband away from Ryder and Cato, his mouth open and his mind blown.

"You've got quite a family, Princess."

Samson captured both of her wrists in his hands and Ryder felt a thrill shoot through her. "I want you to meet my daddy."

Allowing her to pull him along, Samson followed to where the patriarch of the McCoy clan was observing his family with his nurse at his side. He wasn't surprised to find the old man's eyes were following their progress across the room.

"Daddy, Olivia, this is my friend, Samson Duke. Samson this is Christian McCoy and Olivia Danvers."

"Hello, Ma'am and Sir." Samson greeted them, kissing Olivia's hand, then squatting next to Christian's wheelchair. "It's a pleasure to meet you, Mr. McCoy. I am looking forward to getting to know you well."

Christian eyed Samson with a stoic expression. "I know who you are, you're OuterLimits, aren't you?"

"Yes, sir. OuterLimits belongs to my brother, Gideon, and me."

At the mention of Gideon, Ryder felt her heart stutter. She missed him. Even though she was more than happy to have worked things out with Samson, knowing that Gideon wasn't in the picture made her feel like she was putting together a puzzle and a critical piece was missing. *Stop it*, she told herself. *Look what you have. If this is going to work, you'll have to accept Gideon in the role he wants to play*. It wasn't like they'd never see him; he wasn't gone forever. But before he returned, Ryder knew she'd have to school her heart and emotions to look at him in a different light.

"Are you dating my daughter?"

"Yes, sir. I am."

"Are your intentions honorable?" Ryder gasped at the same time Olivia whacked Christian on the shoulder. Leave it to her father to go right to the crux of things, no pussy-footing around.

"Strictly honorable, sir. I would do anything for your daughter."

Hearing the words from Samson's lips caused Ryder to sway on her feet.

Samson caught Ryder to him.

"I'm counting on you to take care of her, if not you'll answer to me." Christian folded his hands in his lap.

"If he doesn't take care of her, he'll answer to all of us."

Ryder jerked her head around to see Heath, who'd spoken, standing next to Philip, Jaxson, and Tennessee.

Samson symbolically stepped in front of Ryder, shielding her from everyone in the room. "I expect nothing less from you and your family, Heath. But from now on, I'll stand between Ryder and anything that might cause her pain."

No one in the room missed Samson's message. He wouldn't put up with anyone hurting Ryder – not a stranger, not himself, and not her family.

"Now, if you'll excuse us, I think I'll drive Ryder home. Are you ready, sweetheart?"

The question seemed momentous.

"Yes." She was ready for whatever the future would bring.

Or…at least she hoped so.

Giving everyone in her family a kiss, Ryder left the hospital with Samson Duke.

CHAPTER SEVEN

"What happens next?" Ryder asked Samson as they headed north from Austin back toward Falconhead and Highlands.

The Lamborghini ate up the miles, a streak of blue lightning streaking across the Texas Hill Country highway. "I'd love to take you home with me," Samson murmured, holding her hand in his, rubbing his thumb across the soft flesh of Ryder's palm.

"I would like that too."

Samson steeled himself to be strong. "But that's not how we're going to play it. Since we're going to be a traditional couple, we're going to do things in the traditional way.

Ryder smiled. "Sounds boring."

Her comment made Samson throw back his head and laugh. "I will make keeping the excitement level high enough to please you as a personal challenge."

Ryder laid her head on his arm. "I don't doubt it, but I was just teasing you. Just being with you is going to be excitement enough."

"Just wait until you hear my plans. I intend to sweep you off your feet." As he was preparing to tell Ryder what he had in store for them, Samson felt a familiar warm flash in his mind. Gideon. For a microsecond, he tried to mentally grab onto the sensation, needing to feel something of his brother's presence. How was he doing? The realization that this was the first glimpse of a connection since the day he'd left hit Samson hard.

"Tell me," Ryder urged.

"Well...tonight, I'm going to give you the best goodnight kiss at your door you've ever received."

His teasing tone made her giggle. "That won't be hard to do. I haven't received very many. Usually the light is on and one of my brothers is sitting inside with a deer rifle across their knee."

Now it was Samson's turn to smile in amusement. "I'll keep that in mind. Good thing we're going to beat them home."

"What else?"

"Tomorrow, if you're not busy, I thought we'd go for a little ride in my helicopter, then take a spin on my boat."

"I've never ridden in a helicopter." She looked forward to that. "Instead of your fishing boat, do you want to take Heath's houseboat on the lake? We could float downstream and check out more of the eagle's nests."

"Oh, I'm not talking about a boat on the lake." He brought her hand to his lips. "I'm talking about my yacht. How does a moonlight sail off Galveston Island sound?"

"Heavenly." Ryder sighed.

"This weekend we'll fly to New York for dinner and if you want, we'll plan a trip to Paris soon." Maybe they could meet up with Gideon, but he didn't want to mention that just yet. If they were going to go this alone, he wanted time to get them used to being without him. Samson shook his head, even thinking about embarking on this grand venture with Ryder without Gideon was difficult. Not that being with Ryder wouldn't be amazing and life-changing, the culmination of his dreams – but he always thought he'd be sharing those dreams with his brother.

"I need to tell you something, Samson."

"What's that?" he asked, not sure if he wanted to know.

"I'm happy just being with you, we don't have to fly all the way across the country or the world. I'd be just as happy going to the movies with you."

"I know you would," Samson said, pulling beneath

in the Highlands gate. "And that's one of the reasons I...can't stop thinking about you."

"Me either."

Samson swallowed hard. He'd almost said that he loved her. An overwhelming sense of rightness and ultimate panic crashed together in his head like two runaway steam engines meeting head to head on the same track. Too soon. He knew it was too soon, but the words were on the tip of his tongue. He bit them back, he didn't want to scare Ryder off.

Zing!

He felt another warm flash in his brain. Gideon as reacting to his feelings, but he couldn't read his brother's response. A sudden urge to talk to him came over Samson. He resolved to do just that when he returned to Falconhead.

Parking in the circular drive, he helped Ryder out of the car, strolling up to her door – hand in hand. "The sun will be up soon. You need to get some sleep."

"I'll try," Ryder murmured, so aware of Samson's big body touching hers that she trembled. "It's going to be hard, I'll probably dream about you."

Samson groaned. "Don't say that word."

"What? Dream?"

"No. Hard. I'm so hard for you." He lowered his mouth and pressed it to hers in a kiss that he fully intended to be gentle and of short duration. But something happened...

She pressed herself to him, as if she wanted to verify his claim. She went up on tiptoe, clasping him around the neck and began to move against him – wild and hot. Nothing in Samson's imaginings prepared him for Ryder's passion. To his immense satisfaction, she took control, lowering her hands to his chest and pushed him back against the door. Her lips never relinquished his for a moment. She kissed him with a fierce, feminine hunger that delighted him to his very soul. This time, Samson surrendered, letting her take everything she wanted and giving her everything he had.

When she withdrew her lips from his, letting them slide down his jaw to his neck, he sucked in a harsh breath – then gasped when she bit him. "My God, I am he luckiest fuckin' man in the world," he growled. "You're going to burn me alive, aren't you?"

Ryder blinked at his whispered words. She'd been operating on instinct and need. "I'm going to try." Her breathing was shallow and fast. "You know what?"

"What?" He brushed a lock of hair off her face.

"I'm standing on the front porch of the house I've lived in with my family for years." She gave him a sweet smile. "But being in your arms, it's like coming home."

Samson shut his eyes. Nothing she could've said would've made him feel any better. "I'm glad. You know why?"

"Why?" She nestled against him and he clasped her close.

"Because I feel exactly the same way.

* * *

Just as he'd promised, the next few days were a whirlwind of surprises and fantastic dates. If she thought Samson had paid her a lot of attention when he'd been trying to change her mind about him, that was nothing compared to this. The only difference was the absence of Gideon. Ryder knew it was wrong, but she couldn't not think of him. Even though their time together was perfection, the things they did incredible – she was still conscious of it being just the two of them…instead of three.

Stop! she told herself. Gideon made his decision, and

even if he hadn't – this was the only reason she and Samson were together. If Gideon hadn't…

A sharp and painful thought lanced through her mid-section. What if?

"Hey, are you having a good time?"

Samson's voice broke through her train of thought.

"Of course I am." She looked up as he came down the aisle from visiting the pilot in the cockpit. They were on their way home from a wonderful weekend in New York City, where they'd stayed in the penthouse suite of the Langham Hotel. The view from their window was the iconic Empire State Building. He'd treated her to every luxury imaginable, buying her new outfits, escorting Ryder to the finest restaurants and treating her to several premiers. She'd never had a better time in her life.

Unless it was the week before, when – as he'd promised – Samson had whisked her off on his private helicopter to his and Gideon's yacht, The Gemini. A one hundred sixty-four foot Sunseeker luxury vessel where they'd spent five sun-filled days sailing from Galveston to Padre Island. They had swum in the surf, snorkeled in the depths, and sunbathed on the deck. Nothing Ryder could imagine wanting had been lacking. She'd been pampered, petted, and spoiled – given everything Samson could even imagine her wanting.

Except one thing.

On both romantic trips, in all the time they'd stayed together, even though they'd spent hours in one another's arms – kissing, necking, petting – whatever you wanted to call it – they hadn't made love. Not because she didn't want to.

To be honest, Ryder wasn't sure why they were waiting.

"We'll be landing at Austin Bergstrom in about ten minutes," Samson informed her as he settled down beside her in the reclining Captain's seat of his private plane. "I suspect you're tired. Why don't I take you home so you can check on your new nieces and tomorrow you can fly with me to Florida. I've got a little business down there you might be interested in."

"Me?" Ryder couldn't imagine. "I'm not sure what you mean. That's not to say I'm not interested in everything you and Gideon do."

Ryder almost covered her mouth – almost. Samson's brother's name seemed to come so easily to her lips. When would she stop thinking of them as a set? Guilt tightened her chest, a knot formed in her throat.

Sensing her discomfort, Samson set her mind at ease. "Stop it. I don't expect you to ignore Gideon or what you felt for him. I love my brother. Our situation, while it may not be what I anticipated, will always include him." He held out his hand for her to grasp, and she did. "Don't worry, we'll work out the dynamics as we go along. So, how about Florida? Can I tempt you to join me in a quick trip to the Sunshine State? We'll only be gone one night."

"I wouldn't miss it," she assured him. "I look forward to going on a business trip with you." The one thing she wasn't looking forward to was facing her brothers. When she'd returned from the trip to Galveston, Heath had given her the third degree and she'd had to remind him that she was over twenty-one. After her older brother almost wore a hole in the rug, pacing back and forth, Ryder relented and confessed that they hadn't been alone on the yacht and she'd slept in her own cabin. Since she'd never lied to her brother, and he knew it, Heath took her at her word, calming down a bit.

While they were coming in for a landing, Ryder stared out the window at the fluffy clouds, realizing how her life had changed. Still…she didn't think she could rest until she asked the question that was bothering her. She had faith in Samson, but to ease her own mind, she wanted to hear what he had to say. "Samson, why haven't we made love yet?"

If Samson hadn't been buckled up, he'd have fallen out of his chair. He heard her question, but he also heard what she didn't say. For a split second, he wondered if he were reading Ryder's mind. Probably not. His date was drawing the same conclusion that any feminine mind would. "I want to make love with you, Ryder. I fully intend to make love with you."

"When the time is right." She finished for him, putting just a tad of resignation in her voice.

"Princess, look at me." He leaned over far enough so that his massive shoulders were mostly on her side of the seat. "This is too important to rush. I want you to know how highly I value you. We're not having an affair; we're embarking on an adventure that I hope will last a lifetime."

Ryder gave him a tremulous smile. "I appreciate your thoughtfulness. In my heart, I knew that," she said, pausing, her cheeks blushing pink, "I just needed to hear you say it. I thought maybe that without Gideon, it was so different for you…"

Samson chuckled. "I think I can figure it out by myself."

Ryder ducked her head. "Of course you can, I didn't mean to imply…"

As the plane started losing altitude, preparing to land, Samson brought her hand to his lips. "I know what you meant." What Ryder thought was partially true – not in the technical sense – but emotionally. While he couldn't fathom his life without Ryder, he was having an equally hard time knowing how to proceed without Gideon. "I'm planning the perfect time and the perfect place. Trust me."

Ryder squeezed his hand as the plane's wheels

touched the tarmac. "I do. Completely."

* * *

Gideon sat in a smoky bar, sipping on a glass of world-class vodka. "So tell me, Nikita, how many rockets did you sell Leonid Oleg?"

"Enough."

The bewhiskered Russian stared at Gideon with bleary eyes. "A man takes care of himself first and foremost, Duke."

"True." He raised his glass in a salute. "What do you know about the threats being made on our lives?"

"Why would I know anything?" Nikita Brezhnev shrugged his stooped shoulders. "I'm sure there are many who would like to stop you from sending that spaceship off to Mars."

Gideon glanced around the room, sensing more than one set of eyes on him. "Samson and I intend to insure mankind is a multi-planet species."

Nikita bent his head and whispered to him. "There are those who say your mission has a military motive."

"We're transporting a greenhouse, seeds, and a gel nutrient. What we're doing is providing insurance for the inhabitants of Earth's survival, and I don't mean just Americans. This isn't a nationalistic effort; this is a humanitarian mission."

"Blah. Blah. Blah," Nikita yammered. "So you say. Words are cheap."

"Nothing about this is cheap."

"That's not what I hear." Nikita pointed his dark bottle of beer toward Gideon. "I hear you've perfected a method to reuse your rockets."

"Yes. We did. Our aim is to make spaceflight routine and affordable. Not cheap. Affordable, there's a difference."

"True. Did you turn down Oleg's offer?"

"His offer to buy our company was an insult, a cover story he's concocted for when he succeeds in killing us." Gideon laughed, lowly and wryly. "Only he's not going to succeed. He's not smart enough and he's not wealthy enough. Who does he work for?"

Brezhnev's eyes widened. "I have no idea what you mean."

"Yes, you do." Gideon edged forward and put his elbows on the table. "Tell me, and I'll make it worth your while."

Shaking his head, Nikita Brezhnev kept his eyes on Gideon. "By sparing my life? I know you're not alone." He let his eyes scan the room. "How many goons do you have with you?"

Gideon lifted a corner of his mouth. "About half the room."

Nikita laughed. "So, about a dozen."

"Give or take." Gideon waited. "So, what's it going to be? Deal or no deal?"

Draining his bottle, the Russian set it down hard on the table. "I'll tell you what I know, which isn't much. The money isn't coming from Russia and I don't know his identity, all I know is what they call him."

"Sounds mysterious." Gideon gave him a half smirk. "All right, I'll bite. What do they call him?"

"My price?" Nikita held out his hand. "One million."

"That's quite a price to pay for something I might not even want."

"Everything worthwhile comes with a high price."

Gideon knew about paying high prices – his brother and Ryder's happiness for his own. "You'll get your money when I evaluate the information's worth."

"Are you asking me to trust you, American?"

"Yes."

Nikita looked all around, then said one word. "Rasputin."

"Rasputin." Gideon let the name roll off his tongue. Rising, he tipped his black Stetson to Nikita Brezhnev. He knew how out of place he looked in this snow-covered country where everyone else wore thick parkas and woolen hats. Gideon Duke didn't give a damn. "Don't call me, I'll call you." As he walked out of the bar, he considered calling his brother. Anytime he had news, good or bad, Samson was the first person he thought of.

But Samson wasn't alone – and he was happy.

Gideon knew this because he could feel it. He could feel his brother's happiness. The abyss he'd created between them prevented Gideon from seeing or knowing details, but he could sense Samson and his joy. Stepping out into the icy weather, he pulled the collar of his coat up around his face. No one who saw the big cowboy would think he was anything other than what he appeared – tough, in-charge, self-sufficient, and confident. In a few days, he would be going home. And when he did, neither his brother or Ryder must know how empty Gideon felt inside.

* * *

"Hey, jet-setter, what's up with you?" Pepper tapped on Ryder's door, but entered before Ryder could invite her inside. "We've been passing one another like two ships in the night ever since the night Ella and Ava were born."

"I'm good." Ryder smiled, packing yet another suitcase. "Actually, I'm better than good. I'm wonderful. Samson is amazing"

"Really?" Pepper came to sit on the edge of the bed. "Just Samson? I didn't see Gideon at the hospital. What's going on?"

Ryder's hand stilled in her packing, dropping a top to the bed unfolded. "Gideon is out of the picture."

"What do you mean?" Pepper inquired, searching Ryder's face, seeing the disquiet on her sister's features.

"Samson came to the hospital to tell me he couldn't live without me."

"So…what about Gideon?"

"Samson said that when I left that day, after telling him that I couldn't risk my father's health or defy my family, Gideon came to tell him he couldn't do it either." Ryder's voice dropped. "He said he didn't think he could commit to being part of a threesome…permanently."

Pepper jumped up and placed her hands on her hips, her long blonde hair swaying behind her. "Just like that? Out of the blue? I thought you said this was part of their heritage and they always share, that this was their plan for the future."

"Yes, this was a shock." Ryder turned around and sat on the bed, Pepper standing over her. "Samson came to tell me the news." She buried her face in her hands. "On one hand, it freed him and me to be together without upsetting anyone's applecart of propriety. But…"

"On the other hand, this changes everything for all of you." Pepper stroked Ryder's hair. "Is this what you want?"

Tears began to well up in Ryder's eyes. "I want a life with Samson. God, yes." She shuddered at the thought of giving him up.

"But…?"

Pepper's prompting didn't get very far. Ryder refused to go there. What was the use? "But, nothing. I've always wanted to have my cake and eat it too, but this is the way it is. Gideon is happy. Samson and I can be together." She stopped, wiped her eyes and rose. "I need to count my blessings and be happy."

"Oh, I want you to be happy." Pepper wrapped her arms around Ryder's waist and squeezed. "Whatever it takes, that's what I want for you."

Ryder held her sister for a few seconds, before disengaging to complete her task. Brightening her voice, she told Pepper her plans. "We're flying to Florida. Samson has business down there." She smiled, her eyes twinkling. "I think he has another surprise for me. Although, I have no idea what it could be."

"You are so lucky, girl. Samson Duke is a prize." Pepper didn't add what she was thinking. Gideon's timely retreat seemed a bit too convenient. Something seemed amiss.

"Oh!" Ryder exclaimed as she zipped the top of her case. "How did your date with Oliver go?"

Pepper groaned. "Don't ask. The whole thing was a total disaster." She laughed, covering her mouth. "You wouldn't believe how awkward it was. The man doesn't seem to be part of this century. Do you know what he asked me?"

"What?" Ryder couldn't imagine what Pepper was about to say.

"He wanted to know how much acreage would come with my hand."

"What?"

"He also informed me that he wanted four children and we needed to begin right away."

"Oh, my goodness." Ryder couldn't help but laugh. "What did you say?"

"I told him he was crazy and I called a cab." Pepper's expression was one of amused disgust. "Can you imagine? And all of this was before the second course! I didn't even get dessert out of the man before he started planning the family and counting my dowry."

Ryder shook her head. "I'm glad you escaped before

he started divvying up the cattle and horses."

"Yea, me too." She pointed at Ryder's case. "So, is Gideon going to Florida with you two?"

"No." Ryder sighed. "He's in Europe, working on something to do with one of their launches. I'm not sure when he'll be back." Or how it would work when he did return.

"Have you had any confrontations with big brother or any of the others since the hospital?" Pepper asked, fingering a silky blue dress Pepper had laid out on the bed to change into.

"No, Heath seems to be preoccupied with some type of business deal. I'm not sure what," she said, then grinned. "Did you hear what Cato told him about being pregnant?"

"Yes!" Pepper clapped her hands. "I did hear her. They've made no further announcement, but I have my fingers crossed. I've been helping Molly with the girls. Soon, this is house is going to be full-fledged nursery!"

A tinge of guilt prickled Ryder's conscience. "I'm sorry, maybe I shouldn't go."

"No!" Pepper almost shouted. "Absolutely not! You go on and have a good time with Samson, you deserve it. There are enough of us here to keep everything going as it should be. Molly and Ten are so taken with those girls, the rest of us have to make an appointment to see them."

Ryder didn't look quite convinced. "After this, I'll slow down a bit. We've been gallivanting all over. You called me a jet-setter and I think I do have a bit of jet lag."

The grandfather clock striking the hour downstairs caused them both to jump. "How silly." Pepper giggled. "How many times do you think we've heard that noise in our lifetime?"

"Thousands," Ryder said, nodding. "Hearing the hour tells me I'd better hurry. Samson will be by to pick me up before you know it."

"I'd tell you to go ahead and make yourself pretty, but you're already gorgeous." Pepper gave her one last hug. "Be careful on your trip and I hope you two have a grand time."

"Thanks." What the future held, she wasn't certain. The only thing Ryder knew was that she didn't want to miss a minute of it.

* * *

"What kind of a business trip is this?" Ryder held onto Samson's hand as they ran down the beach, laughing as they splashed through the surf.

"A very important one. Look." He pulled her in front of him, wrapping his arms across her, pressing Ryder back against his hard chest. She lifted her eyes and followed his pointed finger. In the distance, to her amazement, she saw a rocket begin to lift off. "Oh, my gosh!" she squealed in amazement. "Is that yours?"

He kissed her on the cheek. "It's ours. The Ryder-I, carrying a payload to the International Space Station."

"She's magnificent!" Ryder gasped in sheer amazement as the rocket soared up into the sky, leaving a trail of smoke behind her.

"Yes, she is," Samson agreed, but he wasn't watching the rocket, he was gazing at her.

"I can't believe this! You named it after me!"

"They'll all be named after you. Each and every one of them."

The pride in Samson's voice touched a chord within Ryder. He really cared for her. Ryder had no doubt of this. "You are so wonderful! Thank you." She turned in his arms to kiss him passionately.

When they were joined on the beach by several others, Samson broke the kiss but kept her close. "This isn't all. Later this evening, we'll watch our girl return. I plan on setting her down on a drone ship in the middle of the ocean. The first vertical landing of a reusable rocket. Ryder-I will go down in history."

"Mr. Duke! Mr. Duke!"

The eager voice caused them both to jerk around. A reporter began taking photographs. "Will you answer a few questions?" Two of Samson's men moved forward to stop the eager journalist, but Samson held out his hand to imply that his interruption would be allowed.

He didn't usually do impromptu interviews, but today Samson was in a good mood. Holding onto Ryder's hand, he gave the reporter some inside info on their plans. When asked why Gideon wasn't with him, he was evasive.

Ryder was relieved when they were finally alone. "Does this happen often, the media attention?" She knew it must, the brothers were famous, super rich and ultra-good looking. If she were going to be with Samson, Ryder knew she'd have to get used to it.

For the rest of the day, he took her on a tour of the OuterLimits facilities, introducing her to his people – the techs, the engineers, and all the other specialized employees. And as promised, after they'd watched the rocket's progress via satellite as it disconnected from the cargo capsule, they monitored its return. Just before Ryder-I's return to earth, Samson flew Ryder in his helicopter so they could watch it reenter the atmosphere and land like a dream on the barge-like surface of the ship. Ryder was stunned at the beauty and the power of what she was seeing. "Thank you," she told him. "I'll never forget that sight as long as I live."

"You won't get a chance to, you'll be seeing them often," Samson told her, clasping Ryder's hand as they strolled to his car. "Now, how about dinner and dancing?"

"Sounds wonderful. You're so good to me."

"Nothing is too good for my girl."

True to his word, they spent the evening in Cocoa Beach, feasting on fresh crabs and dancing in the moonlight at a seaside café.

"What's next?" she asked, her head lying on his chest, happier than she could ever remember being. It was so strange, the way her emotions danced around. Ryder couldn't deny the complete contentment she experienced with Samson, while at the same time part of her soul yearned for Gideon.

"I have a house near here," he began, but stopped when his phone buzzed. Holding up one finger, he indicated that he needed to take the call. "Gideon?"

At the mention of the other brother's name, Ryder felt her heart begin to pound in her chest. She froze, waiting to see what Samson had to say.

"It's good to hear from you, man." He laughed. "Yea, we nailed the landing."

She watched Samson's face, trying to read his emotions. A shadow passed over his handsome features and Ryder dug her own fingernails into her palms.

Silence on his end.

"I see." Concern clouded his eyes. "That doesn't sound good." A pregnant pause. "What time?" He glanced at his watch. "I'll meet him there. No, it's fine. I'll fly back tonight."

Ryder waited, tense, until he ended the call. "What's wrong? How is Gideon?"

"He's fine." Samson kissed her cheek. "Something's going down with our Mars mission, we seem to still be having a problem with someone who'd rather it didn't get off the ground. He's sending someone to talk to me with information that has to be delivered in person."

"Oh, okay. I'm so sorry. Please, be careful."

"I will and I'm the one who's sorry. Would you mind if we flew home tonight?"

"No, of course not. Whatever you need to do is fine with me." The only question she really wanted to ask Samson was why he hadn't told Gideon she was in Florida with him.

* * *

"So, tell me about Anatoly. What do you know about him?" Jimmy Dushku asked Heath as they rode down the rough dirt road in Heath's old red pickup. Occasionally, they both had to hold on to the door or the window frame. The road was bumpy and the shocks in the truck were shot to hell.

"Not much. He's interested in introducing some environmental concerns in his homeland, as well as supporting some of our work here in the states." Heath put on his blinker and they turned onto the main road. "Roll up your window, I'm getting hot. I need to turn on the A/C."

"Well, if you didn't insist on wearing that blue jean jacket everywhere, you wouldn't get so bloomin' hot, cowboy," Jimmy, who was cold-natured, grumbled.

Heath grinned. "Cato likes me in this jacket, she thinks I'm sexy."

Jimmy groaned. "You'd better hang onto Cato. She's one of a kind."

"I plan on it. Why do you ask about Anatoly?"

"No reason."

"Shoot, with you, there's always a reason."

"I don't know, something just seems to be off with him." Jimmy watched as a road runner scooted across the highway ahead of them. "Well, I thought I'd use my vast resources and my massive technical ability to do some digging on him. You know who else I don't trust?"

Heath barked out a laugh. "You're such a conspiracy theorist. Who?"

"Scott Eagleton. Something's fishy about him."

"What do you mean? The man has a sterling reputation. His great-grandfather was a steel magnate, his mother's wealth came from South African diamond mines, and he's a former Ambassador to Russia. He also walks a fine line between supporting energy and wanting it to be green. The man is loaded and I want some of that money to help back my conservation efforts."

"I think you wanted him for a brother-in-law. Am I right?"

Heath blew out a disgruntled breath. "I think he would've been good for Ryder. He's stable, he's conservative, and he would've fit into our family well."

"So, when are you meeting with him again?"

"Soon, I hope. Anyway, I appreciate you looking into things for me. I've missed you, Dushku. What's in Hong Kong that you can't find in Austin?"

"Geishas."

"You perv."

"Hey, you must be developing a taste for pervs. After setting the bar at Eagleton, I can't believe you're letting Ryder date one of the Dukes."

"Awww, you're just jealous because they're richer than you, Dush." Heath chuckled. "Honestly, I can't stop her. I tried. I don't think Duke's a perv, though."

"No, seriously. They do stuff that I don't do." Jimmy smirked. "I'm into BDSM, but those two share."

Heath frowned, keeping one eye on the road. "Share what?"

"Women... Hey, watch it!" Jimmy bounced around, holding onto the dash as Heath ran off the road.

"They share women!" Heath bellowed. "What the fuck?" Then, he calmed. "I'm not sure what that means."

Jimmy shook his head. "You need to get out more." Slowly, he drew Heath a mental picture. "Being richer than God, the lives of the Dukes are a constant source of fascination with some people. And one of the things that's common knowledge in some circles, is that they share women…with each other. Always. No exceptions. So, if Ryder is involved with one Duke, she's involved with both."

The explosion could be heard in the next county.

CHAPTER EIGHT

"Ryder, are you all right? Is Duke in there with you?" Heath stood at the edge of the drive as she climbed from the limousine, his hands on his hips, his jaw jutting out and his nostrils flaring.

Gervis answered for her. "No, sir. Mr. Duke had urgent business. I escorted Miss Ryder home."

"What's this all about, Heath? I phoned and told Pepper when to expect me. If something had gone wrong I would've sent word to you." Ryder had no idea what her big brother was angry about, but she'd seen this look too many times before to mistake it for anything else. "What's wrong with you?"

"What's wrong with me! What's wrong with you!?" Heath yelled, stomping toward her as he big black car pulled away. Before Ryder knew what was happening, her brother had her by the arm. He wasn't rough at all, but when she tried to pull away, he wouldn't loosen his grip. "Let me go, Heath!"

"Heath, you don't want to do this," Cato's voice came from the open doorway.

"Stay out of this, baby. This is something we have to do."

"We? What are you talking about?" Ryder went with Heath, climbing the steps – not like she had any choice. This whole thing felt familiar. She'd been here before, but it had been years, a lot of years. Heath had only spanked her once when she was fourteen for climbing to the top of a rickety old windmill. He'd told her she scared ten years off his life.

Well, she hadn't been climbing any rickety windmills lately.

"If you don't let me go, we're going to have a problem. I'm not a teenager anymore, I'm a grown woman. I don't know what grass burr you've got up your ass, but…"

"Watch your tongue, little girl." Heath led her through the door and the question of who the 'we' was – was answered. Her whole family stood waiting on her. Her brothers on one side and her female relatives on the other. And none of them looked happy. Jaxson, Ten, and Philip looked disappointed and Cato, Pepper, and Molly looked peeved. They were glaring at the men like they were on separate sides of a paintball war.

"Where's the twins?" Ryder asked, trying to make sense of what she was seeing.

Ten answered, "Olivia's watching the babies. We didn't want them here for the intervention!"

"Intervention!" Pepper spat at the same time Ryder yelled the same word in the form of a question. "Intervention?"

"I'm not doing anything that needs to be intervened in!"

"Oh, I beg to disagree." Heath spoke in a loud booming voice, worthy of a legal orator proclaiming his case before the Supreme Court. "Now, is the time for us to step in and insure that you don't do something to permanently scar your life!"

"Now, just hold on a gol-darned minute." Ryder again tried to struggle, but Heath led her to a straight back chair in the middle of the living room and urged her down. All four of her brothers proceeded to sit in a straight line in front of her – while the girls stood defensively at her back.

"No, you hold on." Heath pointed his finger at her. "I've just learned these men you're seeing are involved in all manners of sexual deviance."

Ryder pressed her lips together. So, this is what all the hell was about. "Who told you that?"

"Oh, so you're not denying it!" Heath pointed the same finger in the air as if he'd just scored a point of some kind.

"Denying what?" Ryder's anger flared. "I haven't done anything wrong."

"You're spending time with Samson Duke!" Heath fired back.

"I am, Samson is a wonderful man."

"Well from what I hear, if you're dating one of those Dukes you're dating the other one too. Do you have a clue about what you're doing?"

"Yes, I do." Ryder let her gaze go from one brother to another. Philip looked contrite, Ten, and Jaxson were backing Heath all the way. Pepper and her sisters-in-law seemed fit to be tied, they were almost as angry as she was. "I'm living my life in the way I see fit."

"No, you're disgracing this family, that's what you're doing! Jimmy says if you're sleeping with one Duke, you're sleeping with them both!"

"Heath…" Philip cautioned.

"Heath McCoy, this is your sister!" Cato admonished her husband.

He gave both his wife and his brother barely a glance. "If you think I'm going to allow you to ruin your life, Ryder, you couldn't be more wrong."

"I'm not the one who's wrong, Heath." Ryder understood what he was saying. He was fulfilling her worst nightmare, doing exactly what she feared would happen. "For your information, I haven't had sex with anyone." She stood to her feet. "Not that it's any of your business, but I'm still a virgin." She let her eyes rove over her brothers. "Look at all of you. We've all got our own little soap operas going on, don't we?" She shot a look at

Cato and Molly. "I'm sorry." Then, she centered her gaze on Heath. "How did you treat Cato?"

"Let's leave Cato out of this," Heath bit back at her.

"You agreed to a fling with an expiration date." Heath started to respond, but Ryder rounded on Ten. "And you! You wouldn't believe your own wife. You accused her of unspeakable things. You're lucky to have her and those two babies!" Before Ten could say something, she turned to Jaxson. "And who knows what's up with you? Do you think we don't know you pushed Tamara away because you felt sorry for yourself!"

"Ryder…" Pepper cautioned.

Throwing up her hands, she lashed out at them all. "You're wrong, I'm not involved with both Samson and Gideon, just Samson. But you know what?" She didn't wait for a corresponding question. "I wish I was involved with Gideon too! I'd give myself to both of those men in a heartbeat!"

Heath reeled at her words and there were several gasps heard around the room. "So, you want to throw yourself away on likes of the Dukes of Hazzard? You could've had a respectable man like Scott Eagleton. What kind of woman are you?" Her big brother was so mad his ears were red.

"I know exactly what kind of woman I am! A mad one!" She picked up her bag and slung it over her shoulder. "I might as well be hung for a sheep as a lamb."

At Jaxson's perplexed expression, Philip murmured an explanation. "When people used to be hung for sheep-stealing, the thought was that if you're going to die anyway, you might as well take a full-grown sheep rather than a little lamb. So…she's saying if she's going to be condemned for the crime…"

"I might as well commit the crime!" Ryder finished for their 'absent-minded professor' brother. "Good day to you all, I'm out of here." She strode out of the room with her back straight and her head held high. "And I don't know when I'm coming back!"

Pepper ran after her. "Ryder, wait. Heath didn't mean all of that, he's just worried."

"Our brothers' are asses." Ryder hugged her sister quickly. "Check on Daddy for me. But if he gets wind of this, it won't be because of anything I did."

"Be careful," she urged.

"I'll be fine." She headed for the garage door. "I'll be with Samson. Don't let anyone follow me, Pepper. They won't like what they find."

* * *

Ryder was so angry; she could barely see to drive. Her brothers had just proved her every instinct to be right. As the tears streamed down her cheeks, a small, sad gasp of laughter slipped from her lips. "God, what all did I say?" She tried to think. "I told them I was a virgin and that I wished I could make love with both Duke brothers." Ryder hiccupped another sob. "I guess that about covers it, at least I didn't lie."

When she'd covered the short distance between Highlands and Falconhead, it occurred to Ryder that Samson didn't know she was coming. What would he think? Would she be welcome? Once she pulled up to the guarded entrance, the gate opened automatically. Her car and face was familiar to all the Duke's employees. She gave the men admitting her a slight wave, then used the same hand to swipe at her damp cheeks. "I bet I look a mess."

Not giving herself time to change her mind, she jumped from the car, not giving Gervis time to reach her door. Thurgood was a bit more prompt, greeting her with concern. "Are you all right, Miss Ryder?"

"Could you tell Samson I'm here?"

"Certainly." The butler brought her indoors, but that was as far as they got before Samson came rushing up.

"Ryder?"

He opened his arms and Ryder ran to him. "Oh, Samson. Can I stay with you?"

"Forever."

His unequivocal acceptance was exactly what she needed. "Thank you."

Samson wrapped his arms tightly around her. "I'm so glad you're here. I've wanted to ask you to come, but I didn't want to rush you." He held her for a few more moments before guiding her farther into the house. "Come in and let's make you comfortable."

Ryder hadn't turned him loose. "If you still have business to attend to, please don't let me take you away from it."

"My visitor left just a few minutes before you arrived." Samson drew her to the couch, pulling Ryder down into his lap. "Having you here is such a wonderful surprise." He lifted her hair from her neck. She was obviously upset. "Now, tell me what happened."

His total acceptance freed something inside Ryder. She buried her face in his neck and everything just came pouring out. "Heath and the others, they confronted me over what you and I and Gideon were doing."

Samson felt his anger rise. He knew this was what she'd been so afraid would happen. Cradling her close, he apologized. "I'm so sorry, sweetheart." He wanted to defend her honor, protect her feelings, and hide her away from the world so no one would ever make her cry again. "I guess you explained to him that it's just you and me, that Gideon isn't involved."

"I told them I was still a virgin and that I was leaving to be with you. But I also told them I wish it was all three of us, that I'd be with both of you in a heartbeat if it were possible." She held onto him his shirt so tight, her knuckles were white.

Samson was stunned. He didn't know which piece of information hit him the hardest. Her words felt like a fist had just been planted in his solar plexus. Air was forced from his lungs in a harsh breath. A virgin? He'd suspected, but hearing the truth from her lips did something to him. And she still longed for Gideon? A mass of emotions roared over Samson. Triumph. Joy. Regret. Hope. He didn't get a chance to formulate a response before Thurgood rejoined them with a drink for Ryder.

"Ma'am, this will make you feel better."

"Thank you, Thurgood." She accepted the hot toddy and sipped it, holding the warm mug with both hands.

Samson ran a comforting hand down her back, trying to assimilate the data he'd just been given. None of this should have been a surprise. Ryder had a sexy but untouched quality about her. Even after he'd loved on her for hours – just kissing and petting, she'd still look at him with those big, innocent doe eyes that turned him inside out. Hell! Having confirmation that no other man had touched her but himself and Gideon was a massive turn-on. Primal possessive instincts rose in his chest.

And hearing she wished Gideon were back in the picture?

This shouldn't have been a surprise; Ryder had said as much when she'd come to tell them goodbye after her father was hospitalized. Somehow, in the intervening days, he'd pushed this truth from his mind. "Better?" he asked gently.

"Yes." She lifted her head, revealing a line of milky goodness all along her upper lip. He couldn't resist licking it off. "What else can I do to make you feel better,

Princess?"

Ryder quivered, the ugly events of the evening catching up with her. She wanted to forget. She wanted to feel safe and wanted. "Would you make love to me?" A flare of doubt blossomed in her mind. "I know you said we should wait. So, if you don't want to, I'll under…"

Samson silenced her with a kiss. "I want nothing more." With that revelation, he placed her drink on a nearby table and gave her no further chance to speak. Taking over, he didn't abandon the silky heat of her mouth long enough to begin to undress her. Samson kept their lips fused together as he slid his hands under the lace camisole she wore, slipping it up and over her head. Their petting sessions to this point, discounting what he and Gideon had shared with her at the Driskill Hotel, had been fairly chaste. For some reason Samson had held back, like he was waiting for something.

But the time for waiting was over.

Ryder had chosen to gift herself to him and Samson was ready to claim her. She belonged to him. His desire ran so high, his hands fumbled as he unfastened her jeans, helping her yank them down and off. She helped him, making tiny sounds of frustration and passion.

"Hurry," she murmured. "I want you so much."

Her obvious arousal, her desire for him sent his own need off the charts. Reaching around Ryder, Samson unhooked her bra, drawing the thin straps from her shoulders, slowly unveiling the delicious globes of her breasts. "I've dreamed about this moment, don't think I haven't."

A blush rose in Ryder's cheeks, a heat that swept down her neck and over her chest, even making the swell of her breasts pink. "Oh, me too. I've touched myself every night, imagining you and…"

She stopped – but Samson filled in the blank.

Gideon. "It's okay, honey. I understand. I wish I could give you…"

This time it was Ryder who stopped him from speaking. She stopped the flow of his words with a kiss, pressing her naked breasts to his chest. "Hush. Don't you ever think that you're not enough – you're everything to me." She groaned in frustration, dipping her head to rest on his shoulder. "I can't explain it."

"You don't have to. I, of all people, absolutely understand." Sliding a hand down her back, he let his fingers pass beneath the band of her panties, lifting her up long enough to push them over the round, firm cheeks of her bottom, and down her legs. Once he was through, she was totally – gloriously nude. "If I live to be a thousand, I'll never tire of feasting my eyes on your beauty, Princess." His gaze boldly caressed every exquisite inch of her body, from her long brown tresses to the pink tips of her toes. Bending his head, he pressed a reverent kiss on each nipple, loving the bob and sway of her tits as they moved with every breath. She was utter perfection. Unable to resist, he sought out the velvet of her pussy, caressing her mound, rubbing the soft narrow trail of fuzz that led to paradise.

"Love me, please," she whispered, trembling in his arms like an Aspen leaf in the wind.

Sweeping her up in his arms, he carried her through the house and up the stairs, knowing Thurgood wouldn't disturb their progress. Resting his chin on her hair, he strode purposefully to his suite. Placing her down on the bed, his eyes met hers the moment she lifted her head. "Never doubt that I want you, that I cherish you."

The approval and heat in his gaze chased away the tiny bit of trepidation in Ryder's heart and mind. "I don't. I trust you, Samson."

Samson bent to kiss her once more, as if he couldn't

resist. No gentle kiss this time – no, this was a possessive claiming, stroking his tongue in and out, eating at her lips, giving her just a taste of the pleasure to come.

"I need to touch you, to see you too," she gasped when he pulled away to rip off his own clothing, taking little care with the expensive materials. As he stripped, his ego couldn't help but respond to her stare, to the appreciation and feminine curiosity in her eyes. Having women like the way he looked was something he was used to – but their shallow admiration paled in the light of Ryder's innocent yearning. He'd always prided himself in pleasing a woman, but this time was critical – imperative – giving her pleasure was far more important than attaining his own.

Lying down next to Ryder, Samson faced her, their legs tangled together. One hand skated up the smoothness of her hip, caressed the indention of her waist, before finding its way up to palm her breast. "I thought you wanted to touch me." he teased her as he played with a nipple, tweaking and rubbing it between his fingers.

Ryder trembled, her whole body straining to be nearer to him. She let out a soft sigh and laid her cheek against his. "I do, it's just so hard for me to think with your hands on me."

"Let this be my time. Okay?" Samson kissed her forehead. "I'm so glad you're here. Your face is so beautiful." He feathered his lips over her eyelids and nose. "Your eyes, your lips." Running his fingers through her hair, he locked her gaze with his. "Your hair is like silk and you smell like a dream."

Ryder giggled. "What do I smell like?"

He pretended to think. "Hmmm, chocolate chip cookies." With a playful growl, he nipped her neck, then settled across her to suckle at her breast.

Closing her eyes, Ryder luxuriated in his attention,

cradling his head as he moved from one nipple to the other. "I fuckin' love your breasts, I won't ever tire of licking and sucking them."

Ryder felt another blush bloom on her body. She tried to repay him by stroking his back and shoulders, rubbing the sole of her foot up and down his leg. "You make me feel beautiful, Samson."

Raising his head, Samson looked at her with his warm amber eyes. "There is no part of you that isn't exquisite, Princess, but what I adore most about you is your kind heart, your amazing mind, and your sweet sense of humor. I also love that you're brave and willing to stand up for those you love…"

"Shhh, we can talk later," she quieted him, layering her lips over his. He chuckled and she captured his laughter and giggled herself. "Make love to me, Duke."

"Yes, ma'am." Taking control, his kisses became aggressive, masterful. Ryder shivered at his dominance. He didn't stop at her lips but moved down her body, his lips closing over a nipple, which he lavished with licks, nips, and suckles. The other breast wasn't neglected by any means, he cupped it with his other hand, brushing his thumb over the sensitive nubbin until it was swollen and distended, begging for his mouth. By the time he'd feasted to his heart's content, she was writhing beneath him.

"I'm ready for you, Samson. I need you so much," she begged, lifting her hips and opening her legs, urging him to take her.

"Soon, don't rush me, I'm having too much fun." Leaving her breasts with one kiss on each puckered, pink nipple, he moved lower. Licking a path down her middle and past her navel, he made for a place he'd been dreaming about since the last time he'd tasted it. Spreading her thighs, he buried his face in her pussy, licking and nuzzling, using lips, teeth and tongue to bring her to the very edge of control.

"Samson!" She gasped his name, raising he head so she could see him worshiping between her legs. "Feels so good! she keened, her hips bucking, her fingers tangling in his long golden hair.

With a long, drawing suckle to her clit, he insured she was wet, wild, and eager to be taken. Rising over her, Samson blanketed her body with his, resting his weight on his forearms. Cupping her face, he gave her long, deep kisses, his tongue sliding over hers – committing the moment to memory.

"Now?" she asked when he paused for a breath, kissing her neck and nipping at her collarbone.

"Now, impatient wench." He was glad they'd had the birth control conversation earlier, he had no desire to dull the heaven of being inside of her with an artificial barrier. Lifting his hips, he spread her thighs with one knee. "Give me your eyes, Ryder. Look into my soul as I make us one." Seeing her eyes widen and the look on her face become uncertain. "Don't be afraid, it's me. I'd never hurt you."

His expression became so gentle and tender that all she could do was smile and lift her hips, inviting him to come inside of her. She gasped, biting her lip, when she felt the head of his cock probe at the well of her vagina. "I haven't even touched you there yet," she whimpered.

"There'll be time, plenty of time," he whispered, as his cock began to sink into her softness.

Ryder clutched his shoulders as she felt him inch forward. He didn't power in, he didn't just shove in fast, he moved slowly with great patience and care. Her eyes widened. "You're too big," she worried softly.

"It's your first time, precious. You're tight. We're perfect for one another. Never doubt it."

She lifted a hand to his face, seeing how tense he was – how hard it was for him to go slow. His unselfish tenderness touched her heart. "Move, Samson. I want to know what it's like to love you. Don't hold back." Wrapping her legs around his hips, she lifted herself, trying to impale herself on his cock.

"Easy, baby, easy," he growled the words, trying desperately to hold on to his last shred of control.

"But I need something…" She moved her hips again, seeking that perfect angle she'd felt just a moment before.

"God, I love this," he said as he bowed his head and kissed her passionately as he pushed forward, burying more of himself. The relief of being inside of her was absolutely breathtaking.

Ryder raked her fingernails over his back as her body accepted more and more of him. Her whole body was on fire, her blood fizzing in her veins. "More, Samson, give me more."

Samson groaned, perspiration beading at his hairline. She was moving beneath him, contracting her little pussy muscles around his cock. He didn't think she had any idea what she was doing, but she was driving him fuckin' mad. "You're amazing. I'm never letting you out of this bed again. Did you know that?"

She gave him a seductive little smile and raised her hips, offering him to sink to the hilt. "It feels so good, baby," she whimpered.

Samson groaned, his cock swelling even larger at her declaration. Bracing himself over her, he began to move. She was fully aroused now, he was embedded deep, and there was nothing to hold them back. Over and over he pumped, pulling in and out of her, making her toss her head in ecstasy. As he made love to her, Samson kissed her mouth – hungry, possessive kisses that left her panting each time he gave her enough leeway to breathe.

"Let's try this, see if you like it," he said, moving up so he could ride higher on her body. When he did, the friction on her clit caused Ryder to cry out, her whole body clamping down on him – arms, legs, and pussy walls.

"Oh, God, yes, please," she begged, hanging on to him for dear life. She was trembling, heat building in her core, a hunger rising so hard and fast that she knew she was about to explode. "Please, please, please," she began to chant as he moved harder and faster – plunging into her with such force that her whole body moved with his on the bed. And all the time, he watched her, he kissed her, he made her feel like she was the very center of his world.

When the wave broke, Ryder shattered, calling out his name in complete abandon. "Samson!"

Her ecstatic cry caused his orgasm to swell. Sliding his arms beneath her, Samson raised her up, crushing her to him, as he rode a powerful swell that rose and rose until it crashed into a glorious wild surge of pleasure. Bellowing his release, he buried his face in her neck, absorbing the shudders and jerks of her body as she floated, awash in a warm sea of aftershocks and pulses of ecstasy.

Rolling them to the side, he molded her body to his. She moaned when his manhood slid from her, but sighed when he cuddled her atop his broad chest, rubbing her back. "Thank you," he murmured, "thank you for trusting me with such a precious gift."

Ryder sighed, nuzzling his chest, stroking his hard pec with the pads of her fingers. "You belong to me now, Samson." She didn't know what the future held or how she'd mend things with her family – but this, this was right and good. The only thing that could make it better was if…

Samson kissed her reverently. "Yes, you are mine

and I am yours." As he rubbed his mouth across her, he became aware of a bit of dampness. "Ryder? Are you crying?"

"I'm happy." She told him, throwing her arms around his neck.

He cradled her close, reading between the lines. Yes, she was happy. "I'm happy too." But they both knew something – or someone – was missing.

* * *

"You aren't going over there, Heath. You just can't do it." Cato knelt at her husband's feet. "I know you're worried about Ryder, but you've just got to give her some space."

"She's going to get hurt," Heath growled, his head bowed, his hand stroking his wife's hair. "It's my job to prevent that from happening if at all possible, you know that."

She stroked his face, giving him all the comfort she could. "From what I can tell, Samson Duke is a good man. Don't judge him and his brother based on gossip and innuendo. Your sister is in love with Samson." She didn't mention Gideon, there was no use adding fuel to the fire. "My every instinct tells me that he feels exactly like you do. I don't think he would hurt her for anything."

"How can I be sure?"

Cato worried. She couldn't hear his voice, so she didn't know if he sounded tired but his face showed strain. "You can't, but I don't want you to hurt her – and you can, Heath. She dotes on you. Don't make her choose between her family and her happiness. Please?"

Heath smiled sadly, cupping Cato's face, mirroring her own gesture. "This goes against every instinct I have, sweetheart. I'm a fixer – I want to make everything right, prevent bad things for happening in my family. I feel like

I've failed."

Cato rose and entwined her arms around his neck. "You haven't failed, my love. Ryder knows you love her." She kissed him on the cheek and sank back down so she could read his lips. "You have another meeting in the morning with that Russian guy and Scott Eagleton has agreed to meet with you too. Don't you think we ought to go to bed? It's getting awfully late."

"Yea, it is. I sure would like to reel these big fish in, they could make all the difference in the world to whether we can get backing for this green energy bill I've got my heart set on. I also need to get myself settled so I can fulfill the contract I have with the Dukes. Strange, that's all the Russian wants to talk about - the Dukes. I wish I'd never let it slip I had a contract with them." He tapped her lower lip with his forefinger. "You know? No matter what - you make everything perfect for me. No matter what storms are blowing around me, I know I can hold onto you and my world will right itself."

"Good. I want you to hold me all night long." She rose to her feet and took him by the hand. "I love you, Heath McCoy. More than the oceans could hold."

As she led him to their bedroom, he knew she couldn't hear him. But that didn't matter – he'd told her a thousand times before and he'd tell her with the last breath he drew. "I love you too, sweetheart. More than anything, even my old red truck."

* * *

Gideon rubbed his eyes, the flight had been tiring. He carried his duffle over his shoulder as he made his way to the back of the house from the heliport. Maybe he should've stayed away longer, but he needed to speak to his brother face to face. They had some decisions to make and some facts to ferret through.

As he moved across the patio, he glanced at his watch. Five a.m. Samson would be up in about an hour or so, he might as well wait. Trying to be quiet, he let himself into the kitchen, easing the door shut. A cup of coffee sounded good. Flipping on the light, he was met with a very feminine squeal.

What the hell?

Whirling around, he was shocked out of his boots to see Ryder – a very sexy, tousled Ryder. She was wearing a well-loved-on look and very little else, just one of Samson's shirt.

"Ryder?"

She gasped, clasping a hand to her breast. "Gideon!" With unrestrained joy, she ran to him, throwing her arms around his neck. "I'm so glad you're home!"

Gideon felt like he'd been hit by a sledge hammer rather than a small, delicate woman. He raised his arms to welcome her, then dropped them. What was he supposed to do? His every instinct was to take what she seemed to be offering. Every part of his body responded – his heart and his cock were on the same page – only his mind seemed determined to remember the rules. "What are you doing here, Ryder?"

Like he didn't know.

His question served to wake her up – not from slumber, but from an impossible dream. Immediately, she backed out of his embrace. "I'm staying with Samson." She pulled on the bottom of the shirt, which only came to mid-thigh. "I'm sorry. I shouldn't have done that – for just a second I forgot that you had decided you didn't want…this…."

Gideon frowned. He stepped behind the granite island, shielding his errant erection from her view. "Didn't want what?"

Ryder ran a nervous hand over her hair, pushing it

back over her shoulder. "Nothing, I'm sorry. I should go back upstairs."

"No! Wait!" Gideon shouted, loud enough to rouse the dead – if not Thurgood. "What do you mean?"

Footsteps at the door caused them both to jerk their heads around. Samson stood there in a pair of lounge pants, no shirt. "What's all the commotion?" He looked from one to the other. "Gideon! You're home." He smiled at his brother, then went to Ryder and placed a protective arm around her shoulder, tilted her head up for a kiss, then whispered in her ear. "Last night was the best night of my life."

Seeing Samson and Ryder together, seeing their intimacy, knowing he couldn't be a part of it – hurt like hell. "I am." He stared at them, trying to settle his heartrate. "Sorry, I should've called."

"Nonsense. This is your home; this will always be your home." He kissed Ryder's cheek again. "As you can see, because of you, we worked things out. I owe you one."

Ryder blushed and Gideon didn't say anything.

Samson could feel the tension in the room, you could cut it like a knife. He knew how Ryder felt, she still longed for Gideon, the fact that she was trembling in his arms attested to her feelings. Her loyalty to her family and the fear of their finding out had created this impossible situation…but all of that changed when the McCoy's confronted her. She'd told her family and she'd told Samson – that if she could, she'd be with them both.

But what about Gideon?

"Come on, let's sit down and have coffee. I'm sure you're tired after your long journey, brother." Feeling like he was walking on eggshells, he pressed his palm to the small of Ryder's back.

"Maybe, I should change," she whispered, anxious to

get some distance. Ryder couldn't believe she'd launched herself at Gideon like some lovesick school girl.

"Okay." Samson gave her a kiss. "We'll be here. Hurry back."

Ryder made her escape, hurrying away, her bare feet padding on the travertine tile.

"Sirs, you should've woke me!" Thurgood came bustling into the kitchen, still wearing his nightshirt and nightcap.

His visage caused both men to smile. "We're fine, go back to bed," Samson told him and Gideon nodded. The old man rubbed his eyes and retraced his path, grumbling something about night owls under his breath.

As soon as they were alone again, Samson went to the cabinet and took down two mugs, selected some K-cups and began to brew them each some coffee. While the last cup filled, he set the cream and sugar in front of Gideon who was sitting at the bar. Without letting on, Samson probed Gideon's mind. Their lives had been in such turmoil; he hadn't really noticed until recently that he wasn't picking up on his brother's thoughts and feelings the way he had in the past. But now – at this moment, Gideon was in turmoil and he could feel it – he could sense it – Samson could read his twin's thoughts as clear as a bell. As soon as the mug was full, he picked them both up and faced his brother. "Did you think I wouldn't figure it out?" Gideon's face looked like it was made of stone and as he met Samson's eyes, Samson could feel his brother's attempt to rebuild the wall between them.

"Figure what out? Something about the Russians?"

Samson turned a chair around and straddled it, studying his brother's face. "You look like shit, man. I think there's more bothering you than what's going down with our space mission. Want to tell me about it?"

Taking a sip of coffee, Gideon evaded the question, then asked one of his own. "How long was I gone before you and Ryder got together?"

Samson answered in his mind. *Hours. I couldn't stay away. She still wants you, you know.*

Whereas Gideon had been looking down, his eyes lifted and he locked his gaze with Samson's.

"Let me repeat my previous question. Did you really think I wouldn't figure it out?"

Gideon rose. "I'm not playing this game with you, brother."

"This isn't a game, Gideon. This is our lives, our happiness. This is Ryder – our destiny."

"Your destiny. Not mine!" Gideon shouted. "She can't accept us both, I heard what she said that day. It's you, she wants, not me!"

Samson stood up and shouted right back. "Apparently, you didn't hear the whole conversation. You sacrificed yourself, Gideon! A sacrifice that is no longer necessary!"

"What's going on?"

Ryder's small voice caused them both to freeze.

When neither answered, she came up to them, looking from Samson to Gideon and back. "Are you talking about me?"

"Yes, baby," Samson grasped her hand. "We all need to talk. We need to clear the air. I think you and Gideon are operating under some mistaken assumptions."

"I don't think…" Gideon began.

"No, you're not thinking." Samson fired back.

"Please, don't fight over me," Ryder pleaded. "I'm just not worth it."

Her statement drew their simultaneous attention and an audible growl from both.

"Not worth it?" Samson exclaimed.

And Gideon agreed, "Making the two of you happy is what this was all about!"

"I'm sorry, I don't understand any of this." Ryder spread her hands. "Should I go home?" She didn't want to, but she didn't want to be the cause of problems at Falconhead.

"No, I can leave." Gideon grabbed his duffle. "I shouldn't have just shown up unannounced, not after I told you I'd make myself scarce."

Samson stepped between them, holding his hands up in a defensive posture. "Stop. Neither one of you are going anywhere. Let's sit down and discuss this." He grabbed his head, his fingers rifling through his hair. "I can't believe I'm the only one who can see what's going on?"

When neither Gideon nor Ryder made a move, Samson sat first. "Please."

Ryder and Gideon cast one apprehensive glance at the other, then Ryder spoke up. "Samson, I'd like to speak to you privately."

"Yes, of course," he agreed, but he looked pained, as if he didn't want to delay the conversation at hand.

When Gideon started for the door. "I'll give you two the privacy you need."

"No!" Ryder moved to stop him. She grabbed his arm, let her hand slide down to clasp his. "Don't go, I want to talk to you. Just wait one moment, that's all I ask."

As he stared into her beseeching eyes, there was no way Gideon could tell her no. "I'll be here."

To Gideon's surprise, she hugged him again. He met his brother's eyes over her shoulder – and seeing his encouraging look – this time he hugged her back.

With a soft, quick kiss to the cheek, she went to Samson, who guided her out of the kitchen and down the hall. "Where do you want to go?" he asked.

"Here is fine." Ryder pulled him into the formal dining room. "What's going on? I feel like I'm missing something." She walked up to him, fully expecting his arms to open and hold her tight – they did. "Are you giving me the green light to ask Gideon if he wants to…"

"Yes," Samson spoke unequivocally. "I'll explain it more later, but Gideon overheard part of our conversation the day you came to say goodbye. What he heard convinced him that you wanted to be with me only. He backed off so we could be together, not because he didn't want to be with you."

Ryder searched Samson's face. "I'm scared, Samson." She nestled against him. "But the one thing I do know, is that I want you and I want Gideon too. Like your mother tried to tell me, what I feel for your brother doesn't lessen what I feel for you one iota, and what I feel for you, doesn't change how I feel about him. I cherish you both. Equally, but differently."

"You are saying exactly what my mother always said, what my grandmother always told us. Love enough for three." He kissed her on the forehead. "Go tell him. This is between the two of you."

"Shouldn't you be there?" Ryder asked, not wanting to do anything that would cause either of her men a moment's pain.

Her men. The thought thrilled her.

"No. Gideon knows how I feel, he's always known. What needs to happen now, is for the two of you to find your footing. You are the heart of this relationship, Ryder. Go to Gideon and let him know how you feel. Show him how you feel."

"Do you mean…?"

"Yes, last night was our first time, this will be your first time with Gideon." Ryder shivered and he rubbed her arms, giving her the assurance she needed. "I'm going to give you the privacy you need and take care of some business. I'll be back later tonight and we'll all go out to dinner together."

"All right," She agreed, raising her lips for his kiss. "I want this, I want you, and I want Gideon. Please don't ever let me do anything to hurt you."

Samson framed her face. "The only way you could hurt me is if you would leave me." He kissed her tenderly. "Please don't ever leave me, Ryder."

"If I ever do, come look for me. I won't have left you by choice," she vowed.

Samson gave her an encouraging smile and the nudge toward Gideon she needed. "I'll always look for you, sweetheart – now go get your man." As he sent her on her way, Samson felt the oddest thing – a chill swept over him, like a foreboding wind blowing through his soul.

CHAPTER NINE

Gideon waited, staring out the window. He'd almost left, but a promise to Ryder wasn't something he could easily break. "Dammit!" he whispered, stuffing his trembling hands in the front pockets of his jeans. "What a big fuckin' man-baby." Gideon felt like he was waiting for the executioner. Why were they torturing him like this? Ryder hadn't changed her mind; she wouldn't turn her back on her family. Her father's health was too delicate for her to risk upsetting him and causing damage to his health.

"Gideon?"

Her soft voice caused ripples of awareness to cascade down his spine. "I'm still here." He stepped into her line of vision. "Where's Samson?" he asked, noticing she was alone.

"He left, he wanted to give us time alone." She approached him, almost shyly. "Could we talk?"

Gideon nodded. "Sure." Why this long, drawn-out goodbye? Didn't she realize he was human, that he could be hurt? Despite his angst, Gideon couldn't help but appreciate how lovely she looked, dressed in tight blue jeans and a red sweater that hugged her mouthwatering curves as tight as he'd like to hold them.

Ryder cleared her throat, trying to garner her courage. This was so important. She hoped to high heaven she and Samson weren't misreading the situation. All she needed to do was humiliate herself with Gideon. She wanted a future with him so bad she could taste it. "Could we go somewhere the staff won't hear our conversation?"

Gideon wanted to ask her to his private suite, but that probably wouldn't be wise. "Let's go into the study." He led the way, wondering what the next few minutes would bring.

Ryder hugged herself, feeling more nervous than she had in a long time. He held the door open for her and she entered ahead of him, barely aware of the rich woodwork and fine leather furnishings. Since getting to know the brothers, their wealth played a much lesser role in comparison to the forcefulness of their personalities and her feelings for them as individuals. "Thank you for speaking to me."

"Here, sit." He held out a chair, then went to sit on the desk, bowing his head. "God, baby, of course I would speak to you." Gideon stopped, not knowing what else to say.

Ryder sat on the edge of the chair, her hands clasped in her lap. "Let me try to explain what happened." Seeing that he was waiting, she swallowed hard and continued. "The day of Dad's episode, when you two left after your plant caught on fire, I went in to speak to him and he essentially told me that all of the family's ups and downs had taken their toll. He told me that I was his good girl, the only one that he could count on not to break his heart."

Gideon could see what this was costing her, emotionally. "Look, Ryder, I understand."

"No, wait." She held up her hand. "Let me finish."

God, this was killing him. She was looking at him with her heart in her eyes, but he didn't know what she wanted from him. "Go on."

"I didn't know what to do." She pushed her hair behind one of her ears. "I panicked. That's when I came here and told Samson that I couldn't be with the both of you."

"I know. I heard. You said that you could love him, but you couldn't be with us both." Even as he repeated what he'd learned that day – his heart ached like a son-of-a-bitch.

Ryder frowned. "You were listening? Why didn't you come to me?"

Gideon shook his head. "Why would I? You don't feel about me the same way you feel about Samson. I didn't want to interfere."

"Interfere? I told Samson that I could love him and I could love you, that if I had my way I'd be with you both." She was talking fast, trying to convey the turmoil she'd been dealing with. "I just didn't know how to have it all – you, Samson, and my family." Bowing her head, she thought about all that had happened. "You know Samson would have never come to me that night, knowing the impossible situation I was in…if you hadn't told him you didn't want me."

"Wait!" Gideon knelt in front of her. "Whoa!" He grabbed Ryder's hands, which she was wringing in her lap. "The only reason I ever made Samson think I didn't want to be in this relationship was because you said being with both of us was impossible, I heard you say you could love Samson, and I knew without a doubt he wanted you."

"Oh, Gideon, in the next breath, I said I could love you too. I wasn't choosing. The whole thing was breaking my heart because I wanted you both."

He cupped her cheek, understanding dawning in his stubborn, hard head. "And Samson, thinking I wanted out, saw an opportunity for the two of you to find some happiness."

"Yes." She leaned into his touch. "But never for one moment did I forget you."

Hope was blooming in his heart. There was just one more question. "So, has anything changed? You're with Samson, now. But you're also sitting here with me. Why? If your family could never accept you being with both of us, why are you tempting me with something I still can't have?"

Ryder shook her head, a cascade of emotion making her shake. "Somehow, Heath and the others found out about your…reputation. They confronted me, tried to perform some type of stupid intervention. I told them I hadn't done what they accused me of, I'd never even been with a man at all. Samson had been a total gentleman. I also told them that if I could, I would be with the two of you in a heartbeat!" She gave him a wry smile. "Then, I promptly marched out and came straight here."

"You and Samson hadn't…" God, he couldn't even bring himself to say it.

Ryder's cheeks tinged pink. It was still hard of her to be so honest about things she considered intimate and private. But…if she was going to have two men, she needed to get over that apprehension. "Samson made love to me last night." Lifting a hand to caress his scruff darkened cheek, she gave him a shy smile. "I'm tired of worrying about what my family thinks. I know what I want. I want you and Samson. Do you still want me?"

Gideon felt a flash of exultation. Steel bands of despair broke their hold on him and he could finally draw a full breath of air into his lungs. "God, yes, I want you." He stood to his feet, pulling her up with him. Drawing her into his arms, he covered her mouth with his and she flowered open, granting him access. They'd kissed before – but this was different, an undertone of certainty, of confidence in one another. Their tongues danced together and he could taste her surrender. There was no holding back, no hesitation. Ryder's hands slid up his chest and around his neck, her fingers kneading his nape, moving up to weave through his long, dark hair.

This was it as far as Gideon was concerned, he didn't intend to back away again. He would ingratiate himself so deep into her life and thoughts that she wouldn't be able to remember not having him around.

Ryder clung to him, feasting at his mouth. This was what she'd needed, what she'd been missing – Gideon. She didn't try to understand, didn't try to justify what she felt. Having him in her arms and knowing Samson completed their trinity only brought her joy.

Double the joy.

"Take me to bed, Gideon," she whispered as she slid her lips from his mouth to rub against his five o'clock shadow. "God, I love to touch you, you're so sexy."

Chuckling, he slid an arm beneath her knees and picked her up, his lips only leaving hers for a moment. "I'm glad you think so. The feeling is more than mutual." Gideon knew he wasn't the eloquent one in the family. No matter, what he couldn't tell her with words, he'd show her with actions – loving and worshiping her body with everything in him.

As he carried her to his suite, she gazed up into his face. "I'm so glad you're here. I was happy with Samson, but having you makes me complete."

"I know, baby." He nuzzled her neck as he carried her into his domain. As they'd always dreamed, he and Samson would share the woman of their dreams – but right now was his time, where he could cherish her in a private world for just the two of them, a domain where she would be his queen, the object of his desire.

Carrying her into his room, he set her down, backing her toward the massive bed. All the while, his hands explored her body. As he'd remembered, her skin was silky smooth to the touch. "Sit here." Gideon urged her down while he divested himself of his clothing, anxious to make her his.

Ryder watched, enraptured. "You're so beautiful." Her dark prince. Broad of shoulder, narrow of waist – a chest rippling with muscles that she planned on tracing with her tongue at the earliest opportunity. And when he removed his jeans and briefs, Ryder moaned and reached for him. "Closer." Gone was the trepidation from the night before. Samson had introduced her to the ecstasy of lovemaking, now she wanted that same knowledge of this man who'd captured her heart as completely as his brother.

Gideon moved closer, almost between her legs, offering all of himself to her. When her delicate fingers touched him, grazing his thigh, her lips pressing to the heated skin below his navel; he closed his eyes, immersed in the ecstasy of the moment. And when her small hand closed around him, he groaned in gratitude. "No more, witch. I don't want this to be over so soon. I have to please you first."

"Awww," she protested, as he came over her, his big body pushing her back on the mattress.

Rolling to one side, he brought her on top of him. "You've got on way too many clothes, Princess."

His calling her by their special pet name was almost Ryder's undoing. "Let me help," she began fumbling with the zipper of her jeans while he worked on the buttons of her sweater. Soon she sat on top of him, clad only in a lacy bra and panties. He wanted to make her comfortable, so he began to pet her, with long, slow caresses. Ryder responded to his attention, luxuriating in his touch. She reminded Gideon of a kitten, purring when she was stroked.

When she began arching her back, wordlessly offering her breasts to him, Gideon couldn't resist. Using both hands, he hooked his fingers into the cups of her bra and pulled down. Her breasts popped out and Gideon growled, "Damn, Princess."

Sliding his hands around her waist and up her back, he pulled her toward him so that her tits dangled in his face. Giving her a dazzling smile, he rubbed his face against the quivering globes. "I'm going to enjoy you so much," he murmured as he sucked one tender bud into his mouth. Ryder shuddered, kissing the top of his head while he fed on her breast. Seemingly, unable to be still, she undulated on top of him, scrubbing her feminine center against him.

"Hungry, baby?" he asked her.

"Uh-huh," was all she could say. "I need you."

His cock ached, throbbing in anticipation of making her his. Knowing his control would be negligible, Gideon needed to please her first. "Lie down for me." He helped her, reversing their position, lowering Ryder to the bed. Enjoying the view, he slipped off her panties, tossing them to one side. "You are so perfect," he said, leaning forward to kiss the valley between her breasts, then moved lower, taking his sweet time to reach his ultimate goal. "I only got one small taste last time and I've dreamed of this moment ever since." He couldn't wait to learn the things that would bring her the most pleasure.

"Me too," confessed Ryder. "I've relived the kiss you gave me there, over and over." She reached out and rubbed her hand on his chest. "You'll never know how torn I've been, wanting you, fantasizing about you, even when I felt completely committed to Samson." She chewed on her lower lip, feeling vulnerable, yet freer than she'd ever been. "You, Gideon Duke – all of this is the stuff of dreams."

Going to his knees by the bed, he eased her body into position. "Let me make your dreams come true." Gideon brushed his mouth over her mound, inhaling the scent of her excitement. It aroused him beyond measure.

Just his breath on her flesh caused frissons of anticipation to dance across her skin. Ryder whimpered as his mouth hovered over and teased her pussy. "Gideon, don't make me wait. I'm dying here. Kiss me, please."

Feeling triumphant, Gideon lowered his mouth and kissed her soft center. When he felt her desire coat his tongue, he groaned. All his intentions to tease and prolong their play flew out the window. His own hunger spiked, he was starved for her. Parting the pretty lips of her labia, he set out to seduce Ryder by learning and worshiping her pussy with his tongue.

The sensation was so wonderful; she couldn't be still. As he held her open, licking and feasting between her thighs, she moved restlessly beneath him. He placed a steadying hand on her abdomen, to keep her hips in place. Still, she tossed her head and clawed at the silky sheets.

"Feel good, Princess?" he asked, realizing that pleasing her was a heady experience, surpassing his own quest for fulfillment. Sliding one hand beneath her bottom, he lifted her for a better angle. With long strokes of his tongue, he laved her slit, teasing the opening to her vagina, spearing deep, relishing Ryder's taste. Her clit was swollen and peeking from its hood, he swirled his tongue around it, flicking and sucking – loving the way she keened and jerked rhythmically, seeking her own release.

"So good…so good." Her moan escalated, rising into a crescendo when he sucked her clit between his lips and curled two fingers deep inside her channel. "Gideon!" she exclaimed as her body tensed and her orgasm hit hard.

"That's my girl," he praised her as he continued his onslaught, forcing her to squeeze every ounce of pleasure she could from her climax. When she finally stilled, her chest heaving, he kissed a path to the top of her mound and gave her a gentle nip. "Birth control?"

"Taken care of, come to me." Her eyes met his and she gave him a dazzling smile. "I am the luckiest woman in the world.

With a growl of possessive hunger, he stared down at her body. "You belong to me, Ryder. Don't ever doubt it. She was glorious. No other woman he'd ever known even compared. "Scoot back a bit, make room for me."

Make room. Ryder eagerly moved up in the bed, her eyes eating up Gideon's fine form. "There's plenty of room," she told him. And there was. In her heart. In her life. Room for Gideon. Room for Samson. Ryder felt rich beyond her wildest dreams – and it had nothing to do with the Duke wealth and everything to do with the Dukes themselves. "I'm ready," she announced with a grin, spreading her legs invitingly.

Gideon chuckled, fisting his cock. "Temptress." Equal portions of joy and lust consumed him. "I can't wait to get inside you."

"Don't."

She raised her hips, palmed her breasts, and drove him mad. Gripping her hips, he lined up his cock and thrust inside. "God, yes," he moaned. This was what he'd been longing for – what he thought would never happen. The desolation he'd felt was gone, the bleakness of a future apart from his brother and their woman was dispelled. Here – in their home, with this woman was where he belonged.

"Closer, come closer," she beckoned him. When he lowered himself to her, pressing his big body to hers, Ryder's arms came up to clutch his shoulders. "Don't ever leave me, Gideon. I couldn't stand it." She wound her legs around his hips and thrust her pelvis up to meet him.

"Not gonna happen," he murmured. Unable to hold back, he began to move – working his way deeper. "God, you're tight, baby." He undulated his hips, slow luxurious figure eights, making room for himself in her body and in her life. Over and over, he plunged in, then dragged his cock back out. The amazing friction, the way her little pussy grabbed on to him, all of it was so intense, Gideon found it hard to breathe. In and out. In and out he took her, his body moving in the timeless primal rhythm of masculine domination. Riding her hard, every pass his body made over hers ground his pelvis against her clit. She wasn't still, didn't just receive – Ryder moved with him, accepting all he had to give and demanding more.

Parrying his thrusts, she bucked her hips up to meet him, matching her movements to his. "I love this, Gideon," she whispered, nipping his shoulder, his neck.

"I love it too, baby," he assured her, completely awash in ecstasy. He'd always associated paradise with his home in the islands, and now he knew the word would mean something else to him. Paradise was here – in her arms. Leaning over to kiss her, Gideon knew he was right where he was supposed to be. "I'm mad about you, Ryder. Fuckin' mad."

Once he lifted his head again, Ryder smiled at him. As he moved over her, she let her hands rove over his chest, tracing his muscles, raking her nails down his abs. "I'm gonna cum soon, will you cum with me?"

"Hell, yeah." He ceased trying to hold back. The heat in her eyes was his undoing. Gideon went wild, fucking between her thighs in utter abandon. Over and over. Again and again. In and out until they were both balancing on the razor's edge of a precipice so deep and boundless that when they fell over – both knew they'd never return to the place they once were.

This was new. Uncharted territory.

"Cum for me, love," he encouraged. "Show me you are mine."

His request sent her over – tumbling, flying, free-falling as wave after wave of bliss cascaded over her. "Oh, God, Gideon!" she cried.

When she clamped around him, her back arching, her eyes closing – her body shuddering as she moaned her pleasure and his name – Gideon let go. He thrust three more times, reveling in the way she milked him, then buried his cock to the hilt. With a shout, his balls drew up and he spilled himself within her. Every cell in his body was electrified with euphoric energy.

They froze – drowning in pleasure, bodies tingling, hearts pounding, eyes meeting. Both knew what this meant. They were joined. This was real. Soon, Samson would join them and they'd embark on their journey together.

Giving her one kiss after another, Gideon absorbed her shudders, loving the way they were still joined, their limbs tangled together. "Are you okay?" he asked, holding most of his weight off her, yet close enough, she could feel the comforting press of his body.

"I'm perfect," she whispered. "I'm ready for everything."

Gideon nodded, easing himself to one side and pulling her with him. "I agree. This is the beginning and I can't wait to see where life takes us."

"All three of us," Ryder whispered, kissing his shoulder. She wanted to mark him, claim him, ensure that no one ever forgot Gideon belonged to Ryder. Yes, she was greedy. She wanted two. She wanted them both.

Forever.

* * *

The minute Samson returned to Falconhead, he knew everything was all right. He'd no more than stepped through the door and handed Thurgood his jacket before he heard it.

Laughter.

Ryder's feminine laughter could be heard mingling

with Gideon's masculine amusement.

"They've been at it all day, Sir."

Samson couldn't help but smile. "Do I want to know?"

Thurgood grimaced. "They're baking cookies, Sir. They're making a mess of my kitchen." He lowered his voice to a crackling whisper. "Flour handprints on the black Italian marble counters."

"Oh, no," Samson whispered, commiserating with his old butler. "I'll see what I can do. How about if I get them out of your hair for a while?"

"Thank you, Sir," he breathed a sigh of relief. "I'll be eternally grateful."

As Samson headed through the house, he couldn't help but smile, listening to his brother and their love.

"Gimme a bite," Gideon coaxed. "I'm still hungry."

A fit of sweet giggles.

"Here, open your mouth. I'll give you one more cookie."

"Who wants a cookie?" Manly growls and a feminine squeal. "I want you!"

Samson slipped up to the door, watching them play. Thurgood was right. Their once immaculate gourmet kitchen was now strewn with ingredients, an unwashed mixer, cooking racks full of cookies…and crumbs on the counter. But what made Samson happy was the game of tag he was witnessing. Ryder was managing to stay just ahead of Gideon, who was stalking her like a hunter after prey. They both looked so carefree and his twin looked happier than he'd ever seen him.

"Do you have any cookies left for me?"

Hearing Samson's voice, Ryder twirled around and ran to him, launching herself into his arms. "You're home! I'm so glad!"

Samson cradled her close, meeting his brother's gaze

from across the room. "I'm glad to see you two getting along so well."

"Oh, we are!" Ryder hugged him tight. "I'm so happy I could faint!"

Samson and Gideon exchanged amused glances. "Well, don't faint, we enjoy your company too much." He took the time to capture her lips in a long passionate kiss.

"Any word from Oleg?" Gideon asked once Samson and Ryder ended their embrace.

"I do have some information," he told Gideon, then cupped Ryder's chin. "I've made reservations for the three of us to go out to dinner. While we talk business, why don't you run upstairs and find something to wear for an evening out? I took the liberty of having some clothes sent to you. Go to the suite of rooms between mine and Gideon's, you'll find plenty of surprises awaiting you."

"Yes! I'm excited!" She gave them both hugs and kisses, then took off to get ready.

As they heard her footsteps padding up the stairs, they came together for a rare hug. "So, from what I saw, things are good," Samson said aloud, even as he sent a private message to his brother. *This is the way things are supposed to be.*

Gideon followed suit. "Things are better than good." *I didn't want to be on the outside looking in.*

"You're never on the outside." Samson placed his hand on his brother's shoulder. "I'm sure we still have work to do. We must mend fences with her family. Right now, she's coming to terms with what makes her happy, but soon, she'll want to reach out to them."

"And when she does, we'll help her build the bridge. How are things with Heath? Is he following through on our methane fuel contract?"

Samson nodded. "Yes. McCoy, for all his bluster, is a professional."

"True, and at the same time he's an over-protective, overbearing bear," Gideon observed, beginning to wipe down the counters.

"Might as well leave the cleaning up to Thurgood and his staff. They gave you privacy, but I think they're eager to get in here and reclaim the kitchen…" He waved his hand at the clutter.

Gideon laughed, running his hand through his hair. Looking around, he raised an eyebrow. "We had more on our minds than maintaining order."

"I'm glad. So, are we of like minds?" *Do we pursue a commitment?*

"We are." *I'm sorry I locked you out.*

Samson turned to look out the window. "I see what you were doing now, putting us first. At the time, I was too torn up to focus on the lack of a connection with you." Turning, he faced Gideon. "Please don't shut me out again."

"I don't intend to." Gideon picked up the plate of cookies he and Ryder had baked. "Try one." He waited for Samson to pick up a cookie and take a bite. "I can't say I noticed at the time, but you were conspicuously absent from my head this morning while I was with Ryder."

Samson took the time to swallow before answering. "For the same reason I left the estate, I wanted you two to forge your own bond without my influence. I wanted there to be no doubt in your or Ryder's mind that what you have between you is as strong and right as what Ryder and I share."

Gideon nodded. "I knew that and thank you." He gave his brother a broad smile. "I'm proud to say that it worked. I'm ready to press forward and start to build our life together with her as the center – the heart of our lives."

"Good. Now, while our beautiful lady gets ready for our evening out, let's you and I work on insuring our quest to get to Mars doesn't get sidelined by those who want to get there ahead of us."

"They won't succeed, Samson," Gideon spoke with assurance. "They can't buy us and they can't beat us."

"Right," Samson agreed. "They have nothing to threaten us with, nothing to hold over our heads." He smiled with the full knowledge they'd succeed. "There's nothing they can do to stop us – and they know it."

"True." Gideon let out a long harsh breath. "What they're doing makes no sense and that's what makes them so dangerous."

…Upstairs, Ryder didn't know whether to be thrilled or feel guilty. When Samson told her he'd had a few outfits delivered for her to choose from, she'd pictured just that, two or three dresses in a garment bag. What she found was two portable racks filled with beautiful gowns and two trunks full of shoes and accessories. The name on the side of the trunk was Neiman Marcus. While she and Pepper had never done without anything they'd truly wanted or needed, their lifestyle hadn't necessitated designer wear or luxury items.

And the high fashion clothing was just the beginning.

The room Samson directed her to had an obvious use. She'd stood at the door and surveyed what was in front of her. This was a romantic haven, the place where they would share her. The bed was vast, not just a king-size, something like a king and a half. "Oh, my goodness." Truthfully, all of this excited her, but it also made her a bit nervous. What was she doing? Could she fit into their world?

A buzzing noise alerted Ryder to grab her cell. As if

thoughts of her sister had conjured her up, she saw the caller was Pepper. For a millisecond, she considered not picking it up. What would she say? She had no intention of reversing her decision, her family had forced her hand and she was glad of it. She'd made her choice and they were just going to have to deal with it. "Oh, fiddle-foot!" Ryder grumbled, pressing the button. Her curiosity was just as great. Besides...she didn't want it to be her dad. An instant of guilt knifed through her breast. What if?

"Pepper."

"Ryder! How are you?"

Without answering her question, Ryder asked one of her own. "Is Daddy okay?"

"Yes," Pepper quickly answered. "How about you? I've been so worried. I called thirty times last night."

"My phone was dead." She'd neglected charging it, she hadn't wanted to talk to anyone.

"Philip followed you, he wouldn't let Heath and Jaxson go, so you owe him one. At least we knew you'd gotten there safely. He came home with the surprising news that you have a protective unit shadowing you. Did you know that?"

Ryder sat down on the edge of the humongous bed. "Yes," she sighed, still not used to the idea, "they've had a guard on me since the car bombing incident. They were afraid someone would think I could identify them. Obviously, no one did. I'm still here."

"Thank God," Pepper exclaimed. "So, what's going on?"

The curious lilt in her voice told Ryder exactly what Pepper wanted to know. The details. All the sordid – or maybe explicit was a better word – details. "I don't know what you mean." No use making it easy for her.

"Oh, yes, you do. So, did you and Samson do it?"

Ryder blushed to the roots of her hair. "Pepper!" she

chided her sister.

"Of course you did. You're nobody's fool." She paused for effect. "Didn't you?"

"Yes," she whispered. "And with Gideon too. Separate, not together. Yet."

"Whooooooooo!" Pepper yelled, loud enough to wake the dead. "I thought you said Gideon wasn't part of the deal."

"He just said that so Samson and I could be happy. When he came home unexpectedly and found me here, things sorta…changed." Ryder was whispering, her heart skipping beats. She'd always shared stuff with her sister, but this was critical – life-changing. "Don't tell the boys."

"Oh, I won't. But don't you think they're going to find out sometime?"

"Yea, but this is too new. Too…important. Like you told me, Pepper, this is my life. I want to be with these two men. I don't know if it will be forever, but I'll never forgive myself if I don't see where it leads."

"I think you're right. I'd do exactly the same thing. I'm so happy for you."

Her simple statement of support made Ryder cry. "I love you, Pepper-pot. How are things with you?"

"Oh, I think I'm going to collect stray cats and take up knitting." She giggled. "I love you too, Ryder. And don't worry about Daddy, he might never find out. And if he does, we'll cross that bridge when we come to it."

"You're too young to be an eccentric cat lady." Ryder stood and walked to the window. From this vantage point, she could see Highlands in the distance. The sight made her feel funny – looking from the present to the past, her heart tugging in two directions. "I would never want to hurt Daddy. I just don't know what else to do."

"Just be happy, Ryder. That's all you need to do.

Everything else will take care of itself."

After the phone call was over, Ryder cradled the phone to her breast. "I hope so, Pepper," she whispered in the silence. "I hope so."

...A couple of hours later, Ryder and her two men were seated at the best table Brazos had to offer. Samson and Gideon were exceptionally dashing in black tie, while she felt elegant in a scarlet, backless Vera Wang original.

"Champagne, Princess?" Samson asked, while the waiter stood in attendance.

"Yes, please." She sat between them, completely pampered, the center of both their attentions. No one had to tell her she was the envy of every woman in the room. Any female alive would be thrilled to be with either of them, and here she was with both. "Samson took me to Cape Canaveral to see the Ryder-I make its maiden voyage."

"Did you enjoy yourself?" Gideon asked indulgently, his hand resting atop hers on the snow-white tablecloth.

Ryder's eyes widened. "I was honored, shocked, and flabbergasted. This wasn't a last-minute decision, you two came up with this a while back. Didn't you?"

Samson covered her other hand with his. "The day after you saved our lives."

She didn't know why it felt necessary to point this out, but she didn't want them waking up one day and wondering how they got here – with her. "You two do know that the whole fate thing is just a good story. Your mother told you something to inspire you, to give you hope for a perfect future. My role in all of this is purely coincidental. Please don't put me on a pedestal, I'm a total klutz. I will fall off."

Ryder said all of this with downcast eyes. When she finally looked up, it was to catch Gideon staring at her with a heated gaze. "And when you do, we'll catch you and put you right back up there." He stopped while the waiter poured their champagne, then put the bottle in an ice bucket, waiting for one of them to approve their choice.

Samson gave the drink a taste and the waiter a thumbs-up. Once he was gone, Samson took up the case. "While we don't discount mother's vision, we do trust our own instincts."

"You captivated us from the very first." Gideon buttered a bit of bread, then placed it between her lips. "Isn't that right, brother?"

Samson grew serious. "We're meant to be, everything is working to bring us together – from the way we met, to the way you selflessly saved us, to the circumstances that caused you to leave your home and come running to Falconhead. None of this is an accident."

Ryder leaned over and hugged Samson, giving him a kiss. "See, you do believe in fate and I want to. But what I do believe in – is you." She turned to Gideon and kissed him on the cheek. "And I believe in you." A scuffle near them caused Ryder to jerk her head around.

"Don't worry." Gideon assured her. "It's just a reporter, trying to get a photo. Gabriel stopped him."

"This is normal for you, isn't it?" Ryder continued to watch over her shoulder, seeing the men who guarded the Dukes confronting a man with a camera. This commotion caused every person in the room to focus on their table. "You two are celebrities."

Samson rubbed her arm. "Don't worry, darling. The attention span of most people is very narrow. Even the news cycles for major stories are short. In a few moments, most of these folks will forget we're in the room. Besides, we're just dining, nothing to see."

Ryder nodded, but she wasn't sure she agreed. Samson and Gideon were too dynamic, magnetic, and handsome for anyone to ignore – especially females who made up at least half the crowd surrounding them.

As the evening progressed, they dined on sumptuous food – lobster, beef tenderloin, and chocolate soufflé. Their conversation was equally delicious.

"So, tell me, what happens next?" she asked, totally enchanted by their attentiveness…and maybe the champagne. She'd never been happier.

Samson leaned over and kissed the corner of her mouth. "Soufflé," he said with a smile. "Our plans are to include you in our life. What we do, you'll do. Where we go, you'll go. Of course, you have complete freedom to come and go as you please, Falconhead is not your prison, it's your castle. If you want to spend time with family and friends, that's what you'll do. Just understand, Gabriel or one of his men will watch over you, we wouldn't have it no other way. You will be their number one priority." He saw apprehension in Ryder's eyes and sought to dispel it. "I have no doubt that we're going to fit together perfectly, but we want to give you time to come to the same conclusion. We want to keep you safe and make you happy."

"Keep me safe from who? Are you still being threatened?" Even as Ryder asked the question, she thought she knew the answer.

"Unfortunately, people in our position always have to be careful. We can't afford to let our guard down," Gideon said, lowly and calmly. "We have the very best team possible and we have a hardline rule - we don't negotiate with terrorists. Ever. This common knowledge about us keeps a lot of nuts from doing something stupid, they know it will be for naught. But don't worry, nothing will happen to us or to you. I promise."

Ryder knew he couldn't promise such a thing. No one knew what life had in store. But tonight, wasn't a night for apprehension. "Tonight is a night for celebration. Let's think happy thoughts."

"Agreed." Samson rose. "May I have this dance?"

She smiled, took his hand and let him help her to her feet. "Yes, please," she answered, but glanced at Gideon for approval.

"Go, enjoy yourself. Just save the next dance for me."

His contented smile convinced Ryder that all was well. As she moved to the dance floor with Samson, she considered the dynamics of her unique relationship. Well...it was unique for her, not unique for them. They had done this before, two men attending one woman. A hint of jealousy flashed through her mind. She quelled it. Those other women were gone and she was the one with them now.

"Come close." Samson pulled her into the circle of his arms as they began to slow dance to the romantic music. Ryder laid her head on his shoulder and sighed with contentment. "No matter what I might worry about, when you touch me, everything falls into place."

Samson nuzzled her temple with his lips, feathering a soft kiss against her hair. "What are you worrying about? Anything I can do?"

"No." She rubbed her thumb against the material of his sleeve. "I was just noting the uniqueness of our situation, yet reminding myself that I'm not the first."

"No," Samson whispered in her ear. "You aren't the first, but if I have my heart's desire, you'll be the last." He squeezed her gently. "Have no fear, you are an exception. We have never brought a woman into our home before."

"But...I saw the bed," she blurted the words, then blushed.

Samson frowned, then smiled. "Oh, in the suite

where I put the clothing from Nieman's." When she nodded, he continued to speak. "And the bed you saw, we had it special made in anticipation of finding the one woman we could build a future with. And that woman is you. When we share it with you, it will be the first time we've used it."

"Oh." She blushed prettily. "I see. And thank you for the clothing. This dress is magnificent."

"Only because you're wearing it." He caressed her cheek, looking into her eyes. "We want you to keep any and all of those things, consider them your homecoming gift."

"That's too much, Samson," Ryder protested. "I do have my own clothes." A shiver of apprehension wafted over her body. She needed to pay a visit to Highlands to collect some of those things – and make peace with her family. Her brothers were not going to approve of her moving into Falconhead – that went without saying.

"Allow us to do things for you, Ryder. It makes us happy."

His simple explanation stole any further protest. "Okay," she acquiesced, relaxing in his arms. They swayed to the music, moving around the dance floor, oblivious to others who might be watching them. Ryder felt like they were in their own little world. "I want you to be happy."

"Oh, we will be." Samson rubbed his hand over the smooth skin of her back. "We do have some work to attend to, but we're going to make sure we have plenty of time for you. I have a few ideas of trips we can take and tonight..." He stole a chaste kiss. "Tonight, we want to share a bed with you."

Ripples of awareness caused Ryder to quiver against him. "I remember how good it was, that first night at the Driskill. I can't wait."

"Good." Samson enfolded her close.

When the music ended, Gideon stood near. "May I cut in?"

"Of course."

Samson relinquished her to his brother, who drew Ryder into his arms. She felt like she was floating in a sea of fantasy. "No woman has ever been luckier than I," she whispered against his chest. "I'm so glad you're here." She clutched his shoulder, digging her fingers into the material and the muscle below.

Gideon's arms tightened around her. "Me too. I know this is new for you, I can just imagine how confused your heart must be."

He caressed the exposed skin at the small of her back, the same place Samson's fingers had lingered only moments before. "My heart isn't confused; my heart knows exactly what it wants."

"And what is that, love?" he asked, needing to hear the truth once more from her lips.

"I want you. I want both of you, Gideon. Samson and you." Her voice dropped to a bare whisper. "But I also want my family to accept us, I want my daddy to be okay with this." She looked up into his face. "I can't stand the thought of hurting my daddy."

Gideon kissed her cheek. "I'll do whatever it takes to protect you."

She lifted a hand to his cheek, just touching him gave her comfort. "Just don't leave me again. Promise?"

"I won't." Gideon let out a long breath. "There are ways. We can make this work. No one will know."

A close flash in their faces caused Ryder to jerk in Gideon's arms. He immediately put her behind him.

A man dressed as a waiter stood near, a cell phone in his hand. "Yea, we can make this work. Everyone will know."

Ryder gasped, she recognized his face. This was the same reporter who'd talked to them on the beach in Florida.

"So, you're Ryder, Ryder-I, makes sense now," the reporter sneered.

"Step back!" Gideon ordered.

The reporter took another shot, holding up his phone. "It's true, isn't it? The Duke brothers have a kink. Sharing a woman."

"Stop!" Gideon lunged for him, knocking the phone to the floor, and hitting the guy in the face with his fist.

"Gideon, no!"

"Come on, Sydney, let's get outta here," a female voice sounded near. "We've got what we came for."

In the next heartbeat, everything turned to chaos. Gabriel Kahn and his men descended on them, providing a buffer between Ryder and the reporter. "Gideon!" she cried.

"Come with me," Samson's voice sounded in her ear. He took her by the arm, leading her from the dining room and out the back way.

"Where's Gideon?"

"Gabriel is with him. He'll be along shortly. Let's get you to the car." Another man in a suit, one of Gabriel's crew, went ahead of Samson and Ryder, clearing the way.

Ryder's heart was hammering in her chest. "What will happen? Will he press charges on Gideon?"

"I don't know," Samson admitted, taking her hand as they made their way outside to the limo. "Don't worry, we have a team of lawyers. They'll take care of everything."

Once Ryder was settled into the seat, Samson climbed in beside of her. He took her hand in his, but he was holding his cell with the other, trying to reach Gideon.

"Hey, everything okay?"

Ryder waited, impatient and shaken. "How is he?" she asked as soon as he disconnected the call.

"He's fine. We'll pick him up in the front. The guy isn't going to press charges."

Ryder thought this sounded like good news. "Why don't you look happy about it?"

Samson shook his head. "Oh, I am. I'm just surprised, that's all. The reporter gave up too easy. Gabriel said there was nothing on his phone."

"He wasn't alone, Samson. There was a woman with him." She didn't know exactly what that could mean, but she had an uneasy feeling about it.

"Hell," Samson muttered. "So, we don't really know what's out there."

As the limo pulled to the front to pick up Gideon, Ryder tried to think. "What's the worst that could happen? We didn't do anything wrong. We were just dining and dancing."

Samson smiled at her. "You're right. Let's not worry. This night is too special to spoil it by worrying."

The door opened and Gideon entered. "Are you okay?" Ryder asked.

"Of course." He soothed her with a kiss. "Gabriel and our legal team will handle everything."

Ryder said there was a woman with him. Whatever the reporter got is still out there.

Gideon met Samson's gaze. *Yes. I don't know how bad it is, maybe nothing to worry about.*

I just don't want Ryder hurt.

Neither do I.

"You two look upset," Ryder observed, looking from one to the other of them. "Are you sure everything is okay?"

Samson decided to be honest. "It's as okay as we can

make it at this moment."

Ryder relaxed. "No one can ask for anything more." As she nestled between them, she clasped onto their hands, holding tight. "Let's go home."

"Home, Gervis," Samson announced. "We have important business to attend to."

At Ryder's inquisitive, slightly perplexed expression, Gideon chuckled. "Don't worry, Princess. You're our business, our most important business. We're about to attend – to you."

CHAPTER TEN

Ryder stepped out of the spa-like shower, wrapping herself in a thick, luxurious towel. Even though she was surrounded by opulence, nothing impressed her more than the thought of the men who awaited her in the adjoining room. They'd given her time to prepare – more like time to settle her nerves. Samson and Gideon had to know how momentous this was for her. As she spread scented lotion on her body, Ryder gave herself a pep-talk. "This is what you've been dreaming of, girl. You are on the verge of falling head over heels for not one, but two perfect men. All you have to do is walk in that room and give yourself over to your greatest fantasy. Nothing is going to happen that you don't want." She giggled a little at her own logic. "And I want it all."

Taking a steadying breath, Ryder slipped on a gorgeous white lacy gown. The cutouts and lace were specifically designed to bring a man to his knees. When she'd unpacked the trunks of items the men had given her from Neiman's, this and other pieces of exquisite lingerie had been included. After smoothing the silky material down over her hips, Ryder took one last glance into the mirror – big eyes, rosy cheeks, lips plump and pink from being tortured by her own teeth, and a body that was more than excited - if the state of her nipples was any indication. "Oh well, this is who you are." Taking a deep breath to steady herself, Ryder left the bathroom to go meet her two men in the decadent suite with the bed big enough for three.

"Hello, princess, how beautiful you look." Samson's deep voice both soothed and seduced her, calling to mind the pleasure she knew he could give her. He looked so good, waiting by the bed, for a moment she couldn't breathe. Everything about him was so familiar, yet so impressive. She let her eyes rove over his broad shoulders, rigid pecs, and washboard abs. A curl of excitement wound its way through her body, as she noticed the boxer briefs that did little to conceal his huge cock.

"Thank you." Blushing, she looked away – then realized they were alone. "Where's Gideon?"

Hearing the panic in her voice, Samson pointed to the door. "Look."

Ryder did as she was told, letting out a sigh of relief when she saw Gideon coming through the door carrying a tray filled with champagne and three glasses. "Did you miss me?" he asked.

"Yes," she admitted. "I thought you'd changed your mind."

Gideon set the tray on a table near the bed. "Not a chance in this lifetime, sweetheart." Coming to her, he took both of her hands in his. "You are, without a doubt, the most beautiful woman on the face of the earth. Don't you think so, brother?"

"I do," Samson agreed wholeheartedly.

Gideon released her hands to shrug out of his clothing, while Ryder ate him up with her eyes. He didn't stop at his shorts, but shed them unabashedly for her. Her eyes widened. Even though she'd seen him before, the sight still made her breath hitch in her throat. He was big, the head of his manhood wide even when not fully hard. His balls hung heavy and she licked her lips in anticipation of touching him.

Seeing where her eyes were focused, Gideon gave her a wink. "You can touch me anytime you want to, what you see belongs to you."

"That's right." Samson came behind her, lifting her

hair and kissing her neck. "You can touch us and we can touch you. Why don't you satisfy your curiosity with Gideon?"

Hearing Samson give his approval; Ryder sank to her knees in front of Gideon, aware that Samson had done the same thing behind her. She didn't know what to expect, but she knew what she wanted. Ryder let her fingers graze Gideon's thighs, her eyes on his cock. Because of her perusal, he was now thick, long, and ready. She shivered at the thought of what she was about to do, savoring the moment. Her nipples were aching and her sex was weeping with excitement.

"Go ahead, baby. I've got you." Samson body blanketed hers from behind, easing her up to sit on his thighs. "This way I can play and please you while you take care of Gideon."

Ryder was so aroused and happy that she was trembling. "Okay, I'll do my best." Taking Gideon's cock in one hand, she lowered her head, licking her way up his length, loving how he reacted – with a groan and the shaft becoming even firmer and thicker in her grasp.

"Your best will kill me, I'm afraid," Gideon whispered, tangling his fingers in her hair.

As she laved the length of him, sucking and nipping her way up to the tip, Gideon widened his stance and began pushing deeper into her mouth. With a whimper, she enveloped him completely, loving that he bellowed in agonized pleasure and bucked his hips in helpless response.

"That's it, love, take him deeper," Samson praised her, kissing her neck and working the gown she wore up over her hips. "This way I can run my hands all over your body." He could sense Gideon's pleasure, sense the velvety touch of her tongue, the pull of those sweet lips. *Amazing. She's incredible.*

God, yes. I can't think. Touch her, Samson. "Deeper, baby. Take me deeper," Gideon ground out the words, his eyes closing in abject ecstasy.

Ryder stretched her lips to accommodate him, achingly aware that Samson's mouth and hands were busy on her body. As she tended to Gideon, Samson was playing with her breasts, massaging the nipples, plumping and kneading the quivering globes. He was also kissing her neck and shoulders, whispering sweet erotic things in her ear.

"You're so perfect. I love your breasts. You are the sexiest woman alive. I can't wait to bury my cock deep into your softness. You're driving us both wild, Princess."

Needing to please them both, she pressed back against Samson. Beneath her bare bottom, she could feel him – equally bare. He'd lost his shorts and she could feel his big cock beneath her. Parting her thighs, she made room for him, hungry for the feel of him against her feminine core.

"Look up, I need your eyes," Gideon instructed. With a hum of agreement, she did as he asked, hollowing her cheeks as she sucked harder, meeting his hungry, intense stare. He tasted so good, she hoped she was pleasing him. The only point of reference she had for this were the books she read and the practice sessions she and Pepper had held with a cucumber. The thought made her smile around Gideon's cock.

"What are you smiling about?" Gideon asked, not expecting an answer.

"Maybe it's me," Samson said, his hands still on her breasts, his cock sandwiched between the lips of her labia. "If I move this way, the head of my cock nudges her clit." He bucked his hips and Ryder moaned. "See? Our baby is so sensitive and responsive."

Ryder shivered, her hands moving around Gideon to clutch his ass, her fingernails digging in. His reaction was to grab her hair, twist it around his fist, then pump into her mouth with a hard thrust. She did her best to give him what he needed without gagging. Like she'd read in the books, Ryder tilted her throat and breathed through her nose, still licking and lapping at the underside of his shaft. Each time he pulled out, she swirled her tongue around the tip and tongued the spot she'd always heard was sensitive underneath.

God, she's killing me, Samson.

I can't wait. I've got to be inside of her.

Is she wet?

Ryder was super aware of them both. As she cradled Gideon's cock on her tongue, she took him even deeper until he was touching the back of her throat and her lips were near the base. Then she worked her way up and back – up and back. Until…she felt Samson lift her and touch her between the legs. Letting go of Gideon, she exclaimed. "Oh, God!"

Yes. Wet, creamy, and hot. She's on fire for us. "Sit on the bed, beautiful. Gideon, help her."

Gideon, knowing what Samson intended, helped Ryder get into place between his thighs, so she could hold onto him while his brother took her from the back.

Ryder closed her eyes as she felt Samson's hand delving between her thighs. "Relax, I'm just going to play a while."

"I hope I can do this," she whispered, amazed at the wonder of being the center of this sensual experience.

"Yes, you can," Gideon assured her. "There is no test, no standard. We just want you – no holding back. No reservations."

Ryder nodded. This was where she belonged, between the two of her men - them pleasing her, her pleasing them. She took Gideon back between her lips, bobbing her head slowly, taking as much of him as she could in her mouth, then working her lips toward the crest once more. Concentrating hard, she tried to ignore the ache that was building inside of her. Samson was ever-present – his hands were everywhere. As he kissed her shoulders and neck, his palms were rubbing her thighs, caressing her breasts, then dipping between her legs to finger her pussy. She began to tremble – needing him to do something to alleviate the building pressure, the hunger to be filled – to be fucked.

"Do you think she's ready?" Samson asked Gideon.

"I do." Gideon looked down at Ryder, running his fingers through her hair, lifting it off her neck. He reached down with one hand and tweaked her nipple, pulling on it while she pulled on his dick. The more eager she became, the more eagerly she sucked him. He groaned, this was so good, he might lose consciousness.

Ryder kept going, sucking Gideon, pushing back against Samson's hand. Her nipples were crested hard, willing victims to their seeking fingers.

Take her, I can't last much longer. Her mouth is just too sweet.

Samson heard Gideon. *None too soon. I need to be inside of her.*

Ryder felt the head of Samson's cock as it came to her opening. She held on to Gideon and suckled hard on his cock, as if pleasing one would equate to the other pleasing her. When she felt Samson begin to work his way in with short sharp jabs – each one giving him another inch to glide into, she arched her back and tossed her head, rejoicing at the raw pleasure of the moment.

As Gideon filled her mouth, Samson thrust his cock home. The sheer joy of being taken by both men, giving pleasure to both, rushed through her, lighting up her body like nothing she'd ever felt before. In utter happiness, she lavished all her energy on Gideon's cock, worshiping him, licking the head, sucking him deep.

Gideon couldn't take any more. "Fuck, baby." He cradled her head and gave over to the ecstasy. "I'm coming," he bellowed, attempting to pull out, but she held him fast. As he felt the cum jet from his cock, he was aware she accepted him, swallowing every drop, then turned him inside out when she licked him clean.

Samson was aware of it all. He felt Gideon's pleasure, he felt his wonder, he saw the woman of their heart give him an indescribable gift of acceptance.

Reward her, brother, Samson said. *Show her how wonderful she is.*

Gideon understood. Slipping from Ryder's mouth, he ignored her little groan and went to his knees at her side. "Face me, baby. Hold on to me."

Ryder allowed them to arrange her once more, this time Gideon's mouth met hers while Samson gave her what she needed, plunging into her from the rear – harder, rougher – like he couldn't hold back – giving her one powerful, shuttling pump after another.

God, she's so tight, Samson groaned.

Ryder mewled into Gideon's kiss, holding onto him as he reached between her thighs from the front – swirling over her clit, pinching the tender little bud. "Gideon! Samson!" she cried their names as the stars began to fall.

Samson didn't let up – he pounded into her until he felt himself swell – felt his orgasm grip him tighter and tighter until the cataclysm hurtled him out into space.

Ryder held onto Gideon, accepting his kiss, his caresses – even as her womb pulsed with the gift of Samson's seed. The rush to ecstasy was so fierce that the explosion sapped her strength and the ability to hold upright.

No matter, she didn't have to hold herself up – there were two strong men to do it for her. Giving herself over to them, Ryder felt surrounded, cherished, taking comfort as their hearts beat as one.

"Take her to the bed, I'll get something to clean us up," Gideon instructed.

"Come here, Princess." Samson swept her up in his arms and placed her in the middle of the mattress. "We didn't even make it to the bed."

"The night's still young," Ryder muttered, too tired to hold her eyes open.

Samson chuckled, taking the warm, wet cloth from Gideon's hand.

"What did she say?" he asked.

"She's wanting a repeat performance." Samson laughed, wiping himself off as Gideon placed the warm rag between Ryder's thighs.

"Well, we'll just have to see what we can do to make our woman happy," Gideon mused. *Yes, she's our woman, Samson. We've got to do everything in our power to take care of her. To make her glad she chose to be with us.*

"I am happy," Ryder murmured, sleepily. "Get in the bed with me, please."

Tossing their cloths, Samson and Gideon climbed in. One on one side and one on the other. Once they were in place, Ryder snuggled between them, her head resting on Gideon's shoulder and Samson spooning her from the back. "Now, this feels right."

And it did – it felt right for all three of them.

* * *

As requested, Samson and Gideon woke Ryder up in the early morning hours and loved on her again. This time, she took Samson in her mouth as Gideon feasted between her legs.

Even later they awoke her anew, unable to keep their hands off her. Gideon spooned her, his cock buried to the hilt while Samson made love to her breasts.

By the time they were finished with the second round, Ryder was famished. Samson placed a call to the kitchen to have Thurgood bring up a cart of food.

When Samson began to speak, it wasn't long before Gideon and Ryder picked up on the fact that something was wrong.

"How bad?" Samson rose, reaching for his clothes.

"What is it?" Ryder jumped up, frantic. "I should've kept my phone with me. It's not Daddy, is it?"

Once Samson finished the call, he assured her. "No, baby, it's not your daddy."

Feeling relief, she ran to the bathroom to dress. "Okay. I'll be right back, then I'll help you do whatever needs to be done."

The men found their clothes, their conversation not quite so evident.

What's going on? Gideon asked. *I can feel your turmoil.*

We're all over the news. She's all over the news. Whatever that reporter had is now out there for everyone to see. You know how these damn cable networks are, the more salacious and damning they can make anything, the higher their ratings.

There's no way we can hide it from her, Samson.

No, as much as I wish there was, there isn't anything we can do. Even if we sued, it won't stop her from seeing it – or her family from seeing it.

I guess this is baptism by fire. Gideon worried, finding the remote so he could turn on the television that was hidden behind the doors of the entertainment center.

By the time Ryder rejoined them, she could hear the

words of the reporter before she even came through the door.

"So, what we've heard about the billionaire Duke brothers, is true?" asked a woman reporter who was grinning from ear to ear.

An equally thrilled man was leering at the camera. "Yes, we won't go into details, we'll leave that for the Entertainment shows like Hollywood Access, but suffice it to say that where there's smoke, there's fire. And it looks like Miss Ryder McCoy of Highlands Ranch, a huge property just north of Austin, is fanning the flames for these two. Our sister program, same channel, same network has exclusive photos of her dancing with both brothers, kissing them – and the conversations they're having clearly paints the picture that they are a definite…sexual item."

"I wonder if we'll hear wedding bells for the lucky…ménage a trois?" the woman asked, about the time Ryder grabbed for the door facing.

"I'm going to be sick," she muttered, turning pale as a ghost. "I can't believe this."

Gideon made a grab for her, pulling her down on his lap where he sat on the couch. "Don't worry. We'll do whatever it takes to get this mess off the air."

"I'll call our lawyer right now." Samson rose and walked across the room, so he wouldn't disturb them with his conversation.

"It's too late. Everyone will have seen this." She buried her head in Gideon's shoulder and began to cry. "My daddy will know everything."

"Come on, let's go downstairs to get you some coffee and something to eat." He was watching her face, seeing the hurt – the disbelief – the fear that colored her features.

"I don't know if I can eat," Ryder whispered. Her stomach was clenching into a tight knot.

Gideon understood she was hurting, but he also understood what was at stake – his life. "Ryder," he clasped her hand, pulling her against him, "please don't give up on us. Don't give up on me. I need you. Don't leave me."

Ryder let him hold her. "I don't want to leave you. I just don't want Daddy to be hurt."

Samson came to them. "Let's go down, we'll see what can be done."

They made their way downstairs where Thurgood waited with coffee and breakfast for them. Ryder sat down at the beautiful table, filled with expensive crystal, fine china, and food fit for a king. She knew she needed to eat, yet she seemed unable to take a bite.

"Please, Princess. For us?" Samson joined her with a flaky croissant in hand. "I'll butter it and decorate it with strawberry jam?"

She gave him a sad smile, accepting the pastry. "I'll try." Truly, Ryder didn't know what to do. As she took a small bite, she weighed her options. Should she call home? Should she go to the ranch? Or should she run to the airport and buy a ticket to Timbuctoo? A tear rolled down her cheek. What she wanted to do was stay here – right here with these two men who were looking at her with their hearts in their eyes. "I'm scared," she admitted.

There was no time to mull over the questions in her head, the answer appeared at the front door of Falconhead.

Bang! Bang!

Samson's phone rang. "It's the front gate."

Thurgood hurried to the door.

Ryder sat up straighter, certain that Heath and her brothers were about to come barreling through the door with guns blazing. She just had no idea what they'd propose. A shotgun wedding? Somehow, she doubted it.

But it wasn't her brothers. It was Pepper. And the first words out of her mouth aged Ryder a good five years.

"Daddy wants to see you. He saw the news report."

* * *

Seeing how upset the two girls were, there was no way Samson or Gideon would let them drive alone.

"We'll take you and we'll wait outside. We won't disturb you. Your father won't even know we're near," Samson had promised.

"Yea, unless there's a reporter lurking around," Ryder murmured softly, her voice sad.

Gideon cursed, grabbing the phone. "Go ahead of us to…" he waited until Ryder gave him the address. "401 Champion Drive and make triple damn sure no reporters are anywhere near."

After that, Ryder gave over, letting the brothers take care of her and Pepper. As the limousine headed south, Samson took another call. This one seemed more positive. Once he was through, he made the announcement. "Looks like the March launch is a go. The Ryder-III is ready and waiting, the engineers have given us the green light, all we're lacking is final specs on the methane delivery from your brother."

"When will this happen, the Mars launch?" Pepper asked.

"In a little less than a month. We're already putting the pieces into place, arranging for the launch, getting the thrusters shipped to the site, and making sure the remote ship will be in position. Once this process starts, it's like dominoes – stopping it would be expensive as hell."

Pepper nodded, seemingly interested in the conversation. "I can remember reading in history about the space trips and the moon walk, all of it seemed to take months and months to get ready. But every time a mission was sent off into space, the whole country sat on the edge of its seat."

Ryder didn't contribute anything to the conversation; all she could worry about was speaking to her father. "What did Heath say?"

"About the fuel?" Pepper asked, innocently.

Ryder groaned. "No. About the crap on television."

Pepper grimaced. "Oh. Well, he yelled, threw a fit, and said he was right all along. Typical Heath."

"Oh, Lord." Ryder ducked her head. "This is awful, truly awful." When no one responded to her exclamation, she glanced up at her two men who sat across from the sisters. The absolute devastation on their faces caused her heart to sink. "No, wait." She reached across to take their hands. "You've got to understand something. This changes nothing. I'm not going to leave you, not unless this is a battle you don't want to have to face."

"It isn't going to be a battle, Ryder, not with Daddy. He loves you."

Pepper's chiding voice, coupled with the Dukes disappointed faces made Ryder feel even worse. "I didn't mean that, either. I just…didn't want it to happen this way. I don't want to be the cause of anyone's pain."

Samson leaned forward, forever optimistic. "Ryder, you belong to us. And we belong to you, even if you decide to walk away."

Ryder sought Gideon's eyes. He didn't look optimistic, he looked haunted. "I understand, but I don't intend to go anywhere."

"Sirs, we're here." Gervis announced through the speaker.

When they pulled up the townhouse, Pepper offered to go in with her.

"No, let me go alone." She didn't want anyone else to be witness to the conversation she had with her father.

Before she exited the limo, she kissed both brothers. "I'll be back. Don't leave without me."

"Never," was Gideon's only response.

As she walked up the ramp, built next to the stairs, every step seemed harder to make. Ryder didn't know what to expect. At least he was here and not in the hospital. Ringing the doorbell, she waited to be admitted.

Olivia opened the door. "Ryder, how are you?"

She studied Olivia's face for some clue. "Not so good. How are things here?"

"Fine. Come in." Her father's companion was absolutely loyal to him, so she could read nothing beyond a placid welcome.

She followed Olivia through the house and back to her father's sitting room. Ryder hesitated to make the final corner, she felt the same way she had as a small child the day that she'd left the gate open and her father's prize mare had gotten loose and was missing. She hated disappointing her father. "Daddy?"

"Ryder, come join me."

...Inside the limo, Pepper folded her arms and stared at Ryder's men. "Well, this is a fine kettle of fish, isn't it?"

Gideon looked down and Samson blushed a bit.

Their reactions caused Pepper to laugh. "Don't look so guilty, I'm on your side."

"I'm not sure we have a side," Gideon spoke slowly. "This is who we are, it's who we've always been. We love Ryder."

"Have you told her that?" Pepper asked sharply.

"Not yet," Samson admitted. "We've come all around it, but we haven't said the words."

"Why not? Don't you think that your commitment would've made this easier for her? She's put herself on the line, put her relationship with her family on the line –

not even knowing for sure whether you're in this for the long haul!"

Samson and Gideon looked at one another. "We thought we were making it easier. We've known Ryder was the one for us since the day of your family's cook-off," Gideon admitted.

"Hell, I knew the day I brought her home the first time, the day the snake almost bit her."

Samson's whispered words touched Pepper. "Take heart, even when she pulled away from you, she never for one moment stopped longing for you." At their softened expressions, she explained further. "If Ryder has a fault, it's wanting everyone around her to be happy. She's always been this way – the peacemaker, the diplomat, the negotiator. If any of the brothers were at odds, she wouldn't let up until she found a solution, made them listen. The reason this is so hard for her, is that she feels responsible for all of our happiness, yours included."

"She is our happiness." Gideon stated flatly. "I can't stand this…" He looked toward the door. "I wonder what they're doing to her in there?"

Pepper laughed. "Relax. If there's anyone who loves Ryder more than you, it's Daddy. He won't hurt her, I promise."

…Back inside, Ryder faced her father. She stood still for about three seconds, then she broke down and ran to him, kneeling at his feet. "Daddy, oh Daddy, I'm so sorry for disappointing you."

"Fiddle-faddle." Christian McCoy patted Ryder's hair. "Stop that crying, get up here and sit by me."

Ryder raised her head and wiped her tears, a realization dawning. "You aren't in the wheelchair!" Her father was sitting in a regular recliner. This was the first time she'd seen him out of a hospital bed or a wheelchair since right after her mother was killed.

"No, I'm not. I'm improving every day. Thanks to good doctors and my Olivia."

Ryder sat back on her heels. "I'm so glad."

"Now, what's all of this I saw on the news. You're dating someone?"

"Yes..." she said slowly. "As I'm sure you're aware," she held up her two fingers, "I'm dating two someone's."

To Ryder's shock, Christian laughed. "Some things never change."

"What do you mean?" Ryder asked.

"Get up off the floor." He pointed to a chair. "Pull that over here and sit by me."

Ryder did as she was told. "Why aren't you mad, Daddy? I just told you I'm dating two men, at the same time. I'm not speaking of just having more than one boyfriend, these men and I are..." She stopped at a loss for words.

"A committed threesome." Christian explained with a straight face.

"Polyamorous." Olivia supplied.

"That's it!" Christian smiled. "I can't ever remember that word."

Ryder looked flummoxed. "I'm not sure why you would need to know that word."

He spread his hands. "Obviously, I should. My daughter is involved in such a relationship. Right? An intimate relationship with more than one partner, with the knowledge and consent of all."

"Oh, my goodness." Ryder covered her eyes. "What did you mean that nothing changes. I haven't done this before. Although, they're good men, Daddy. They're the best." She kissed his cheek. "Almost as good as you."

"Ryder, I don't know if you remember, but one of anything was never good enough for you. You had to have two kittens, two puppies, two cookies, two Easter dresses, two candy bars, two chicken legs…"

Ryder laughed, burying her head in his shoulder. "Stop, Daddy. You make me sound like a greedy grabber."

"You are a greedy grabber." His voice went solemn. "Your mother always said it was because your heart was so big."

"And apparently, my stomach."

"Regardless, Carolyn always said you had love enough for two." He kissed her on the forehead. "And your mother was always right."

Ryder was so shocked, she just had to ask. "Are you sure you're okay with this? You do understand what I'm doing? I'm living with two men…having…"

"Stop!" Christian held up his hand. "Please don't draw me a picture. I may be old, but I'm not dead. And I'm not a prude." He held up his hand and motioned Olivia to come to him. "What do you think Olivia and I have been doing all this time, playing tiddlywinks?"

Ryder's eyes widened. "I'm not sure I want to know what you and Olivia have been doing."

"But you want me to be happy, don't you?" He took Olivia's hand in his and kissed it.

"Yes," Ryder answered unequivocally.

"And I want you to be happy also." He rubbed Ryder's back. "Now, when can I meet these two men of yours?"

"Well…they're outside. How about now?" she asked tentatively.

"Good. Olivia, darling, would you ask our other guests to join us?"

"Certainly."

Once Olivia was gone, Ryder looked at her father. "You're being wonderful, but I know this had to have been a shock. I'm sorry, I should have told you first. After what happened to you a little while ago, when you had to go to the hospital, I didn't know how. I was afraid it would set you back."

"And you wanted to be my good girl, didn't you, sweetheart?"

"Yes." She gazed at her father lovingly. "I always want to be your good girl."

"Well, don't worry about me, or your family. What I want you to do is get out of town until this crap dies down. In a few days, something else will catch people's eye. Just have those Duke boys take you on a nice trip. Then, come back and we'll have Thanksgiving together, the whole family."

Thanksgiving. Ryder hid a grin. The Indians and the Pilgrims managed to sit down together for a meal, but she didn't know if a holiday meal between the Dukes and the McCoys would be nearly as peaceful.

"What about Heath?" Ryder couldn't help but ask, as she heard the front door open and shut.

"You let me worry about Heath. I'm still the patriarch of this clan." He motioned at the door for Samson and Gideon to enter. "Now, you girls go on and let the men talk."

Ryder started to just give her men a small smile, but after speaking to her father, she didn't hold back. She hugged and kissed each one. "Everything's okay," she whispered to them, then she left to join her sister and Olivia in the kitchen.

Left behind, Samson and Gideon sat down in front of Christian McCoy.

"I hear you're dating my daughter."

The gruff voice came as no surprise to either man.

"Yes, sir. We love your daughter very much," Gideon said.

"Huh." Christian looked at Samson. "I remember you telling me at the hospital that your intentions were honorable."

"Yes, sir." Samson nodded. "They still are. My brother and I are totally committed to Ryder."

"Have you asked her to marry you?"

Samson sent a direct message to Gideon. *Nothing like being put on the spot.*

I say we go for it, ask for his permission to propose. Are you ready for this?

I am. How about you?

Completely.

"Not yet, we were waiting for the right time," Samson said, by way of explanation.

"May we have your blessing, Sir?" Gideon wanted to waste no time.

"I would say the time is right, and yes, you do have my blessing. I do have a favor to ask of you."

"What's that?" Gideon asked at the same time as Samson said, "Just name it."

"I think you ought to take my girl out of town, get her away from anyone who would know her. Not for long, just a few days. I happen to know something's about to go down that will take everyone's mind off romance."

Samson and Gideon caught one another's eyes. "What do you mean?"

"I can't say, just know for certain that no one in this part of the world will be thinking about something so important as two billionaire space explorers dating one woman."

"Good Lord," Gideon mused. "What's going down? Is Texas about to secede from the union?"

"Close." Christian laughed. "Not quite as dire, but close."

"Thank you, sir." The Dukes stood to shake

Christian's hand. "You won't ever have to worry. We'd die for your daughter."

"I expect nothing less."

When they left to find Ryder, she was waiting at the far end of the hall, watching. Running to meet them, she threw herself against them. "Is everything okay?"

"Perfect. Your father understands and has given us his blessing," Samson blurted out.

Hey, don't blow the proposal. Gideon chided him in his mind.

Ryder searched their faces. "His blessing?"

"Yes, he is happy you're happy." Gideon tried to smooth things over, at least until they could buy a ring.

Ryder let out a long, relieved sigh. "Good. Can we go home now?"

"You mean Falconhead?" Samson asked, needing to make sure.

"Yes…unless you've changed your mind. We'll have to give Pepper a ride, of course."

"Oh, we haven't changed our minds at all," Gideon assured her. "But when we get home to Falconhead, we'll only be staying long enough for you to pack a bag."

"Oh, really? Daddy said we should take a trip until the gossip dies down. Where are we going?" Ryder couldn't help but be excited. This was all turning out so much better than she'd feared.

"You took us to paradise last night," Samson whispered for her ears only. "How about we take you to paradise today?"

"Hawaii!" she squealed. "Really? I get to meet the dads?"

Loving how she thought, Gideon pulled her close. "Yes, you get to meet the dads. And they're going to love you. No doubt about it."

CHAPTER ELEVEN

"Paradise, Hawaiian style." Ryder sighed, staring out the window as the Duke's private plane began its descent toward the big island. "Hawaii looks like a string of emerald beads in a lapis sea."

Samson and Gideon watched her indulgently. They'd spent most of the trip working on the Mars launch, making sure all the paperwork was up to par. The only break they'd taken was to fulfill a wish on Ryder's sex list. A threesome in the mile-high club.

"Is there anything special you want to do while we're here?" Samson asked. He and Gideon had already arranged several surprises for her.

She shook her head, never taking her eyes from the scene below. "No, I just want to experience your Hawaii. I want to see the islands through your eyes."

Samson sent a mental message to Gideon. *Is she perfect or what?*

She is perfect. Did you call about the ring?

I did. We pick it up tomorrow.

"What are you two doing?" Ryder asked, causing the brothers to jerk their heads toward her. She wagged one small finger at them. "I know. You're doing that brain/psychic thing, where you're talking to one another. Aren't you?"

"How can you tell?" Gideon asked, surprised.

Ryder smiled. "Well, it's simple, really." She made them wait a couple of seconds before she explained. "Samson gets this cute little wrinkle in his forehead, right over his nose. I guess he's concentrating too hard."

Samson looked disturbed. "Really?"

"What do I do?" Gideon asked, intrigued.

"You rub the cleft in your chin. Like this." She showed him.

"Damn." *We're never going to be able to hide anything from her.*

Samson laughed as Ryder pointed at Gideon. "You're doing it again!"

"Don't worry, Princess. We were just planning a surprise for you," Gideon assured her.

"Really, I want to see your home. Meet your fathers. Go for a long horseback ride on the beach. Maybe see the volcano…and surf. I want to surf."

Samson looked disturbed. "All of those things are a yes, but the surfing. Surfing can be dangerous." He'd never gotten over Gideon almost drowning and he never would.

"Oh, please, just dog paddling in the surf?" She looked so cute and hopeful, that Gideon relented. Almost.

"Maybe."

"Maybe?" Ryder asked, her eyes wide.

"We're going to keep you busy making love with us," Samson murmured with confidence.

"Maybe," Ryder said, causing both men to roar with laughter.

"I think we can tempt you into changing your mind." They were both tantalized by Ryder's sensual appetite, she was always as eager for them as they were for her.

Ryder didn't argue with her men, they were right. "Oh, we're about to land!" She smiled, staring out the window. "I think I see your parents. They're waiting for us!"

"Mom and the Dads are here?" Gideon was surprised. "They never come meet us."

We've never brought a girl home before.

"True," Gideon said out loud. "Are you sure it's them?" He wasn't sitting where he could see out the window.

"Well, I recognize your mother." Ryder explained. "And the men look just like the two of you."

The guys looked at one another and shrugged. "Can't argue with that. I do look just like Solomon and Gideon is the image of Kona. You can't see Mother in either one of us."

"I can," Ryder said with complete confidence. At their inquiring looks, she explained. "You both love like she does, with her whole heart."

…A few minutes later, Ryder was met by three people who all wanted to hug her at the same time.

"Aloha, beautiful." Solomon placed a lei around Ryder's neck.

"Thank you." She gave him a kiss. "I'm so pleased to meet you."

"Aloha, nani." Kona placed another lei around her neck.

"Aloha, sir. I remember nani means beautiful, thank you." She gave the big Hawaiian a kiss on the cheek.

Lastly, she gave Leilani the longest hug. "I'm not wearing white, are you still glad to see me?"

"I'll always be glad to see you. The wedding will come."

Ryder didn't argue, she didn't know what to say. She, Samson, and Gideon had done a lot of planning and a lot of dreaming, but no one had mentioned marriage. Ryder was afraid to wonder why.

"Let's go home. We brought the SUV. We can all ride together. I'll drive." Kona led the way.

"Why are you driving, Dad?" Gideon asked. "You hit all the potholes."

Kona chuckled. "Reminds me of an amusement park ride."

They all climbed in and held on as Kona drove them

toward home.

Solomon made a circular motion with his hand, pointing out all the windows. "All this, as far as the eye can see is Lani."

The pride in Solomon Duke's voice was unmistakable. "I can't wait to see everything. I'm more thrilled to be here than you'll ever know," Ryder said excitedly.

Leilani and her sons exchanged a glance, leaving Ryder questioning whether they had some sort of psychic connection with their mother. She quit worrying about it quickly, however. The tropical paradise out her window drew her whole attention. Driving from the private airport, they crossed over fields of green grass and by ponds of bright blue. Cattle and horses dotted the pastures, a familiar serene scene. Lani would have reminded her of home, except for two very important things. The volcano to her left and the ocean to her right. Palm trees completed the picture. Ryder couldn't quit looking around. She was completely and totally impressed. Entranced. "I love it here; this is the most beautiful place I've ever seen in my life."

"Welcome home, Ryder." Leilani gave her a meaningful glance. "Once you've had a taste of paradise, it's hard to walk away."

Ryder knew this to be true, she went to paradise every night in the arms of her two men.

"The place looks the same," Samson noted. "I have to tell you I'm relieved." He looked at his dad. "Mother said you and Kona made some changes. Want to tell me about it?"

"No talk of business until after dinner." Leilani made the edict and no one refuted it.

"Is that your house?" Ryder asked, seeing a home up ahead.

"Yes, isn't it lovely?" Leilani had no qualms stating her appreciation of their home.

"It is. And it looks like nothing I expected." She craned her head to see better.

"What did you think Lani would be like?" Gideon asked, curious to know what Ryder was thinking.

She shrugged. "I don't know, a glorified beach house. A big, luxurious treehouse." Instead, she saw a huge white bungalow with a wrap-around porch. The yard was a lush mass of flowers – hibiscus, orchids, plumeria, and big tall birds of paradise. "You have a beautiful home." She addressed Samson and Gideon. "I know the business reason you say you came to the states, but truly – I don't have a clue how you could even consider leaving this place."

"We left to find you," Samson stated simply, causing Ryder to almost swoon.

"Awww, you three are so mushy. Reminds me of the two-finger poi I had for supper last night," Kona murmured, laughing at them.

"You got mushy with me last night, big man," Leilani teased.

Gideon held up his hands. "TMI! TMI! I remember the real reason why we moved away now."

"What is two-fingered poi?" Ryder asked. "I mean, I know poi is like mashed potatoes."

Everyone in the car appeared to be shocked at what she said. "Bite your tongue, Princess," Gideon chided her playfully. "Poi is our traditional food, sweet as ambrosia. It is not only traditional, it is sacred. We are descended from the god of Poi. Out of respect, anytime it is placed on the table all arguments must cease."

"Wow, then it's sort of like Texas BBQ, we consider it sacred too."

Samson and Solomon laughed at her joke. Kona,

Leilani, and Gideon didn't seem to find it quite as funny.

"How about the two-finger part. Is that something magical?"

"No." This time it was Kona's turn to laugh. "Depending on the thickness, or how much water is added, you might have to use one to three fingers to eat it."

"Oh, I see. Thank you for explaining." Ryder smiled, feeling happy. She also felt peaceful for the first time since seeing that stupid news report on television. Her father had been right, she needed to get away. Lani seemed to be a place where trouble could never touch her.

When they arrived at the house, they were welcomed inside. "Our wing is in the back. Mother and the dads keep it for our use, almost the way we left it."

Ryder turned in a circle, trying to take everything in. The house was light and airy. Sunshine and the breeze from the ocean could enter the home from its many windows, patios and courtyards. Blue and white were the primary colors, but there were accent pieces, like pillows and artwork, in jewel tones of green, orange, and yellow.

"Go rest, explore. Just be back in time for supper," Leilani instructed, giving each of them a kiss. "And be careful, the nightmarchers come tonight."

Ryder was about to ask what the nightmarchers were, when she heard a very feminine squeal, then had to stand aside to keep from being knocked over by a rotund older woman who ran straight through the house and right into Samson and Gideon's arms. They were standing close together, and the move seemed to be one they had done many times.

"Kali! Calm yourself!" Leilani scolded the woman, but her voice was full of affection. "Let the boys breathe."

Ryder couldn't look away. The older lady was crying and her men were obviously glad to see her; they were all smiles. "Kali, there's someone we'd like to introduce you to." Samson wrapped his arm around Kali and turned her to face Ryder. "Ryder, this is Kali Hale, our god-mother. Her husband is the local priest; he knows us all and loves us just the way we are. Kali, this is Ryder McCoy, our lady."

Our lady. The term made her feel warm inside, it felt to be more than a mere girlfriend. She gave the men a special smile, then braced herself as Kali came to hug her with almost as much enthusiasm. "Hello, Kali."

"I'm so glad to meet you, Ryder. I can tell my boys are happy just by looking at them." After squeezing her for a few more moments, Kali pulled away. "The best years of my life was spent taking care of these two." She whispered to Ryder, "they call me their godmother, but I was really just their cook and housekeeper. But nobody, nobody except their parents have loved Samson and Gideon more than me." Leaning nearer, she spoke even softer, "until you. I can see it in your eyes."

"Turn her loose, Kali. We want to show our girl around." Gideon gently extricated Ryder from Kali's embrace and steered her toward the rooms they'd be staying in. Ryder was totally captivated by the home. "Is this an antique?" she asked as they passed a huge hall tree that looked more like a throne. She stopped to run her hand over the gleaming wood.

"Yes, the home is full of antiques, furniture and art dating back a century and more. Mother has this idea to allow the public to tour Lani, but we're against it," Samson explained as he moved ahead of them down the hall, opening a door at the end and waiting for them.

"Why?" Ryder asked. "The idea sounds responsible to me. This place is too beautiful to hide away from the world."

Gideon set their bags down and walked across the

spacious room, throwing open the French doors to allow the sound of the surf to be wafted in on the cool ocean breeze. "Our business dealings have created a few enemies for us. We can provide security for our folks, but we don't want to take responsibility for a visiting public."

"No, I see. You're right." Ryder sometimes forgot how powerful and influential they were. To her, they had ceased being the billionaire Duke brothers and had become – hers.

As soon as they were settled in, Samson announced he would bring around Solomon's Jeep and they would go exploring around the ranch. "You two meet me out front." He gave Ryder a quick kiss. "Wear a bikini underneath your clothes, you're going to need it."

"Okay," Ryder agreed, happily. "Are we going down to the beach?"

"No. Better," Samson promised as he left the two of them alone to get ready.

Ryder tried to hurry, despite Gideon's attempts to get her attention by posing in front of a mirror and flexing his muscles. Every time she made a little headway, she'd have to stop and give him a kiss. "You are way too distracting, Duke."

He seemed pleased by her observation.

A tap on the door interrupted their fun. "Samson's waiting out front. He keeps blowing the horn every few seconds," Kali announced from the other side of their door.

"Okay, we're on our way!" Gideon grabbed her hand. "Why did you make us late?"

Ryder giggled and swatted him with her floppy beach hat she brought to keep the sun out of her eyes. "My fault? You think it was my fault?"

By the time they arrived at the Jeep, both were giggling like school kids. Ryder had never been happier in her life. "What are we going to see first?" she asked as she climbed in the middle of the wide bench seat.

"A very special place," Samson said. "Our own private waterfall."

As they traveled, Ryder was mesmerized. "I've seen photos of Hawaii all of my life, but I never knew it was so diverse. You have everything!" She could look to her right and see pineapples growing in fields and palm trees full of coconuts. To her left, she could view the massive volcanic mountain, belching steam and releasing orange-red streams of lava to flow down the sides.

"This is a beautiful place," Gideon agreed. "And it will always be ours, we can come here anytime we like."

As they drove farther west, they came upon a jungle-like setting. These foothills were set apart from the volcano and were covered in lush vegetation. "Let's park here and walk the rest of the way. Get the bag I packed, Gideon," Samson directed as he maneuvered into a flat spot where they could begin their journey.

Ryder was so excited, she had the hiccups. They loved the cute noise she made. "Sorry, this always happens when I get over-stimulated."

"I don't remember you getting hiccups in bed." Samson frowned, teasing her.

"Good thing, since my mouth's always full."

Her frank response caused both men to laugh. Holding her hands, they entered the jungle and headed toward the sound of falling water.

When they arrived at the waterfall, Ryder was stunned. "We have a waterfall at Highlands, only it's about twelve feet high." She craned her neck to look up. "And this one has to be…"

"Over a hundred feet," Gideon supplied. "Samson and I used to jump from the top and land in the pool below."

"That had to have been dangerous," Ryder fussed. "How could Leilani let you do that?"

Samson tugged at her clothes. "What Leilani didn't know..."

"We could get away with," Gideon finished his brother's thought, shucking his shorts and T-shirt.

"Is that the way it's going to be with me?" she asked as Samson finished undressing her. She'd lost all her inhibitions with these men.

"No." Samson tugged off his own clothes. "We will always be honest with you. Our highest priority is to make you happy and keep you safe."

Ryder heard his declaration, but she'd lost the urge to debate. Stepping close to Samson, she took his long, thick cock in hand and began to stroke it in her fist, loving the way he capitulated to her touch, his face going slack with ecstasy. "This is what will make me happy."

"Come on you two, let's go behind the falls. Remember, Samson? We always fantasized about bringing a woman here."

Ryder reluctantly relinquished her hold on Samson to dive into the sparkling blue water. For a few minutes, they cavorted like children – splashing and swimming – diving beneath the clear surface, only to pop up and cling to one of the surrounding rocks. She played a game of keep-away with them, teasing, evading their clutches, loving the moments when their hands slid over her body.

"She's our little mermaid, Gideon. If we take her up on land, maybe she'll turn into a woman with two beautiful legs we can get between." Samson lunged for her and Ryder flailed back, landing right in Gideon's arms.

"I think you're right, brother. Let's take her behind the waterfall and have our wicked way with her."

Ryder didn't fight them, she wanted this as much as

they did. Holding their hands for support, she followed them out of the water, across some huge boulders, and behind the wide ribbon of water cascading down. "Wow, look at this," Ryder whispered, seeing the natural cave. "I love it here."

Gideon had retrieved the bag he'd thrown on the edge of the pool when they arrived. He pulled out a big blanket and spread it on the floor. "You're going to love what we do to you more."

His tone intrigued Ryder. "I always love what you two do to me. I'm totally addicted to your touch." She joined them on the blanket, sitting between her two Greek gods – one dark, one light. Both precious to her. "Would you let me play a bit?"

Not what we had planned, brother.

Oh, be adventurous, Gideon. Nothing she will do could ever disappoint us.

No, I just want to prepare her.

Following her directions, they lay on the blanket and she sat between them, surveying her options – her choices – all of them mouthwatering. With a seductive smile, she set out to drive them mad. Taking turns between them, she kissed their chests, rubbed their cocks, caressed their shoulders, thighs, and arms. Ryder neglected neither man, nor any part of their bodies, continuing to tease them until they were rock hard and ready to make love to her.

"Ryder, we need you," Samson implored, bringing her down on top of him. Settling her between them – he to her front, Gideon to her back, they let their hands and mouths explore to their heart's delight. Samson suckled at her breasts, toying with the tender tips, making them rosy and swollen from his hungry lips and fingers. Gideon kissed a trail down her back, knowing he had a destination and a mission in mind.

From where she was sitting, astride Samson's thighs,

she had access to his manhood. So, as he attended to her breasts, she was fisting him – up and down, up and down. Soon, Ryder couldn't stand the wait. "I need you," she whispered, rising and sinking down – impaling herself on his cock. "Oh, yes," she whimpered. "This is what I needed."

"Good, baby?" Gideon spoke, so close his hot breath fanned her neck. Not to be left out, he rubbed her shoulders, her arms, and her back. Finally, he allowed himself to sample what he'd been waiting on – he palmed her bottom, cupping the globes, kneading the silky, firm flesh. As their woman rode his brother, Gideon dipped his fingers between her cheeks – letting her know for the first time what he yearned for.

"Oh!" Ryder squeaked, bracing her hands to Samson's chest. Neither one of the men had ever touched her there before.

"Easy, baby, easy." Gideon kissed her nape. "You take care of Samson; I just want to play."

"Okay." She'd read about this, but she'd never seriously contemplated trying it. But with two men, she guessed this would be expected. "I don't know if I'm going to like this," she warned Gideon.

"We're not doing anything today, Princess," he assured her. "I just want to see how you respond."

"Look at me, Ryder," Samson's voice held a hint of domination. "We will never do anything to you that you don't love. Okay?"

Ryder nodded, turning herself over to the people she trusted most in this world, even more than her family. Closing her eyes, she made love to Samson – riding him, undulating – moving up and down – back and forth – milking his cock as she caressed him with the hungry walls of her vagina. And all the while, Gideon's fingers and lips were never still. While she took her pleasure with

Samson's body, his brother never ceased to kiss her, rubbing his lips across her neck and shoulders, his fingers teasing her secret spot, dipping into the tight ring of muscle – pushing in – pulling out, ringing the sensitive place, amazing her with the knowledge that it felt good – it felt right.

Samson couldn't take his eyes off Ryder. He could see her acceptance – her appetite for them and for whatever they wanted to do with her. As she rose and fell on his cock, he raised his hand to swirl and twirl around her clitoris, adding more fuel to the fire.

And Gideon – Gideon was hypnotized by her response. Even as she kept up the rhythm designed to drive his brother mad, she pushed down on his fingers. Her little body was demanding more and more. He was so turned-on; he couldn't hold back. With one hand, he introduced Ryder to new delights and with the other, he stroked his own cock, long, strong pulls. As his balls tightened, his voice rose, moaning, "God, Ryder, what you do to me!" The finish was inevitable and in sight.

The dual sensations – Samson feeling the wonder of Ryder's surrender to Gideon – Gideon sharing the pleasure his brother felt while enveloped in her tight pussy – all of it together propelled them to a tidal wave of rapture. As they rose to the apex, both brothers increased their efforts to please their woman.

Ryder was mindless in her quest for release. Samson plucking at her breasts and torturing her clit would've been enough to catapult her into ecstasy. But when Gideon was added to the mix, teasing her backside, scattering kisses and nips along the sensitive skin of her nape – nothing in the universe could've prevented her from screaming their names – "Samson! Gideon!" She felt her whole being, body and soul, fly apart. Only the hands of her lovers, kept Ryder anchored to this world –

a paradise for three that she never, ever wanted to leave.

* * *

After making love behind the waterfall, the trio rinsed off in the natural pool. "Are we going back?" Ryder asked as she pulled on her clothes, glancing around nervously.

"No, I thought we'd take you to the Fern Grotto. It's a special place for our family," Samson answered, slipping his sandals back on his feet.

"And don't worry, Ryder, there's no one about. This is private property," Gideon reassured her, having seen her nervous survey of her surroundings. "We wouldn't let anyone see or take what belongs to us."

"That's right, you're always protected. Even when we're not around, there will always be someone watching out for you."

As Ryder took her place in the Jeep, she felt complete contentment. For the first time in a long while, everything seemed to be going the right way for her and for her family. "Tell me about the Fern Grotto."

"It's not far," Samson explained, "hidden in a natural grotto, deep in the jungle. This particular place served as a heiau, for our ancestors. The old ways were outlawed under King Kamehameha, but this heiau survived."

Once they were on the road, Ryder watched the passing landscape with rapture. "What's heiau?"

Gideon took this question. "A heiau was a temple, built on high-rising stone terraces or enclosed in hidden grottos. They were adorned with stone carved gods and were a source of great power, called mana. The temples were restricted to the king and to the kahuna, the priests.

"Well, if it's restricted, how can we go there?"

Samson chuckled. "Well, we no longer adhere to the old ways, for one thing. And for another, we have our priest with us. Gideon and Kona are descended from the kahuna and our mother is an ancestress of the King."

"You have your bases covered then. So, the only outsider will be me." Ryder wasn't worried, she knew her men wouldn't take her someplace dangerous.

"You aren't an outsider. You are ours," Gideon reminded her. *And tomorrow, we'll show her how serious we are when we ask her to marry us.*

She's going to have questions, Gideon. How this will work. The legal ramifications.

We'll tell her whatever she wants to know. The only important thing is that she agrees.

"Is that it?" Ryder pointed to a dense grove of trees. As they approached, a flock of birds lifted from the trees and flew into the sky.

"We're getting close, yes," Samson answered, finding a place to leave the jeep.

"I'm glad there aren't any snakes here," Ryder observed as they began their trek through the thick undergrowth.

"Well, that's not exactly true," Gideon began to explain, "there are a few brown snakes brought by boat. They've made themselves at home…" He grunted when Ryder jumped into his arms, climbing him like a monkey going up a palm tree.

"Ha!" Samson laughed. "A mention of those snakes might come in handy someday."

Gideon didn't care, he gladly bore his sweet burden until they came to the grotto. Their family took care of this sacred place, treating it and its history with respect. "Here you go, sweetheart." He stood her on her feet. "Let's look around."

As they ventured closer, Samson began to tell her the meaning of it all. "Our ancient religion is called kapu, or taboos. There was a right way to live your life, to worship the gods, and even a correct way to eat." He tugged on a lock of Ryder's hair. "For example, women weren't allowed to eat with men."

They laughed at Ryder's sweet grumble. "I'll remind you two of that the next time you want oral sex."

"No!" Gideon yelled. "That's not what it meant at all."

"Uh-huh, sounds right to me," Ryder teased. "What else was taboo?"

Samson picked back up on his lecture. In many ways, he reminded her of Philip.

"Well, no one could touch the king's shadow, if they did, his power could be stolen. The kapu system grew in strength over the years, culminating in a time where human sacrifice was practiced."

"Ewww." Ryder shivered. "That seems unnecessary."

"Mankind is always seeking a way to display their power over someone else," Gideon added as an aside. He held up a banana leaf and allowed Ryder to move in closer.

"What kind of gods did they worship here?" she asked as her eyes roved over the small stone figures surrounded by lush ferns, their fronds partially hiding some of the statues. The figures looked a bit childish to her, with their rounded heads and crude facial features.

"Ku was the God of War, Kane was the God of Life and Light, Kanaloa was the God of Death and Lono was the God of Peace." Samson listed the main deities.

"What about Pele?" Ryder was quizzical, hugging herself. She didn't want to tell the guys this, but the fern grotto made her feel a little creeped out. For some reason, she felt like they were being watched.

"Pele, yes, she is the Goddess of Fire. Her sister Hi'iaka is the Goddess of Water."

Ryder held onto Samson's arm as he spoke, at least she enjoyed the sound of his voice.

"All of Hawaii's mystical world allows for nature to be explained by the existence of gods and spirits."

As they stood still, absorbing the unique atmosphere, the sun began to sink behind the mountain.

Out of nowhere, Ryder heard a haunting sound. A conch shell blew, and in the distance, she could hear the sound of drums and chanting. For a long moment, they stood frozen, listening. "What is that?" Ryder asked, rubbing her arms to dispel the chill bumps on her skin.

"Nightmarchers," Gideon murmured, almost reverently.

"They'll come through the grotto, brother. I didn't realize how late it was getting to be." Samson drew Ryder into his embrace.

"What's that smell?" Ryder asked, holding her nose at the strong musky odor that had arisen out of nowhere.

"I'm not sure," Gideon said, "it just comes with the experience."

"You've seen this before?" Ryder asked, a little nervous.

"He has. We won't." Samson turned her with him, his body blocking any view she might try to find.

As she quaked in her lover's embrace, Ryder could see the lights from torches dancing against the trees as whoever, or whatever, drew closer.

"What's happening?" she asked in fear.

"They're coming. The warrior ghosts and the king. They have marched this same trail for centuries."

His voice was solemn, but unafraid. "Why doesn't he turn around?" she whispered to Samson. "I don't want anything to happen to Gideon."

"He knows what he is doing, he is one of them, more so than me. You and I are not permitted to see the nightmarch; he is not taboo."

Soon, the pounding of footsteps could be heard – drawing closer and closer. Ryder scrunched her eyes together, and when she heard a voice shout, "Na'u!" she jumped.

"It's okay. That's a good sign, a sign of acceptance. Someone recognized Gideon and shouted, mine! If you are in the nightmarchers bloodline, no one in the procession can hurt you."

They stood as still as the statues in the fern grotto as the procession of the dead passed by. Ryder had never known anything like this. Instead of terror, she felt awe and wonder.

Paradise was a magical place.

Once they were gone, the three made their way to the Jeep, saying little. Only when they were on the road, did Ryder raise her arms over her head, and shouted one word. "Na'u!"

Samson and Gideon both looked at her in confused amusement. "What are you doing?" Gideon asked.

"I'm claiming the two of you in your own language. "Na'u! You are mine!"

Neither Duke could argue with that.

* * *

Back at Lani, Ryder felt more trepidation than she had with the spirits of the Hawaiian warriors. Leilani still intimidated her. "I should have returned to help you prepare the meal."

"Nonsense, Kali did most of it."

Again, Samson and Gideon's mother was regal in a peach sarong, her blue-black hair coiled up on her head in an intricate design. The Dads were much less fearsome, dressed in shorts and colorful shirts, they lounged with their sons and discussed the changes they were making on the ranch.

The discussion continued as they seated themselves around a huge teak dining table, laden with all manners of tropical delights. Pork, fish, poi, pineapple, chicken and rice, and sweet potatoes. "This looks wonderful," Ryder complimented Leilani.

"Thank you. So, what did you think of our home?" she asked politely as she began to pass the food around the table, family style.

"Magnificent. We went to the waterfall." As soon as she said the word, an unbidden memory of what they'd done there made Ryder blush.

Seeing her discomfiture, the brothers began to smile and chuckle – which led to the dads picking up on their train of thought. Soon, everyone was laughing except Ryder. She kept her gaze firmly planted on the white china plate in front of her. Hoping to quell their amusement, she finished her tale. "Afterwards…we visited the Fern Grotto and the nightmarchers came."

At that revelation, Leilani gasped. "I told you to be careful. Samson and Ryder are not protected like you, Gideon."

"We were careful, Mother. We turned our backs out of respect. No harm was done."

"What did you think of the nightmarchers, Ryder?" Kona asked as he began to eat his two-finger poi…with two fingers.

Ryder shrugged. "I loved it. I'm originally from Louisiana. Spirits and ghosts haunt the countryside there, as much as your nightmarchers do here."

"I like this girl." Solomon pointed his fork at her. "So, how did you get from Louisiana to Texas? I thought you were from a family of cowboys."

Ryder briefly explained about Hurricane Katrina and losing their mother. "Moving to Texas was a way we could be relatively close to home and continue our way of life. Belle Chase, the plantation where I grew up, was basically a cattle ranch – with the addition of crops such as rice, sugar cane, and crawfish."

"Very similar." Kona nodded. "We raise cattle, along with pineapple, coconut, and sugar cane."

"So, what are these changes you're proposing?" Samson asked his family, unable to ignore the topic any longer.

Seeing their son was more than curious, Solomon laid his napkin in his lap. "Nothing earth-shattering. We want to maintain the status quo, but add some environmentally friendly additions – like a processing plant to convert saltwater to fresh water, solar panels, and some turbines to take advantage of the winds off the ocean."

"Oh, my brother Heath would love you," Ryder stated unequivocally as she munched on a piece of succulent pineapple. "We call him Mr. Green Jeans."

Leilani laughed at Ryder's little joke. "We've always tried to keep up, even when living in such an ancient and grounded place. My boys have always dreamed big. When they announced to me they wanted to travel to the stars, I never doubted them."

After the meal, Ryder insisted on helping Leilani in the kitchen – where an uncomfortable topic came up. Out of nowhere, the matriarch of the household announced – "I know about the news expose, Ryder."

"You do?"

"I'm sorry that happened, but I think it's for the best."

Ryder didn't really disagree, but she wanted to know the reasoning behind Leilani's comment. "Why do you think so?"

"What you feared most has come to pass and you

survived it with your life, your family, and your heart intact. Am I right?"

"Yes, you are correct." She began placing the crystal glasses back inside the hutch. "I was very fearful things would not work out so well. I was very fortunate. My father is very understanding." She sighed. "I haven't spoken to my brothers. I shall have to do that as soon as I return home."

As they finished up, Ryder considered what the future held for her. She was happy. Happier than she'd ever been. Samson and Gideon spoke often of the future. They never hesitated to assure her that she had a place in their plans.

Yet, no words of love had been spoken.

Many times, the words 'I love you' had been on the tip of her tongue. She'd had to bite them back. Saying them first was such a scary thing. Still, she did love them. And soon, she needed to tell them so.

Did they love her as much as she loved them?

CHAPTER TWELVE

"Where's Gideon?" she asked. Ryder knew she shouldn't be uneasy when one of them wasn't around, but she couldn't forget how it had felt when Gideon was estranged from them.

"He's just taking care of a little business. He'll be back, I assure you, Princess." Samson hooked an arm around her neck and kissed her cheek. "And while he's gone, I'm taking you on a little sight-seeing trip."

"Where are we going?" The mention of another excursion caused her heart to bounce. She loved seeing the island.

"We're taking a helicopter up to the volcano."

The news he conveyed made her shiver. "Is it safe?"

"Yes, it is. I'll make certain of it," Samson stated with authority. "We've done this same thing hundreds of times." He had just one main objective today – to entertain Ryder while Gideon traveled into Honolulu to pick up Ryder's engagement ring from a custom jeweler. If it had been possible, they would've asked for a delivery, but Haiku was old, he couldn't make the trip. His craftsmanship and one-of-a-kind designs were well worth the effort to fly over and pick up the ring.

Flying in a helicopter wasn't something Ryder had done before becoming involved with the Dukes. Now she was becoming an old hand at it, not blinking an eye as she boarded and prepared for lift-off. Samson gave the pilot some directions and they lifted off. She enjoyed the birds eye view of the ranch, pointing out a couple of things and asking Samson what she was seeing. "What beach is this?"

"Our private beach, we call it Ahina, for the white

sands. In fact, that spot," he indicated a rock-strewn area, "is where we'll be meeting Gideon in a few hours. We're going horseback riding together."

Everything sounded good to Ryder. She didn't want to talk much while they were in the air, the things she wanted to say, weren't really for the pilot's ears.

"Look, Ryder." She followed Samson's gaze and gasped at her first sight of the volcano. "Wow. I've known ranchers who owned their own mountain, but none with their own volcano." She held her breath as she watched plumes of smoke rise high. The closer they came, the more amazed she became at the sheer size of the crater. "This is sort of scary," she admitted when she saw the bubbling cauldron. In a way, it didn't look real to her. Even more intriguing were the rivulets of orange-red snaking their way toward the ocean. They stood out like neon signs against the backdrop of black volcanic rock. "How close can we get?"

"I can take you to a magma stream, but you'll have to do exactly as I tell you," he cautioned.

"Yes, sir," she agreed wholeheartedly.

Once they were on the ground, Samson led her from the helicopter. "We have a short hike ahead of us, about a quarter of a mile. Feel up to it?"

"Of course," she told him, then waited while Samson spoke to the pilot, telling him how long they'd be gone.

When they were on their way, hand in hand, Ryder broached a subject she needed to discuss. "Samson, is it normal for me to feel more comfortable talking to you about some things than Gideon?"

Samson considered her question for a moment. "I suppose. Our relationship is a bit different, due to the circumstances when Gideon left us for a while. But I don't like to think of you trusting one of us more than the other. I don't think that's right."

"Oh, I don't," Ryder assured him. "It's just that Gideon did something to me yesterday, and I don't really understand it."

Samson thought he knew where this might be headed. He hid a smile. "Well, I'll be glad to speak with you about it, on the condition that you talk with him also."

Ryder frowned. "Okay, I just don't want to disappoint Gideon."

"You can't. He only wants what's best for you. Now, what's your question?" All the time they were talking, Samson kept them headed in the right direction.

"When we were making love I was on top of you."

Samson felt himself begin to grow hard. "I remember."

"Gideon was kissing and touching me."

Samson groaned. "All right, let me stop you right there and let you know that we will be having an erotic session where you'll talk dirty to us."

Ryder giggled. "I'm not talking dirty."

"No, you aren't. I'm teasing. Go on."

"He…put his finger in my…bottom."

Samson glanced over at her, loving that her cheeks were pink and her eyes were shining like jewels. "Did you hate it?"

"No, I didn't hate it." She felt her cheeks grow even warmer. "I liked it, it didn't feel like I imagined it was going to feel."

"How so?" Who needed to see a volcano when he was walking next to Miss Hot-stuff herself? Samson pulled on the leg of his jeans to give his burgeoning package more room.

"I thought it would hurt and I didn't expect there to be…pleasure centers there."

"I'm glad you liked it, in a relationship like ours, sometimes we will want to take you at the same time."

Ryder sighed. "I want to do that, but I'm worried." Before Samson could say more, she just came out and said it. "I think both of you are way too big to fit back there. When he had one finger in me." She held up her forefinger. "One finger! How will I manage anything more? You men are hung!"

Gideon, you're missing out, man.

What's going on?

She's worrying that we're too hung for anal sex.

Hahahahahahaha! You can tell her I picked up an extra surprise today.

"I think being hung is a good thing. Right?"

"Yes, but my other parts seem to stretch better, Samson."

"Oh, both your parts will stretch just fine. Gideon is bringing you a little surprise home today. Something you can wear down there that will make taking us a lot easier."

"A butt plug?"

Samson tripped over a rock and almost went sprawling. Ryder giggled at the sight. When he was back on a firm footing, he frowned at his lady love. "You know about a butt plug? How do you know about a butt plug?"

"I read."

Her simple answer sent him into gales of laughter again. "Ah, those erotic romances. I think we need to monitor your library."

"Oh, no. I love my books. I've learned a lot from reading. You can thank some of my favorite authors for your blow jobs."

Again, he laughed, then turned and took Ryder by the shoulders, kissing her hard and long. "I bless the day I found you. You are worth everything to me. I'd give the last dollar and everything else I own for you in a heartbeat."

Ryder hugged him back. "I feel the same way, but

I'm not looking forward to wearing a butt plug."

He squeezed her tight. "Well, try it. For Gideon. From what I've heard, wearing it stimulates your…erogenous zones."

"Hmmmm, okay." Then, she looked up. "Oh, my goodness!"

He followed her gaze and realized she was seeing the volcano for the first time. "Did it sneak up on you?"

"Yea, I had forgotten about the lava and the volcano, I was just thinking about riding your cock and Gideon touching my nether regions." Ryder hid a smile. She was perfectly aware of what she was doing. By the look of the bulge in his pants, if she kept going in this vein of conversation, there would soon be an eruption of another kind.

Moaning, Samson protested. "Stop it, Princess. I can barely walk now."

She grabbed his hand and pulled him forward. The closer they went, the warmer the air became. Soon, they were standing at the base of a great mountain. Off to one side, ribbons of magma were trickling down the sides. "Talk to me, tell me what I'm looking at."

He brought her hand up and pressed it next to his chest, holding it tight. "This particular volcano spews magma constantly. Right now, it's concentrated on the east slope."

"How fast does it go?" She was totally entranced, easing along, just in case the small river of lava decided to change course and come after her.

Samson could tell what she was thinking. "If the level of output doesn't increase, it stays inside the existing lava flows, moving between two and twenty yards per hour."

"That isn't very fast, I could dodge that, if I needed to," Ryder observed as she cautiously approached with a stick in hand that she'd picked up along the way. "Let's get closer so I can poke it."

Samson smiled again. "Okay. Yes, a person can get out of the way of the flow, it's other things that pose a problem." He pointed toward the ocean. "Of course, that's not the case with our volcano, but some have been known to eat up houses and entire towns in the path of the lava flow."

"I'm sure it can be a hazard." She spread her arms wide. "But I think it's magnificent." Ryder looked all around. "Your home is magnificent." Coming to him, she threw her arms around him. "Thank you for bringing me. I'll never forget how good you and Gideon have been to me."

Samson enfolded her close. He didn't particularly like the sound of that comment, there was a hint of temporariness in her words. As far as he was concerned, Gideon couldn't get home fast enough with that ring.

* * *

Gideon's heart was beating faster than the horse's hoof beats on the sand. He was riding to their rendezvous spot, leading a mount for Samson and one for Ryder. They were supposed to meet him here after their trip to the volcano. The ring he'd purchased earlier was burning a hole in his pocket. Would she love it? Would she say yes?

The wind was a little high, but the tide was low. Their ride along the beach should be romantic. He'd left instructions with Kali for her to hire caterers to set up a tent and a table with a candlelight meal on the sandy beach.

Getting close, brother? he asked Samson.

Look up.

Gideon did and he saw the helicopter in the distance,

the beating of the blades barely discernible at the point.

I see you. How's our girl?

Perfect, but I'll be glad when we get a ring on her finger. Something she said today bothered me.

What did she say?

She thanked me for being so good to her. Said she would never forget it.

I don't like the sound of that.

Neither did I.

Well, come on. Let's take her for a ride, then set the stage for romance.

By the time the helicopter was on the ground, Gideon was waiting for them, standing under a palm tree, holding the reins of their horses. His eyes were hungry for the sight of Ryder. He could tell the moment she spotted him, she turned loose of Samson's hand and began to run toward him. When she reached him, he caught her sweet body close and drank from her lips like he was dying of thirst and she was his only hope of survival.

"I missed you!" she told him once her mouth was free to speak.

"I missed you too. Did you have a good time?"

"We did."

She began to describe what she saw – fast and in great detail. When she paused to take a breath, he kissed her again. "Sounds like you enjoyed yourself."

"Yes, I'm enjoying every minute of everything." She met his eyes, then gave him a mischievous smile. "Where's my surprise?"

Gideon jerked his head up, meeting Samson's eyes.

She's not talking about the ring, Gideon.

Oh!

Gideon looked at her in all innocence. "What surprise?"

She held out her hand. "My butt plug."

"Ah!" He laid his palm across her outstretched one. "You'll just have to wait until the right time."

"Dratz. I was going to see if I thought I could handle it."

Samson shook his head. "Don't deprive us of the pleasure, love. We want to be the ones to initiate you into this particular joy."

"Yea, we'll lube it up, then lube you up, doing all manners of sexy, kinky things to your sweet, little body before we slip it in."

She squirmed in her tracks, her eyes closing. "Don't. You're turning me on!"

"Turn-about is fair play," Samson reminded her. "That's exactly what you were doing to me on our walk to the volcano."

"Oh, my goodness, what's a girl to do for an orgasm around here?" She teased them unmercifully.

Gideon had all he could stand. Handing Samson the reins to Ryder's horse, he mounted his, then pulled her up to sit in front of him in the saddle – all before she could voice a question or a word of protest. "Never let it be said that a Duke doesn't deliver."

Go for it, brother. "You two ride on ahead. I'll be bringing up the rear," Samson assured them with an amused smile and a casual wave.

"What are we doing?" Ryder asked, breathlessly.

"Giving us both what we need." Urging the horse forward with his knees, he pulled Ryder's T-shirt out of her pants. Running his hands up from her narrow waist, he slid them around and unhooked her bra, freeing her breasts for his hungry hands.

"Oh, Gideon," she breathed, closing her eyes in ecstasy.

This time he didn't take it slow, he wasn't gentle. He covered her tits with both hands and began kneading –

plumping, rubbing, massaging – weighing them in his palms, then tweaking and twisting her nipples until she was arching her back, pressing her head hard against his shoulder. "Like that, little girl?" he asked, then returned to sucking at a soft spot beneath her ear.

"God, yes, Gideon, give me more." She opened her legs, hoping he took the hint.

He did.

Cupping her mound through her jeans, he began to massage the pad of her pussy vigorously, causing her to writhe so much the horse danced to one side – wondering what the hell was going on in the saddle.

"Holy snickerdoodles," she gasped.

Gideon smiled. He was getting to her. "Does your little clit need playing with?"

"I'll give you two free blow-jobs." She set out to strike a bargain.

"Deal." Unzipping her jeans, he nipped her earlobe. "Don't think I won't hold you to that bargain."

"Get to it, cowboy, I'm dying here."

Behind them, Samson came along slowly, enjoying the experience second-hand, but enjoying it nonetheless.

Gideon worked his big hand down the front of her pants. She lifted her hips just enough so he could wedge his palm over her mound, slipping his fingers into her creamy, hot pussy.

"Gideon!" She brought her hands up over her head and around his neck. "Harder!"

"Gladly." Dipping his fingers deep, he pushed them up inside of her, moving in and out until her breath was coming hard and heavy. After every three plunges, he would swirl around her clit, then back – creating a seductive, erotic rhythm that soon had her gasping from a climax so hard, she was shaking in his arms. And all the while, the surf pounded, the winds blew and a huge

Hawaiian sun sank beneath the horizon.

"Are you okay, baby?" He held her close, his cock so hard he could've pounded nails.

"I'm good. I want more later, though. That was just an appetizer."

Gideon smiled. "Samson and I will make sure you get everything you need. Just down the beach, a beautiful tent is set up. We'll eat and then we'll make love to you in the surf. We've got an important quest…"

"Gideon!" Gideon heard Samson's voice in his head and in his ear.

Gideon pulled up on the reins with one hand while he straightened her shirt with the other. Turning the stallion sideways, he looked back at his brother. "What's wrong?"

"We've got to go."

"Where?"

"Texas. Our lead engineer on the Mars project was just killed in a car wreck."

The ring will have to wait, Samson said with regret.

As will the proposal. Damn.

A few hours later, the trio was fairly subdued on the flight home. There was a solemn feeling in the air. Ryder hadn't known the man who was killed, but Samson told her he had a family, two little girls aged three and five.

Once the call came through, they'd returned to the house to say goodbye to Leilani and the dads with promises all around that a new visit would happen soon.

Now, they were winging their way over the Pacific, headed back to Texas. Ryder knew when they landed her men would be busy. She intended to make good use of her time alone, Ryder intended to go see her family.

Somewhere over the ocean, Ryder closed her eyes, trying to sleep. At her request, they'd moved to a large sectional sofa so she could sit between them. Feeling their body heat, the press of their big forms against her, made Ryder feel safe.

When she'd finally dozed off, Samson and Gideon whispered to one another, trying to make sense of what had happened. "Gabe and his team are on the job. We'll know more soon," Samson spoke low, so as not to disturb Ryder.

"They don't think Ralph Ellis's death was an accident, do they?"

Samson shook his head in the negative. "No, he was run off the road."

The low buzzing of a cell phone caused Gideon to turn around to grab it quickly before the noise woke Ryder. Samson put his arm around her when her body jerked, soothing her so she didn't fully awaken. He could tell by his brother's expression and the waves of disquiet he could feel rolling off him that something else was going on. He didn't have to wait long to find out.

"There's been an explosion at Cape Canaveral. One of our rockets was blown to smithereens."

"We have another. This won't stop us." Samson was livid. Only Ryder's presence soothed him, so he kept one hand on her, absorbing strength from her small, still body. "So, this has to be the work of Rasputin."

"Who the hell is Rasputin? Why haven't we been able to find out? I'm damn sure Anatoly and Oleg aren't doing this on their own. But who's backing them? Do you think Rasputin could be Putin himself?"

"I don't think so, Gideon. Putin may be involved, but he's got someone else doing his dirty work. Call them back and give our team strict orders to keep the news of the explosion strictly in-house for as long as possible. All we need is negative publicity, not that it will stop our mission, but we're dependent on private contracts. If companies lose confidence in OuterLimits, our customer base will dry up."

Gideon did as Samson asked, moving to the back of the cabin so he could speak freely. When he returned, he laid the phone on the table. "I can understand competition, the battle for the upper hand. But this is terrorism, plain and simple, Samson. What will be next?"

"They've already tried to take us out once, we've got to make damn sure they don't do it again, especially if our Ryder is near."

"Yes, but if it's one of us…just remember our rule. We'll come after one another, we'll send an army if necessary – but we don't bend to the pressure. We don't pay ransom and we don't compromise." Gideon's voice was full of conviction, rising above a whisper. By the time he was done, he was almost shouting.

An emotional second or two passed before Samson and Gideon realized Ryder was crying. "No, please, no. Don't say that. I'd give anything I had to save either one of you. Even my life."

Samson cursed under his breath, gathering Ryder into his arms. "Oh, honey. Nothing's going to happen. Our testosterone is just riding high because we're upset. Everything will be okay."

"I don't know, so much is happening. I'm scared!"

Gideon took her from Samson's arms, adding his comfort. "Don't be scared, baby. We're sorry. We were just two men carrying on in the heat of the moment. We won't take any unnecessary risks."

"No, you're serious. I know you." She clutched Gideon's shirt. "Take me to the bedroom. I need you both to hold me. I'm shaking and cold. I don't feel like I'll ever be warm again."

Samson and Gideon did as she asked, leaving the couch and escorting Ryder to the bedroom on the private plane. Once behind closed doors, they undressed her and themselves, slipping beneath the covers to cradle her close between them.

Ryder shivered, lying on her back. She held onto them, her arms linked to theirs. Her men laid on their sides, facing her, soothing her with kisses and caresses.

"You'll be careful, won't you? I can tell you're worried."

"Yes," Samson promised her. "We'll be careful. Now that we have you, we're going to do everything in our power to keep you safe and to keep ourselves safe for you."

"That's right, Princess." Gideon put his arm around her waist. "We'll take care of this tomorrow, then we'll come home to you. Promise."

She closed her eyes and prayed, willing that all would be well.

* * *

Heath hung his black Stetson on the hat rack in his office at the resort. He was waiting on Scott Eagleton. He'd finally been able to tie the man down for a meeting. Even though they'd been acquainted for a while, Heath didn't really know the guy that well. In addition to his views on the environment, he knew Eagleton was an adventurer of sorts. Like Philip, he'd traveled the world. His reputation was that of a cat with nine lives; he'd survived a plane crash, one of the terrorist attacks in Paris, a gunshot wound from a would-be burglar, and a poisoning attempt from a disgruntled employee. Heath admired the man's resiliency. Eagleton was hard to kill.

As he headed to the dining room, Heath stopped to speak to a couple of customers. He made nice, asking how they were enjoying their room and the food. "Have you gone on the paddleboat tour to see the eagles?"

"No, we haven't! But we'd love to." A woman

gushed, giving him a flirty smile.

"Well, my wife and I highly recommend that you go. Just check at the concierge desk, and they'll book you a reservation."

The lady looked a tad let down. Heath guessed the wedding ring he wore sorta got lost on his big ole hand. Maybe he needed to wear a sign around his neck that said, *Happily Married, Baby on the Way."* Yes, he was gonna be a daddy and Heath couldn't be happier.

In fact, things were looking up all around. He'd received a text from Ryder. She and...those damn Dukes were on their way home from Hawaii. The thought of those two goons putting their four big mitts on his sister still gave him a migraine. At least their father was handling the situation better than he was. Heath still intended to talk her out of this nonsense, but at least he was going to get the chance to sit down with her and address this mess face to face. When he answered her text, he issued a civil invitation and she agreed to come to the ranch for dinner that evening. Heath was keeping his fingers crossed that he could talk some sense into his baby sister. If not, he might just have to hog-tie her and put her in the barn for a spell until she cooled off.

Hearing his phone buzz, he looked down and grimaced. "Goddammit!" Another meddling, supposedly well-meaning friend had sent him a You-Tube link. He started not to click on it, assuming it was a link to that damn libelous video revealing the fact that Ryder was the Dukes' current flavor of the month. "Hell, I hate this."

But, when he took a closer look, it was something else entirely. "Wow. Great!" He was relieved on more than one count. This piece of information was going to spread like wildfire. And if people were talking about this...they wouldn't be spending their time gossiping about Ryder. Another valid point was that this was legitimately good news. "Excellent! Kyle Chancellor has announced he'll run for the Presidency in 2020." Everyone he knew, everyone who knew Ryder, would find this tidbit of news irresistible.

"Heath!"

Heath turned on his heels to find his guest had arrived. "Scott, good to see you, man!" He went to shake his hand. "I appreciate you making time for me, there's a lot I'd like to discuss with you."

"Always glad to see you, Heath. I respect what you're trying to do for our country."

"Climate change and protecting our environment are passions of mine." He escorted Scott into the dining room to the best table Canyon of the Eagles had to offer. After placing an order for drinks and hors d'oeuvres, he began to lay out his plan.

"As you know I've spent years building my energy company to be as green as possible. I've been diversifying, not putting all my eggs in one basket. Solar, wind farms, hydropower, and I'm even working on devising a way to use methane cleanly. I've recently signed a contract with OuterLimits to provide methane for their rockets. You know, they think they can refuel on Mars using the methane that occurs naturally there."

Heath was used to people zoning out while he talked, he didn't usually care, as long as he got their support and their money, he didn't care if they were entertained or not. But - Scott seemed animated, excited. "You work with the Dukes?"

"Yes." This wasn't exactly what he was aiming for, but he'd take what he could get. "Samson and Gideon are very concerned about the environment. It takes people with the kind of money that you and the Dukes have to bring awareness to the rest of society."

"What can you tell me about the Mars launch? When

is it? Is everything in place?"

Heath shook his head. "Not much. I only know about the fuel."

"Do you think you can get me a meeting with them?"

Scott's face took on an intensity that Heath couldn't define. "Well…"

"I will tell you that I have several million dollars to allot for one of your programs…if you can get me an audience with the Dukes."

Heaven above, Heath never knew he could use a member of his family this way. "I can try." Lie. Lie. "My sister is dating one of them and she's coming to dinner at Highlands tonight. If you'd like to come to join us, I can see about getting Samson and Gideon to stop by."

Scott sat stock still, mesmerized, like he'd just been offered the keys to the kingdom. "I can see Ryder at dinner…" A myriad of emotions clouded Scott's countenance. "I've always been drawn to your sister, McCoy. I saw that hideous video. None of that can be true, can it?"

Heath shook his head. "Of course not. Ryder is dating Samson only. I'm not worried, though. She's still playing the field. My baby sister is too young to get serious about anyone."

A pleased smile split Scott's face, transforming it from handsome to almost skull-like. "I see. Well, in that case, I accept your invitation. Seems like I'll be able to kill two birds with one stone."

Heath didn't return Eagleton's smile. It wasn't clear to him what constituted the two birds. "Great. I look forward to seeing you. Be there at seven…and bring your checkbook."

Hell, he was just trying to garner money for a good cause.

So…why did he feel dirty?"

* * *

Back at Falconhead, the Dukes and Ryder arrived home safely. During the night, Ryder had calmed down after being reassured repeatedly by her men that everything would be fine. The sweet, gentle way they made love to her went a long way in accomplishing their goal.

Just before landing, Ryder relented and contacted Heath. She didn't apologize, but she did make an overture by asking to come visit him. Her older brother surprised her by suggesting she come to dinner. How odd that felt – being issued an invitation to her childhood home. Ryder couldn't deny she was anxious to see everyone. Even though it had only been a few days, this was the longest she'd been away from them all. Even on vacations or trips, someone in her family had normally accompanied her. At least she hadn't been totally incommunicado with the clan. Since the visit to their father's home, Pepper had called her several times and Molly sent pictures of the twins daily. Cato texted her, sending Ryder encouragement. Philip had even contacted her in his odd way, vacillating between sending GIFs of baby pigs to articles on obscure archaeological finds he thought she might be interested in. Following their elder brother's example, Jaxson, and Ten hadn't reached out to her at all, and this bothered her. Especially Jaxson. She'd always been so close to him. Since his accident, however, that had changed. Jaxson had changed. Oh well, it wasn't like she was running out of time. Ryder knew she had fences to mend and she was ready to try.

All in all, things looked brighter to her this morning.

The only ones who weren't happy she was returning to Highlands were Samson and Gideon. She understood how they felt, she wasn't anxious for them to venture out in all the turmoil that was going on. "I know you need to go take care of things," Ryder told her men, "I'll just miss you. Don't worry, I'll be fine. I'm just going to have supper with the family, then I plan on inviting Pepper back here for an impromptu slumber party. I've missed our gossip sessions."

"We'll be back as soon as we can. Most of our security team are at the plant or on other assignments, but one of Gabe's men will be here to take you to Highlands and bring you home when you're through." Samson buttoned her sweater. "The temperature is dropping; you might need to wear your gloves."

"Samson, Highlands is next door. I could walk over there in ten minutes."

"No." Gideon added emphatically. "You are to take every precaution. We still don't know who's behind all of this. The only people we trust is us, our team, and your family."

"Okay." She gave them a loving smile, resting a hand on each of their chests. "I'll walk on eggshells until you get back. And then…I want my surprise."

"We look forward to giving you that surprise." Samson gave her a grin and a wink.

"As well as another one, an important one." Gideon ran a loving finger down the side of her beautiful face. "So, you take care of what belongs to us, Princess. Our future is just beginning."

* * *

Gideon sat in the passenger seat of the Lamborghini, holding Ryder's ring box in his hand. "This wasn't how I planned on spending the day."

"Me either," Samson mused. "She understood and she'll be waiting for us when we come home."

"I can't wait to get this ring on her finger. You know,

we need to decide how we're going to handle this. We've always talked about marrying the love of our life, but we both can't – not legally." Gideon glanced over at his brother. "How are we going to manage this?"

"Well, I've given it some thought." Samson tapped the steering wheel. "One of us will marry her openly, in front of her friends and family."

"That should be you," Gideon said immediately.

Samson frowned. "No, I think it should be you."

"Listen. You've dated her. If you marry her, no one will blink an eye. If I'm the one, people will be more likely to believe the video or wonder if we're feuding."

"Okay." Samson could see his point. "I don't want to leave you out though, best man status is not enough for you."

"I'll be married to her in my heart, either way. This ring is proof of that." He opened the box and stared at the ring, designed to complement the necklace they'd given her – one big Princess cut diamond flanked by two huge round stones. A picture of their future.

"Why don't we have two ceremonies? One can be legal and public, the other can be private and personal."

Gideon smiled. "Perfect. We'll just need to find someone to perform the second ceremony."

"You leave that to me," Samson said. "I'll find someone we can trust."

"How about Kali's husband? He respects the old ways. We could fly them over with the folks." Gideon's voice was excited now. He had a plan.

"Perfect. Just perfect," Samson agreed, changing gears on the Lamborghini to make a sharp curve.

"Great." Gideon put the ring box back in his pocket, then patted it. "Everything's settled. Nothing can go wrong now. We won't allow it."

CHAPTER THIRTEEN

"Ellis was targeted to stop the mission. There's no other explanation."

"For the same reason they blew up the rocket and the cargo capsule. They don't know we have multiples. The plans we've put into place aren't the norm for the industry. We've perfected a way to produce rockets cheaper, therefore our eggs aren't all in one basket." Samson shook a folder at Gideon. "That lack of insight is the only thing that keeps me from suspecting this is an inside job. How the hell are they getting inside our property to do this much damage?"

Gideon stared at the wall of their office at Cape Canaveral. "I don't think they are. Everything that's happened – the fire, the explosion – all of this could've been handled remotely. Hell, they could've used a drone to do their dirty work."

Samson tugged on his hair in frustration. "You know what we should do? You know what would be the ultimate 'fuck you'?"

"What?" Gideon was intrigued.

"We have all the components in place. This is an unmanned mission. The trajectory is mapped out. Losing Ellis was a blow, but his second-in-command is up to the job. All we need is for Heath to deliver the fuel. Let's move up the launch. Crap is going to continue to happen until we've put the matter to rest. Let's go to Mars now."

Gideon smiled. "I agree. All systems are go."

...Meanwhile on their way to Highlands, Ryder was receiving a lecture by the youngest member of Gabe's team. His name was Laramie Goodnight and he looked less like a bodyguard than anyone she could imagine. He was dressed completely in cowboy gear and spoke with an East Texas drawl. "All I'm asking ma'am is that you let me check things out."

"This is my home, Goodnight. The only place I'm safer is when I'm lying between Samson and Gideon."

Honest to God, Laramie covered his eyes. "Oh, please don't say things like that, ma'am. I blush easy. All I'm asking is that you let me do my job. I don't want to let Mr. Gabe or the Dukes down."

"All right." Ryder gave in. "Do whatever you think is necessary. You can even join us for the meal if you'd like." She looked up toward the driver. "Gervis, I'll send you out a plate."

"Not necessary ma'am. Thurgood made me a ham sandwich." He lifted the plastic wrapped packet. "While you're visiting, I'm going to park down by the lake, enjoy my meal, and wait for your call."

Since the trip was so short, there was no further time for conversation. "Whose limousine is that?" Laramie asked, automatically taking his phone in hand to check the plates.

Ryder sighed in disappointment. "No need to look it up. I recognize the car. It belongs to one of Heath's friends, Scott Eagleton." How could he do this? "I'm going to strangle, Heath," she muttered. "He hasn't accepted anything, he's still matchmaking!"

"You're right, Scott Eagleton, former Ambassador to Russia, business mogul. Single. Thirty-two. Weight, one-eighty."

Ryder leaned over. "What kind of database has all of that information?"

Laramie pulled it to his chest. "Mr. Gabe has many resources."

She had to smile. "Well, I'm glad Mr. Gabe works for Samson and Gideon."

When they pulled up to the house, Gervis held the door. "Thank you." She gave him a smile. "Come on, Laramie. Let's get this show on the road."

The next few minutes were full of joy and frustration.

Ryder's reunion with her family was a happy one – for the most part. She kissed the babies, she hugged the girls – she even had a meaningful moment with Jaxson and Ten. Philip, as always, tried to be the peacemaker, escorting her from one member of the family to the next, as if she might've forgotten their names.

But when it came to Heath – she stood before him like a petty thief in front of a magistrate. But why? She had no reason to feel guilty. "Heath."

"Ryder."

"Glad you could make it."

"Thanks for inviting me."

Catching a glimpse of Scott standing a few feet behind Heath, she narrowed her eyes and whispered, "I thought you invited me here because you'd finally accepted my decision, not a final attempt to talk me out of it."

"Oh, this isn't my final attempt," Heath murmured with equal intensity. "I'll never accept you being Daisy Duke to the Hazzard brothers."

"I think you've mixed up your metaphors." She jerked her head toward Eagleton. "And you're matchmaking, again? Have you lost your mind?"

"I'm fundraising, for your information. The fact that Scott still has a crush on you is a bonus." He looked over his shoulder at Laramie Goodnight. "Who's the kid? Don't tell me you've brought a fourth into your dirty little triangle."

Ryder had to clench her fists to keep from punching her brother. "That's my bodyguard."

Heath's eyebrows raised to the roof. "They think you

need a bodyguard in your own home? With us?"

"If I remember correctly, you made me so miserable I had to leave my own home."

"That was your decision, missy."

"Hey, guys, settle down." Cato tugged Heath's sleeve. "We have company, you know."

After that, the family gathered around the big dining table. Ryder found herself sitting between Heath and Scott Eagleton. She sent Pepper a look that pleaded for rescue.

"We'll escape soon," Pepper mouthed to her.

Cato, who was sitting across from Ryder kicked her under the table. "I'm sorry about this. He does love you, give him a chance to come around." Her sister-in-law didn't say the words out loud, she signed them.

Ryder signed back. "I love him, too. Beyond that, I don't know how this will end."

"The food is delicious, Pepper." Ryder complimented the meal. "You made chicken and dumplings, one of my favorites." There was also a huge beef roast and all the trimmings – mashed potatoes and gravy, green beans, a multitude of salads, fresh rolls, and coconut cake for dessert.

"Molly and Cato helped. Ella and Ava even got in on the act. They sat in the carriers and laughed at the mess we made."

Pepper's recounting made Ryder a little homesick. "Sounds fun." As she looked down the long table, she noticed Laramie appeared to be enjoying his food. "Who's the man sitting by Laramie?" she asked her brother.

"That's Scott's assistant. I'm not sure what his name is, I don't think he said."

Heath's response didn't satisfy her. She stared at the man who met her eye and gave her a smile. "He looks familiar. I've seen him somewhere before."

"This food is excellent," Heath answered between bites. "Maybe he was with him at the cook-off, I'm not sure."

"Maybe. Now, while I've got your attention. What's it going to take for you to accept Samson and Gideon in my life?"

"Pass the salt, Ryder." Scott touched her arm and Ryder jumped.

"Sure." She gave it to him, inching further over in her seat toward her brother.

"I don't know what it will take – a miracle maybe," Heath grumbled to her left.

To her right, Scott tried to strike up a conversation. "So, I hear you're dating Samson Duke?"

His question stunned Ryder. "Yes, I am," she answered slowly, half expecting Scott to join Heath in his attempt to dissuade her. "I love them...him very much." Ryder cut her eyes up to see if Scott had caught her slip.

He had. An odd smile came over his face. "I see. Will your men be joining us today? I know they are usually inseparable." Eagleton gave her a pointed stare, letting her know he knew more than he was saying.

"Yes, that's a good idea, Ryder. I think it's time we all had a nice sit-down. Why don't you call and invite them over for dessert?"

Ryder looked between them, trying to ascertain if they'd both lost their minds. "How gracious, but that will be impossible. They're out of town on business."

Scott frowned. "What a shame."

For a few minutes after that exchange, things leveled out. Ryder was able to participate in the general family conversation around the table.

"Ava and Ella are finally sleeping through the night," Ten announced proudly.

"That's great!" Ryder celebrated with the proud papa.

"Mostly thanks to the new nanny we've found," Molly added. "Maxine is a dream. She's upstairs with the girls now."

"I'm so happy for the both of you. What other good news do we have? Jaxson?" She looked at her 'favorite' brother expectantly.

He opened his mouth to say something, then shut it, shrugging. "The only thing worth mentioning in my life is the new bull we bought last week. He's going to make some fine calves."

"I'd love to see him before we go." She glanced at Laramie who was speaking to the stranger, whose familiarity plagued her memory. "How about you, Philip? Are you still seeing the mysterious Shell?"

Philip laid his fork down and clasped his hands together, his gaze moving from one family member to the other. "No, I'm not seeing Shell. I invited Racy Monahan out to dinner. Our first date is tomorrow night."

Pepper dropped her fork, which clanked against the plate. "Racy!"

"Racy!" Ryder echoed her sister's surprise. "That's wonderful!"

A plethora of outbursts and questions were thrown at Philip. Heath, on the other hand, seemed determined to talk business with Scott Eagleton. Ryder had to lean back to give them room to converse.

"Scott, I wanted to tell you about my work with methane."

Ryder closed her eyes. "Do you want to trade seats with me?" she asked her brother.

"No." Scott clasped her arm. "You stay right where you are."

This didn't deter Heath. "Natural gas is the cleanest

burning fossil fuel we have. As you know, its main ingredient is methane. There's a great environmental benefit to using methane, by mass it produces more heat and light energy than other fossil fuels, including coal. It also produces less carbon dioxide and other pollutants. This means the more natural gas we use, the less greenhouse gas emissions and smog related pollutants we produce. I think we can develop a process to capture some naturally produced methane to use as a fuel. For example, methane from waste water treatment plants or dairies could be collected and used. We'd be able to reduce the amount of methane in the atmosphere as well as reduce our dependency on fossil fuels."

Ryder's eyes were crossed and she was amused to see Scott's were as well.

When Heath's cell phone rang, she and Scott shared a sly look of relief.

"Yea?" Heath pinned Ryder with a stare. "Samson. What can I do for you?"

Heath listened for a moment. Ryder and Scott leaned closer, trying to hear what was being said.

"Hell, yes. I can be ready. If you want to move up the Mars launch, I'm ready to help you. Yes, she's right here. Safe and sound. Would you and Gideon have time to stop by?"

Next to Ryder, Scott tensed.

"I understand," Heath concluded. "No problem. My brothers and I will set the ball rolling. We'll have that fuel delivered to you in no time." He handed the phone to Ryder, his smile disappearing from his face. "Samson wants to talk to you."

Ryder took the phone. "Hey, baby. What's up?"

As Ryder listened to Samson's excited voice, Heath stood and addressed his brothers and guests. "Philip, Jaxson, Tennessee – we need to have a quick meeting out in the ranch office building. All of my specs are out there."

The brothers rose and threw down their napkins, ready to help their sibling.

"Scott, I hope we can do business." Heath shook hands with the former ambassador. "I think this launch is going to prove the value of our work and my plan."

Ryder tried to concentrate on Samson's voice as he relayed what sounded like good news. "We're moving up the launch, that should quell the trouble once and for all. Once the rocket is on its way to Mars, that should take the wind out of their sails."

"When will you be home?" She wanted them to accomplish their goals, she just needed to be with them. "How about if Laramie brought me to you?"

"That sounds like a plan. Let me talk to Gideon and we'll call you back with arrangements."

She hung up, distracted by something going on at the table. Scott was on the phone, whispering. Cato looked alarmed, watching him. The man at the end of the table was standing up, saying something to Laramie. Scott hung up his phone, then he stood also - speaking to his assistant in a language Ryder didn't understand.

After that – things were a blur. Scott and his friend pulled a gun. To her horror, he pointed the gun at Laramie and pulled the trigger. For a moment, Ryder didn't comprehend that there was a silencer on the gun. Only the red blooming on Laramie's white shirt convinced her the man had actually fired the weapon. All the women screamed as Laramie fell to the floor. Ryder tried to punch redial on Heath's phone, but Scott snatched it from her hand. "Sorry to do this, sweetheart, but you're coming with me. We have some long-standing business to attend to."

"What?"

"No!" Cato screamed.

"Help!" Pepper screamed as hard as she could – but there was no one to hear her.

Molly looked horrified, glancing toward the stairs, seeming to gauge if she could make it to her babies. Ryder knew she was praying that Maxine couldn't hear and didn't come to investigate

Ryder felt like she was living in a nightmare. She didn't understand. "What's this about, Scott? We need to call an ambulance!" As she panicked, her gaze lingered on the man at the end of the table, the man who'd shot poor Laramie. Then – the truth hit her like a bomb blast – he was the same man who'd put the bomb beneath Samson and Gideon's car. "You! It's been you all the time! You're the one who's been trying to stop the Mars launch? Why?" In horror, Ryder looked toward the door. Should she scream? Why didn't Heath and the others come back? Hadn't they heard the commotion?

No, of course they hadn't heard. They were halfway across the property by now at the ranch office.

"Yes, I'm the one. I'm the one who set fire to the plan. I'm the one tried to end this fiasco early by blowing them up with the car bomb! I'm the one who killed the engineer, the one who blew up their damn rocket. And I'm the one who's going to stop this damn launch. If anyone gets to Mars, it will be me and my people!" Waving the gun around, Scott began to issue orders. "What room can be locked?" When no one said anything, he pointed the gun at Cato. "Quick, I'm losing my patience. What room can be locked?"

"The study." Ryder finally offered. "Take the women in there and lock them up, Oleg. Cut the phone line if there's one in there and make sure they don't have a cell phone with them. We need to buy time to get out of here."

Ryder watched in terror as Oleg herded Pepper, Cato,

and Molly to the study to lock them in. "All right, let's move."

"What are you going to do? Where are we going?" She almost stumbled as he pulled her along.

"Did you know I've always wanted you? How could you give yourself to those two perverts instead of me?"

"Because each of them are a thousand times the man you are!"

"If you think that, you're dumb and blind, Ryder. I could've given you everything. But no – you chose them over me." He got to the door and waited, giving Oleg a chance to catch up. "I'm going to use you to get what I want, Ryder. Since the Dukes have moved up the launch, it's fortuitous to have this opportunity to use you as collateral."

"What do you mean?" Ryder cried as they began to drag her to the limousine. "Help! Help!" she screamed, hoping that someone – anyone – would hear her. Where were all their hands? Where were Gabriel's men. In despair, she remembered Samson saying that his team were all out checking leads, only Laramie had been left behind to help. "Poor Laramie," she whimpered. "Do you think he's still alive?"

"Who cares? If the Dukes don't cooperate, you won't live to see tomorrow."

"I don't understand. What do you want?"

"For your safe return?" He barked out a laugh before shoving her in the back of the white limousine. "One hundred million dollars and the canceling of the launch – permanently."

A sinking feeling hit Ryder in the pit of her stomach. "There's something you don't know, Scott." Part of her was sad – and part of her was triumphant that this idiot wouldn't get his way. "The Dukes don't negotiate with terrorists. You won't get anything you want."

"Well…we'll see. Once we're a safe distance away, I'll call your brother and make my demands. He can relay them to your lovers. That will be a little extra revenge – forcing them to work together to save you." He laughed, a bitter, hard laugh. "But they'll fail, they'll never find you. If they don't meet my demands, I'll have you out of the country and on a Soviet sub before they ever know what happened."

* * *

"Never let it be said that a locked door can stand in my way." Cato struggled to get the screen off the window. "Here, Molly hold this shutter back, let me see if I can get my big butt through this opening."

"God, Cato, do you think they're gone?" Molly sounded scared to death. "I can't believe none of us had a phone!"

"Hey, it was your idea that we needed to have family time without anyone checking their messages."

"Yea, it's the new mother syndrome."

"Got it!" Cato announced as her feet touched the ground. "Here, give me your hand." She helped Molly through the window. I know you want to get to those babies, but be careful. Make sure they're gone before you head through the door. I'm heading over to the office to alert Heath. Pepper, you check on that poor boy and call an ambulance, too."

"Hurry, Cato!" Pepper urged, following her sisters-in-law out the window. "We need to get Ryder back!"

Cato hurried. She ran as hard as she could – across the yard, down the road, and by the barn. By the time she reached the office, Cato was out of breath. "Heath! Help! Heath!" She began to scream as she bounded up the steps. "Help! Heath!"

The door flew open and Heath stood there, his face

white. He could tell panic in his wife's voice when he heard it. "What's wrong, baby?"

"It's Ryder! Scott Eagleton pulled a gun on us. His friend shot Ryder's bodyguard."

"What about Ryder?" He urged her to get to the point.

"Scott took her, he's the one who's been sabotaging the Duke's Mars mission."

"Fuck, fuck, fuck!" Heath dry scrubbed his face, pulled Cato into the office, then turned to face his brothers who looked as horrified as he did. "I brought the fucker into our home! How could I have been so blind?"

Tennessee took off running. "I've got to get to Molly and the babies!"

"They're fine, Ten!" Cato called, but he didn't wait to hear more.

"Jaxson, Phillip, you two take off and see if you can catch Eagleton. Take your guns!"

The two brothers immediately followed his instructions. Heath moved into the office and grabbed his phone. "I'll call the cops and the Dukes. God, we don't have a clue where he's taken her. You know he won't go home. He'll take her somewhere to hide her until he can get his dirty work done."

Before he could dial the number, the phone rang in his hand.

"Eagleton," Heath said as he recognized the number. "You son-of-a-bitch, bring back my sister!"

"Tut, tut," Scott said with malice in his voice. "Not going to happen. Listen to me, friend."

"I'm not your friend!" Heath shouted.

"That's what you called me when you wanted my money. Listen to me carefully, if you ever want to see your sister alive again. I want you to call the Dukes to deliver a very important message. Tell them I want a hundred million dollars and I want them to scrap their launch – immediately and permanently. I not only want them to scrap it, I want them to destroy all their components, their factory, their plans – I want it all obliterated. If they don't, I'll kill your sister. She tells me the brothers don't ever negotiate with terrorists – well, this time they need to reconsider."

Heath thought he was going to throw up. He knew the Dukes could be ruthless businessmen. "Please, Scott. Don't do this. What you're asking might be impossible. Could you kill Ryder? Could you destroy your life like this?"

"I have a life that you know nothing about. The authorities will never find me. Even if they do, I'll be where no one can touch me."

"Well, I'll find you, you son-of-a-bitch. You'll have to go to Mars to escape me? Do you hear me?!"

"I hear you making a lot of noise, McCoy. Give this number to the Dukes and tell them I await their call. I'll give them an account number to deposit the money in and I want visual evidence of the destruction of their property."

"Don't hurt my…"

The line went dead in Heath's hand.

"Oh, God – what have I done?"

* * *

"I'm glad we went to see Ellis' widow. The money we gave her will go a long way to helping those little girls have a good life." Samson felt optimistic.

"Everything else is falling into place. I've promised time and a half to everyone involved. Once Heath gets the fuel delivered, we'll be ready to rock and roll. We won't call a press conference until the last possible minute. We don't want to alert Rasputin – whoever he is – to our plan." Gideon was excited. "Let's go home. I think we can take care of the rest of this over the phone, don't you?"

"You're just anxious to get back to Ryder? Samson observed dryly.

"Well, aren't you?"

"Hell, yes! We need to call Thurgood and get him to prepare something special. We want a romantic dinner to set the stage for our proposal."

The sound of the cell phone cut off Samson's line of thought. He glanced at the screen. "It's Heath. Hello? Something wrong?"

As Samson listened, Gideon picked up on the darkest tide of emotion he'd ever felt come from his brother.

"**Fuck, no**!" Samson screamed, jerking the Lamborghini off the road. "*Fuck, no. Fuck. Fuck.* Heath, let me put you on speaker. Repeat what you just said so Gideon can hear."

"Scott Eagleton took Ryder. He's the one behind all your troubles."

Samson and Gideon looked at one another. They'd never felt so devastated. They'd never heard Heath sound so hopeless. "What does he want, Heath?"

"One hundred million dollars and for you to scrap the launch. Not only scrap the launch, but destroy everything – he wants OuterLimits to cease to exist."

"Done," Samson said flatly.

"Scott said Ryder told him that you don't negotiate with terrorists."

Gideon gave his answer. "We're not going to negotiate with the terrorist. We're going to meet his every demand. This is Ryder. There's nothing in this world we wouldn't give up for her in a heartbeat."

"I have a number for you to call to talk to Eagleton." He gave it to them. "I want to be there with you when this goes down. This is all my fault. I'm the one who invited Eagleton into our home."

"Meet us at Falconhead. We're on our way now."

"Hold on."

Samson and Gideon could hear Heath talking to someone.

"Cato told me to tell you two things. First, your man was shot, the one who came with Ryder."

"God, no," Gideon said, clutching his fists in anger. "Is he still alive?"

"I don't know, yet. Tennessee has gone to check on the folks up at the house. We were down at the office, working on the fuel transport plan. That was why all of this went down – *Fuck*!" he cried out again.

"What else?" Samson urged. "Was there something else?"

"Yea, Cato read Eagleton's lips while he was making a phone call. She thinks Eagleton took Ryder to Galveston. He's always wanted her. He's been obsessed with her for years."

"He's planning on getting out of the country!" Gideon exclaimed.

"Yes, and if he doesn't kill Ryder first, he'll take her with him." Samson slammed his palm against the steering wheel. "Okay, Heath. Change of plans. Gather whomever you trust and we'll bring our team and meet you on the island. Come to the Galveston Yacht Club on the bayside, the Gemini is docked there."

"We've got to get her back."

Heath's voice was weak with fear. Samson and Gideon understood, they felt the same way. "I won't tell you not to worry, Heath. We're worried. We love Ryder with our whole heart. What I can tell you is that we will get her back safely – anything else is unacceptable.

* * *

Samson and Gideon wasted no time. Even though their world had just crashed at their feet, they refused to give an inch. They fully intended to do what needed to be done. Even as they set out to catch their plane to take them to Galveston, they sat side by side ready to place a call to a person who was their enemy in every sense of the word.

"I want to kill him." Gideon didn't beat around the bush.

"I know the feeling," Samson agreed, "but we've got to keep our head. We need to do what this man says, but at the same time, we need to put into motion a plan to save Ryder. I don't trust this man's word."

"You know what kills me?" Gideon whispered, pain lancing through his heart.

"What?"

"We never told her we loved her. We were waiting on the right time, waiting to give her the ring." In anguish, Gideon looked at his brother. "Right now, in her heart, Ryder doesn't think we're coming for her. She thinks we won't negotiate for her release. She might expect her family to come for her, but she has no hope we will."

Samson groaned. "Don't say that. Surely she knows."

"I don't know, Samson. With all our bluster, with all our money, we've failed to make the one person we love more than anything in the world aware of her value. She's everything to us."

"Everything!" Samson repeated. "When she's back with us, when she's back in our arms – this must be our greatest priority."

Taking a few seconds to get a handle on their emotions – Gideon placed the call.

In a few seconds, there came an answer. "Rasputin, here. Is this the mighty Dukes?"

"Eagleton, we want Ryder back."

"Uh-uh, not so fast. You know my demands. Here's the account number." Scott rattled it off. "I expect one hundred million to hit there in one hour. That's your down payment. The rest – the disassembling of OuterLimits, you have twenty-four hours to set it into motion."

"You know that's impossible."

"And you have to know I mean business. I want video evidence that you are destroying rockets, capsules, computers – everything. I want you out of the commercial space travel business."

Samson looked at Gideon. "Why don't we just give it to you? Legally. Lock, stock, and barrel. You give us Ryder and we give you everything we have."

In the background, they heard a gasp.

Thank God, Eagleton had them on speakerphone. At least Ryder knew the truth. They would give everything they owned for her safe return.

Their offer seemed to stump Eagleton.

Gideon kept his eyes on Samson. They were in total agreement. "Just give us a place to make the exchange. We want Ryder and we'll give you a deed to OuterLimits. We'll walk away."

"How do I know I can trust you?"

"The same way we know if we can trust you! We don't!" Samson yelled. He swallowed, this time lowering his voice. "Look - we give you our word. The only thing more valuable than our word to us, is the woman you've stolen from our arms – Ryder McCoy."

"I'll call you back."

When the line went silent, Samson and Gideon closed their eyes in prayer.

…When the McCoys needed to rally their troops, they could raise an army. Within a few hours, men were flying into Galveston from every direction. The Highland

McCoys converged with the Tebow McCoys. Their Cajun friends – all former Seal members, together with Harley LeBlanc, a foremost bomb expert, all gathered their arsenal and set out for Texas. The Equalizers assembled, including the Texas Governor who'd just announced his candidacy for President – all super-qualified – all potentially deadly. But their secret weapon was already on the island. Equalizer Jet Foster, a Navy Seal Black Ops diver, was sitting on his pirate/treasure hunting ship, checking to find out exactly who was on the island and what ships were docked off-shore.

With him was Jet's best friend, former Intelligence guru, Micah Wolfe. "We've got this, Kyle. I've got a bead on this bad boy. The intelligence community is abuzz." Micah lounged on the deck of Jet's boat, his computer in his lap, his phone to his ear. "Eagleton, or Rasputin as he likes to call himself, is Putin's boy. And get this, my friends in Navy intelligence tell me that we have a Russian nuclear sub in the Gulf. It's lurking just off the coast of Mexico and appears to be waiting for a signal."

"What the hell?" Chancellor exclaimed. "I've got a damn nuclear sub off the coast of Texas? Do I need to mobilize the state National Guard?"

Micah sipped a colorful alcoholic drink through a straw. "Not yet. We don't want to alert them to the fact that we know they're here, not till we get Ryder back. Plus, I don't think we want to trigger an international incident. You know, back in 2012, a Russian sub armed with long-range nuclear missiles meandered all over the Gulf and we didn't know it until after they left. Thanks to that fiasco, we've kept a closer eye on the area or we wouldn't be in the position we're in today."

"God, what a mess!"

"Boss!" Jet hollered from across the way.

"Hand him the phone, Wolfe. Tell Jet I can't hear

him bellowing from Austin."

Micah handed his cell to Jet Foster. "Here, Champ, the Guv wants to talk to you."

"Boss, I just got some new info. My sources on the island tells me that Eagleton has a house down on the far end of West Beach. One of those big fuckin' mansions with a wall built around it."

"Will that be a problem?" Kyle asked calmly.

"No, I have the address. Do you want me to go get her?"

"No, I want you to wait until everyone else gets there – including me. By the time we put our plan into motion, Eagleton won't know what hit him."

* * *

"Why do you call yourself Rasputin, Scott? I don't understand." Ryder was trying to make him talk. He was making her nervous, pacing up and down the floor, walking to the window and looking out toward the pounding surf of the Gulf of Mexico. He'd brought her from the Hill Country of Texas to Galveston Island. Now, she sat in a straight back chair, her hands tied behind her back, her feet bound together. At least he hadn't gagged her – yet.

"You don't need to understand."

"Talk to me, Scott. We used to be friends."

"We were never friends!" he barked at Ryder. "I was nice to you. I asked you out. You ignored me. You treated me like shit."

Ryder frowned. "I'm sorry. I didn't really date anyone before…"

"Until you whored yourself out to two sexual deviants!" Scott slashed his hand through the air. "I'm not interested in your excuses. That ship has sailed."

"Why are you doing this, Scott? What is this

Rasputin stuff? Why are you threatening Samson and Gideon?"

Running right up to her, he screamed. "Because I can!" Shaking a finger in her face, his expression contorted with rage. "Do you know who I am? No. You never took time to care."

"Scott...please."

"I can buy and sell the Dukes. It's abhorrent to me that they think they should be the pioneers to a new world. That they should be the ambassadors to a new planet." He pounded himself on the chest. "I am the ambassador. I am the friend of Presidents and Kings. I am Rasputin. Do you know who Rasputin was?"

Ryder shook her head. "Some Russian quack who tried to save one of the Czar's kids from hemophilia?"

"No!" Scott bellowed. "Rasputin was the Royal Vizier to the Czar..."

"Oh, like Jafar in Aladdin."

Slap!

Ryder reeled from Scott's blow to her face. "No! Not some cartoon character. I am Putin's right hand. He wants the honor of reaching Mars first and I will give it to him."

"My men will come for you," Ryder spoke with certainty. What she'd heard on the phone had laid her fears and doubts to rest.

"Let them come. I welcome them. I would love to pit myself against them. I am invincible!"

"You wouldn't win."

"Like Rasputin, I have beaten the odds. They tried to kill him – he was gutted, poisoned, shot, and strangled. They finally tried to drown him beneath the ice, but he didn't drown, he died of hypothermia."

"He wasn't so tough after all, I guess. Didn't they cut off his cock?"

Slap!

Ryder wanted to cry, but she wouldn't give him the satisfaction.

"They tried to destroy me also – I walked away from a plane crash, lived through a terrorist bombing, and survived a gunshot. Like Rasputin, not even poison could harm me."

"But Rasputin was defeated and so was Jafar, I think they stuffed him in a lamp, didn't they?"

Slap!

"You will keep your whorish mouth closed!" He grabbed Ryder around the neck and began to squeeze, only the buzzing of his phone saved her life.

Scott tore himself loose and looked at his phone. A creepy smile covered his face. "Ah, sweet. I'm one hundred million dollars richer, thanks to your stooges." He shrugged. "Not that I needed the money. I just wanted to take it away from them. After all, one can never have too much money, can they?"

"Perhaps not, I think you have more money than sense, though."

Scott was just about to slap her again when his phone rang this time. "Hello?"

"You have your money and we have a preliminary deed. It's as conclusive as we can make it in this amount of time. I can send my lawyer in with it, if you're ready to make an exchange."

"Samson! Gideon! I love you!"

Slap!

"Don't you touch her!" Samson bellowed, understanding the sounds that he heard. "Let me talk to Ryder."

"No!" Scott walked to the far side of the room.

Ryder was scared. Scott was crazy. He was like a toddler with a hand grenade.

"When can we make the exchange?" Samson

pressed, realizing there was zero chance Scott was going to let him talk to Ryder. But he did know she was alive – and that she loved them. He needed to give her that same assurance more than he needed to breathe.

Scott pressed his hand to his head, a dull pain thudding behind his eyes. "Text me the contract and I'll get back to you if I think it's legit. But sign it first – sign it, so if it's good, all it will require is my signature."

"You know the law well enough to know that a contract like this has to be witnessed, it has to be notarized. The transfer of a one-hundred-billion-dollar business can't be done on Docu-sign."

"Send your lawyer! Just your lawyer to…" he repeated the address. "But if you send anyone else – she dies."

Even Ryder knew this was a mistake on Scott's part. The Dukes were nobody's fools. For the first time in hours, Ryder felt hope bloom in her heart.

CHAPTER FOURTEEN

Destry Cartwright was a man who wore many hats. A military sniper, former clerk to the Supreme Court, current Attorney General to the great state of Texas and above all, an Equalizer – he was ready and waiting to be the frontline in a daring rescue. "God, I love this kind of stuff."

"Well, don't have too much fun without us. From what we've gathered from satellite imagery, there's just three men with him. What we don't know is how the house might be booby-trapped. After all, one of these guys almost took out the Dukes with a car bomb." Micah finished affixing a wire to Destry's chest. "So, you keep your head on straight and your eyes open."

"That's right, the rest of us won't be far behind. They're going to be watching the road – but we're going to come at them from the air and the sea. They won't be looking for us there."

About that time, a door slammed open. Samson and Gideon came rushing in. "Are we ready?" They were the last to arrive. Of course, they'd had the farthest to come.

"Not quite. Almost." Micah tested the connections, making sure the microphone was working properly. "Give me and Saxon about ten minutes to make sure we've got a clear connection."

"Easy, Duke," an authoritative voice spoke from deeper in the cabin. "We're going to get this done."

"Governor." Samson stepped forward to clasp the politician's hand. "I'm so grateful you're here."

"No problem." Heath spread his hands, gesturing to a group who'd just come through the door. "We're all here." The Gemini was a big boat and it would have to be to hold the entire group. "Have we notified the local authorities on what's going down?"

The Governor waved his hand in dismissal. "Got that covered."

Gideon marveled at the group. "Ryder has many friends. Powerful friends." He saw her brothers. Heath. Tennessee. Philip. Jaxson. But there were many others.

"Gideon, Samson, I'd like for you to meet our family and friends." Heath proceeded to introduce everyone. "This is Aron, Jacob, Joseph, Isaac, and Noah McCoy, our first cousins. And this is Patrick O'Rourke, Revel Jones, Beau Leblanc and his wife Harley, our Cajun friends. Harley's talent as a bomb expert is rivaled only by Jet's. And you've met some of the Equalizers, but this is their leader Kyle Chancellor, whom I'm sure you recognize, Destry Cartwright, Saxon Abbott, Tyson Pate, Jet Foster, and last, but not least, Micah Wolfe. I won't even try to explain what all these people can do. Suffice it to say they've taken down drug cartels and serial killers. This small-time Russian mafia will be a breeze."

Samson and Gideon were suitably impressed. "I don't know how we'll ever thank you."

"No thanks necessary, they're here for Ryder." Heath's tone was still accusatory.

"I understand. Anyway, the ransom has been sent and the deed is ready. We're prepared to exchange OuterLimits for Ryder."

Heath nodded his head. When all of this was over, he was going to have to eat crow concerning these boys. He was wrong. They did love Ryder. They were suitable candidates for her hand in marriage. God, he hated the taste of crow.

"I'd like to say something," Jet spoke from the sideline. He was big, gruff, holding his automatic rifle, scruffy beard on his face. He reminded Samson of

Rambo…and Gideon.

"What's that, Champ?" Kyle asked.

"I don't think this guy is gonna exchange Ryder. I think he's planning on taking her. That vessel I told you about is moving this way. If she gets on that Russian sub, we'll have a hell of a time getting her off."

Gideon almost swallowed his tongue. "A Russian sub?"

"A Russian nuclear sub." Jet nodded. "I say we go in with guns blazing and finish these guys off like we did the drug cartel."

"I agree," Patrick O'Rourke spoke up. "But like Micah said, we need to check for bombs. There has to be some, they can't expect to defend themselves with a few guys and their guns."

"But remember," Saxon pointed out. "They're not expecting an army, not an army like we are, anyway."

"Whatever we do, let's do it soon," Gideon begged. "Every minute we leave her there, her life's in danger."

Aron McCoy stood to speak for the first time. "Kyle has a plan; he always has a plan." Everyone looked to the Governor, the least-likely politician any of them knew of. "You tell us who goes where and what we're doing when we get there. We're ready to roll."

…Back at Eagleton's beach house, Ryder wasn't feeling so well. "Can I have some water, Scott? I'm really thirsty."

"No! You don't need water where you're going."

That didn't sound good. "What do you mean? I thought I was going with you."

"I've changed my mind. I'm going to take my money and my deed and I'm headed back to Moscow. As soon as possible, we'll begin to dismantle OuterLimits and move all the assets and engineering to Russia. Then, we'll get our own spaceship headed to Mars."

"You'll never get out of here alive. I'm sure Gideon and Samson have been to the police. They probably have roadblocks set up."

Scott smiled at her sickly. "We're not leaving by the road. My friend, President Putin, has taken care of everything. My carriage awaits – a nuclear sub will be just off-shore. A boat is ready for us as soon as we get the deed in hand. We're just waiting for the Dukes' lawyer to arrive, then we're out of here."

"I thought you said you wanted to review it before you make the exchange."

He sneered at Ryder. "I am a lawyer. I'll be able to tell if it will hold up in a court of law. But…there'll be no exchange." He sighed loudly.

"What do you mean?"

What he told Ryder broke her heart. She was going to die.

* * *

About an hour later, everyone was in place. Destry would head in first, then Kyle would fly part of them over in the Duke's plane and they'd parachute in. The second wave, fittingly, would come from the sea. The Gemini was almost in place and Jet, Harley and a few others would swim in. As requested by Scott Eagleton, Destry Cartwright would be the only one to come in by land.

"Are we ready?" Samson asked for the second time that night.

"Yes, let's let Destry get in the door, then we'll start our assault." Kyle spoke to them all through his headset. "Let's let Jet and Harley lead the way, they have the equipment to detect any explosive devices. We do know we can trace Destry's steps, that path will have been cleared. Our first task will be to take out the outer guards. This will be Boris Anatoly and Leonid Oleg. Keep your eyes open, though. There may be support personnel there that we don't know about. Part of the house is concrete; we can't be sure what is behind those walls."

The next ten minutes was radio silence. The plane was circling; the ship was in the right position and Destry's car arrived at the gate. "Hello, I'm Ben Matlock and I'm here to deliver some paperwork to Scott Eagleton from Samson and Gideon Duke."

"Get out and let me pat you down. Can't let you in if you're armed."

Destry grimaced. He wasn't armed, he was wired – he also stunk. A trick he'd learned in the service. "Sure, but pardon me. I was out drinking all night and I didn't get time to take a shower."

As soon as he got out of the car, the guard stepped back. The stench of BO and stale liquor was almost unbearable. "Sorry, fella."

The guard waved him on. "Just get outta here."

Destry smiled and continued on his way. "I'm in."

After passing through one other check point at the door, he was inside and being led to Scott Eagleton. "Looks to be a piece of cake."

"All right, phase two," Kyle announced and men began dropping from the plane, floating soundless through the sky as several amphibious personnel jumped from the Gemini and swam toward shore.

Inside, Ryder watched Destry Cartwright as he spoke legal jargon to Scott Eagleton. He was wearing a disguise and some awful smelling…something. If she hadn't been feeling so hopeless, she would've smiled. The glasses were a nice touch, but the wig was a little over the top. As she listened to him lay out what Samson and Gideon were giving up, she couldn't not speak up. "Tell them not to do this. Tell them this isn't necessary. Tell them not to come, if they're planning on it. It's not worth it, he's not going to let me go."

Destry tried not to have any reaction. "I only do what I'm told, ma'am."

"Shut up!" Scott stalked across the room and slapped her again. "One more word out of you and your surprise comes sooner rather than later."

Ryder almost...almost told him to go fuck himself. But she didn't want Destry to be hurt in the blast.

Everyone on the team heard what Ryder said. "What did she mean?" Jacob asked as he shrugged off the parachute.

"There's a trap," Revel answered. "Probably a bomb if I had my guess."

"Harley will handle it," Beau assured them. "And she'll come through with flying colors. She has to, we have a new baby at home that needs her almost as much as I do."

Samson shook his head. "I can't believe you're risking yourself and your wife. I am so honored and thankful."

"Hey, this is what we do. We're family." Beau pulled down his night-vision goggles, ready to rumble.

There was another ten minutes or so of silence while everyone got into place. "What's our status?" Kyle asked.

"There's no trip wires, no IED's that we can see. I don't think the perimeter is booby-trapped." Harley reported.

"I don't like this," Gideon muttered. "Something doesn't feel right."

"Let's go with it. Team One, you take out the guard at the gate. Team Two, you come over the wall and take out the guard at the door."

Kyle's instructions were followed to the letter. Samson, who was with Team One, held his breath as they came through the gate. He was close to Ryder, she'd be in his arms soon, and that was all that mattered.

Gideon, who was with Team Two, was first through the door and into the house. He held his breath, expecting men with guns to pop out at any moment. All he wanted to do was run through the halls, shouting her name, but he held back – determined to follow orders. This was too important for him to mess up with his knee-jerk reactions.

"All right – Team One, go through the first floor – room by room. Team Two – take the second floor – go."

Methodically – room by room they searched the beach house. Experts. Soldiers. Professionals. All with a single, solitary, goal in mind. Rescue Ryder McCoy.

"Kyle, we've got a problem," Patrick O'Rourke spoke up, at the same time Jet Foster chimed in.

"Kyle, we've got a problem."

"Shit. Talk to me," Kyle spoke from his post on the Gemini.

It took a few seconds for Samson's brain, who was with Patrick, to register what he was seeing. "Oh, my Lord God." The whole place was set to blow.

Patrick didn't lose his cool. "We've got a tunnel beneath the beach house. We're about to check it out, but I presume it goes to the beach. And looking though this thermal imager, someone just came through here only moments ago."

"Go after them, it has to be Eagleton. Foster, can you confirm this?"

Even as Jet was answering, Gideon was moving across the floor to Ryder, who was tied to a chair.

"Roger that, Destry is down, he's alive, but Eagleton is not here."

"We've got to get everyone out – now!" Kyle ordered in a commanding voice. "Jet, you and Revel go with Patrick – find Eagleton. There's several ships anchored out here, I presume one of them is here to take him to the sub. But unless he's an Olympic swimmer, you should be able to catch him."

"What about Ryder?" Samson shouted over the headset.

"I have her. I have her," Gideon spoke as he knelt in front of her. Her precious face was bruised. "You're safe, darling, we've got you. You're safe." He bent over to hug her, but she stopped him.

"Don't. Please don't."

Gideon froze. "We came as soon as we could, Princess. I'm so sorry this happened to you."

She lifted her eyes to his. They were full of tears. "I'm so sorry you lost your company, your money. For me. For nothing."

"Shhhh, everything is okay."

"How is she?" Samson came rushing up. He didn't even wait; he ran behind her to undo the ropes.

"No! Don't! The chair is wired. If I get up, if my weight shifts, it's going to blow."

"Fuck!" Gideon shouted.

"I love you, I love you both so much. I want you to know that I'd do it all again. You were worth it, you were worth it all," she told them, her words coming out fast, punctuated by sobs.

"I love you, Ryder McCoy, more than anything." Samson needed to put her mind at ease. "We aren't going to let you die. We won't allow it."

"I love you, Ryder McCoy, more than the whole world and the universe beyond," Gideon cradled her cheek. "We'll get this damn bomb off this chair. We have help."

Harley came up behind them. "There's no time." She checked her watch. "The bombs in the basement are set to go off in six minutes. There's more of them than I can diffuse. We've got to get out of here."

"We're not leaving her!" Gideon screamed.

"We'll stay with her," Samson said, not a doubt in his mind. "I'm not leaving her alone."

Heath and her brothers came through the door. "Pull a rabbit out of your hat, Governor!" Heath shouted to Kyle.

Harley went to her knees, examining the bomb affixed to the bottom of the chair. "I can't cut the wires, this one needs to be frozen. I need liquid nitrogen."

"There's no time," Samson whispered. "No time."

Harley held up her hand. "Let's get her out of here."

"What's the plan, Harley?" Kyle asked over the headset.

"Pick up the chair and carry her out, but it's got to be done slowly and evenly...and the clock is ticking. Kyle, have someone get some liquid nitrogen and meet me outside in the empty lot across the street."

"All right. Listen up. One person carries her out, the rest clear the way, then get the hell out of the way. This is a one-man job."

Heath spoke up, "I'll do it."

The other brothers spoke up, all volunteering.

"No, this is our place. Our honor," Gideon said calmly and evenly.

Samson agreed. "Yes, our privilege. This is a two-man job."

Ryder's heart was so full of love, it broke. "If you two get killed, I'll never forgive you."

...Tick-tock. Tick-tock. Gideon's heart beat in the same rhythm as the damn ticking clock. Tick-tock. Tick-tock.

He and Samson moved in tandem, each carrying two legs of the chair that held their hope – their future – their life. "Don't you worry, darling. We're going to make it."

One-step. Two-steps. Easy. Easy. "You're damn

right we're going to make it."

"Three minutes. How's it going?" Kyle's voice sounded in their ear.

"Halfway down the stairs, then out the door," Gideon spoke with confidence. There was only one way this could end. Only one way he would allow it to end.

"What about your money? Your company?" Ryder whispered.

Tick-tock. Tick-tock. "To hell with the money. To hell with the company. We don't care about it. You are all that matters," Samson said, feeling for the next place to put his foot.

Ryder wanted to cry. She wanted to scream. "I don't want it to end this way."

"You want me to tell you how it's going to end?" Gideon spoke to her gently, tenderly. "You're going to sleep in our bed tonight and tomorrow will be the first day of the rest of our lives."

* * *

Across the road, a safe distance away, Ryder's brothers were slowly going crazy. "Where are they?"

"How much time do they have?" Jaxson voice tore from his throat. "I can't believe I ignored her, punished her by not speaking to her. What kind of a fuckin' fool am I?

"One minute," Harley said, evenly. "They'll make it. You don't know how long sixty seconds can be when a bomb's ticking."

"Not fuckin' long enough." Philip stood with his heart in his throat, standing and waiting to see their sister again.

"Let's go back, let's just go back in after her." Ten started to cross the road, but Micah stepped in.

"No, you need to have faith in Ryder's men. If we

ran over there now, we'd just get in the way. She has to be brought out slowly and evenly, our presence isn't going to change anything – one way or the other."

Heath squatted down, his hat in his hands. Closing his eyes, he offered a prayer.

Dear Lord, this is Heath. I know I don't talk to you often enough for you to remember who I am, but this is Heath McCoy and I'm coming on my knees with my heart in my hands. Please, Lord, save my sister. She's one of the best people you ever created. I don't know what I can offer you in trade, that you'd want. My love. My devotion. My faithfulness. And God, if you'll just save her, I'll be better. I won't be such an as...astounding jerk. Please. Well, that's all I got to say. Talk to you later.

As Heath stood, the house in front of them blew. Every person in their little army gasped and cried out. The explosion was so loud and so jarring that it shook the ground where they were standing. "Oh, God, oh God." Jaxson began to cry.

"Fuck it all!" Philip screamed, the profanity pouring from his mouth so unlike him.

"Why? Why?" Ten yelled. How could this be?

Heath couldn't breathe. He couldn't cry. He couldn't look away from the rising flames and the billowing smoke. It seemed if he could just stare hard enough...he'd see... "Look! Look!" he yelled. "There they are! They're alive! Thank God! They're alive!"

...Once they stepped through the cloud of smoke, tears began to run down Gideon's cheeks. "We made it. We made it."

Samson urged his brother on. "Easy, we aren't there yet. Let's make it across the road and set her down easy so Harley can work her magic."

Ryder began to cough and the men had to stop and hold the chair still, despite the jerking of her little body.

"Oh, baby, baby," Gideon didn't know what else to say, all he could do was make his body a rock so he could keep her alive.

Tyson ran up to them with a small portable oxygen tank. "Here, breathe."

Ryder took it, inhaling the clear air.

Samson and Gideon continued their journey, the few remaining steps until they were free and clear of the smoke and debris.

Once they had Ryder on the ground, the rest went quickly. Harley sprayed the bomb with liquid nitrogen, then cut it from the chair. A collective sigh of relief filtered through the crowd when the bomb was off and placed in a special container for transportation to police headquarters.

"Get her off that damn chair," Gideon demanded.

Heath and Micah cut her loose and she briefly hugged her brother, but in the next breath she was in the arms of Samson and Gideon. "I love you two, so much!"

"We love you too, baby." Gideon hugged her so tight she could barely breathe.

"We love you more than life, Ryder," Samson blanketed her from the back, kissing the side of her face.

"I can't believe you two did that – you risked your life for me!" She was still shaking, the horror just now hitting home.

"Every time," Gideon promised. "We'll be there for you – every time."

After that, Ryder doled out hugs and kisses. She was so happy to see her brothers, to see her friends. The police came and she had to make a statement, but the presence of the Governor and the Equalizers made the process go smoothly.

Jet, Patrick, and Revel came from the direction of the beach. They were leading a very bedraggled, very angry

Scott Eagleton. "Damn you! Damn you all to hell! I'll get my revenge! Don't think this is over, because it's not."

No one even dignified his outburst with a response.

When it was Harley's turn to wish Ryder well, she whispered to her. "I have this power. When I touch things or people, I get these images. I want you to know how much you're loved. There are very few people in the world who will ever know such love and devotion as you have been granted – not in one person, but in two. You are doubly blessed." Harley kissed her cheek. "I know. I can recognize this gift you've been granted because I have it myself."

Ryder thanked the woman who'd done so much to save her life. "We're two very lucky women, very lucky."

When Harley stepped away, Heath was waiting to speak to her, Samson, and Gideon. "Next week is Thanksgiving. I can't think of a better reason to give thanks than what we've witnessed here tonight." He shook the men's hands. "This is an official invitation to dinner. Come hungry and come ready to play football." He winked at the newest members of his family, because that's how he thought of them now. "I just think you ought to know - we cheat."

* * *

"Don't you want to know where we're going?" Samson asked as the cab they were riding in traveled down Galveston's seawall.

"We aren't going home or to the yacht?" she asked, murmuring against his shoulder. Gideon's hand rested on her knee and her hand held his arm in a grip that hadn't lessened since they left the site of the explosion. She was holding tight to both men.

"No, home is too far and we're not staying in the yacht until that Russian sub is as far away from us as the east is to the west." Gideon pointed ahead. "Samson and I thought we'd stay a couple of nights at the San Luis Resort. We've got a little unfinished business to attend to."

"Business?" She made a sad little face. "Will you get your company and your money back?"

Samson tapped her on the nose. "Yea, I'm sure the lawyers already have everything all lined up."

Ryder let out a long breath of relief. "I'm glad. I didn't want to be the reason you lost everything."

Gideon put his hands around her waist, picked her up, and sat her in his lap. "Let's get something straight – for the last time. The company and the money are irrelevant."

"That's right," Samson agreed, taking her other hand and twining their fingers together. "Compared to you, anything else is immaterial. We can always make more money, there is only one you."

She bowed her head, the tears overtaking her. "I was so afraid."

Gideon cradled her. "I know. It's over. It's over."

"I was so afraid you'd die for me." Ryder almost choked over the words.

"Why would we want to live without you?" Samson asked as the cab came to a stop in the circular drive of the hotel.

"I would want you to. This has just been crazy." Her mind was still muddled, but she needed to know more. "How's Laramie? Did he make it?"

"He had to have surgery, but he's alive. He'll have some rehab time, but he'll be fine," Gideon rubbed her back as they entered the hotel.

Ryder waited while her men booked the penthouse suite. Looking down at her clothes, she had to admit she wasn't dressed well enough to stay at a homeless shelter, much less the penthouse suite of a nice hotel.

"Don't worry about your clothes," Samson said, noticing she was staring down at her soiled and torn clothing.

"Why?" she asked, following them to the elevator. "I look like a ragamuffin."

"Because you aren't going to be wearing any," Gideon whispered with a twinkle in his eye. "And if you do, we'll provide. We'll always provide you with what you need."

"Thank you." She liked the idea of that. "I'm sure looking forward to a bath. I smell almost as bad as Destry. How is he, by the way?"

"He'll be okay. Probably has a concussion. He wasn't shot, just pistol-whipped." Samson pressed the button for the penthouse.

The ride couldn't be over fast enough for Ryder. She felt that if she could just take a shower, she'd wash all of these bad memories away. "What kind of business do you have to do tonight? Will it take long?"

"You'll see," Gideon promised. "You'll see."

…A little while later, Ryder felt like a new woman. A shower was just what she'd needed. After she toweled off, she was glad to see one of the men had found her something to wear, a pretty blue dress, too pretty to just lounge around in, but she didn't care. Ryder pulled it over her head gratefully.

The penthouse suite was amazing, offering a breathtaking view of the ocean. While Samson and Gideon took care of whatever business they had, she was going to stand on the balcony like Kate Winslet on the bow of the Titanic – arms spread, thrilled to be alive.

"Samson! Gideon!" she called out, coming around the corner. "I'm here!"

"We're waiting, Princess."

When she found them, the scene she beheld took her breath away. A table was set with beautiful china. There were candles in the center of it and all around the room. A bottle of champagne stood at the ready. But what caught her eye the most – were her two men, dressed in black tie and tails. "What's all of this?"

"Our unfinished business." Samson held out his hand. "Making you ours."

Placing her hand in his, she said simply, "I am yours. I belong to both of you. Completely."

"We need to make it official," Gideon said, going down on one knee.

Samson followed suit. "We don't want to wait one more minute without putting our ring on your finger."

Ryder's knees went weak. "You're asking…"

"Well, we'd rather just tell you," Samson laughed, "but we'll do whatever it takes." He held up a ring, a beautiful ring.

"Oh, it looks just like my necklace," she said in wonder, her hand reaching out so they could place the ring on her finger. "I don't know if my heart can hold this much love."

As tears flowed from her eyes, Gideon kissed them away. "I think the love's overflowing, sweetheart. So, will you marry us?"

"Will you complete us, Ryder? Will you be ours?"

Ryder sank down on her knees between them, her arms going around their necks, pulling them close. "Yes, yes! I want nothing more! I want to belong to the two of you forever."

As the waves crashed to the shore – as the stars shone in the sky – three hearts became one.

Slowly, purposefully, they undressed themselves, then they tenderly undressed her. No words were needed. No words were spoken. With grateful hands and seeking lips, they kissed and caressed her entire body. Not an inch was overlooked. While one worshiped her mouth, another suckled at her breast. When one kissed her between the thighs, she rode the other to heaven and back. Before their night was over, she'd made love with her men in every way possible…but one.

* * *

"We've gathered together to ask the Lord's blessing." Christian McCoy stood to offer grace. The family had watched with pride and love as their father walked on his own two feet for the first time in over a decade.

"This bounteous table is full of food, for which we are grateful. And sitting around this table are the people who we all love. Our family."

"Amen!" Heath said, happier than he could ever remember being.

"I'd like to propose a toast." He held up his glass. "We've had quite a year and much to be thankful for."

Everyone lifted their glasses as the elder McCoy gave his blessing.

"To Heath, my oldest and to his beautiful wife, Cato - I'm thankful you found one another and I look forward to seeing my third grandchild. Thank you for taking care of this family so well and so faithfully." Heath and Cato lifted their glasses in salute.

"To Tennessee and Molly. How grateful we are that you two found one another again. How lost we would be without those two precious girls you've given us - Ava and Ella. I wish all four of you a lifetime of joy and happiness." Ten lifted his glass and Molly wiped tears from her eyes.

"To Philip, the only child who inherited my amazing brain."

Everyone laughed – except Philip. He raised his glass a little higher in agreement.

"Philip, I'm thankful justice was served and you are with us tonight. I never want to be separated from my children, not even for one day."

"To Jaxson, my child of the land. You inherited your mother's heart. She valued the earth beneath her feet more than money in the bank. I'm thankful for your strength, we all depend on you to keep the ranch – and us, going."

Jaxson raised his glass and nodded to everyone as they seconded their father's sentiments.

"To my beautiful Pepper, you are the light of our lives. You give us laughter and you give us sunshine. I am thankful for your smile. Congratulations on your graduation. I can't wait to see what you accomplish."

Pepper blew her father a kiss.

"To Ryder, my beautiful daughter. My good girl. How thankful we are than you are…" He choked up. "How thankful we are that you're alive. And to the men who sit on either side of you. Samson. Gideon. We owe you an eternal debt of gratitude and we want you to know that we are thankful for you, not just for saving our Ryder…we are thankful for your character, for your friendship, and for the beautiful way you love our Ryder. Welcome to the family."

Everyone clapped and Ryder beamed happily.

They thought Christian was through, but he surprised them. "I have just a couple more things to say. One, is that I want you to appreciate your family. I was separated from my brother until it was almost too late. I know it was a surprise to you when you found out that Sebastian and I knew of one another, that we had met – secretly. We didn't get to spend too much time together before he and Sue were taken from us." He stopped and reached back for his chair. "I think I need to sit down. Sue found your grandmother's Bible in the attic of Tebow Ranch. Inside that Bible was my name and a note, a note asking for the promise that if we found it and found one another that we would keep their secret. I can't say I understand it, I can't fathom how two people can turn their backs on someone so completely that they don't even want their own children to remember them. But…that was her wishes. Sebastian chose to ignore them. He came to me – not once but three times, and we were just about to bring the two families together when he and Sue drowned in that tragic flood. This Christmas, I'm going to make a special announcement, so I'm asking all of you to plan on spending Christmas at Tebow Ranch with the other branch of our family. I've been waiting to give you some news for a long time."

When they all began to talk at once, he held up his hand. "No, no, there's no use to ask – I'm waiting until Christmas to tell you the rest. My surprise isn't quite…ready yet. But I do want to tell you what I've learned from this experience."

They all leaned in, watching the old man whom they loved with all their hearts.

"Family is everything. Let's never let life come between us. Let's promise to never get so angry that we push one another away. If we commit ourselves to loving one another, nothing will ever defeat us."

He raised his glass and the family broke out in applause, then they rose to their feet, giving their patriarch a standing ovation.

"Oh, one more thing." He stood again and held his hand out to Olivia, who sat on his right. "I have another announcement." Christian paused for effect. "Olivia and I are getting married!"

After that – everything just dissolved into laughter,

congratulations, and good times. Ryder kept shifting in her seat, trying to find a comfortable spot.

"Something bothering you, Princess?" Gideon asked, in all innocence.

"No. What could be bothering me?" She squirmed a little more.

Our girl can't be still, Samson.

"Ryder, do you want a cushion?"

Ryder slapped Samson and Gideon on the knees closest to her. "You two be quiet! I don't want everyone to know."

"Know what?" Gideon persisted, enjoying the heck out of the moment.

"That I'm wearing a butt plug!" she said – just a little too loud.

Luckily, no one heard her – except Cato, who was reading lips again. She busted out laughing and Ryder had to give her the evil eye to make her be quiet.

"Just wait until we get home," Samson whispered in her ear, provocatively.

Ryder stood. "You two need to go play football with the other guys."

"Okay, okay." Gideon held up his hands. "We'll go – but later, later you're all ours."

They didn't get very far. Philip came through the house, rounding everyone up. "Picture! We need to take the family Christmas card picture!"

A huge wave of déjà vu hit Ryder. This was once a moment she dreaded, now it was about to become one of her most precious memories.

For as the family assembled, while Philip set the automatic timer, while they all arranged themselves and yelled the word – "Cheese!" Ryder wore the biggest smile of all.

For the picture included all the Highland McCoys.

The whole family.

Even Ryder…and her two men.

CHAPTER FIFTEEN
EPILOGUE

Ryder's wedding day was perfect. Two grooms. Two ceremonies. And one very happy bride.

She really hadn't given the actual wedding much thought. Some women obsessed over the day itself – over the ceremony, the dress, the flowers…the pomp and circumstances.

Ryder just obsessed over her men. She didn't care how or where she married them.

She just wanted to be – Mrs. Ryder Duke.

The first ceremony took place at the neighborhood church, well attended with all their family and friends. The chapel was full and many people came out of curiosity.

But the curious found nothing amiss.

Dressed in a beautiful white gown, surrounded by her sisters and her brothers, Ryder married Samson Duke.

Their best man was one special guy. Gideon.

The second ceremony took place at Falconhead. It was attended by family only, and a few very close friends. Kali's husband, Honi, married them in an ancient ceremony, blessing them with a special blessing:

This is the day for which you have longed. Love has come to you. What you were seeking, now you have found. Someone to share your days, someone to share your joy. You three are now one. Today is your wedding day.

As Ryder stood between her two men, they each placed a lei around her neck, and she placed one around each of theirs.

Honi explained the meaning to all assembled. "Leis are a symbol of love. With its handpicked flowers, each blossom is twined to the others with love, a reflection of how your own lives will begin to weave together."

Samson had given Ryder a ring in the first ceremony, but in this one, they would all exchange a ring. Leilani brought up a wooden bowl and gave it to Ryder. Kona and Solomon gave Samson and Gideon a conch shell filled with water from the ocean. Honi took a ti leaf and dipped it into each man's conch shell, then he placed it in the wooden bowl. "The ring, by nature of its shape, is the perfect symbol of eternity. The circle has no beginning, nor has it an end. These rings will symbolize your devotion and commitment to one another from this day forward."

Ryder took the rings from the bowl and placed one on Samson's finger and one on Gideon's. They, in turn, each placed a narrow gold band on her finger to rest atop the engagement ring.

Gideon spoke first. "With this ring, I promise to grow with you. I promise to build you a world of love. I promise to listen to you and cherish you for all the days ahead."

Samson spoke next. "I promise from this day forward that you shall never walk alone. My heart will be your sanctuary and my arms shall be your home."

Ryder began to cry. "With these rings, I thee wed." She laughed. "Both of *thees*." Gazing at the precious rings on her finger, she told them what was in her heart. "We will feel no rain, for we will shelter one another. We will feel no cold, for we shall keep each other warm. We shall never be lonely, for we have one another. We are three, who shall live as one."

Honi joined their hands, Ryder's between the two of theirs. "By the power vested in me, I now pronounce you husbands and wife. You may kiss the bride." When they both made a move toward their bride, he laughed. "One at a time, please."

Ryder kissed Samson, then she kissed Gideon, then she kissed them both again.

Leilani cried, while Solomon and Kona looked on with pride. Ryder's own family clapped with joy. Pepper was her maid of honor at both ceremonies, but at the last one, she sang for Ryder. Pepper didn't sing often, but when she did the angels cried. She sang an old favorite of Ryder's, Elvis Presley's *Blue Hawaii*.

At the end of the day, when everyone else had gone home, Ryder and her two men stood at the top of the tower. From this vantage point, they could see all of Falconhead and beyond, they could see Highlands.

This was their home.

"Are you ready to go to bed, love?" Samson asked.

"Yes." She turned to Gideon. "Are you ready to go to bed?"

"I am." He swept her up in his arms while Samson led the way.

A trinity of passion, a trinity of love.

Three was Ryder's favorite number.

SECRET EPILOGUE – Shhhh…

Ryder was delirious with pleasure. Samson and Gideon were taking her higher than they ever had before. Her breasts were swollen from their kisses; and they'd feasted between her thighs until she screamed in delight.

And now…

"We're going to take you together, sweetheart. Are you ready?"

"God, yes, I'm ready. I've worn that little red…"

"Shhhh," Gideon laughed, putting his hand over her mouth. "Such language."

Arranging Ryder on her side, they took their places – one in the front, one in the back.

She placed her leg on top of Samson's as he slid his throbbing cock into her pussy. "Oh, that feels so good. I'll never get used to this, it just gets better and better."

Gideon pressed against her back, kissing her shoulder. "That's because we love you more and more every day." With the greatest care and the utmost gentleness, he eased his aching cock into her backside.

"Oh, sweet heavens," she cried, feeling Gideon push into the place they'd been carefully preparing for weeks. She reached back and grasped his thigh as he worked his way past the tight ring of muscles.

"Are you okay?" Gideon whispered, his eyes closing in ecstasy. "You're so tight, I might pass out from the pleasure.

"I feel so full, so complete." Ryder just gave herself over to the experience. She was right where she wanted to be, between her men. Surrounded. Protected. Loved. As they moved within her, the feeling was so right. She pressed her face into Samson's chest, while Gideon feathered kisses on her neck and shoulders. "I won't last, this feels too wonderful," she gasped, her body tingling, ecstasy radiating out from her sex, to her nipples – to her toes.

As they moved in tandem, loving their woman, the breaking news on the television announced that the Ryder-V had made a successful landing on Mars. History had been made. The Dukes had gone where no man had gone before.

"Are you cumming, sweetheart?" Gideon held her tight, his own release only seconds away."

"Oh, I am, I am!" she cried. "Come with me, Samson! Come with me, Gideon!" They met her sweet demands, giving her everything they had, all the love she would ever need.

For long moments after, they lay together, their hearts beating as one. Finally, Ryder sighed. "Whew, that was intense! I can't believe I was afraid. I loved it. I don't know why I couldn't just trust you two to take care of me."

"We'll always take care of you, Ryder," Samson said, staring into her big, blue eyes. "Always," Gideon vowed.

Ryder's surrender to love was complete.

THE END

Sign up for Sable's Newsletter
http://eepurl.com/qRvyn

Thunderbird:
Hell Yeah! (Equalizers)

Soulmates. Twin souls. Two people destined to be together. Their journey to love is never an easy one, but when they meet – their hearts beat only for one another.

Kyle Chancellor is a hero, an honest to God hero. After winning the Heisman, he turns down a lucrative career as a professional football player to fight in Afghanistan. Not many know he enlisted because his heart was broken. When his time is up, Kyle comes home to form the Equalizers with the members of former Seal Team 7, they band together to fight battles for those who cannot fight for themselves.

Hannah Montenegro is a woman who has sacrificed her life to help her family, never knowing the joys and freedom a young girl should enjoy. She lives in constant fear of being discovered in a country where she has no citizenship and no hope for the future.

But fate has a plan…the night Kyle comes back to Texas, they meet in a bar where he is drowning his sorrows and she is spreading her wings to learn how to fly. From the moment they touch, the heat between them is undeniable. But unfortunate circumstances separate them and neither dares dream they will see one another again.

Kyle is from a powerful Texas family. Because of his work with the Equalizers, his stance on stem-cell research and internet security, he is the only one surprised to find the people of the Lone Star state want him to run for Governor. Many get behind him, including the McCoys. But the one person he wants at his side eludes him.

Hannah is always on his mind. From the beginning

their relationship is complicated, but when she comes back into his life, he grabs onto her with both hands. Politics, a sex tape, immigration issues and a baby complicates their pathway to happiness. But Kyle is the Thunderbird and Hannah is his soulmate in the truest sense of the word. Their journey to love is one you'll never forget.

A modern day Cinderella story with a twist...

Burning Love :
Hell Yeah! (Cajuns)

Beau's passion burns hot for Harley Montoya. When he discovers that the woman who has enflamed his libido is the girl he fell in love with so long ago in a runaway shelter, he is overcome with joy. But Harley - or Nada as he knew her - has been burned by tragedy. They both live lives full of adventure. He builds custom weaponry and owns a reptile preserve, and she is an EOD expert - Harley defuses bombs for a living. But nothing is more explosive than the love they share.

Beau is determined to show Harley that he is worthy of her trust and that he is willing to protect her from anything that would cause her harm. But Harley has a mad-man on her trail and she can't walk away from her responsibilities. Bombs, alligators, haunted plantations and Louisiana lore spice up their life, and danger and ghosts from their past threatens to tear them apart - but nothing can put out the white-hot flames of their Burning Love.

One Man's Treasure:
Hell Yeah! (Equalizers)

Jet is a hero—Special Forces, an Equalizer, a motorcycle riding MMA fighter who is part pirate and all man. No one messes with Jet.

He is formidable—the tall, dark, and deadly type.

In One Man's Treasure, he's on a quest for gold. Jet travels to Mexico to fight a challenger before he sails the Sirena to bring up a fortune from the sunken Spanish galleon, San Miguel. As usual, Jet is in control, master of his destiny. Until...

Jet meets Sami.

Sami waits tables at a club in Veracruz. Jet can't help but notice the slight, shy bartender. It angers him when customers give Sami a hard time.

Only problem—Jet assumes Sami is a boy.

Sami is actually Samantha. She's come to Mexico to find healing and the truth about what happened to her best friend. When she has to leave town fast, she stows away on Jet's boat.

Imagine his surprise when he finds Sami...and then discovers she's a woman!

Beneath a silvery moon, Jet watches a mermaid play in the sea and discovers that

One Man's Treasure can be more than diamonds and gold.

One Man's Treasure is love.

Forget Me Never:
Hell Yeah! (Cajuns)

Some truly lucky people experience a love so great that nothing can separate them. Distance, misunderstandings or even death are not powerful enough to stop the longing and the hunger and the desire to be together. Patrick loves Savannah. He is a Marine who faces danger on a daily basis and his greatest fear is to be forgotten.

Savannah loves Patrick. Because of the circumstances of her birth, she has grown up never knowing what it is like to be touched or hugged or accepted by anyone. The haunting mists of Louisiana, the ravaging horrors of war, and the remnants of an ancient disease will try to pull them apart, until their destiny draws them together and they discover a love so perfect that it will last forever.

The Key to Micah's Heart:
Hell Yeah! (Equalizers)

Micah Wolfe is one cocky, sexy, son-of-a-gun. He wears many hats–former intelligence officer, Equalizer, rancher, and a secret career that's about to become public knowledge–erotic writer Don Juan. To most he seems like an open book: flirtatious, audacious, and devil-may-care. But there's a side of Micah that he keeps locked away. He's been hurt, suffered loss, closed away parts of his heart so no one will have the power to hurt him again. But the winds of change are blowing…

Madison Fellows is at the end of her rope. For every step forward she gains, life knocks her back two. She can't even stay in her own apartment because she doesn't feel safe from her flighty mother's abusive husband. But sometimes the storms in life push us to the perfect place at the perfect time–Cinderella meets the man of her dreams when she least expects him. Madison runs to a homeless shelter where Micah is volunteering. Seeing her struggle to protect what little she has, he loans her a simple item that will become an unlikely symbol of their love. A lock. An ordinary lock.

Micah has no shortage of beautiful women; he attracts them like flowers draw bees. But there's something different about Madison–she's real, she's sweet and he fast becomes addicted to her taste. Join them on their journey of love fraught with adventure, intrigue and steamy to-die-for sex. The quintessential bachelor meets the woman he can't forget–the woman who'll hold The Key To Micah's Heart.

You Are Always on My Mind
Hell Yeah! (Cajuns)

We all like to think we have a soulmate. Unfortunately for some of us, we miss them, passing unseen like two ships in the night. Revel and Harper were among the lucky ones, they knew without a shadow of a doubt that they were meant for one another. In a perfect world, they would've enjoyed a 'happily ever after'. But this isn't a perfect world.

Harper is haunted by her past, a past so tragic and so unthinkable that she can't even imagine confessing it to Revel. And she knows from past experience, that when he learns the shameful truth about her – nothing will be the same. So, to protect him, she walks away.

Harper underestimated Revel's love for her. From the moment she disappeared, he set out to bring her home. Their journey to love is one fraught with ghosts from the past, both real and imagined, and a demon from their present who is intent on making sure she has no future. But those ghosts and demons have never met a hero like Revel Lee. He is determined to give Harper exactly what she needs...until Harper realizes that all she needs is him.

If I Can Dream:
Hell Yeah!

The moment Tennessee McCoy lays eyes on Molly Reyes sitting astride a horse in the desert sun, love hits him like a bolt of lightning from out of the blue. She is his soulmate, his other half. They speak the same language, they want the same things. Their attraction is complete, the passion they share nearly consumes them. Knowing she is meant to be his, Ten can't wait to make her his bride. The future seems bright until happiness slips through their fingers like grains of sand.

When all seems hopeless, sometimes all we have left is our dreams. Ten can only believe what his eyes can see, what his ears can hear. Molly can't seem to find the words to make him understand that she would rather lose her soul than betray him. Now both Tennessee and Molly must learn to place their faith in one another, to hold fast to love and trust their hearts.

Their journey back to love will be one you'll never forget.

Because I Said So
A Hell Yeah!/ Texas Heroes Crossover

This book will break your heart…then mend it back together again.

BECAUSE I SAID SO crosses the world of the TEXAS HEROES with the beloved characters of Hell Yeah! to teach the eternal lesson that everyone deserves a second chance at love.

As far as Brodie Walton is concerned, his life was over the day his beloved fiancé was killed in a senseless mass shooting. He doesn't deserve happiness. He doesn't even know how to go on. To give his life meaning, he seeks to save others as a first responder, so their loved ones won't face the sorrow that he lives with each day. His plan seems to be coming together…until he meets his new partner.

Shane Wilder jerks the rug out from under Brodie Walton, sending him reeling – awakening feelings and emotions that he has no desire to experience again. This baptism of fire brings out the worst in him. He lashes out at her, when all he really wants to do is hold her close and never let her go.

Shane has been through the emotional wringer herself. After her divorce from an unfaithful husband, she's sworn off men…until she meets her handsome, cantankerous boss. When Shane discovers why he's thornier than a bramble bush, she sets out to show Brodie he has a right to be happy, she wants nothing more than to give him a reason to live.

Yes, sometimes…Love Hurts.

And sometimes, it's the only thing that will save you.

T-R-O-U-B-L-E:
Texas Heat

Trouble comes calling on Kyler Landon. He falls hard and fast for his beautiful, mysterious neighbor after she saves him from a rattlesnake attack. The sexual tension mounts between them with each sensual encounter, but he soon realizes that Cooper has been hurt and is leery of men. So, he sets out to teach her that a real man can be gentle, loving, and sexy as hell.

Trouble seems to follow Cooper, and Ky makes it his mission to protect her from her past. Kyler would move heaven and earth to keep her in his bed and in his life.

A Breath of Heaven:
El Camino Real

Cade and Abby have a history. Years ago they were in love. Undeclared and unrequited, Cade waited until Abby was old enough for him to declare his love. Abby wanted nothing more than she wanted Cade.

But something happened.

Abby pushed Cade away and he never knew why. Since then, sparks fly when they're together. Antagonizing one another has become their favorite sport. The only problem is… it's all a front. They bicker because they both want the same thing – each other. A wedding brings them together and Cade is determined to learn Abby's secret. He'll do whatever it takes to win her love.

Meet the King Family of El Camino Real – five brothers, one sister and a legacy as big as Texas.

Sable Hunter's
Hell Yeah! Kindle World
has launched!

http://sablehunter.com/hell-yeah-kindle-world.html

Join The Hell Yeah! Kindle World Facebook Group
https://www.facebook.com/groups/1730952817180627/

Hell Yeah!: Man of My Heart
by Desiree Holt
http://amzn.to/2bkwWCr

Hell Yeah!: Until There Was You
by Ciana Stone
http://amzn.to/2aYEJDr

Hell Yeah!: Cadillac Cowboy
by Cynthia D'Alba
http://amzn.to/2bkuQSU

Hell Yeah!: Saddle and a Siren
by Randi Alexander
http://amzn.to/2aRYe2t

Hell Yeah!: The Song Of Her Sighs
by Lana K. Dempsey
http://amzn.to/2aRYEFN

Hell Yeah!: Her Hell Yeah Cowboy
by Donna Michaels
http://amzn.to/2bvfBmo

Hell Yeah!: Boardroom Cowboy
by Kandi Silvers
http://amzn.to/2aRZbYB

Hell Yeah!: Cowboy's Break
by Lexi Post
http://amzn.to/2bveG5y

Hell Yeah!: Gun Shy
by Sabrina York
http://amzn.to/2aYGHE4

Hell Yeah!: Seducing Sarah
by Maddie James
http://amzn.to/2aYHXqD

Hell Yeah!: Cowboy Kinky
By Jodi Redford
http://amzn.to/2b530uG

Hell Yeah!: Chasing Butterflies
By Jennifer Labelle
https://amzn.com/B01MQFKA4S

Hell Yeah!: Audacious
By Beth Williamson
https://amzn.com/B01MXHQK3R

Hell Yeah!: Letting Go
By Rhonda Lee Carver
https://amzn.com/B01N8WMVO2

Hell Yeah!: The Pink Rose of the Prairie
By Ginger Ring
https://amzn.com/B01MXHQOUH

Hell Yeah!: Cowboy Collision
By Kandi Silvers

https://amzn.com/B01N3X9DV2

Hell Yeah!: Thunderstruck
By Amanda McIntyre
https://amzn.com/B01N8OECBF

Hell Yeah!: Don't Mess With the Bull
By Sidda Lee Rain
https://amzn.com/B01N0AAM7L

Hell Yeah!: Taboo Frequency
By Gem Sivad
https://amzn.com/B01N3X9FJ4

Hell Yeah!: Sensing Love
By Tamara Hoffa
http://amzn.to/2eBu4gV

About the Author:

Sable Hunter is a New York Times, USA Today bestselling author of nearly 50 books in 7 series. She writes sexy contemporary stories full of emotion and suspense. Her focus is mainly cowboy and novels set in Louisiana with a hint of the supernatural. Sable writes what she likes to read and enjoys putting her fantasies on paper. Her books are emotional tales where the heroine is faced with challenges. Her aim is to write a story that will make you laugh, cry and swoon. If she can wring those emotions from a reader, she has done her job. Sable resides in Austin, Texas with her two dogs. Passionate about all animals, she has been known to charm creatures from a one ton bull to a family of raccoons. For fun, Sable haunts cemeteries and battlefields armed with night-vision cameras and digital recorders hunting proof that love survives beyond the grave. Welcome to her world of magic, alpha heroes, sexy cowboys and hot, steamy to-die-for sex. Step into the shoes of her heroines and escape to places where right prevails, love conquers all and holding out for a hero is not an impossible dream

Visit Sable:

Website:

http://www.sablehunter.com

Facebook:

https://www.facebook.com/authorsablehunter

Amazon:

http://www.amazon.com/author/sablehunter

Pinterest

https://www.pinterest.com/AuthorSableH/

Twitter

https://twitter.com/huntersable

Bookbub:

https://www.bookbub.com/authors/sable-hunter

Goodreads:

https://www.goodreads.com/author/show/4419823.Sable Hunter

Sign up for Sable Hunter's newsletter

http://eepurl.com/qRvyn

SABLE'S BOOKS

Get hot and bothered!!!

Hell Yeah!

Cowboy Heat

Hot on Her Trail

Her Magic Touch

Brown Eyed Handsome Man

Badass

Burning Love

Forget Me Never
With Ryan O'Leary & Jess Hunter

I'll See You In My Dreams
With Ryan O'Leary

Finding Dandi

Skye Blue

I'll Remember You

True Love's Fire

Thunderbird
With Ryan O'Leary

Welcome To My World

How to Rope a McCoy

One Man's Treasure
With Ryan O'Leary

You Are Always on My Mind

If I Can Dream

Head over Spurs

The Key to Micah's Heart
With Ryan O'Leary

Love Me, I Dare you!

Godsend (Hell Yeah! Heritage)

Because I Said So
(Crossover HELL YEAH!/Texas Heroes)

Ryder's Surrender

A Guide to the Hell Yeah! Kindle World

Hell Yeah! Sweeter Versions

Cowboy Heat

Hot on Her Trail

Her Magic Touch

Brown Eyed Handsome Man

Badass

Burning Love

Finding Dandi

Forget Me Never

I'll See You In My Dreams

Moon Magic Series
A Wishing Moon

Sweet Evangeline

Hill Country Heart Series
Unchained Melody

Scarlet Fever

Bobby Does Dallas

Dixie Dreaming
Come With Me

Pretty Face: A Red Hot Cajun Nights Story

Texas Heat Series
T-R-O-U-B-L-E

My Aliyah

El Camino Real Series
A Breath of Heaven

Loving Justice

Texas Heroes Series
Texas Wildfire

Texas CHAOS

Texas Lonestar

Texas Maverick

Because I Said So
(Crossover HELL YEAH!/Texas Heroes)

Other Titles from Sable Hunter:

For A Hero

Green With Envy (It's Just Sex Book 1)
with Ryan O'Leary

Hell Yeah! Box Set With Bonus Cookbook

Love's Magic Spell: A Red Hot Treats Story

Wolf Call

Cowboy 12 Pack: Twelve-Novel Boxed Set

Rogue (The Sons of Dusty Walker)

Kit and Rogue

Be My Love Song

Audio
Cowboy Heat - Sweeter Version: Hell Yeah! Sweeter Version

Hot on Her Trail - Sweeter Version: Hell Yeah! Sweeter Version, Book 2

<u>Spanish Edition</u>
Vaquero Ardiente *(*Cowboy Heat)

Su Rastro Caliente (Hot On Her Trail)

19855856R00191

Printed in Great Britain
by Amazon